Ruin Mist:

Elf Queen's Quest

Robert Stanek

Ruin Mist Chronicles

Ruin Mist: Elf Queen's Quest

Copyright © 2002 by Robert Stanek

First Edition, November 2002

Reagent Press

Published by Virtual Press, Inc.

Cover design & illustration by Robert Stanek

ISBN 1-57545-041-0

Also by Robert Stanek

Ruin Mist Chronicles
Keeper Martin's Tale
Elf Queen's Quest
Kingdom Alliance
Fields of Honor

Ruin Mist Heroes, Legends & Beyond
Magic Lands & Other Stories
Sovereign Rule

Praise for Ruin Mist

"A gem waiting to be unearthed by millions of fans of fantasy!"

"Brilliant… an absolutely superior tale of fantasy for all tastes!"

"It's a creative, provoking, and above all, thoughtful story!"

"It's a wonderful metaphor for the dark (and light) odyssey of the mind."

"The fantasy world you have created is truly wonderful and rich. Your characters seem real and full of life."

The Reaches

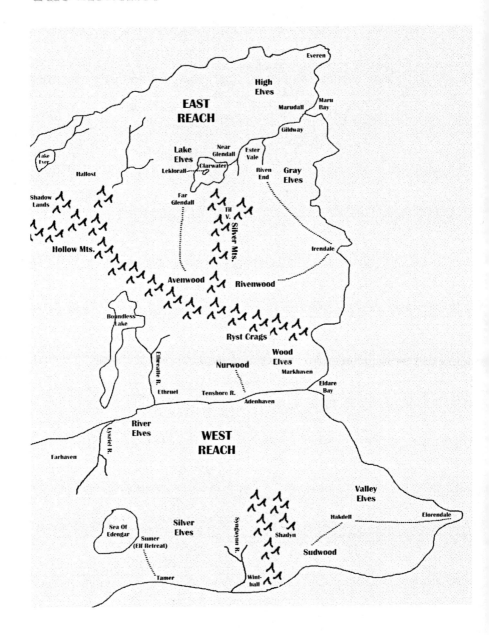

Great Kingdom

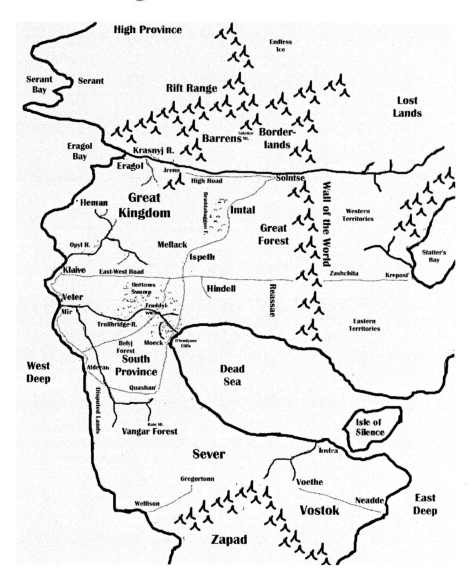

Under-Earth (Lands of Greye)

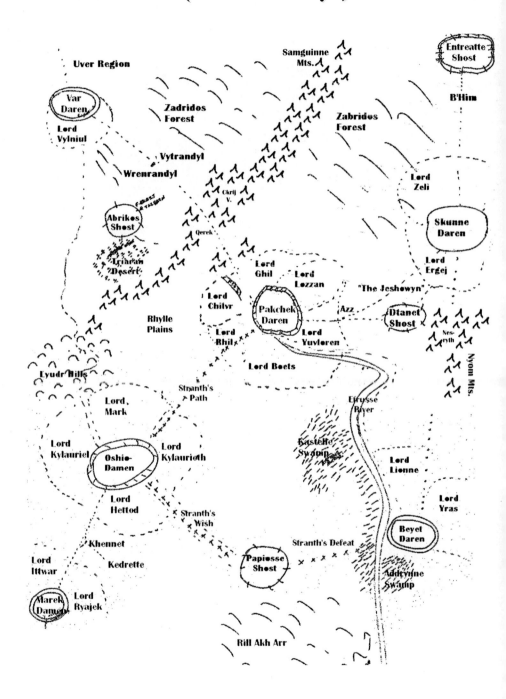

After the Great War that divided the peoples, the kingdoms of men plunged into a Dark Age that lasted five hundred years. To heal the lands and restore the light, the great kings decreed that magic and all that is magical, be it creature, man or device, shall be cleansed to dust. Creatures born of magic were hunted to extinction. Any who dared call magic to their hands were butchered in the streets and afterward their kin were cast out of the known lands or hunted in the blood sport. The cleansing raged for so long that no human could recall a time without it and it is in this time that the Dark One, the one called Sathar, returned from the dark beyond.

The one hope of the peoples of Ruin Mist was Queen Mother, the elf queen of old. She saw a way out of everlasting darkness, a path that required the union of the divided peoples. Yet the Elves of the West did not share her vision. They thought her mad and answered her call for help with a call to arms. Now for the first time in recorded history the armies of the West are marching toward the sacred city of the East and an unholy war where elf must fight elf is inevitable. To turn back the tides of one war and prepare for another, Queen Mother must send her most trusted warriors on a perilous journey across the Great Sea, but what the elves will find if they can reach the far shores cannot be known for certain.

Prologue

Seth glanced at the piles of scrolls and tomes spread across the desk. No matter what Queen Mother had told him, there was no way he could remain unaffected by such writings. The fact that she wouldn't listen to his protests only served to agitate him.

Focus, he told himself, setting one of the leather-bound tomes before him while trying to convince himself that he wanted to read it. After a long pause, he opened it. The book was entitled, *War of the*

Races, Chronicles I.

Seth read the first page and no more. He pushed the book away. He couldn't continue to study the perversity of Man. His thoughts were cluttered with all that had happened yesterday.

He focused his thoughts on the breeze blowing outside the protected fields of Sanctuary. The wind ran dry and hot over the parched earth. A simple projecting of his will and he was racing with the swells, dancing in the swirls and accompanying a river of currents into the heavens. There was moisture in the clouds. This was good.

Peace swept over Seth. The will of the land found him. He looked down from the heavens and raced toward the jagged wall of mountains in the distance. Everything was calm and the troubled thoughts were nearly forgotten.

Seth laughed as he reached the mountains for the breeze turned suddenly cool, his voice echoing over the land before it died in his throat as the breeze became icy. Pain followed; white-hot it swept through Seth's mind and then as if he had reached the edge of the earth, the breeze stopped and all the air was gone.

Suddenly, Seth found himself back at his desk, his eyes wide and the book before him. It took what seemed an eternity for him to recover his wits and for the pain to recede from his mind.

As the pain faded so did the memory of its presence. Soon all Seth could remember was the book before him, which he started reading after a momentary self-protest.

Without announcement a figure clad in red burst into the room. Seth looked up from his studies only long enough to see it was Galan. He glanced up once more to see her disrobe and prepare for a bath, then his thoughts returned to the book.

You study too much. You need to relax… whispered Galan's soft voice in his mind, *You should join me. The bath is soothing.*

Seth looked up again to see Galan standing naked before him. *I wish I could.*

Is it true then what I've heard? Galan sent strong emotions with the words, longing and curiosity.

For the first time as he looked at her, Seth saw Galan as different, beautiful. The silver of her skin danced within the rays of sunshine streaming into the room, and all the while he watched the lavender of her eyes and the gentle swaying of her body called to him. Suddenly uneasy and not understanding why, he stared down at his books. *Their strange ideas pollute my mind even now.*

Galan replied, *Then it is true.*

Seth sent her acknowledgement, but did not look up.

Galan's thoughts raced. *What do you find most odd about them?*

Seth smiled. Only Galan would ask what he found most odd about humankind. *I find them most odd. Everything about them is odd.*

Why is that? Galan scratched at her breast and Seth was again drawn to her eyes. *Why has Queen Mother told you to study their ways? It has been five hundred years since the Race War, why now?*

Seth sought to change the subject. *Will you stand my watch again this day?*

Galan answered not with words, but with feelings. She sent him thoughts of impatience.

Seth got up, walked around to the front of the desk. *An hour away from my studies will do more good than harm.*

Galan smiled, a smile that was short-lived as the voice of Queen Mother pervaded her thoughts. The will of Queen Mother could reach across the land. She called to Seth.

***

Seth guardedly walked beside Queen Mother, his mind carefully searched while his eyes scanned every shadow the two passed. As First of the Red, her safety was his responsibility. He was against remaining in Sanctuary, but Queen Mother wouldn't speak of leaving.

For reasons that escaped him, she wanted to use Sanctuary's High Hall. Its crystalline walls were specially attuned to reflect the feelings of a particular host despite even the best efforts of a mental block or mind shield. This was a feat Queen Mother could have easily performed herself though she said she wished to conserve her will power. For what, she hadn't said.

Seth sent his thoughts into her mind as they walked. *Queen Mother, is it true?*

Her thoughts were silent for a moment and then she replied. *Even now he joins forces with King Mark of West Reach and still others flock to his banner. It is as we most feared.*

Will there be war? Seth asked.

Queen Mother regarded Seth. *I will miss you in my thoughts.*

The words caught Seth by surprise. He didn't understand. The link between protector and queen was unbreakable. He was the watch warden of her body and of her mind. He felt her pain. He knew her anguish, her every anxiety. This was the link. *My Queen, I don't understand.*

Queen Mother paused momentarily and gazed into his eyes. *In time, you will. Even traditions that stem from ages past cannot remain forever. Soon it will be time to guard my own thoughts and my own being just as the first queen had to do.*

Seth was confused and the troubled emotions he cast along with his words showed it. *But my queen, you mustn't. You must direct your will to protect land and people.*

Queen Mother quickly returned, *Centuries ago we abandoned our ancestral homes. We fled to this barren land out of fear. We have lived in fear of repeating the past and only succeeded in repeating it. Still, the day may come when all Elves will smell the green life of our ancestral forests again.*

Seth was about to reply when she silenced him.

Say no more. We are at High Hall, she bade.

With a simple projection of thoughts, the two passed through the outer antechambers and entered High Hall. Seth remained at Queen Mother's side. He was pleased to see Brother Ry'al seated behind Brother Samyuehl, First of the Blue Order.

Greetings, sent Seth to Ry'al, guiding the thought solely to Ry'al's mind. Seth had not seen Ry'al since the two had been together under

Samyuehl's tutelage, a time during which Seth had learned a great deal.

Just as Queen Mother took her place and sent her own greetings to the foremost six, each dressed in the appropriately colored robes of his or her order—Yellow, Brown, Blue, Black, White and Gray—Seth momentarily contemplated the hundred and one seasons of tutelage under Samyuehl's watchful eye. Being of the Red Order meant that he had to endure the seven teachings as a member of each order—and he had, thanks to Samyuehl.

As all was in order, Seth took his place two paces behind Queen Mother. He noted that she attuned High Hall's crystalline walls to her own mood, which at first was both pensive and somber. Reflecting this, the walls shone mostly in shades of black and gray.

Queen Mother's expression became grim and determined as she levitated into the air above the gray satin-pillowed couch that dominated the center of the immense hall. The gray of the couch again reflected the somberness of her mood.

For a few moments before he settled behind the shields in his mind, Seth knew and felt Queen Mother's thoughts. She was reminding herself that she had been annoyed this morning and had been annoyed many times over many previous days, but not now. Now she needed to keep her mind clear and her thoughts focused. She needed to keep her emotions centered and directed.

She chose her words carefully now and directed her thoughts outward. *Greetings to wise council. Thank you for a speedy assembly.*

Those thoughts were the last Seth heard before he entered the quiet solitude of his mind. His duty was to be present and not to listen in unless directed to. Instead, he would follow her feelings to know her mood, and if she needed him her feelings would reflect this.

He had many other things to concern himself with besides squabbles amongst High Council or the First Brothers. Again, he feared for Queen Mother's safety and wondered what would come of his fears.

Time passed.

Within the folds of his mind, Seth was only aware of the world beyond High Hall and of Queen Mother's mood, which was growing more somber. His will guardedly watched the winds. Far off in the fields beyond Sanctuary he heard the scurrying of a mouse. Then for a single instant, it was as if a breeze had entered his mind. It was a presence in his thoughts.

Seth opened his eyes and turned to Queen Mother. She regarded him for a moment and then dismissed him with a nodding of her head. Seth stood his ground, the indignity he felt at the dismissal showing briefly on his face. Then he exited High Hall, speaking not a word.

Call Brother Galan to my chambers, Queen Mother whispered after him. *Return to your studies.*

***

Following the unspoken whisper, Brother Liyan entered the room. The gray of his robe was a symbol of office, unlike the white of Queen Mother's robe that was a symbol of her whims and mood. Brother Liyan nodded to Galan who stood watch just inside the chamber. Her dark lavender eyes regarded him for a moment and she felt a chill run the length of his spine, and then she softly re-entered Queen Mother's thoughts, doing what she wasn't supposed to do but felt compelled to do.

The hue of the walls slowly adjusted to reflect agitation. At first they dulled and darkened to a metallic bronze and then settled on a murky brown. Taking note of the falling and deepening of the cubicle's glow, the wonderful silver of Brother Liyan's eyes turned dark as the coal that stoked the great furnaces of Sanctuary.

My queen, Brother Liyan said as he stepped into the room. He kneeled appropriately, and awaited her response to make further comment.

Once more Queen Mother responded only with feelings: displeasure and annoyance.

Brother Liyan looked up into Queen Mother's eyes and uneasily rose from his knees. *My queen, a thousand pardons for the interruption, but this matter is urgent. You did not address it directly during the assembly, but I gather that Brother Seth prepares for the journey?*

Queen Mother responded quickly, *Yes, that is so.*

Brother Liyan's response was returned just as quickly. *Why Brother Seth, First of the Red? His strength is needed here, especially now.*

Queen Mother held her position, her long white robe cascading to the clean, cold floor. *It must be.*

Brother Liyan continued his protest. *You yourself said the chosen wouldn't survive the ordeal. Brother Seth must not go. Who would protect in his stead?*

Queen Mother replied in thought. *Only those of the assembly know the fate of the chosen. It is my wish that the Red are the ones.*

Brother Liyan paled visibly. *My queen, the Red are your protectors.*

Shielding their thoughts, Queen Mother slammed the cubicle's door. Black walls mirrored her increasingly somber mood, for these were the very thoughts she had sought to cleanse away through meditation.

Precisely, was her response and Brother Liyan's eyes went wide.

My queen, Brother Liyan began, then his thoughts scattered to the winds as Queen Mother's will fell upon him.

Queen Mother stopped levitating and stood beside Liyan, staring into his eyes. *If I as Queen Mother, the heart and soul of my people, cannot pay the dearest of prices for the ridding of the greatest ailment, then I and all fail the greatest of tests.*

Brother Liyan struggled to recover his wits. *I truly did not know or understand, forgive me.*

Queen Mother returned, evident sadness in her words. *We each have our parts in this and we must play them out. We have waited too long. Our people return to the lands of Man. There will be no further discussion.*

Queen Mother called out to Galan. Galan opened her eyes, her thoughts in juxtaposition with Queen Mother's. *Yes, my queen?*

Leave us now, Queen Mother directed to Galan alone. *Tell Brother*

Seth I await his presence.

Galan fixed her eyes upon Brother Liyan. Remember your place, her glare warned. Then she rushed out of the chamber.

***

Seth returned from a bath to find Brother Everrelle waiting for him.

Everrelle whispered to his mind, *Queen Mother wishes you to return to High Hall and would have you wait in the antechamber until her summons to enter.*

Seth excused himself and rushed off. Today was the third day of secretive meetings in the hall and now he was to be invited in? He couldn't fathom why.

Seth found the antechamber empty. He waited, his thoughts flowing with the passing of time.

Hours passed. The walls of the antechamber oscillated through casts of gray, hovering just slight of brilliant silver then fading to quasi-black. Oblivious to this light show, Seth sulked. He had seen it a thousand times before and would see it many thousands more. The subtle but swift changes were supposed to be soothing, but he wasn't soothed.

Seth felt utterly helpless as he waited. He considered eavesdropping on those behind the closed doors. It would have been an easy enough feat to do, a simple projecting of thoughts, nothing more. Those within would not have gone to the trouble of masking open thought. He would have only to reach out.

The notion tempted Seth for a time before his thoughts turned to Galan. As they had walked to the bathing pool distress had replaced her usual playfulness. Later she told him she had not masked her thoughts during a conversation between Queen Mother and Brother Liyan. She had heard, seen and felt everything through Queen Mother's eyes.

Galan had told him privately, *I am afraid for you my brother, but I cannot say why. Will you promise to return to our quarters afterward?*

Seth had said he would, though he had been aghast at her deed.

For a time his thoughts became unfocused, and just when he thought he could wait no more, the doors swung open and the summons came. He was shocked to see all the members of the three councils in attendance and that many others streamed in through the far door. Many eyes were directed at him and he did not know why.

An unusual amount of energy filled the air, accompanied by a strange silence, which to his prescient mind was like an unwholesome numbing. People fidgeted around in their cushioned seats or floated agitatedly just above them, carefully controlling the flow of their thoughts.

Seth was beckoned to the fore, not by the flow of words or feelings to his wildly spinning mind but by the briefest stroking of his senses, a presage bundled in the form of a picture and thrust upon his mind with such a force that it would have felled most others. This was done for effect. It was such an overpowering tool that only Queen Mother would have ever resorted to its use. Sure, Queen Mother could have directed him with wordless thoughts, but any child could have done that. Apparently, she wanted to stun him and she had.

Head slightly lowered, eyes wide and upturned, Seth lurched to a perplexed halt. Words whisked through his mind as through a dream and then an avalanche of voices followed. Seth could only stare blankly ahead, still half in stupor as he sought to digest the multiple conversations.

Queen Mother lowered her gaze and when their eyes met a smile passed her lips, and only in that instant did Seth realize none of the others knew what she had done to him. In a way, she had stolen his words before he could offer protest. When he finally did start to protest it was already too late, only Seth had the misfortune of not realizing it immediately.

How can this be so? he demanded.

"Brother Seth, the decision of the High Council is final." The voice that permeated the air of the great hall was Brother Liyan's. It was not often that one of the Brotherhood spoke aloud, but this too was done for effect.

Immediate silence followed.

"It was I who offered your services. The Red Order shall serve in this undertaking." the voice, again spoken aloud, was Queen Mother's and now audible gasps crisscrossed the chamber. In the thousand seasons Queen Mother had spoken aloud only once before.

Seth was just as purposeful when he responded in thought as when Queen Mother had spoken aloud. *What of the Brown? Is this not a duty of the warrior order?*

It was a small defiance, but it was a defiance far greater than offering his opinion when she had obviously warned him that she wanted to hear little more than his silence. The presage had been her warning to him and now Seth had defied her, yet those of the council were not privy to her earlier act. So while gasps passed around the chamber, Queen Mother fixed her open gaze upon Seth. Under the weight of her stare he must hold his tongue, and listen carefully.

"Brother Seth, their part will come. It is not now," Queen Mother again spoke aloud. "Why do you think you have been studying their ways these many past weeks?"

A trace of anger passed over Queen Mother's face; her naked rendering of such a strong emotion in the company of the Council and so many others was in itself significant enough to make Seth's knees tremble. It wasn't so much that he feared her wrath. Queen Mother held no malice within her. Her eyes held only caring and her heart only love. A greater pain than physical pain was shame and dishonor.

Who will accompany me? Seth asked, breaking the silence and risking all.

Brother Liyan responded aloud to return respect and order to the council room. "The choice is yours, Brother Seth. I know it will be a difficult one but I have confidence in you, Brother Seth of the Red, First of that order, Queen's Protector. You are the chosen one."

***

Brother Liyan was silent for a time, his gray robe cascading to the floor ruffled in the breeze he played about the room. *Brother Seth, you have hardly committed an unforgivable transgression.*

Seth sent Liyan tortured thoughts. *I told her I needed her beside me when I made the journey. I told her and then I kissed her. These ideals of Man corrupt my thinking.*

Brother Liyan settled into the thickly cushioned couch beneath him. *Brother Galan will forgive you. I have been your mentor for only one season now, my appointment at Queen Mother's request. Just now I understand what it must have been like enduring the teachings of the seven orders and after every phase of the training beginning anew like a child and always in training with children. I am suddenly less afraid of the mysterious and powerful Red.*

Seth started to interrupt.

Brother Liyan cut in before Seth's thoughts could flow. *Let me finish, Brother Seth. It is Mother-Earth herself that corrupts your thinking. Have you never been beyond Kapital or Sanctuary?*

Seth returned, *I have traveled the canals of the city from end to end with Sailmaster Cagan, and I have traveled the road to Sanctuary. Is there anything beyond I would care to see?*

Brother Liyan bowed his head. *Now I understand why you fought so hard in High Hall. You are genuinely afraid of venturing into the world and I have perhaps discovered the one thing that can bring true fear to one of the Red. You ask what is beyond Sanctuary and my answer is that the whole of the world is beyond these walls. Sights so marvelous you could hardly begin to imagine them all. And never forget that what you call Kapital, the people call Leklorall.*

Liyan sent Seth a mental image, the green of a forest against the backdrop of a white-capped mountain, the sky so blue it was almost purple. *That is our ancient home. Is it not truly beautiful?*

Brother Seth held the picture in his mind's eye for a time before responding. The homeland of his people was indeed beautiful. *What of my act? Are my thoughts polluted?*

Brother Seth, I will tell you a secret I have never told another. Liyan waved his hand and brought the light breeze in the room to a standstill. *Just as you fear what you do not know, I have always feared the Brothers of the Red. In fact, terror is a better word to describe the emotion.*

Seth quickly replied, *That is an emotion we are trained to evoke. It ensures obedience to our wishes and safety for Queen Mother.*

Brother Liyan nodded contemplatively. *It is something you would do well to forget as you journey into Man's world and while it explains much, it is not the point I am trying to make. We all have our fears and what we fear most is a thing unknown to us. From birth your kind is secreted away from all of society. By the time you complete your training you are passed youthful adolescence and then we dub you Protectors of the Queen, never thinking that up until now all your dealings have been with teachers and children.*

Seth, you were wrong about the Brown Order. They were the chosen warriors only out of necessity. Before the Brown, there was always the Red. During those dark centuries when the races turned against each other, the Red remained first and foremost the warrior-protectors of Queen and people.

Perhaps it is a good thing Queen Mother wishes you into the world, and a good thing that you studied the ways of Man. Their culture is not so different from our own that you could not learn from it. With Elf kind, mating instinct often skips generations for reasons only Great Father and Mother-Earth truly understand. Your feelings are not wrong Seth; they are as natural as the four winds.

Brother Liyan crossed to Seth and put a hand on his shoulder. *With Brother Galan, I would suggest you follow your instincts; perhaps it will bring good. There is however, one thing you should know—these feelings may never find her. It is a tragedy of our kind. For now, you should turn your thoughts to the journey ahead. You must ask yourself: Are you prepared to greet the world? Is the world ready for you?*

Chapter One

Lying to the council was hard, though not because lying went against her principles. No, the ability to pass off a falsity was a virtue. Still, when one stretched what was already a lie, there was little room for the new lie, and she had to be careful not to be caught in the folds of that second or third lie. She had told so many lies of late that she was unsure which was the truth and which was the lie. She could tell that the First Priest, Talem, had not believed her.

Her loyalty had been questioned. She was a priestess of Mother-Earth. So why did she aid the Priests of the Dark Flame? What was her connection to the frantic rounds of cleansing sweeping the kingdom? These were the questions that had been put to her repeatedly, and each time she had stated that there was a fine line between loyalties and that she, Midori, held loyalty to the greater of the causes.

She was tangled in the web deeper than anyone knew or could guess. Now she had only to maintain the facade one more day and then she would be safe, safe from all probing eyes and prying hands. She wouldn't care what Talem did or said then. The council would be unable to touch her and she would be safe in High Temple.

Midori would have left that very night if she had been able to, but Talem was always pushing, always questioning. He would not discover her secrets no matter how hard he probed and no matter what tools he used to wrest those secrets from her. She knew this.

The private chamber she paced and schemed in seemed a tiny prison. She knew Talem had his spies that watched her through hidden peepholes. She did not care. Let them watch her, let them watch her all they wanted, she taunted in her mind. They would discover nothing. She was too clever, too quick, and had but a single night until freedom.

She inspected her bags to ensure they had not been tampered with and smiled as she ran her hands over a subtle seal. Talem would never have guessed that she would have the audacity to bring her secrets with her to council, but she had. Her heavy bags concealed two scrolls; there had been three but the first had already been given to a trusted messenger and delivered long ago. The last two were for her to handle alone. One she was to read after she spoke to council, which was now. The last, she was to deliver. To where, she did not yet know.

The impulse to pull the hidden scrolls from her bag ebbed as she forced herself to find control. She would wait. She had nearly succeeded and there was no need to be hasty when her goal was so close.

"Do you want an eyeful?" she whispered to those unseen.

Casually, she untied the belt about her waist and let the loose-fitting, black robe slip from about her shoulders and cascade to the floor. A water basin stood in a corner. Midori dipped her long, black hair into the gently warmed waters.

Herbal scented soaps lined the wall to her left, but she took the plain, unscented bar to her right and used this to wash her hair. She moistened a cloth and dabbed it across her body to remove the day's sweat and grime. It had been a long day. Rinsing in the warm waters was soothing and allowed some of the tenseness of the day to slip away.

A few more hours, she reminded herself as she lay down upon the bed, just a few more hours.

Only minutes later, a heavy knock at the door awoke her. She brushed her hair back casually and crossed to the door, opening it without hesitation. She looked on unwavering at the one who stood in the doorway. "Why Talem, do come in," she said calmly.

Talem stepped into her room. "I will forgive you this day's transgressions," he began, "for I know how the times of equinox affect your kind. But do not try my patience thus in the future."

"What kind would that be?" Midori shot back without thinking. She was so wrapped up in her current situation that she had forgotten to stay the flow of emotions within her, and this realization came to her just when she thought she was being so careful. Equinox was a time when the flow from the Mother was so strong that it could overcome her priestesses and drive them to do the irrational and spontaneous. There were many benefits to this, but they were not without certain disadvantages.

She didn't let the priest speak before adding, "Do not worry, Talem. I am done here. Did you come to wish me a safe journey?"

"I know you hide something," he said, stepping toward her. "I will find out what it is and then I will personally see that you are brought before the council."

Midori was confident. "If I were hiding something, the council would have discovered it. I hide nothing, Talem. I spoke the truth and am exhausted of telling the truth. Now if you will please excuse me, I have a journey ahead of me tomorrow that demands an early start."

"There is plenty of time to sleep. What I have to say will be quick, do not worry." Talem took another step toward her and grinned. "Do you know that you are quite striking in your way?"

Midori backed away from him, shaking her head. Talem took another step toward her and flung her onto the bed. Midori shouted at him, "Do you seek to defile this vessel of the Mother?"

Talem drew up to his full height, an act that made him somehow appear less vicious. "You just remain still, I do not intend to touch you or to harm you. I merely wish to gain your full attention and I can see that I have it now."

Midori didn't say a word. She would let him think he had won this show of dominance.

"We are much alike you and I," Talem began, "We are both users. We use those around us as tools to gain what we want."

She wanted to scream at him that they were nothing alike, had never been anything alike and would never be anything alike, but she did not. She needed to be more aware of everything she did and said now more than ever if she was going to erase his suspicions.

"We have our moments," she replied.

"Good, that is what I wanted to hear. Our relationship could go far. Do you know how much untapped potential is out there?" Talem chuckled. "Oh, if you only knew."

She did. She said nothing.

"I need you on my side in this. I will forgive your earlier transgressions, just make no more." His last few words lashed out at her with a harsh edge. He started to chuckle to himself again.

Midori looked up at him, her eyes seemingly receptive. She didn't know what sort of game he was playing, but intended to go along with it for now. "I could become persuaded to your cause," she told him.

"Very well then, there are two scrolls in your bag with the shaman's own seal upon them," this was not a subtle Would you fetch them? but a direct command to go get them now.

Midori didn't hesitate or change her expression; yet within her world filled with sudden turmoil. She had been so careful, oh so very careful. She had to think fast and hide the excitement from her voice. "I wish I could, but you must know as well as I that they will not open for any other than the intended recipient, or otherwise you would have broken the seal days ago."

Talem said nothing.

Midori's racing heart slowed, though only slightly. The priest had given her a way out with his silence, or at least she hoped so. "I wish that I could tear them open with my bare hands, but I can not," she said sounding exasperated, hoping she wasn't being overly melodramatic.

"Yes, yes, I know the feeling. The shaman is a snake."

"A vile, treacherous snake," Midori added.

Talem grinned and then said, "It is good that we agree on this." He paused and Midori continued her receptive stare. "Who are the scrolls intended for, perhaps this can shed some light?"

Names, demanded Midori of herself. She had to think quickly. She couldn't let Talem believe she was stalling. She had been close, so close. She had to choose names that would cause no harm to her cause. Deciding, she stated, "One I am to deliver to an innkeeper, I would be certain that it pertains to a long overdue debt and contains empty promises to the individual that he will be paid in due time. The second is bound for High Priestess Jasmine; I do not understand it myself," her aim was to gloss over the first with the more enticing second.

"Jasmine," said Talem as if musing over the name, "that is interesting."

"Yes, quite. Therefore, you see why I hasten to High Temple. If there is any chance that I can be present during the reading, I will surely take advantage of it and I will of course relay the information to you."

Talem seemed pleased at the response. "Good, good," he hissed, "but what of this innkeeper, what is his name?"

Midori had purposefully neglected to tell him this, hoping he would be more interested in the scroll directed to the High Priestess. "I'm not sure. Let me think. Oh, yes. Misha, his name is Misha, but he is harmless. As I have said, I would imagine it concerns a long overdue payment and I might even expect that it tells this innkeeper that he can get his payment from me."

Midori saw Talem's contemplative smile and continued, "I would wager that this is the reason the scroll is sealed. Can you imagine being told that you are to give payment for a debt you do not owe? I wonder what else the scroll promises."

"Yes, I know what you mean," said Talem. "These are trying times… trying times indeed. Our relationship will go far if you continue this honesty with me. I will have the coach drawn up at once; mustn't delay your departure to High Temple any longer. You have done well by me my dear, and I do not easily forget." Again, his last phrasing held an edge and a subtle hint of retribution that would be taken if she crossed him.

Midori was about to respond, when Talem turned about and departed. She sighed.

"One more thing, Midori," said the priest, turning back to her as he passed through the doorway.

Her heart leapt into her throat again, but she hid it well. "Yes?" she replied.

"I would expect to hear from you as soon as possible. Do not make me wait too long. I get impatient." Those were Talem's last words as he closed the chamber door behind himself.

Once the coach was drawn up and she was safely inside it, Midori wouldn't care what he had said to her or what she had said to him; she would be safe and, very soon, far beyond his or anyone's grasp.

***

Princess Adrina waited in the shadows for the guardsman to finish his rounds, her eyes drinking in the sunrise spread across the horizon. As she moved from the doorway, an angry wind blew long strands of hair across her face. The hair, black as the receding night, flowed to her waist. Adrina could see that winter was close at hand for the breeze came from the North and not from the direction of the great West Deep. Fifteen winters in Imtal had thickened her blood and it was much more than the unusual chill in the air that caused her to wrap the woolen cloak tightly about her.

She walked to a place where the wall jutted out and cut its way into High King's Square. Behind her, the palace parade grounds were empty and silent, as were the executioner's blocks in the square before her. The silence seemed a shroud over the whole of Imtal, clear to the green grassy tops of the Braddabaggon where the bandit kings had camped to lay siege to Imtal. Soon the square would fill with sounds as the executioner began his day's work. Palace guardsmen would muster for breakfast. Afterward, the great iron gates of Imtal would grind open briefly to let those that had endured the hardship of the night outside the city's protective walls come within. Later, the skirmishes would begin and the catapults would begin their assaults.

Adrina preferred the quiet moments just before all this happened, for the silence echoed the aching of her heart. She pressed her chin into the palm of her hand, her elbow glued to the stone framework of the wall. To her, Imtal represented death, and life was beyond the gray stones of the walls.

Great Kingdom had many holdings. High Province in the North, where amidst mountains of ice and stone the rivers boiled and filled the air with blankets of fog. South, beyond a forest of great white trees, lay South Province with its capital city hidden in the majestic Quashan' valley. East through the Kingdom along the king's road were the Territories, holdings only the mightiest king of the land could lay claim to. Traders from the East told tales of the walled city of Zashchita, its spires lifting so far into the heavens they were lost in clouds.

Adrina could waste most days dreaming of these faraway lands. However, today she wouldn't pass the time dreaming of things she may never see. Today the weight of her station was heavy upon her shoulders. She didn't understand what difference the passing of a year made. Why did it matter so much that she was a year older? This year seemed the same as the last.

The echo of footsteps against hard stones startled her. It wasn't the guardsman Adrina had seen earlier. She was sure his shift was at an end and no other would replace him until after the morning muster. Her eyes went wide. Would Lady Isador venture to the walls?

Her governess had threatened to do so before. Adrina didn't want to be reminded of all the things she should or should not do so she rushed to the northern tower. At dawn, the watchtower would be empty and she could be alone without fear of interruption. The tower's uppermost room was large and open with broad windows that were normally used to keep vigil on the city's north wall and the fields beyond. The wind streaming through the windows beckoned to Adrina.

As she looked out the tower window, she could see the armies of the bandit kings lining the hilltops of the Braddabaggon and off in the distance she could see long lines of their reinforcements coming from the Bad Lands. In that moment, it seemed to her that life was war and there couldn't be one without the other. The routine of attacks, withdrawals and recovery seemed a never-ending cycle.

The war with the bandit kings was in its seventh year. The bandits had laid siege to Imtal two summers ago and still did not understand that victory over Great Kingdom was not possible. For every man that the bandits sent to the line, the kingdom sent two. For every man that died on the battlefield, the kingdom conscripted three to replace him. For every peasant that was killed as the bandits plundered the countryside, the kingdom executed a dozen prisoners of war. No, there could be no victory for the bandit kings, only defeat and death.

The faint sound of a foot slipping over the stones aroused her senses. She drew her sword, turning to strike with the swiftness her years of training afforded her. Still, her heart and mind began to race. The troubled dream of the previous night came back to her.

She paused her sword at the throat of the stranger. The robed figure moved toward her unafraid, whispering, "Child, I will not harm you."

"Who are you and what are you doing here?" Adrina demanded, brushing back hair from her eyes. "Your face, it is covered in soot. Stop where you are or I will end your life."

The stranger raised her hands slowly and then removed her hood. "I come to speak to you, Highness. I have seen you often."

As Adrina stared into the woman's eyes, she felt a calmness she had never known before. She sheathed her sword, no longer afraid, and then asked, "Who are you?"

The old woman didn't respond immediately; instead she turned to the open window and waved her hands, pointing to the distance. "You will journey beyond Imtal. I have seen you in a far off place. It comes, child, can you not tell?"

"It?" Adrina asked, puzzled.

The strange woman took Adrina's hand and turned her to the window. The breeze still howling out of the north blew Adrina's long hair back from her cheeks. "Change, child. Darkness cannot hold a land forever."

Adrina turned to look at the woman's face. The woman directed Adrina's gaze away, pointing again to the distant horizon. Adrina was afraid now. Change had taken away everyone and everything she cared about. Valam had taken control of the southern armies. Calyin was married to ensure the allegiance of a high lord and that of his family. Midori had entered the service of the Mother. Her own mother was gone, a victim of the poison.

The old woman touched Adrina's cheek and the calm returned. "Queen Alexandria is indeed missed. You have her beauty and her strength."

Adrina wondered if the old woman could reach into her mind, and then she realized the woman was gone. Hearing again what sounded like a foot slipping across the stones of the floor, Adrina spun around and shouted, "Show yourself!"

From the shadows, the woman whispered a warning, "Be careful what you wish for."

Adrina stepped toward the woman. "What do you mean?"

The old woman, her face suddenly appearing aged beyond her years, took Adrina's hand. She kneeled then and as she kissed Adrina's hand, Adrina felt the moisture of tears on her arm. The woman whispered, "For the children, who at the end of the journey will be no more."

***

Evening found Adrina in the East wing of the palace. Since the meeting with the old woman, she had been wandering the quiet halls, alone with her thoughts. For a time it seemed weights were around her shoulders, but slowly Adrina concluded that the babblings of an old woman were just that, babblings and nothing more.

When Adrina realized she hadn't changed into a dinner gown and the evening meal was less than an hour away, she became frantic. She didn't want to be late, especially after avoiding her duties all day.

The private access ways were the quickest way to her room. Adrina ran full stride down these darkened corridors. Since only she used them now, there was no fear of bumping into anyone, and she knew well ahead of time their every turn by the count of her strides. When she turned a sharp corner, she knew she was entering the North wing. A mostly straight stretch of hallway was ahead and then another sharp turn into the West wing.

She slowed her gait to catch her breath; the line of light ahead was from the private door to her chambers. She stopped outside the door and peeked in. Inside her attendants were waiting. When she didn't see or hear Lady Isador, she entered. She quickly discarded her sword belt and her chain mail shirt.

For a time the attendants fussed over her hair and helped her put on her gown. When they finished, Adrina raced through the halls so fast that she nearly ran down the captain of the guard. She stumbled through an apology and then rushed away.

In the great hall, her father was seated at his kingly chair with its high raised back and stout, straight arms in the true fashion of his office. Catching the gleam in his eye as he looked upon her, Adrina smiled then sat. An attendant pushed her seat forward, and she nodded in response. She was not late, though only barely so.

"Good evening, father," Adrina said, while trying to hide the sudden smile that came to her lips. "I trust I am not late."

King Andrew swept his gaze around the enormous oblong table

to the faces of the honored guests. "Only so, dear Adrina. Only so."

Adrina looked to Chancellor Yi standing rigidly behind her father in his rightful place as the king's principal adviser. The old chancellor did not move as he stood there, nor did he ever unless summoned. This was a strange thing since otherwise he was plagued with an endless cold and all the sniffles and sneezes that went with it.

Her stomach rumbled. Adrina looked to the lines of attendants waiting to ferry food from the kitchens, at the honored guest, and at her father. Everyone in the room wanted to pretend that they weren't at war with the bandit kings and to forget that they had only just washed the blood of the day from their hands. Even Father Tenuus who was about to speak on the king's behalf knew the grim details of the day, yet sought to sweep them away with his words.

Adrina's eyes wandered to Father Tenuus as he spoke. He was the only member of the priesthood that lived in the palace. Others of the priesthood, like Father Jacob, King's First Minister, had chambers tucked away in the East wing of the palace, this was true, but they were rarely in attendance. They had other concerns.

When the welcome and invocation seemed finally over, Adrina watched the attendants descend upon the tables carrying plates overloaded with fresh breads, platters with game hens, decanters of wine and an array of steaming dishes carrying wonderful aromas. Her mouth watered as she tucked a wayward strand of dark hair behind her ear and sighed. She looked around the table. Her father, apparently midway through a smile, frowned, yet made no comment. He never did.

The rather pale looking man to her right, clothed in a purple velvet overcoat and blue silk shirt, turned a whiter shade of white as he raised a handkerchief to his puffy red nose. Adrina did her best to ignore him. Courtiers were parasites that fed off crown and land. They only wanted to bend her father's ear to their petty troubles, and the fact that they visited the castle by the hundreds spoke volumes for the times.

King Andrew smiled, apparently at this small show of independence. Adrina knew he liked it, yet she also knew a great deal could be hidden in a simple smile. Its uneasy weight made her turn away from his gaze and back to the bit of honey-glazed hen that remained on her plate. For a moment, her thoughts went to the discussion of duty she had had with Lady Isador and her father. She still didn't understand what difference a year made and why it mattered so much to the kingdom that she was coming of age.

No longer hungry she could have pushed the mostly empty plate away but soon afterward one of the courtiers would have tried to engage her in conversation. She was delighted when Captain Brodst, the man she had nearly collided with earlier, entered the hall and approached the king's table. She was also a bit surprised. The captain of the guard rarely interrupted the evening meal. She tried to listen to the words passed between the captain and her father but could barely hear above the noise in the great hall.

King Andrew furrowed his brow and said something Adrina couldn't hear to which the captain responded by nodding. Then she heard her father clearly say, "Rouse two guards to council doors."

"At once sire," returned Captain Brodst and then he quickly departed.

Adrina waited for her father's further reaction. Her hope was to escape the dining hall and find a strategic position near the council chambers. As time passed she began to think that the matter wasn't too urgent or else her father would have departed immediately; yet sometimes it seemed he mulled over the simplest of decisions for hours—like the color of a new flower to put into the gardens—and then those decisions she assumed he would deliberate over for days were made in the blink of an eye.

As King Andrew laid his dinner knife aside and rinsed his fingers in the dipping bowl for what appeared to be the last time, all eyes around the great oblong table rose to greet his. As the king departed, Adrina paused for a moment and then followed. Most of the courtiers were caught in the tangle of attendants attempting to remove the remnants of the meal. Some of the courtiers guardedly returned to their fare as they always did. Some were already deep in meaningless conversations with whomever was to their right or left. Others were there to watch. They were the eyes and ears of many a lord and even the paid spies of other kings.

Adrina was sure that the courtier who had been seated beside her was not only pretending to be aloof but was also listening to the King's every word. That courtier was not caught up in the tangle of attendants. In fact, he moved rather adroitly through the crowded room and into the adjacent hall.

As Adrina reached the corridor that connected the Central wing of the castle with the West wing, her heart and mind began to race. A voice whispered in her mind, "Change, child. Darkness cannot hold a land forever."

Chapter Two

He awoke, crying out into the darkness and drenched in sweat. His thoughts raced. The whole of his small body shivered uncontrollably. "It was only a dream," he whispered to reassure himself; yet it was a dream like no other, for in the dream his secret had been discovered and the dark priests had come for him.

He stood uneasily and dipped his trembling hands into the washbasin beside his bed. The cool water sucked the pain from his eyes and mind and gently began to soothe and awaken his senses as nothing else could. Only then did he become something other than a frightened child. Only then did he become the boy of twelve whose name was Vilmos. Vilmos, the Counselor's son.

Readying for the day's chores, Vilmos tried to push the last of the dream from his thoughts, but as he leaned down to rinse his face once more in the cool water of the basin it was as though he was sucked into the water and when he opened his eyes, he was in a different place. In this place, there was no moon or stars, only boundless lines of fire cutting into the ebony of the heavens.

At his feet lay a dirt road and ahead beyond a crossroads was a forest of dark trees. The dark trees, glowing with an eerie radiance, called to him. Puzzled, Vilmos clutched his arms about his chest and followed the dirt road toward the strange light in the distance.

Beyond the crossroads was a long stretch of empty road. Vilmos hurried. As he approached the forest, the shadows grew long despite the glow in the treetops. It was within these shadows that Vilmos saw a mass of black darker than all the rest. Slowly the mass took form and it was only as he stumbled through the great ruins that he saw someone sitting within the folds of the great shadow. When the figure looked in Vilmos' direction, two thin beams of light radiated from eyes the color of a silver moon. Stare as he might, Vilmos could only see the strange eyes within the folds of the figure's hood. Vilmos asked, "Is this a dream?"

"If a dream, it is a waking dream." The voice seemed to be that of a man.

"Who are you?" Vilmos asked.

"My name is Xith, you can call me 'Shaman'." The shaman stood. Vilmos was surprised to find he could look directly into the shiny eyes without looking up. The strange eyes, hypnotizing and dazzling, danced as the shaman regarded Vilmos, and then the shaman took Vilmos' hand. The hand in Vilmos' seemed a piece of hardened leather and not the hand of a man at all.

Vilmos repeated, "Who are you?"

"Who I am is not important at the moment." The robed figure lowered his hood to reveal childlike features riddled with lines that spoke of ages past and of hardship. Although few of the ancient ones ever ventured into the kingdoms, Vilmos had read about them in the Great Book. He knew in an instant the figure was a gnome and kin to the mighty dwarves who lived in the bowels of the earth.

The shaman raised his eyes to the fires etched in the skies and then waved his hands one over the other until a glowing orb of brilliant white appeared. Within the orb was a face, the face of a woman young in her years, though still older than Vilmos. Her cheekbones were high and rosy. Her eyes were green and her hair, long and black. In a way she was strikingly beautiful, yet there was such sadness in her eyes and this sadness cut into his heart.

"Who is she?" Vilmos asked.

"A princess and the one you seek," whispered the shaman. For an instant, tension and pain was evident on the shaman's face, and then a new figure appeared within the orb. "Take a long look, Vilmos. He is of a race swept from the world of the seeing long ago. Their legend is recorded in the Great Book of your realm, yet few ever knew the truth of their disappearance. Change is sweeping the land, all the lands, and the kingdoms of elf and human are no exception."

Vilmos beaded his eyes, his heart filled with hatred. "Elves are our sworn enemies."

The shaman grabbed Vilmos' shoulders and shook him violently. "Remember the faces. The two and the one will be drawn together as are the winds clashing against the fourth unseen. Your dreams will bring them together."

As he spoke, the shaman turned to the forest. "The land called Ril Akh Arr and within dwell the shape-changing beasts of the night. Be forewarned, they come for you, for the princess, for all who would stand in the way."

The shaman paused to suck in the heavy air, and then wheeled his hands in a great circle. Just then, shadows swept through the skies blocking the fires of the heavens and the ground beneath Vilmos' feet shook violently. "This place is called Under-Earth and you, Vilmos, are the second. The first was taken from me before I could reach her."

Vilmos was puzzled. Were the stories true? Dare he ask the question that was on his tongue?

The shaman sighed. "My kingdom and people were taken away so many years past I cannot recall the day."

"Your kingdom?"

The shaman grabbed Vilmos' hand, the grip numbing as he drew a jagged blade from a scabbard at his belt. As he spoke, he dug the blade into Vilmos' palm. "Elves, gnomes and humans are all very real. I will come for you, Vilmos. When I do, the dreams end and the journey begins. Remember the faces and forget not that the fourth can blow across the mountaintops. Remember there was another before you and that they reached her before I did. Now return to your affairs. Listen to the one who will lead you to me."

The shaman paused. The shadows directly overhead now blocked out all light from the fire-streaked skies. As a great hand reached down from the heavens to grab them, the shaman hurled a brilliant green orb at Vilmos and spoke a single word, "Awaken."

Vilmos blinked and found he was leaning over the water basin beside his bed, water and blood dripping from his upturned hands. He shook his head, blinked again. In the other room, he heard his mother calling him.

"Hurry," she said. "You must gather the day's wood before breakfast!"

***

Out of breath from the long run, Vilmos doubled over. A good run always made him forget everything he left behind, and the sharp pain in his sides told him the run had been especially good. Vilmos stretched after the pain passed. If his leg muscles were too tense or if he strained, he'd have a tough time getting home. He then slipped on his boots. He preferred to run barefoot; otherwise the boots gave him blisters.

The wind howled up the path parting the dark woods before him. It was then Vilmos noticed how quiet the woods were that morning. He stared long into the dark wood—keeper of his secret. Here his childhood dreams were realized. In the shadow of the great trees, he could slay imaginary elves and dragons while discovering lost treasures and playing with imaginary friends.

Remembering his task to gather the day's wood, Vilmos worked to collect two bundles of firewood from the nearby thicket. Afterward, he secured the bundles with vines, and then laid them aside. The wind howling again sparked his imagination. He started up the overgrown path. He never ventured far into the woods–only far enough to be within their shadows yet close enough to see the sunlight in the clearing beyond.

Just then, he heard movement and then the crunching of leaves beneath heavy feet. He spun around to get a better look but saw only shadows.

An alarm went off in his mind. Fleetingly Vilmos thought of the girl from Olex Village, a girl too young to have been taken by a bear. Vilmos had no desire to share her fate. He stood still, his feet planted in the ground, his heart racing so fast it wanted to jump out of his chest. He picked up a large branch and wielded it before him.

Movement in the shadows caught his eye again. For an instant, he could have sworn he saw an old man carrying a gnarled cane. Holding the tree branch before him in what he hoped seemed a menacing pose, Vilmos crept into the shadows of the dark woods.

The fallen leaves and branches crunched under his boots, bringing a frown to his lips. With all those long days of hunting, he knew better than to clomp through the forest like a troll but he proceeded anyway, unafraid for the moment. It was then that the black fur and black eyes rose before him.

When the great bear reared up on its hind legs, terror gripped Vilmos' mind. His every thought told him to run, but he couldn't. It was as if he were rooted to the spot where he stood. His eyes bulging, Vilmos stared at the bear, sure any moment it would swing one of its mighty paws and that would be the end of it. Again a voice in his mind screamed, "Run!" but he could not move.

Images from his nightmare became real. In the nightmare the dark priests had come for him and like now, he had been unable to run. To save himself, he had lashed out at the priests with his secret power, and then like now, the forbidden came forth from his hands in a great surge.

In his mind, he screamed, "No!" at himself and at the bear. He squeezed his eyes shut and waited.

The great black bear roared. Vilmos squeezed his eyes tighter still. A scream building in his throat died as it escaped his lips.

Silence followed.

Vilmos waited. Thinking that surely the great bear must be charging, he gulped at the air and then mustering all the courage within him, he opened his eyes. To his astonishment, the bear was gone. In its place was a girl covered in mud and blood. She lay there on the ground, unmoving in the place where a moment before the bear had been.

Vilmos couldn't believe his eyes. Where had the bear gone? Was it possible that the girl was the bear? He had heard tales of shape shifters from other lands.

Suddenly remembering breakfast and the woodpile, he turned his gaze to the forest's edge. He saw the sun in the clearing and ran for its safety. Once he reached the clearing, he didn't stop running. He was halfway home before he realized that he had forgotten the wood for the hearth, but by then he wasn't going to return for it.

Soon afterward, Vilmos raced into the house. His eyes wide, he told his mother of the encounter with the bear but left out the part about the girl.

Lillath's face turned white. She swept Vilmos up in her arms.

Vilmos' father put aside the Great Book and stared at Vilmos with eyes that cut into his soul. "Bear or no bear, there is no excuse for using the forbidden."

Vilmos hid behind his mother. "Father, I know. The power just comes to me. I can do nothing to stop it."

"No excuses," his father said. "If you had returned after gathering the wood you never would've encountered the bear. You must resist the temptation to use what no man should possess."

His mother held him for a time, and then knelt before him, placing both hands on his cheeks. The terror in her eyes deepened. "When the tutor comes tomorrow, you will study two extra hours as penance. Understood?"

A flicker of hope to escape punishment was cut short by his father's voice. "Do you want them to come? Do you want them to take him away? This evil must be purged from his soul!"

"No, not again!" Lillath screamed. She moved between father and son.

His father reached for the whipping strap. "The penalty for use of the forbidden is death. Do you wish me to pass that sentence upon our only son? I am the village counselor. How can I make such an exception yet pass judgment on others? No, there must be a penalty paid."

Lillath backed away.

Vilmos gritted his teeth and waited for what he knew must come. The whipping was painful and just when he thought he could stand it no more the leather strap came down again. Tears flowed then and there was nothing he could do about it.

Crying during punishment like magic was forbidden. Each tear that crossed his cheek brought with it the strap. For a time it was as if the tears and the pain were one. Later, it seemed a great blanket of fog was over his thoughts. He knew the strap was upon his back but felt it no more. This was a blessing for when the boiling tonics were poured upon him to exorcise the demons within, he would feel them not.

The room moved and swayed. Vilmos knew he was being dragged to the healing room. He screamed then, his first scream, as he plunged deeper and deeper into the darkness of his thoughts and his soul. Within the darkness was a tiny speck of green and as screams leapt from his lips so did his soul leap from his body.

When he opened his eyes, a deep green valley with steep craggy walls spread out before him. A river with waters that were the deep blue of a sapphire dissected the green of the valley.

Vilmos folded out his arms, walked to the cliff's edge and jumped. As his feet lifted from the granite of the valley wall, talons replaced toes and wings replaced arms. He became a creature of his imaginings.

Alone and free, he flew as the great golden eagle. This was his special place, only his, Vilmos thought. He was the great winged bird, master of all he surveyed, who could swoop and soar, dive to the valley floor, or glide up on a light puff of air.

Vilmos looked out through the eagle's eyes and let out a cry that cut across the valley. The eagle could soar above the pristine valley. It could float on a pocket of air, sink to the valley floor, scouring for prey. It could fill Vilmos with life when pain brought his body to the brink of death, but it couldn't help him forget and it couldn't tell him about the stranger watching from afar.

Chapter Three

The celebrations of the Autumnal Equinox were nearly complete and for Sister Midori-shi the time in High Temple had not been a time of release and cleansing as it had been in previous years. She had far too many concerns on her mind to allow herself to relax and enjoy the celebrations. First Priestess Jasmine had been scrutinizing her every action as she prepared her to take over the position of the ill-fated Sister Shella who until a short time ago had been Second Priestess.

If Midori wasn't acting appropriately at any time, Jasmine told her and as if that alone weren't enough, one final anxiety brought her pacing about in her chamber as she had for the past seven nights, and that was the thought of Talem. He waited for her somewhere beyond the safe haven of High Temple and he expected her to have information for him.

When Midori had first arrived at High Temple, she had had every intention of telling Jasmine of the scrolls she carried with her and thus passing off the burden that she shouldered. Now there was too much at risk. She had been vying with Sister Catrin every step of the way for Sister Shella's position. Every moment brought her closer to the appointed time—a time when she must search her soul and make a decision that would affect her for all time.

If Midori told Jasmine what she was involved in, especially after she had been forbidden to meddle in the affairs of the dark priests, there was no way she would ever rise to the rank of Second Priestess ahead of Catrin. She coveted this standing the way she coveted no other thing. Her appointment would mean that she was only one step away from First Priestess. Soon afterward, no one would stand in the way of her goals ever again.

In trembling hands, she reread the scroll. The final time, she told herself, before she would destroy it as the shaman had told her to do. A low fire was crackling softly before her. By all accounts, she should have cast the scroll without delay into the flames, but after weeks of contemplation she still did not know if she could do what the shaman asked of her. Now was the time when she really could have used the guiding hand of Mother-Earth, yet she could not ask for it.

Outside in the courtyard the priestesses were gathering for the final celebration and she heard singing and the sounds of laughter now. She didn't have much time to make a decision. She glanced to the window, noting the lights and sounds coming from the courtyard below, and then her attention went back to the scroll. She carefully read the lines that told her of a thing she could not fathom. In her mind as she did this, the words rang in her ears and she heard the shaman's voice whispering in a hushed, solemn tone.

The sounds of instruments and the gathering musicians came in through the window now, and mixing with the crackling of the low fire, it began to lull her. The laughter and singing grew and any moment now Midori was certain a summons would come for her. It would be either Sister Jasmine or Sister Catrin and either way it would not bode well for her.

Midori paused in her reading to uncoil the last portion of the scroll and, in doing so, skipped ahead to the end. The shaman had set his mark just beneath the last line, and upon glimpsing it that final time, Midori found the courage to cast the scroll into the orange flames of the fire beside her. She watched the parchment as it burned, the edges of the thick yellow paper consumed in the flames and a slow trickle of brown and black creeping inwards toward the center of the scroll, thinking that just then she had found what she had been seeking. She no longer cared if Talem waited for her, nor did she care if Sister Jasmine thought her unworthy. She would do what she must and hope that in the end this brought her that which she coveted.

As the last remnants of the scroll became ashes in the hearth, Midori scattered them with a poker. She straightened her robes and her hair while gazing into the long, slender mirror beside her dressing table, and then hastened out the door. She hurried along the length of the hall to the long winding stairs that lead to the courtyard below.

The musicians and songstresses gathered in full chorus just as she reached the landing. If she hurried, she could slip unseen into the waiting throng.

***

The siege on Imtal had begun anew. For days, no one had been allowed in or out of the city. This day the catapults and ballistae of the bandits had pounded the outer walls mercilessly since dawn and there was no sign that there would be a reprieve. As the outer walls were more than a mile way, Adrina paid little attention to the battle. Even if the bandits did breach the outer walls, they would still need to penetrate the two inner walls before they could lay siege to the palace.

Adrina glanced at the flowing blue gown Lady Isador busily hemmed. Lady Isador wouldn't hear of allowing a servant to do the work. "Proper hands do proper work," she had said after chasing the servants away. That had been hours ago. It was now well past midday.

The clatter of hooves against the stones of the outer courtyard caused Adrina to jump and turn.

"Stand still, Young Highness," Lady Isador said. "Look now. Look what I've done. I've to begin again."

Still on her tiptoes, Adrina stared down at the courtyard below. The sight of a sweating mount passing to the stables caught her eye.

"Down, my dear," Lady Isador told her, "No wonder that hem looked all wrong. Mustn't stand on tiptoes." When Adrina didn't say anything, Lady Isador stopped her work and looked up at Adrina. "Child, you look definitely peaked. Are you hungry? The day is long. Shall I order the midday meal?"

"Could we finish tomorrow, Lady Isador?" Adrina asked.

"Sixthday is only a few days away, wouldn't want to disappoint his lordship, the son of Klaive, would we?"

Adrina rose to her tiptoes and turned a longing stare toward the stables.

"There goes that hem again," Lady Isador muttered. "My eyes aren't what they used to be, perhaps they do need a rest."

Adrina asked, "Is that a yes?"

"Yes, Young Highness, it is," said Lady Isador.

Adrina quickly changed out of the gown and into her riding clothes. Her goal was to act as though she was heading to the stables, when in truth she wanted to see what had brought the rider racing so quickly into the palace proper. Guards outside her father's private council chambers caused her to duck into the shadows of the hall.

A moment later, the door opened and a figure entered the hall and darted away. He bore Kingdom insignia but was otherwise clad all in black. Immediately afterward, a second figure raced down the hall and into the private council room. Adrina watched him pass. He bore no insignia save one on the upturned collar of a cloak draped over his arm. It was the white and gold bands of a messenger.

Adrina became determined to learn what the messenger was delivering. The last messenger had been in and out before she had a chance to learn anything. Word in the halls was that it had been a personal message from King Charles, and to Adrina it seemed servants knew more about the incident than she did.

She came out of the seclusion of the shadows and walked past the closed chamber doors. Adrina knew the king's guardsmen listened even when they knew they shouldn't. She also knew how to make most of them talk, especially the younger man on the right. His name was Emel and he and Adrina had history. As she walked up the nearby staircase, she was confident that she would be able to find Emel and it was to this place she headed when she noticed the subtle rising of stones in the wall near the top of the stairs.

She stopped and ran her hands along the edge of the stones, quickly noticing that the stones formed a door and that she could pull the stones out from the wall. Checking to see if anyone was watching her, she looked down the stairs and to the end of the hall in front of her. When she was confident that no one was near or watching, she slipped into the doorway, closing the secret door behind her.

Her hand on the dagger at her side, Adrina walked forward into the darkened passageway, stopping at a place where light came up from the floor. Drawn to the light, she looked downward where much to her surprise she could see into her father's private chamber. The messenger was still in the room as were her father and Chancellor Yi. It was then that Adrina noticed the dark stain of blood on the messenger's right side and the way his right arm hung limply. While it was Chancellor Yi who took the scroll from the messenger's left hand after his report, it was her father, the king, who touched the messenger's left shoulder and thanked him before bidding him to leave.

Adrina kneeled now to get a better look as the chancellor set the scroll onto a nearby table. The chancellor twisted both ends of the scroll, bringing the scroll to life with a power Adrina had never seen before. She was about to cry out when she was grabbed from behind and a hand was clasped over her mouth. The strong hands held her as she stared on.

In the light cast by the scroll, she could see her brother Valam and he was speaking now. "Your Majesty, father, I use the power of the old ones as you've instructed. I have secured the things you have asked for and the time is at hand. As your lord of the Southern Province, I beseech you to let me command the broken armies of the North. My generals are faithful; I can restore order after Imtal as no one else in the land can. As your son, I implore you to enjoin the exodus and make your stay with me in the South. Your safety is my utmost concern."

The figure behind Adrina gripped her tighter now and whispered in her ear, "Leave this place at once. Tell no one what you saw or heard. I will join you in the gardens at sunset. You must act as if you haven't seen or heard a thing."

Adrina didn't say a word as she retreated from the passageway and her trembling didn't stop for several hours. She ate the evening meal in the great hall, quickly and quietly, and now as she waited in the garden, she couldn't even recall what she had eaten.

While she waited, Adrina stared into the deadly stillness of the garden. There was a time she had imagined that it contained all the colors of the world. Her mother, Queen Alexandria, had put the array of gardens together, flower by flower, into one great garden. Now her mother too was dead, a victim of the times in which they lived.

Adrina paced as she waited. The sun had already set by the time he approached and by then her tears were long gone. "Your turn at watch at an end so soon?" she asked him calmly.

"Your Highness, you know it is," he said, his voice surprisingly mild. "Sunrise and sunset mark the changing of the guard."

"Guardsman Emel," Adrina said several times, luring him to her. They had been friends practically since birth, and this was her way of reminding him of his place and that he had something she wanted.

"Acting Sergeant, Your Highness," he said abruptly.

Obviously, he was still angry for what she had done to him last summer and in a way Adrina didn't blame him. High Road was a lonely place to spend the winter. She tried to smile, but couldn't. "Acting Sergeant, who'd've guessed?"

Emel's pace quickened. "Just until Sergeant Stytt's group returns from the Free City."

"I could see to it that he is positioned there permanently," she said baiting him as she walked with him to the other end of the garden.

When they entered the shadows at the other end of the garden,

Emel grabbed her arm by the elbow and pulled her as he ran to a side passageway. "What would you want in return?" he asked as he ran.

Adrina replied, "Information, that's all."

Emel grimaced. "You already know far too much. You must forget what you have heard."

"Or what?" Adrina's thoughts swirled. The voice of the lady in the tower echoed in her mind and all she could think about was finding out everything Emel knew. She linked her arm in his.

Emel pulled away from her. "I won't fall for your empty promises anymore."

Adrina edged closer, knowing it was hard for him to be cross with her when she was so close to him.

Emel glared at her. "Why haven't you talked to me until now?"

Adrina wanted to tell him about the lady in the tower. She longed to tell him more than anything but something wouldn't let her. "I've wanted to talk to you since your return. It was wrong for me to let you take all the blame."

"If I tell you the rest of what I know, do you promise to tell no one?"

Adrina nodded.

"I want to hear you say it."

"I promise, Emel. I will tell no one."

"In two days time Warmaster Gabrylle is taking a group of ridesmen out Braddabaggon way. He has chosen twelve to accompany him. He wouldn't say the purpose of the duty, but I can guess. When I return I will know for certain what is at hand. I will tell you then, I promise."

Adrina touched a spontaneous kiss to Emel's cheek and rushed away. She descended the long stairway into the central gardens and moved along the paths without really seeing much of what she passed. When she reached the far end, Adrina stopped and looked back toward the upper balcony.

Barely visible amidst the deepening shadows was a figure bent over the railing. Adrina knew it was Emel. She had always intended to make up for what she had done to him, but the time had never seemed right.

"I am sorry, Emel," Adrina whispered. "I do miss what we had."

Chapter Four

Imtal palace held an unusual silence even for the late hour of the
night. Adrina tossed and turned, enduring a fitful dream from which
she had awoken more than once. Minutes ticked by flowing into hours
as unchanging as the night. An eternity later, the first rays of the day
began to take the darkness from her chamber. It was then that she
heard the voices.

A moment passed when she was unsure if the voices were real or
in her head. She was almost certain the voices were imagined when
she heard the coughs and sneezes of the old chancellor. Soon
afterward, more voices and then the low, baritone moaning of Father
Tenuus arrived. Adrina put on her robe and went to her door.

Far down the hall, she heard the chancellor call out and request
admission to her father's chambers. As she peered out her door, she
could see the guardsmen at her chamber door, standing rigidly at
their post. The hall around them was a bustling thoroughfare as the
king's elite guardsmen marched down the halls. Their shining armor
and crimson breastplates showed combat readiness; they were much
different from the parade uniforms they had worn at the ceremony
the day before.

Adrina knew then that she couldn't go into the main hallway
without being seen, so she went to the rear of her chamber and

opened the secret door that led to the private hallway. The private
hall, however, was not empty and its usual darkness was broken by
torchlight. The one holding the torch was unfamiliar to Adrina, yet
she wasn't afraid.

"The lady sent me," the torch holder whispered, "I am to watch
over you."

Adrina wrapped her robe tightly about her and fully stepped into
the hall.

With his free hand, the torch holder reached out to Adrina and
touched her shoulder saying, "That which you wish to be, can be."

Adrina felt a wave of energy move through her, and then it was as
if she was standing in her father's chamber. She could see and hear
everything. Chancellor Yi was standing beside her father's bed, calling
out to him, "Sire, please wake. Keeper Martin wishes to speak with
you."

"A keeper," said King Andrew, rising up in his bed with a slow
persistence determined by age. "At this hour? What is a keeper doing
here at this hour?"

"Please sire," said the chancellor, "Keeper Martin says it is a
matter of utmost import."

The monarch stretched arms to full length and began his long,
slow turn to put feet to floor, causing the chancellor to scramble for
the royal slippers.

"Keeper Martin did you say?"

"Yes sire, Keeper Martin, head of all the Keepers of the Lore,"
said Yi, sighing with relief, as he just barely placed the slippers as the
king touched his feet to the hard, cold floor.

"What is Keeper Martin doing here at this hour?" King Andrew
cleared sleep from his eyes. "A king needs his sleep you know,
especially at my age."

The chancellor waited for the king to stand, saying, "I assure you
sire, I wouldn't wake you unless it was a matter of import. Though the
keeper would not address the matter directly, sire, there is a look

about him, as if he has just returned from a very long journey—a look of fatigue in the eyes. It is unlike Keeper Martin to have an unkempt beard. He wishes to speak to you alone. Rather mysterious, I must say. I will go talk to him if it is your wish, sire, and tell him to come back at a more appropriate time."

The king raised a hand to the chancellor's shoulder, using it to lift heavy bones from his plush bed. "There will be no need, Chancellor Yi. I am already roused. Tell him I will be along presently."

In her shadow form, Adrina was able to follow the chancellor and king as they entered the hall and joined Father Tenuus. Father Tenuus shot a worried scowl to the chancellor as he whispered, "I told you we should have waited a few more hours. Who is it that is here again, Keeper Q'yer or Keeper Martin? I always get the two mixed up."

"Come along and lower your voice!" said Chancellor Yi.

"Oh, that's right, the Keeper Q'yer is that nice, younger man. Keeper Martin is distinguished and graying… His hair, that is… It must be Keeper Martin that has arrived."

"You're the one that's graying, and it's not your hair," said Chancellor Yi in a barely audible voice as he strode away down the hall. He drowned the priest's further comments by blowing his reddened nose a few dozen times into a long white handkerchief.

While Adrina looked on, a still drowsy king greeted the great Lore Keeper. She chuckled a bit at her father's dowdy appearance in his night robe and slippers, and at his gauche waddle due to the slickness of the smooth floor. The special significance of the meeting struck her suddenly, especially when private chambers were entered without Chancellor Yi. This was further compounded by the arrival of a second visitor shortly after the two had entered the chamber and closed the door.

The distinct robes of office were an easy clue as to the man's identity as he removed his riding cloak and wrapped it over his arm. Father Jacob was first minister to King Andrew, head of the priesthood, and there was no mistaking the great swirling circles of white that decorated the sleeves of his otherwise black robe.

A visit by both men, especially at this late hour, was unprecedented—and in her mind, Adrina found only one answer. As she gasped in despair, the vision ended. She found that she was standing alone in the darkened hall. The torch holder was gone and she was suddenly exhausted.

She returned to her bed and quickly found sleep. Dreams were soon to follow, but at first she didn't see the creature in her dream, only the young man.

***

Vilmos' father did not come home until late that evening. He had been delayed in a special advisory session. Apparently, a series of bear attacks had taken place in Two Falls Village a day's ride to the north and huntsmen and trackers from the surrounding villages were preparing to track down the great black bear before it could kill again.

Vilmos, who had been listening closely, rolled a bit too far in bed and hit his head. Though the sudden pain brought tears to his eyes, he didn't utter a sound. Fleeing from the pain had grown easier over the past few days and the call of the vale was especially strong toward evening. He closed his eyes, forgetting that the return trek was never as easy as the initial folding of thoughts, one on top of the other.

Vilmos inhaled and folded his thoughts. The vale appeared. He walked to the edge of a cliff overlooking the vale. The sunset in the distance was breathtaking just as he had imagined, but a chilling breeze blew through the vale—a wind that had never before been cold.

Something felt different, as if he were not alone. Worriedly, Vilmos scanned the little vale, its steep walls, its large open floor. He found nothing and believed he was indeed alone.

He became a great taloned eagle, fearless and swift. The dive from his favored cliff was accomplished in one powerful leap. Wings sliced the air and made it sing. Down into the vale's depths the eagle swept, its keen eyes instantly spotting its prey. An unsuspecting valley hare was the intruder in his domain. He would crush its life and then he would indeed be alone.

In razor sharp talons, Vilmos swept up the valley hare. The warm and fleshy creature writhed pitifully and cried out for escape. The eagle did not heed its cry, but a part of Vilmos did and he forced the great eagle to release the hare.

"Do you know what it is that you are doing?" called a voice into his mind.

Vilmos was startled. The voice was somehow familiar and momentarily the vision of the eagle faltered. For an instant Vilmos stood on the cliffs staring into a cold northerly wind. Then he was propelled back into the razor-taloned eagle.

"It is called non-corporeal stasis, an out of body experience," said the voice with evident wisdom.

The vision of the eagle faded, yet the cliff was not the place to which Vilmos returned. Instead, he stood in the middle of the valley and searched in all directions for the source of the mysterious voice. "What does that mean? Are you here to take me away?"

"*Look*!" the voice commanded in a tone that was strangely compelling. "Look about you. What do you see?"

Vilmos did as bid. "I see the valley."

"Yes that is correct, now look beyond the valley. Extend your thoughts and open your mind. Now what do you see?" The voice flowed with warmth and again Vilmos sensed a familiarity in it.

"I see only the valley."

"No," said the other angrily, "*Look, look again*. Search beyond the valley. What do you see?"

Vilmos didn't like this game and clenched his fists in anger. "I see nothing!"

"*Open* the window to your soul. You will see."

Compelled to do as told Vilmos looked inside himself, he saw the door to his soul and he opened it. Beyond in the shadows he saw himself, lying in his bed in his father's house.

"What do you see?"

"Nothing!" Vilmos screamed, lying openly.

"*What do you see?*" the voice commanded.

Vilmos said, his voice filling with surprise, "But how, I don't understand?"

"That is what the experience is. Your body remains on the physical plane and your spirit searches beyond. You were truly flying. You really were the lone eagle flying over a valley of your own creation." The ominous voice seemed to close in on Vilmos. "You are a master of non-corporeal stasis, yet do not forget that all things have mirrors on the physical plane."

"How is this possible?" Vilmos asked.

"Think, before you speak. Look within, you know it is possible." The tone of the voice became sinister. "As is everything."

Vilmos felt the urge to go home.

"But Vilmos you are home," said the voice, "This is your home."

Vilmos shivered. "I want to go home; I am afraid."

"Well you should be, Vilmos, you should be very afraid."

Great black eyes drew up before Vilmos.

"This experience leaves your physical self completely without defense, open to attack from any force that wishes to enter."

Vilmos jumped back, his face drawn, pale with shock. His body shivered beyond his control. Everything within him told him to run, to hide, though he could not. It was then he recognized the voice. It was then his panic grew to despair and he feared for his very soul. "It is you, the one from my nightmares. Have you come for me?"

"Yes it is," said the voice with mocking overtones, "it is I."

Vilmos remained absolutely still; only his own gasping breaths broke the silence, nothing more. He looked out over the once peaceful valley, only now regaining the vantage point of the cliff as he fought to focus his mind. He felt alone, very alone, though he knew he wasn't. He cocked his head, left and right, forward and back, searching and waiting to hear the voice again to ensure he wasn't daydreaming.

"Where are you? Show yourself," Vilmos called out.

The only answer Vilmos received was the sound of wind rushing over the point and the returning echoes of his voice as it faded away and blended into the wind. The vale was empty. The ridge, empty.

"Looking for me?" came a voice from behind him.

Vilmos jumped. His heart pumped faster and faster. Breathing became taxing. It seemed he could not grasp any air. He spun around, faltering and falling to the hard, rocky surface of the vantage point. He pulled himself to his feet and shook defiant fists at the empty air.

"I will not hurt you," said the now charismatic voice from behind him.

Vilmos spun around again. "Where are you? Show yourself."

"I am here," returned the voice.

Vilmos turned to look in the direction of the voice and found an old man standing in plain view. He was by far the oldest man Vilmos had ever seen. His appearance was one of such frailty and weakness that Vilmos imagined a heavy wind lifting him from his feet and casting him about in the air like a feather.

The aged man, leaning his weight against a long misshapen walking stick, edged poised lips closer to Vilmos' ear. "Do not let the body fool you, boy. The body is fleeting, the spirit eternal. I will not blow away in the wind."

Instantly a cold, harsh wind blasted across the point. With each passing second, it increased in force until it was a gale of hurricane strength. Vilmos found he could no longer stand. He crouched to his knees and then hunkered down on his belly. The old man did not so much as twitch.

"Please stop!" Vilmos screamed.

"I cannot," said the old man, "Only you may stop it."

The wind dragged Vilmos to the edge of the cliffs. His feet dangling over empty air, Vilmos clawed at the rocks, trying desperately to maintain his grip. "I don't know how to stop it. Let me go, I want to go."

"Then surely you shall perish." The man spoke sternly, his voice lacking any hint of remorse.

Vilmos trembled and never stopped clawing at the rocks. "Do you mean die?"

"As surely as you were born."

Truth in the other's words stung Vilmos, similar to the dirt in his eyes. He knew without a doubt he would perish if he failed. Through a haze of dust, Vilmos saw the man, standing straight and tall, tall as the twisted staff he carried. He faced the wind, his stance still did not vary and then suddenly the man did not appear so aged. Somehow, he seemed different, as if Vilmos saw another standing in the old man's place.

Vilmos' knees went over the edge of the cliffs. He began screaming wildly, "I do not deny your powers are beyond my grasp, but I don't understand the point of the test. I don't know what to do."

"Vilmos, *use* that which you already know. *Use* the skills you possess. *Use them now.*" The man spoke powerfully.

Compelled by the enchantment of the voice and desperation, Vilmos concentrated, trying to make the wind stop. He clasped his eyes together, held his breath, clenching his fists so firmly his fingernails dug into his palms. Nevertheless, the wind continued to lash at him with increasing vigor.

Vilmos slipped further and further over the cliff, only his upper body remaining on the rocks while the rest of him dangled freely over empty air. His fingers pulsating with pain and wary of the approaching drop, he pleaded for help, his head turning wildly. "I don't want to die... please help me... How can you just stand there? Please, I beg you."

"The power lives within you. You have used it many times before, though you didn't know why or exactly how. *You are the power, Vilmos.* It yearns to be released from within you. *Release it.*"

"Please, please help me." Vilmos' plea sounded pathetic even in his own ears. "Please."

"Vilmos, let it go. I am giving you a reason to use your power; I give you your life. *Release it.*"

The voice was again commanding, Vilmos felt compelled to do as invoked. He had to prove he could stop the wind. Somewhere within was the key, a key that must be found. It had been so much easier before. He had never really tried to use the power; it had just come to him.

"Hurry, Vilmos. You must hurry!"

Vilmos found the object of his inward search; the strength was there. Still unsure exactly how he was supposed to make the wind stop, Vilmos decided to let his mind drift. His thoughts wandered until he found a helpful clue. As he anticipated, the solution to his dilemma seemed to seep into his mind.

It had always been there.

"Quickly, Vilmos. *You must release the power now.*"

A test of the power within forced the wind to flicker. Strength flowed to Vilmos unbidden. He bathed in its caress; it felt so wonderful.

Magic isn't bad; it is beautiful.

Vilmos knew what he had to do to make the wind cease and now he would do it.

The man screamed, "Vilmos, release the power, release it now before it is too late!" His anxiety increased with each passing second. "Hurry, Vilmos! *Let it go; feel it flow!*"

Vilmos perceived a peculiar scratching at the back of his mind; something loomed closer. Magic isn't bad, he reminded himself, the words flowing to him again.

"Go on try it," whispered the man, "Set it free."

Vilmos shook his head to rid himself of the irritating scratching. "I will, I will."

Vilmos focused on the wind, shaking his head to rid himself of the irritating scratching at the back of his mind. Was it a whisper?

Seemingly, as if simply acknowledging that the whisper existed was enough, Vilmos heard it. "No, Vilmos, no."

Vilmos shook his head, his concentration faltering. Irritated, the old man grabbed Vilmos about the shoulders and lifted him from the ground, shaking him violently while his razor sharp fingernails ripped into Vilmos' shoulders. "Do as you are told boy!" he shouted.

With untold power captivated in a crisp, clear voice, the newcomer spoke again. "It is a trick, Vilmos. Look closely, see his true form. The fourth comes. *Look!*"

The wind stopped dead. The old man released his grip. Vilmos fell to his knees.

The man said, "No, Vilmos, it is not true. Do not listen to foul lies."

Torn between the two voices, unsure which to follow, who spoke the truth or what to do, Vilmos clasped his hands to his head. His mind reeled with pain. He wanted to curl up into a ball and disappear.

Unchecked, the power within grew to a crescendo, reaching beyond Vilmos' control. His wild eyes stared in disbelief as crazed thoughts continued to spin through his mind. He was the power, the master of all he surveyed; he would release the force within. His arms shot out and he stood with his feet spread wide, bracing against the wind. His eyes were wild.

The second voice screamed, "Vilmos, in the name of Great Father, I command you, *Awaken!*"

Vilmos' eyes jumped open. He was sitting on the edge of his bed, blood dripping from his shoulders and fingers and pooling on the floor. The sound of stifled, irregular breaths fell upon his ears. Realizing the sound was not his own, he shrank into the corner. He would not have been amazed to see the old man sitting beside him, yet as he turned, meeting a warm smile, he nearly wet his pants.

"I thought you would be away until next Seventhday. What are you doing here?"

The tutor seated at a chair next to the bed, stared at him. She whispered softly, "Protecting you, Vilmos. The fourth is upon us."

"Why didn't you wake me? I was having a terrible, terrible dream."

The tutor looked to Vilmos' hands and the blood dripping to the floor. "We both know it wasn't a dream. I am here to help you, Vilmos."

Vilmos turned away from the tutor and then back again. "I don't need help; just go away."

She glanced nervously to the window and then touched a dark yellow stone to the palms of each of Vilmos' hands. "Healing stones," she said quietly, calmly. "They will ease the pain."

"Is it magic?" Vilmos asked.

"In a way," she responded, upturning warm green eyes, "these come from the temple of Mother-Earth."

She touched her index finger to each stone and whispered words in a language unknown to Vilmos. The stones burst into brilliant yellow flames and as Vilmos witnessed the birth of two tiny suns, his fingers tingled. As he watched, the wounds healed and scabs formed. Soon there was no trace of injury, and all the while the dazzling glow of the stones was diminishing until all that was left of the tiny suns were pebbles the color of coal.

She touched a finger to Vilmos' shoulders where the old man's clawed fingers had raked the flesh. He could feel the shoulders throbbing now that the pain from his hands was gone. "I am sorry," she said. "The power of the stones is spent, but I could not have undone this anyway. I must go now. Will you come with me?"

"Wh-wh-where," stammered Vilmos, "are you going?"

"Vilmos, you are special. All you have to do is trust me and let me help you. I am going to meet someone. He has waited a long time for you to be ready."

A voice told Vilmos if he left now he would never be coming home again. "I am afraid."

She offered Vilmos her hand and hesitantly he accepted. Her touch put Vilmos at ease and as he looked up into her soft green eyes his worries faded away. He would go wherever she would take him.

"We have to move swiftly," she said as she led Vilmos from the house. "The woods are a strange enough place with the light of day, let alone without it."

They had just reached the edge of the village when the sound of drums burst into the air. She began to run all out, dragging Vilmos behind her.

"Hurry, hurry," she said. "They come."

The two made the trek from the village to the dark wood at a record pace, the tutor dragging Vilmos behind her. Before them was a path overgrown with weeds and underbrush but still visible to an observant eye. Here they entered the dark wood. Questions flooded through Vilmos' mind. Where were they going? What of his mother and father? What of the drums?

He followed her along the tangled trail. Several times he tried to speak, though no words ever escaped his lips. A sickness welling up from his stomach told him the whole of the world was suddenly somehow different.

By the time they emerged from the dark wood, the sun was low on the horizon and the meadow spreading beyond the forest's veil was shrouded in shadows. Beyond the meadow, rolling hills obscured the horizon and somehow Vilmos knew the place she hastened to lay beyond the hills, somewhere off in the unseen distance. He raced alongside her expectantly now as the echo of drums chased their footfalls.

Chapter Five

After that night Adrina spent days trying to piece together what had transpired. That is, when Lady Isador or Chancellor Yi weren't giving her lessons, and discounting the horrible day she spent with Rudden Klaiveson. The more she probed for answers, the more intrigued she became. No one in the whole of Imtal Palace would talk about the visit—Emel included.

She was working on a plan to change that. Emel would talk. She had only to find the right time and the right words, which she hoped was now as she waited in the shadows. Performing his duties as acting sergeant had delayed Emel, and by the time he had arrived at the palace stables the others of his company had been and gone.

His steed, fittingly dubbed Ebony Lightning because it was jet black and could outpace even stallions bred for the king's swiftest messengers, still waited in its stall. He had known the appointed time of first formation, so he had not hurried. Then he had still had a full half hour.

Before and after every ride, Emel rubbed Ebony down from the poll of its head to the dock of its tail, up and down each powerful leg. In his proud eyes Ebony was the tallest stallion in all the lands and when he rode him, it was from this height that he looked out at the world.

Emel would have given anything to be like the Kingdom huntsmen, free like the four winds. His skills as a tracker stemmed from these desires. He had even pulled several short assignments at High Road Garrison—the last being during the past winter and spring—which allowed him to exercise these desires. He had not been able to take Ebony Lightning with him then, but now things were different. Ebony was his now, a reward for services rendered to the crown.

He was putting the finishing touches on the rub down when Adrina emerged from the shadows. Now he could only watch from afar as the other riders began to file through the outer palace gates and listen to the Warmaster Gabrylle's call, knowing the evident anger in the tone.

From the expression in Adrina's eyes and the saddlebags beside her, Emel knew without a doubt what she wanted. He stroked Ebony Lightning and glared. "Adrina," he began, "I will say this one more time, give me the harness and let me go. They're passing through the palace gates. Damn you and your foolishness!"

Adrina dangled the harness in front of him. It was the only harness that remained in the stables as far as Emel knew. "I'll have my father talk to Warmaster Gabrylle if need be. My horse is already saddled."

Emel regarded her for a moment. She had been trained in hand-to-hand combat the same as he had. She had even bested him once or twice on the competition field. "This is not practice," he said, "This is the real thing. People are dying out there on the fields."

Adrina lost her resolve momentarily and Emel snatched the harness from relaxed hands. By the time he put the harness in place and was in the saddle Adrina was mounted and awaiting him just beyond the stable in the parade grounds.

As Emel rode up to Adrina, he told her, "A dozen other guardsmen will willingly take my position. I must show the warmaster that I know what I am doing."

Ebony whinnied as Adrina edged her mare closer, bringing the two horses side by side. "You know what is at hand. I want to know and I'll be waiting for you when you return. You must tell me everything you know then as you promised before."

Emel nodded acknowledgement and rode out of the parade grounds. Adrina watched him go and then returned her mare to the stables. She passed the hours that followed quietly, taking dinner in her chambers.

Early evening found her atop the palace walls. Every now and again as she looked down into High King's Square, she tucked the errant strands behind her ear. The square was bustling with activity, merchants packing their wares onto pack animals, townsfolk haggling for last minute deals and the inevitable array of jugglers, musicians, fire-eaters and the like who had gathered to make festival of the day's executions.

Adrina disliked the busyness in the square. Nevertheless, the square afforded the best vantage point to witness the return of the riders. She was growing worried. Emel should have returned to the palace an hour ago.

She cast uneasy eyes westward. The sun was already beginning to dip below the horizon; soon it would be dark. As she turned back toward the square, a distant sound came to her ears.

Adrina wondered if it could be the clatter of hooves on cobbled stones. She wanted it to be but knew it wasn't. She heard the sound again, though this time it was even more distant.

Her heart leapt when trumpeters in the palace gate towers and at the city walls sounded off in response to the far off call. Her eyes set with worry, Adrina stared westward. There was no mistaking the distinct call to arms.

Knowing Imtal garrison riders and foot soldiers would soon respond to the trumpeters' summons, Adrina's face flushed white. Emel was out there somewhere with Warmaster Gabrylle and a group of unproven young guardsmen. It was their sixth excursion in as many days and the only one where they hadn't returned before dusk.

Within minutes, another call came from the city walls. This call meant a mounted guard was passing out of the city and into Imtal proper.

Billows of smoke rising in the foothills caught her eye. Near the smoke she could see long lines of troops, rushing across the hilltops of the Braddabaggon. For a moment they seemed a swarm of insects over the land and it was then she realized she had never seen so many in the field. As the opposing lines of troops clashed, the attack on the palace began anew. The enemy catapults and ballistae hurled their payloads at the outer city walls.

The battle raged on as the darkness of the night gathered full. The torches and fiery flames of arrows and bush lit the foothills with an eerie glow. Adrina said a silent prayer then, asking Great Father to watch over the kingdom soldiers. At the last she added a special wish, a wish that Emel would return safely from the fray.

In the distance she heard the crackle of thunder and saw the storm that moved in from the north. Rain followed. Slowly the lights in the foothills faded until there was only darkness and the distant sound of a raging battle she could not see.

***

That night of running through the woods had spilled over into many days and nights of running. Throughout it all the drums had been there, always behind them and seeming to get closer as time passed. Panic had ruled those days and nights but not this night. This night was different for they had arrived at a campfire and the one Vilmos had seen in his dreams was there waiting for them.

Vilmos stared at the peculiar tiny man for a time, still unsure if the things he had seen in his dreams were real—if any of this was real. After a long pause, Vilmos said, "I know you. You are King Gnome."

The gnome's skin was the color of rough leather—and while his face, deep set with wrinkles that covered its entirety, was the best indicator of his great age, his hair, long and black with whispers of gray, neither accented nor subtracted from his appearance of age and wisdom. He sat and motioned for the two to do likewise. Then he said, "Descendent of the long line of Oread though I am, I am no longer king. My people were taken away a thousand years hence and I am all that remains."

Far off Vilmos heard the drums. He saw the tutor glance to the woods. He was silent for a moment and then said, "You know I am afraid; you can sense my fear. Can't you, your majesty?"

"If you insist on thinking of me as a king, you will put my life and yours in great jeopardy. I am a simple shaman, nothing more. You may call me Xith."

Vilmos remembered something that had been gnawing at him ever since he first heard the shaman's voice. "In a vision you told me of Under-Earth and showed me two faces in glowing orbs."

"No vision," he said.

"Then was it real?" Vilmos asked.

"More real than you will ever know," Xith said as he leaned forward and touched a hand to Vilmos' shoulder where the raked flesh was begun to fester with a deep infection. "We will camp here this night. Tomorrow I will answer your questions. Do not worry, for there is nothing to worry about. All fears are behind you for a time. You will *sleep* peacefully this night. You must remember always that history belongs to the teller and is only as reliable as the teller's recollection of it."

Overcome with sudden fatigue, Vilmos found a dire need for sleep. Xith gestured with his hands and the campfire flames became bright with sudden life. The fire's warmth carried with it a healing touch and as soon as Vilmos lay down on the hard ground next to the campfire, he fell asleep.

Xith's silver eyes glowed with joy in the firelight then and as he regarded the tutor, he thought her brave and sincere. "Come here," he bade her, "Let me look at you."

She crossed to him.

Xith took her hand, noticing how the years had matured her. When she started to speak, he silenced her saying, "Promise me that you will forget what you know and what you have seen. Think of the boy no more. He is under my care and this alone should ease your mind. A great change is sweeping the lands and it is no longer safe. Do not return here."

She looked up into Xith's eyes. "Will you be all right?"

He hushed her with a silencing finger. He did not use the Voice on her as he had the boy. "I grant you faith Midori, deliver the final scroll. I know that the journey of homecoming will not be an easy one for you. But it is one that you must make, and one that you will make more than once."

"First do no harm," she whispered.

Xith's face grew dark and shadowed. With a sweep of his hand, he cast her into the winds and though she was far from sight, he whispered after her, "Watch your way with care and I will see you many more times."

Alone now with the boy, he looked to the heavens and the gibbous moon obscured by dark clouds. He did not know if he could cheat fate or even if it was wise to try, though he must try for the future of all the races in all the realms was at stake.

***

Seth's eyes keyed to the impassable line of multi-sailed vessels hungrily waiting. That the ships were King Mark's, he had no doubt. That the five ships, including the flagship he sailed in, would survive the encounter, he had plenty of doubts.

Brother Galan reached out to his mind, *What do we do now, Brother? Two days out of Kapital and already we find the enemy upon us.*

Seth ignored Galan and directed a thought to the ship's sailmaster. *Cagan, we must get through. We cannot fight them all at once. Can we make it to open seas?*

"Perhaps," Cagan said, speaking aloud as was his chosen fashion and the fashion of those who were not of the Brotherhood. "The escort ships should strike the right side of the blockade while we cut straight through and try to make for open seas. With the wind filling our sails this ship can outrun anything."

Bryan stepped forward, his young blue eyes betraying naked anger, *Running is pointless. It would only show cowardice. We should strike the enemy head on with our eyes wide open.*

Galan turned to Seth. *I agree.*

Sailmaster Cagan tugged at his beard, his open thoughts streaming to Seth as his mind worked through the dilemma. Cagan said, "We will strike head on, we just won't stop, and if surviving means running, we must run."

Bryan cut in. *You are wrong.*

Seth raised a hand commandingly. All dispute ended. *Sailmaster Cagan, go ahead with your plan. I trust your judgment.*

Cagan passed instructions to the ship's broadcaster, who in turn relayed messages to the escort ships. A maneuver was dealt out to the small fleet. The escort ships turned sail from their positions, heading directly for the right side of the blockade. Following Cagan's orders, the sailors readied torches and grapples.

As the first of four ships rammed the blockade, the sound of wood and metal twisting and breaking filled the air. Sailors from both sides were washed over the decks. As the cries of battle rose, Cagan passed out orders to the crew of the Lady L. The Lady L, her sails trim, turned with the wind and raced for open seas through the mass of tangled ships.

Including Bryan, Galan and himself, Seth had selected eleven of the Red to undertake the journey. Seth looked down to the lower deck of the Lady L where the chosen were assembled. He knew they were preparing for a fight that must come and they must win. Behind them, pillars of smoke and flames rising into the heavens dwarfed those battling upon the ships, reduced to tiny specks leaping from tiny ships and cast against a backdrop of hungry white sails. The chase was on.

Chapter Six

Unsure what had awoken her, Adrina stirred. The battle in the hills outside Imtal raged on for days without reprieve. In that time, few returned to the city though many left to defend its gates. Emel was still out there, though Adrina did not know where.

The light of the moon, filtering in through an open window, cast long shadows about the room. She brushed a hand across the pillow still wet from her tears.

"Winter is surely coming," she told the attendant who was stoking the coals in the fireplace.

"Sorry, Your Highness," the girl whispered. "I shouldn't have let the fire go out, but I wished not to disturb you. But now it looks to be a cold night and I was concerned."

Adrina nodded absently, her thoughts miles away.

When the attendant finished, she bid Adrina a good night as she left. Adrina slid to the edge of the bed and stared at the fire building in the hearth, waiting for its warmth to chase the chill away and wanting to run to the open window so she could stare out into the darkness of the night.

A knock on the private entry door followed by whispers caused her momentary alarm. She called out, "Lady Isador, is that you?"

"Do I sound like Lady Isador?" came the reply.

Adrina's heart skipped, tears of joy came to her eyes. "Emel?" she called out.

"Of course," the voice said, "Are you going to let me in?"

"Just a minute." Adrina slipped a robe around her and then opened the door. She almost ran into his arms, but caught herself on the first step. "Must remember your station, dear," she whispered to herself. They were Lady Isador's words, not her own.

Emel moved closer to her and then with swiftness Adrina had never before witnessed, he grabbed her and clasped a hand to her mouth. Eyes round and wild, Adrina struggled against the hand raised to her mouth.

"Do not scream," came the ominous whisper in her ear, "I will lower the hand, but do not scream."

The voice was feminine now and Adrina recognized it as if from a dream, and then she recalled a thing forgotten. In that moment she looked up and the face and body were no longer Emel's. She stared then into the dark eyes, seeing the long black hair and knowing without doubt who the attacker was. Her eyes grew wider and her despair edged toward panic.

As the hand was removed from her mouth and the restraining grip was released from about her shoulders, Adrina considered screaming. She could have easily and aid probably would have arrived within moments afterward, but she did not scream. Instead, she regarded the one that stood over her. "Calyin?" she asked.

The other shook her head. "I am not my older sibling though at times I wish for such a simple life."

Though Adrina had only vague pictures in her mind, she knew without a doubt who stood before her. "What are you doing in Imtal?" Adrina demanded, "How did you get into the palace? If you're caught, you'll be ejected from the city or worse, held for treason. Father will—"

The woman touched a finger to Adrina's lips and said, "Father is the one I wish to see."

Adrina regarded her sister. "Are you mad? After what you did to him and to the Kingdom. You were betrothed to Jarom of Vostok. Valam was put to a contest of steel and he nearly died."

"*Silence*", the other commanded, using the voice as simply as she had used the illusion. "Listen to yourself. I am not chattel. I would not wed to Jarom of Vostok for I loved another, and now he is lost and I have sworn my love and my life to yet another." She passed warding hands about the air and added, "You must know what it is to love one that your station does not allow. Do you not, sister?"

Adrina fought the urge to go to her then and ease the pain in her sister's eyes. Then finding strength, she said, "Midori, you must leave. Leave or I'll call the guards myself."

Midori procured a small parcel from beneath her dark robes. "Father must read this. I must know the truth of it. If he is enthralled then there can be no hope."

Adrina reached for the parcel. "Give it to me and then be gone! I'll give it to him for you."

Midori said, "We were sisters once, you and I. Can you not remember?"

"I remember." Adrina spoke the words bitterly and truthfully. "But there was so much pain, and then you made it so the pain swallowed me for three long years while you lived a life beyond these walls, a life without remembrance."

Midori replied, her voice edged with pain, "I remembered it all, just not the way that you do. I lived with the pain and paid for the pain. I am still paying a debt that I never owed. Can you not see that? I had to leave. I had no other choice. Can you not find it in your heart to forgive me?"

Adrina spat at her then. She didn't know why, she just did. "It is not something that I can forgive and father will not see you. To him you are dead; you died the day you left Imtal. He buried you in this thoughts beside mother."

"I am flesh and blood," cried out Midori, "your blood, your kin.

Touch my hand. Can you not feel it? The blood coursing through my veins is your blood. Our family. Our blood."

"I understand," whispered Adrina. She did not take her sister's hand.

"Can't you see, Adrina," implored Midori, "I've paid and I will pay always. The man I loved is no more and now I can never love another. Is that not payment enough?"

"He will not see you," replied Adrina.

"Adrina!" shouted Midori, as she fought to embrace her sister, "I would throw myself from this window if you wished it, but it would not resolve anything. I am asking you, imploring you, to take me to see father. Take him on a walk through the garden to the gazebo. I'll be there waiting and make sure you are alone."

Adrina replied quickly, coldly, "Haven't you been listening to what I've said, I will not help you. You are on your own."

Midori replied, "Sister, it is you who has not been listening. Do you think I would return for petty reasons? I have been running from this place ever since I left it. This is the last place I would ever return to by choice. Don't you see? This is something much greater than you or I, much greater! I must give him this and then the truth of it will be revealed to me."

Adrina could resist her older sister no more. She collapsed into the others waiting arms, the weight of years passed around her shoulders. "This doesn't mean I've forgiven you," she whispered.

"Not at all," the other replied.

***

Vilmos bolted upright, unsure what had awoken him. Thoughts from the previous day came flooding into his mind. The Shaman. Midori. The drums. He heard the drums again and voices, and then for an instant all his thoughts stopped.

No dreams, Vilmos realized. He had slept peacefully and nothing had awoken him until just now. The drums, he heard them again. Vilmos was about to speak when Xith clamped a hand to his mouth.

"Not a sound," Xith whispered. "Take my hand."

Vilmos nodded. His knees were trembling. He sat as Xith indicated he should.

Quietly the two waited. The voices and drums grew steadily clearer and closer. Soon it became apparent whoever was out there was in the hills just beyond the edge of the clearing. Vilmos was ready to run but Xith sat very still, his eyes closed, his face pale and drawn, his hand clasped tightly to Vilmos'.

From high overhead came the call of a hunter. Staring long, Vilmos caught sight of the grandest eagle he had ever seen. It was circling lazily over the hills and as Vilmos peered up at it, it turned a glistening black eye in his direction.

Suspicious, Vilmos eyed Xith.

The eagle called out again, a long piercing call, and then it folded its powerful wings and dove from the heavens. Vilmos held his breath as he watched the eagle plummet downward. It soared over the cliff's edge, down into the depths of the valley.

Afterward the color returned to Xith's face and he released Vilmos' hand. "Hunters and trackers," Xith whispered, patting Vilmos on the back reassuringly. "They are from your village and the neighboring two."

Vilmos turned a watchful eye to the hills. "Are they looking for me?"

Xith shook his head. "As far as I can tell, they hunt an animal of some sort."

"The bear, the black bear," Vilmos said, wide eyed. "It is dead, I killed it and then a girl appeared."

Xith asked Vilmos to explain. Vilmos told him of the recent bear attacks and his own encounter with the bear. He didn't say anything about the girl that appeared after the bear died, however.

Xith said, "Animals of the forest have a keen sense about them. We will have to keep our eyes open as we move north. To be sure, it would not be wise to travel north through Vangar Forest, and a descent into the valley from here shouldn't be too bad."

A puzzled frown crossed Xith's face, his eyes darting toward the hills.

Vilmos said, "You weren't expecting hunters and trackers. Who were you expecting, shaman?"

"No need to trouble over the could-have-beens," Xith replied. "Are you hungry?"

Vilmos agreed he was. Xith removed a thick slab of smoked beef and a loaf of black bread from his saddlebags.

"Eat all you care to," Xith said. "It will be a long day."

Vilmos quickly reached for the bread. "I am going home then? My parents will miss me if I am not home soon."

Xith, busily cutting thin strips of beef, paused and then laid the knife aside. "Many, many years ago, I made a promise to a young couple who were very much in love. Five years they had been wed and still they had no children. They so wanted a child. I told them of a girl heavy with child in need of caring hands."

Xith's eyes lost their gleam and there was evident sadness in his voice. "The girl, your mother, needed a secluded place to stay, a place where none knew her or that her child was without a father. I told the couple they must harbor the child's mother and see the child into the world without harm. Afterward the child would be theirs to keep and raise as their own. I also told them there was a price, for one day I would return for the child, but until that day—"

"I want to talk to my mother," Vilmos cut in. "I'll tell her I am fine and that I am with you. She will understand, though I am sure she will tell you to make sure I am back before the next Seventhday."

"*You will not be home before the next Seventhday, Vilmos, or any other day.*" Xith paused to ensure Vilmos understood. "Your father was among those from the three villages. I could sense his anguish. He knew the day I spoke of those twelve years ago had come. Your feelings for him are wrong, you know. He loves you more than the air he breathes…

"I stayed with them for three days when I escaped from the North with your mother. I told them the signs to watch for, the signs that would tell them I would return." Xith walked to the rim of the valley and gazed across the great span. "Your magic is what brought me to you, Vilmos. It was the reason your father was so exacting. He knew your use of magic would only hasten me to your door. It was his love that protected you from the cleansing that has taken so many other would-be magicians."

Tears in his eyes, Vilmos turned away.

"*Do not be sad,* young Vilmos. To be sure, Great Father and Mother-Earth will not let their sacrifice go unrewarded. *Look now to the future* and the days ahead. You have always known you would leave your home."

Vilmos nodded. Closing his eyes, he pictured long brown hair touched with gray and tired eyes of blue.

Xith turned Vilmos to face him and stared directly into his eyes. "It is time to start our journey. There is much to do, so very much to do. I would ask you now to come into my service. You could think of it as an apprenticeship of sorts. I can teach you of the powers within you and would have you enter my service of your own free will, yet there are things I must first tell you."

Vilmos nodded.

Xith began, clearly and slowly, "Know that you *can* stay if that is your intent. Know also, the fourth comes. It brings the dark priests and they will not be as kind as I. They will bring a sentence of death upon you and upon those you love, as that is the law."

Vilmos shuddered at the mention of the dark priests. Their task was to purge the land of magic, a task they had carried out across the centuries.

"Or you can come with me now. I will do my best to teach you control over your powers. And though I am not human, I *can* teach you the way of the Human Magus." Xith's tone became firm. "A very difficult trial awaits in the coming days, and in this I need your help.

Will you help me, Vilmos?"

"Lillath will be lonely," Vilmos said, wiping tears from wet cheeks. "Will they ever have another child?"

Xith's eyes became distant and it was as if he was searching an unknown place. Time passed and then the long silence came to an end with Xith saying, "In time, Lillath *will* have a child. They will find peace."

Vilmos could sense the truth of the words and questioned no further on the matter. "What of the dreams, are they gone?"

Vilmos watched odd expressions cross Xith's face. Something told him that until that moment Xith had been sure the dreams were gone, but now as he looked into Vilmos' eyes he wasn't sure anymore. Then finally, Xith said, "Have you made your choice, Vilmos?"

Without hesitation Vilmos said, "I wish to go with you."

Xith's face betrayed no emotion, pleased or otherwise. He waved his hand, beckoning Vilmos to follow him.

***

King Andrew regarded the hooded messenger that knelt before him as he returned the bit of parchment to waiting hands. "You are more than a day late with this news messenger. What say you?"

The hooded figure rose, but did not speak.

"What say you?" repeated the king. Adrina raised a hand to her father's shoulder. "How do we know that we can trust such news? What proof have you to anything written in this letter?"

"She is mute father," whispered Adrina in the king's ear.

"She?" inquired Andrew. "As I have said messenger, you are more than a day late with this news. I'm sure King Jarom's spies are already aware of that fact, so you needn't prod for anything more. If you seek proof to give to your master, I will tell you that it is so. Begone from my site...Guards, guards!"

Four armed figures launched out of the shadows toward the gazebo, two with swords drawn, two with readied crossbows.

"Father, you promised no guardsmen!" protested Adrina, "You

promised safe passage."

"Withdraw the hood or one of the guardsmen will do it for you," King Andrew commanded, "and if you raise that blade from beneath your robes messenger—yes, the one you are fingering even now— they will kill you before you take a single step."

"Withdraw the hand slowly," ordered one of the guardsmen stepping up behind the hooded figure, while another stepped between the figure and the king.

Heedless of the warning, Midori continued to draw her hand up from beneath her robes. A shiny handle could be seen protruding from her robes now and one of the crossbowmen moved to get a clearer shot, his finger resting on the releasing mechanism.

"Withdraw the hand slowly," repeated the head guardsman.

Midori took an ominous step towards King Andrew, attempting to get around the guard in front of her.

"No!" Adrina screamed as she launched from her seat at the crossbowman, striking him in the flank and deflecting his shot harmlessly into the courtyard. "You want them to kill you don't you? Are you mad?" shouted Adrina.

One of the guardsmen grabbed the concealed hand, while the other latched onto the hood that concealed the messenger's face. "It is a scroll your majesty, a scroll."

"Yes, that is clear," retorted Andrew, his face turning ashen. "Hand me the scroll guardsman and have your men withdraw."

"But sire," the head guardsman protested.

King Andrew waved his hand; only he had recognized the revealed face that was still partially obscured in a tangle of dark hair and thick hood. Andrew said nothing as Midori returned the hood about her head, though the color did begin to return to his face a short time afterward.

"You should have let them kill me," hissed Midori, pursing her lips and directing her words at Adrina.

King Andrew turned his attention to the scroll. He uncoiled it and slowly began to read. When he finished, he turned back to Midori in a stately manner. He was taken aback by the message contained in the scroll, though you couldn't tell this by his face or by his words, only by his posture. "As already stated, the group departed for the South a few days ago. You are too late."

"I am not a foolish child any more, I know the ways of your thoughts. The decoys are still caught in battle in the foothills around Imtal," returned Midori. "I know you plan another and that this one aims to move the royal household to the safety of Alderan. You must go with them; I have seen the parting paths. As the scroll states, the son will fall before the father and then the kingdom will be lost."

Andrew was silent for a time as the weight of office removed the rigor from his posture. "How do we know this is the truth? What proof have you that the kingdom is so infested with spies and that Prince Valam's life is in danger?"

"Promote Captain Brodst to King's Knight First Captain. He is the only one in Imtal palace that I trust. The truth of the matter will then reveal itself." Midori turned to Adrina as she started to move away from her father-king. Her expression said the thing that she couldn't say. "Heed the warning or not, I no longer care. I have fulfilled my duty."

It was then that Adrina remembered Midori's earlier words about the danger and the journey she would soon be undertaking. "Say something father," she cried out. "Tell her what I know is in your heart!"

Andrew said nothing. He merely watched as Midori slipped into the shadows of the courtyard and then faded from sight.

***

Seth stood silently as Cagan swung the Lady L about to fill the sails, forcing the pursuers to scramble to catch a fresh breeze.

Seth passed to Cagan's mind, *Clever, Sailmaster Cagan, very clever.*

Cagan's retort was swift and his eyes never broke away from the sails or the wheel. "I had some help, did I not?"

The forces of the Mother are at the call of all who serve her. A peculiar sight caught Seth's eye and for an instant his thoughts broke off. A speck along the horizon grew to a dot on the water. *To the east, a ship!* he called out to all on board.

Cagan sighed. "It is over, my friend. One way or another we must move to engage, either to the rear or to the front." The wily sailmaster paused. "Yet perhaps… Yes, if we tack directly toward that incoming ship we will surely catch them off guard."

Seth nodded agreement and Cagan ordered the vessel turned against the wind; their nimble sloop could cut well in the tack. The cutters behind them, on the other hand, were much slower in the turns, and cross-winded the Lady L rapidly approached the ship that a short time ago had been but a mere spot on the water.

All on board readied for the inevitable. Silent prayers were sent to the Father and Mother to protect and to keep them.

"Sailmaster, she has square foremasts and two lateen rears!" yelled the lookout from his perch.

An expression of dismay and fear passed over Cagan's face. His fears permeated the air and flowed to Seth along with his open thoughts. The speed with which the vessel had moved through the water had led him to believe it was another cutter. Cagan had not expected a full-sized war galleon.

Seth was also worried. King Mark was better prepared than they had thought. He only wished he could risk the projection of his will to contact Brother Liyan and warn him. Many skilled craftsmen had labored long on such a vessel as they now faced, which as they drew closer, loomed larger and larger against the pale blue backdrop of the waning day.

The two ships, galleon and sloop, were nearly within striking distance of each other. The Lady L was dead on course for the galleon, and with the other enemy ships reduced to unseen dots to the distant rear, for now it would be just a one-on-one engagement.

Seth was proud of Cagan's sailors. They held no fear in their thoughts, only determination that was strong and growing with each passing moment. They followed Cagan's orders and kept the sails perfectly trim while they rallied for the coming fight.

A questioning voice came into Seth's mind, *Brother Seth?*

Everrelle? Seth said curtly, disturbed by the untimely interruption.

Everrelle's response was strong and firm. *Do you mark any of our kind on board the ship?*

I do... not. Seth paused then gasped.

Nor do I, added Galan.

What if they are merely shielding their thoughts? Bryan offered. *We should probe to make sure.*

Seth agreed. Bryan cast his will into the wind. Cagan continued on a direct course for the galleon. A few moments later Bryan passed to their thoughts, *There is no trickery.*

Seth's grimace turned upward, perhaps the day was not lost.

The galleon captain scrambled to turn the large ship, barking out orders that carried across the darkening waters even above the sound of rising frenzy from both sides. As Cagan turned toward his broadside, he tried gallantly to fill sails for maneuvering speed and then with a resonant rending, sloop and galleon collided. The air filled with the cacophony of crunching timbers and shrill screams.

The battle was joined.

The galleon had received a potentially lethal blow and was gaining water fast. Still her sailors would not go down alone. Grapples were swiftly set and tied off tight. Cut lines were cast back relentlessly, yet this alone was not enough and the two ships would go down together if the sea had its way.

"They do not stand a chance against us!" Cagan cried out to his sailors as he swung across to the galleon's low side on a rope tied to the upper rigging. With a cheer, his men returned his chant and charged, their blades clashing with the enemy and drawing crimson blood.

The eleven members of the Red stood still, waiting until the mournful screams in their minds reached a crescendo. When he could take no more, Seth screamed out the order to attack.

The Red surged over the side, pouring forth like a deadly red rain. A blur of brutal force, they dropped the enemy each where they stood with but a single precise touch. Such was their evident anger and the might of their invoked will.

When the first of the Red fell, a blow from behind piercing his heart, Seth screamed again. He vowed there and then to spare no suffering on the one who had delivered the deadly blow. With a jump and a kick, the guilty was knocked stunned to the deck, his demise not instantaneous like the others before him.

Nine and one of the Red trudged onward toward the galleon's high deck. Three sailors were all that remained of Cagan's once proud group and they protected his rear as he struggled against the galleon's surly captain. Seth tried to push through to reach Cagan but was held at bay. The enemy was strong and wielded their weapons skillfully. Two more brothers fell.

The sight enraged Seth. He pushed forward with renewed vigor, as did his companions.

Seth and seven others reached the high deck to find only Cagan remained standing. All around him were the dead and the dying and his sword lay deep in the enemy captain's chest.

Drained, Cagan stumbled. Seth rushed to his aid. Cagan's clothes, blood splattered and shredded, revealed multiple lacerations. Seth held Cagan from toppling over. He knew there was no time to attend to the wounds and Cagan knew this as well. Two of the pursuing ships were closing in and soon their ranks would sweep over the decks to the place where the last few survivors stood.

"It is only us at the last." Cagan choked on his own blood and weakly added, "my friend."

Seth was silent. The middle decks of the galleon were already being claimed by the sea and their own small ship was beginning to founder. The end was surely near.

As his mind filled with despair, Seth found strength in Cagan's eyes. He turned to the few fated to remain and pointed to the ships closing in. *They are what stand in the way of escape. We cannot fail; we will not fail. Eight against the many shall be triumphant!*

Cagan struggled to his feet. "There are... nine!" he shouted.

Chapter Seven

Three squadrons of garrison troops, one of the Horse and two of the Foot, filed through Imtal's southern gate in ponderously long lines four abreast. At the city's eastern, western and northern gates, a similar scene played out as every available soldier and conscript moved from the city to the fields. This day the city would be won or lost, and the royal household would be moved under guard to Alderan.

As she listened to hooves and boots clatter on the cobbled streets, Adrina knew she would miss Imtal. So often she had looked out her window, stared at its tall gray walls and dreamed of things outside that the lands beyond seemed just that, a dream. She let her mind wander along the city streets and into the shadowed alleyways she passed, pieces of her thoughts falling into every nook and cranny.

Soon afterward, her thoughts went to those she left behind. She would miss Lady Isador and her father-king, this was true, but oddly, she decided that most of all she would miss those tall gray walls. They had housed and symbolized her fears, her loss, her anger, even her hopes and dreams for so long they truly seemed a part of her. The future without them to look out at seemed a frightening thing.

Her dreams had carried her through those three long years after her mother's death, but now Adrina finally had what she wanted and suddenly she felt an overwhelming urge to race back to Imtal Palace.

Returning from her thoughts, her eyes went to the hills of the Braddabaggon. With one hand she held the reins while the other gripped the hilt of her sword, though she had been told that the elite guardsmen around her had sworn their lives for hers should it come to it. She surveyed the battlefields that they passed, the dirt in some areas stained with the blood of the fallen. She longed to be farther south and away from the fighting.

Along with thoughts of the father she left behind, Adrina cast away thoughts of Rudden Klaiveson. Her betrothal to set the alliance and the Barony of Klaive was at the end of the journey. First, she would travel to Alderan by the sea.

The air that morning was fresh and cool. Overhead the sky, besmirched with dark clouds, promised of rain. Adrina took in a deep breath and as the smell of grass and smoke wafted to her nose, she tightened her grip on the reins and bid her horse to speed onward. The sound of hundreds of hooves and thousands of feet plodding along muddy ground filled the air.

***

Four times the trail ended and nothing save the perilously high walls of the canyon loomed before them. To continue the descent, Xith and Vilmos used ropes and when they finally reached the bottom Vilmos was out of breath, panting with sweat dripping from his chin. He sighed and fought to get his breathing under control. He craned his neck up to see the lip of the wall, knowing the hard work had been oddly cleansing.

A breeze cutting through the vale brought cool air swirling beside the wall. Vilmos smiled even though the cool perspiration tingled his nose and sent a chill up his back. "Where do we go from here?" he asked.

"The valley will carry us to the upper bounds of the Vangar," Xith said, indicating the brief rest was over.

Xith spoke as he walked. "From there, it is at most a day's trek to the plains beyond. We do not want to delay long in the forest."

"Beyond?" Vilmos said, turning to regard the shaman.

With the high sun at his back Xith seemed mystical and while it was perhaps the timeworn face etched from the stones of Under-Earth itself, it could have been the troubled eyes dulled by the sun yet still of a silvery gray. "The whole of the greatest kingdom in all the lands is north and it awaits."

"The Alder's Kingdom?" Vilmos asked. "How will we survive the wastes beyond Sever?"

"Great Kingdom to those who dwell there," Xith said as he slung his leather satchel over the opposite shoulder and put the walking stick into his left hand. "The Borderlands are in the far north, beyond the bounds of Great Kingdom, but I suspect our journey will not carry us that far north..."

Xith's voice trailed off. He froze. His face turned pale. He waved his free hand in the air, causing a glowing orb of white to appear and within the orb was a face. At first Vilmos didn't recognize the face but then the image grew clear, as if powerful eyes telescoped inward.

The face was that of his tutor and it was riddled with fear. Her head was swaying about and though her face was all Vilmos could see, he knew she was running scared and something or someone was chasing her.

Xith pursed his lips and blew into the orb. He whispered, "*Run fleet upon the wind, child...*"

His spell of speed and protection cast, the shaman turned his attention to the one that called to him and the image of the warrior elf burst to life within the orb. The raft the elf and his companions floated on was held together with little more than faith and to this, Xith cast a spell of binding so that the makeshift raft may survive the turbulent waters of the open ocean. He could offer little else for the distance was great and his strength was drained.

Chapter Eight

The storm clouds of early morning were blown south by strong winds out of the north and a clear sky quickly replaced dark clouds. Adrina rode quietly, content for a time watching the battlefields fall away behind them.

The swelling rounds of the Braddabaggon quickly replaced the green of the Imtal plains. Adrina kept alert, her eyes wide, watching for signs of trouble. The guardsmen around her were similarly alert. Although she couldn't hear the raging battle in the fields to the north over the din of hooves and feet, she imagined she could and grew anxious for Caption Brodst to quicken the pace.

For a time she thought about the long southwesterly trek to Alderan. The coastal city was a day's ride south of the Free Cities and was rumored to be beautiful beyond compare. In days of old it had been the capital of Great Kingdom and was named after the first king of the land, the Alder. It was once considered the meeting place of the North, South and East or as legend said, the meeting place of the three realms.

Adrina maneuvered her mount between Keeper Martin and Emel. She attempted to spark a conversation with Emel. She didn't know why he was angry with her but she aimed to apologize quickly. She needed someone to talk to. In response, Emel spurred his mount and rode to the front of the party. Her intent hadn't been to anger Emel, only to carry on a conversation with him.

"Dear one," Keeper Martin said, "he will forgive you in time. For now, just let him be. Enjoy the morning."

Adrina was aghast; the Lore Keeper had spoken to her. She didn't have the heart to tell him that she couldn't enjoy the morning under the circumstances. Her reply instead was an easy response of agreement, a few more hours of silence would be tolerable, but just barely so. She hoped Emel would speak to her soon.

At midday Captain Brodst called the column to a halt. The abeyance would only be long enough to give horses and tired foot soldiers a much needed rest and to grab a light repast. Adrina was very pleased to rid her bottom of the saddle for a short time. After dismounting, chasing off an attendant and leading her horse to where Keeper Martin, Father Jacob and a few others were gathered next to a small stream beside the road, Adrina dove into her saddle bags where she found dried beef, still-warm rolls and a skin of kindra-ale.

While she ate, Adrina looked to the Lore Keeper and the King's First Minister. She wondered at Father Jacob's quick approval of the journey. His words on behalf of her father-king had surprised her then and puzzled her now as she contemplated them. Why did a man who spoke directly to Great Father care so? Why did a man like that do anything?

Then there was Keeper Martin. Rumor had it the great keepers communicated in dreams and that is how they recorded the histories of all that went on in the land. Rumor also had it that Martin was unlike his predecessors. The head keeper before Martin never left the Halls of Knowledge. Keeper Martin was forever traversing the land, heading over mountain, braving the wilds of the Territories or journeying to unknown places in the Far South.

"It is impolite to stare, dear," whispered a voice behind her.

Adrina gulped down a lump of half-chewed meat. "I didn't mean to stare. Do you know everything, Keeper Martin?"

Grey-haired Martin chuckled. "No, Your Highness, I don't, though there are those who say I would like to."

Adrina took a sip of kindra-ale, a bitter tasting drink with an unpleasant aftertaste that was strangely satisfying. "Will you be going all the way to Alderan with us, Keeper Martin?"

"I was planning to turn south at the crossroads and press on to South Province with a detachment heading to Quashan' garrison, but I think I will continue to Alderan. It seems my business in the South can wait a few days."

Not knowing what else to say, Adrina smiled and returned to her meal. After eating she wandered to the edge of the stream. There was a small pool here, formed where white waters rushing from upstream found themselves blocked by two large boulders. The twelve guardsmen sworn to protect her followed, only a few steps behind.

Bending down, she dipped her hands into the water of the pool. Finding it clear, she rinsed the dirt of the road from her face and neck. Ignoring the guardsmen, she slipped off her riding boots and dangled her toes in the cool water.

As she looked into the waters of the pool, she imagined that Lady Isador was beside her, chastising her for doing something that wasn't proper. She quickly slipped her boots back on and pulled the collar of her riding blouse into place.

Emel approached her slowly, calling out to her. "Adrina, I'm sorry about earlier. I was just frustrated that's all."

"I would not have believed it myself if I had not heard it from someone I—" Adrina stopped midway through, finding it hard to say that one simple word and then she said it, "trusted."

Emel said nothing though his eyes never moved from hers.

Adrina said quickly, "Congratulations on the field promotion, sergeant. I heard that you performed well beyond Warmaster Gabrylle's expectations out Braddabaggon way."

Emel smiled, pride showing clearly. "It was unexpected but earned."

Hearing the heated discussion of a large group of men, Adrina turned. "What are they discussing over there?"

"Scouts. They left the group a few hours ago. Must've just returned," Emel replied. He cocked an ear in their direction, saying nothing for a time and then he told her. "Sounds like they're worried about something ahead. You see the three approaching just now with the gold lapels?"

Adrina edged toward Emel. "Garrison captains?"

"The one on the right with the grizzled beard is Captain Trendmore. The tall southerner is Captain Adylton. The other is Captain Ghenson. He's quick-witted. I like him."

Adrina grabbed Emel's arm. "Were they just talking about the ship from Wellison?"

"I don't think so. It wouldn't be a prudent thing to do." A horn sounding the end of the rest disrupted Emel's further thoughts on the matter. "Time to mount."

Emel walked away. Adrina grabbed his hand, turning him back to face her as she did so. "Why?"

"It's probably nothing, hardly anyone knows about it."

The horn sounded again. Hurriedly Emel escorted Adrina to her mount. As Emel helped Adrina into the saddle, she glared at him and said, "What aren't you telling me, the truth?"

"Ride with me," he told her, "I want you close."

**

The first night in the valley, Xith and Vilmos camped beneath the stars. Vilmos learned the deep valley was a harsh place without a warming sun. Soon after dusk the land lost all its warmth and the cold only worsened as the night lingered on.

Two hours before sunrise, they started their solitary march, for when the evening sun arrived Xith hoped to reach the river at the valley's center. If they crossed the river an hour or so before nightfall they could, with luck, dry their clothes by the last of the sun's rays. If they didn't reach the river in time, they would camp on the near shore and cross the river the next morning, but this would mean many wasted hours. Hours Xith told Vilmos they didn't have to spare.

Xith set a furiously fast pace. Any rest periods this day would be few and short. Vilmos couldn't be sure but it seemed the farther north they went the more eager the shaman was to quicken the pace.

The sores about his shoulders had grown scabs but still they ached with a dull pain. To Vilmos, the pain was a constant reminder of what waited ahead.

"We walk to teach a lesson, your first lesson," Xith said. Vilmos had been asking him questions ever since they crossed the river this morning and though he was growing irritated, Xith was pleased. Vilmos was genuinely interested in just about everything. "Once you begin a course of action, you must follow it through. Beside, it would be unwise to try teleport to our destination. You would learn nothing and would most likely die in the attempt."

Vilmos thought about Xith's statement for a moment and then asked, "Teleport?"

"Yes, teleport." Xith held back a chuckle, knowing a secret yearning the boy was not aware of. "True teleportation, or moving from one place to another through magic, is very powerful magic. You must understand that. Teleportation is a special kind of incantation that draws heavily upon the threads of the universe, and one must know exactly where they are going in order to succeed. To fail is to bring about your own demise."

Vilmos struggled to keep up with Xith's furious pace. He was exhausted and nearly out of breath. "You don't know where we are going?"

"I do, but you do not," Xith said contemplatively. "For the spell to be successful, to teleport the two of us to where we travel, you must also know precisely the point to which we go. Many magicians of the past lost themselves teleporting those whose thoughts strayed from their destination." Xith stopped for a moment to open the leather bag that he had slung over his left shoulder. "Here, eat this."

Vilmos invoked a sour face in disgust, but he was hungry. "What is it?"

"Dried fish." Xith raised a warding hand as Vilmos started to speak again, waving his hands wildly and pointing to the ground, meaning for Vilmos to stoop low.

"What's wrong?" Vilmos whispered, not moving.

"*Get down!*" commanded Xith using the voice.

The response automatic, Vilmos sank low and moved with Xith to the tall grasses that grew along the river's edge as the air filled with the cacophony of hooves. Vilmos hugged the grasses closely and clung to the ground for safety.

The clash of whips and voices soon became overbearing. Vilmos clasped his hands to his ears, pushing until his head began to pound. Wanting to run became the most prevalent thought in his mind, but would he be caught? What would they do to him if they caught him and where was Xith?

Hesitantly, Vilmos opened his eyes and craned his head up slightly. Wagons were still passing and behind them came many more riders. Carefully Vilmos checked the area to his left and right, his hands never shifting from his ears. Xith was nowhere in sight and now Vilmos was really feeling frightened and alone. The voices he heard seemed harsh and cruel and the cracks of their whips sent shivers down his back.

Seconds ticked by to the pace of his heartbeats. Vilmos prayed to Great Father to keep him safe.

Eventually, the sounds grew distant and as quickly as they had appeared, the men and horses disappeared. Before daring to crawl from the high grass cover, Vilmos waited until he could no longer hear the sounds of movement. Hesitantly he rose from his knees to a half stoop, and stared along the trail in the direction that the sounds had retreated.

He called out then to Xith. Xith's answer was calm. "I am with you," he said.

"Who were those men?" Vilmos asked.

"Soldiers. They are the reason we must travel swiftly."

With his eyes filled with fright, Vilmos asked, "Would they have killed me?"

"There are worse fates than death, Vilmos."

Vilmos brushed the grass and dirt from his clothing. "Where are they going? And why are they in the valley?"

"Most likely they use the valley for the same reason we do. It is safer than the forest."

"Why would such a large group fear the forest?"

Xith turned to stare at the trail of dust rising from the valley floor. "Why indeed?"

Chapter Nine

The rains followed them for several days as they journeyed south, making each day seem like the one before it. This day was no different: Dark clouds early in the morning followed by afternoon rains that at first were only a light mist and then turned to heavy sheets of icy rain as the day waned, causing the roads to turn into rivers of mud that bogged down the travelers in gooey, sticky muck.

Captain Brodst kept the group traveling onward despite the heavy downpour, yet for safety's sake slowed the great column to a crawl.

Despite a hood and cloak pulled tightly around her, Adrina was drenched through. Days of wet clothes and a wet saddle had chaffed and irritated her skin. The growing sores gave her something to dwell on other than her fears.

She turned to look back at the others through the shroud of rain. Father Jacob wore a solemn, thoughtful expression on an otherwise expressionless face. Knowing that the good priest was always like this—true feeling hidden on the interior of a hardened exterior—she wondered what feelings he secreted away.

The rain notwithstanding, Keeper Martin had his eyes wide open. He scanned the horizon ahead. His face, with upturned eyebrows and slightly furled lips, showed little complacency. Clearly he didn't like the rain or the trail conditions, yet as always he sought to maintain a clear awareness of their surroundings. Something troubled him,

Adrina noted.

Besides the ever-present scowl, Captain Brodst had an otherwise expressionless countenance. For Adrina, the scowl signified order. The captain kept his companions and his subordinates in check with it—the guards, the soldiers, not even the distinguished guests, Adrina included, dared to speak their thoughts. They would endure the rain for as long as the captain ordered.

The others in the long line of garrison soldiers fore and aft, still four abreast on the muddied kingdom road, and the elite guardsmen that protectively encircled her, Adrina noted, were disheartened. The rain was bogging down their thoughts. Some of those whose faces she could see despite the murky rain were thinking of other places—perhaps home and loved ones, perhaps just the local ale house—but still it was clear they were watching the fields beyond the road carefully.

Her talent for knowing what others were thinking from their expressions, a gift perfected during numerous court sessions, ended as she turned to regard Emel. She had a hard time discerning his feelings from his expressions. This especially troubled her and attracted her to him. As she considered this, her eyes wandered toward him once more, quickly turning away down the muddied path as her gaze met his. The message in his eyes, mixed feelings—feelings she didn't like—was confusing.

As the rain persisted and the day grew long, Captain Brodst signaled another slackening of the pace. Afterward, he signaled Emel to fall in place beside him. Adrina followed, then after slowing her mount, she did her best to listen in.

The captain rode beside Emel and told him clearly, "Remember it will be a light camp, no tents, so find us a good thick spot in a forested canopy."

To Adrina's surprise, the captain addressed her next. "Sorry, Your Highness, we will be unable to reach an inn. I had hoped we would be able to make up some time, but the rain is slowing us to a crawl. Our file is too long to risk much faster travel."

"You considered stopping at an inn," Adrina said, more to herself than to the captain, "even after what you said before we departed Imtal?"

"Adrina!" yelled Emel, as he urged Ebony to race onward. "Catch up!"

Captain Brodst was part way into a response that was quickly drowned out as Adrina raced to catch up to Emel. She was certain she was right about his constant scowl. It was his shield.

"You see, my father..." shouted Emel, looking back over his shoulder as his horse galloped through the thick mud and rain, "... the captain has a heart after all."

For a long time the two sped along the trail despite the greatly reduced visibility from the rain, diminishing daylight and their speed. Adrina had a difficult time maintaining her focus on the dim figure of Emel ahead. Soon she became completely unaware of her surroundings and watched only for the spray of mud from hastening hooves in front of her.

Emel reined Ebony in. "Even in the rain I know this section of the road like the back of my hand." He stroked Ebony Lightning. "My first apprenticeship was as a king's messenger. I know exactly where we'll find a sheltered site away from the rain."

"Then why are we racing?" Adrina asked.

"Imtal Palace Guardsmen and guests shall have the base fire. The garrison troops will have to fend for themselves. They have their own detachment and squadron commanders. It is my father's way of telling the palace guards he cares. Garrison soldiers will also see him as one who cares well for his own and perhaps there will be more than a few who at the end of this trip will wish to enlist in his service. At the end of a long journey soldiers remember the little things. Food, water and shelter are held in the highest regard. And we race for the sport of it!" Emel said, urging Ebony faster and faster.

Mud and dirty water was propelled high into the air and fell just short of Adrina as she fought to catch up with a flagging mount.

After they had rounded several bends in the road and breached several low hills, Adrina lost sight of Emel. Her heart still pounding from the race, she held her breath as she tried to discern shapes in the dim light. When she spotted a horse and rider racing off the trail, she hastened after them.

Just before he reached the edge of the woods, Emel turned Ebony about and raced back toward her. In one swift move he wheeled his mount along side Adrina's and reaching down, seized her horse's reins just above the bit, bringing the mare to a rigid stop. Not expecting this, Adrina tumbled from the horse into the mud.

Emel dismounted. "Can I help you up, Your Highness?" he asked smugly.

Adrina could see he was trying to contain the humor within from bursting into raucous laughter. Her face was red and tears came to her eyes. Mud clung to her hair, her clothes, her cloak, and frustrated hands did little to remove it. "No, I think you've done enough already. I am quite fine."

Emel tossed her an impish look and if he hadn't burst into laughter, Adrina would have cried deeply. The laughter, a much needed burst of cheer, was oddly cleansing, but short-lived.

"You fool!" She screamed, "You did this on purpose, didn't you?" She was crying now and suddenly screaming at him again. As she realized she was whining and how pathetic she sounded, she laughed and the laughter felt good.

When Emel offered her his hand in assistance, she pulled him forward, and didn't let go until he landed face first into the mud. "Why you," Emel yelled, as he grabbed the retreating foot.

A backwards slip landed her, with a muddled thud, on her backside. She squirmed to get away from him as he dragged her toward him. "Let me go! Let me go!"

Emel continued to drag her by one leg backwards through the mud as she fought to break free while the rain beat down on them in a sudden strong drove. With both hands, she scooped up a large clump of mud and threw it at Emel. It landed with a splat, squarely on target and she finally broke free of his grip. "So that's how you want to play it," Emel said, grabbing a large handful of wet muck.

Adrina returned the volley. "Serves you right!"

The mud flinging continued back and forth until they were both drenched and covered in mud from head to toe. Adrina was laughing so hard she fell backwards into the mud, adeptly tripping Emel as she went down.

As she pushed a sodden handful into his face, both burst into hearty laughter. Content to sit idle, allowing the rain to splash down upon them, the two passed a quiet moment.

"Stand up," Adrina told Emel, offering her hand to him as she stood. "We have to get all this mud off of us before the others catch up. I don't want to get you into any more trouble."

Emel looked at her, eyes agape, as if he had just remembered something that his life depended on. Warily, he accepted her offer, quickly returning to reality from the momentary reprieve. They waited in the rain just long enough for it to wash the majority of the mud from their clothing and then prepared to move under the forest canopy.

Emel said, "Grab your horse, and follow me."

Hurriedly, he led her into the large stand of nearby fir.

Quickly the rain became scarcely noticeable as they entered the thick folds of the shielded canopy, and as they moved deeper and deeper into the heart of the great fir stand the rain was soon only a pleasant sound in the distance. The world became suddenly quiet and calm.

"Gather dry pine needles and small branches for kindling. I'll get the larger branches," Emel said. He loosely tied Ebony's reins to a low branch and retrieved a hatchet from his saddlebags.

Adrina collected the kindling. When she had finished, Emel had already returned with a plentiful harvest of large branches. A tree had fallen nearby and its great boughs would be put to good use.

After a circle was cleared for the campfire, Emel assembled the wood into a neat pile with the kindling at the base and the larger branches at the top forming a huddled triangle. Flint and steel were retrieved from saddlebags and a short while later a spark from the flint stone lit the kindling. A few tender puffs spread the tiny flames and soon a gentle fire was crackling, replacing the soft sound of the distant rain.

Adrina was almost impressed by his expertise. "Pretty nimble," she said, "how much longer before the others catch up?"

"Soon," Emel said, "so hurry up and take off your clothes. We don't have much time."

Both flattered and outraged, Adrina's face flushed and then became bright red. "What do you mean?" she shouted. She slapped his face. "Why I never! What do you mean get undressed?"

Emel swallowed hard and then his face turned bright with embarrassment, a close match to Adrina's. "What I meant to say was, hurry up and get out of those wet things so we can dry them over the fire."

"Why?" demanded Adrina still upset.

"I didn't mean it the way it… I mean, what I'm trying to say is…" said a flustered Emel, "You need to dry your things before the others arrive. Otherwise, you know, it might be difficult for you to get them dry. I'll tie a line up between those two trees for you, and then you can hang your clothes to dry. I'll go watch for the others by the trail, just yell when you are finished."

After a moment of silence, Adrina laughed. Now, she understood what he was trying to say. "I'm sorry Emel," Adrina said, quickly adding, "I mean for hitting you, I'm sorry."

The fire was blazing brightly by the time Emel had tied up a secure line. He would have preferred to gather more wood as he should have done, but he didn't. The great fallen tree was close by though and it could serve as a source for many, many fires to take away the chill of the rainy night. "Just call out when you're done. If the others get here first I'll call out in greeting to them and you'll know they are close. I'll need to build a watch fire near the forest's edge but that will only take a moment."

***

The watch fire built, Emel was hesitant to leave its warmth. Returning with Ebony Lightning to unsheltered skies seemed an unpleasant proposition and he did so with quick regret. Almost immediately, cold rain drenched any part of him that had been partially dry.

An easterly wind blown from the direction of the distant sea made the rain feel that much colder. He knew, even on an evening such as this, the red glow of the watch fire from the darkened wood cutting into the darkened land could be seen from a long distance. He needn't wait here on the trail for the others, for they could have easily followed the building light to its source. However, here he felt safer, safer because he was away from the young princess and the desires of his own young heart.

Safer? Emel asked himself, immediate alarms sounding in his mind. He had just left Princess Adrina alone in the woods. He had not checked for signs of other passersby. Nor had he checked for signs of other creatures seeking shelter from the rain.

Emel mounted Ebony and charged into the thick woods, passed the watch fire, ducking low hanging branches as he went. Dark silhouettes of trees passed by in blurs as he raced for the red of the base fire. Reaching the base fire, Emel found the hollow under the canopy empty. His thoughts spun wildly and a sudden emptiness made its way into the pit of his stomach. Princess Adrina was gone.

Chapter Ten

Two long and uneventful days followed the encounter near the river, and on the eve of their fourth day in the valley Vilmos and Xith completed the crossing to the northern rim. Low bluffs on one side and gentle hills on the other replaced the high cliff walls of the southern rim. The two weary travelers found a small cave nestled in a low wall and they stopped to pass the night. The cave was just as dreary as Vilmos had always imagined a cave would be—damp and dark, offering nothing that appealed to his senses. He almost would have rather slept outside on the hard ground.

"Well," Xith said, "what are you waiting for? I am sure you will find some brush just outside that will make us a good warm fire."

Vilmos considered another time when Xith spoke those words. It seemed now a distant memory—not altogether forgotten, but rather something that had occurred long ago. Yet now he recalled the thought fondly and smiled as he retreated from the cavern.

After a small bundle of twigs and sticks were neatly stockpiled Vilmos went in search of larger firewood and found some not far off. Xith indicated that he need not gather more wood. They would have plenty to carry them through the hours of darkness and to cook their breakfast if they so chose.

Xith started rummaging through his bags, telling Vilmos, "Set the wood in the center of the chamber and start the fire while we still have a little light from the outside."

Vilmos did as Xith asked and built the firebase. Afterward he looked to Xith, waiting for the shaman to give him something to start the fire with. "Are there flint and steel?" he asked.

"We do not need flint and steel this day," Xith said. "This day you'll use that which you have. Do not be afraid to use your natural talents."

Vilmos searched in the dim light until he found two stones he could use to try to make a spark. Xith watched enthusiastically. Vilmos had such determination that Xith almost believed Vilmos would light the fire by striking the stones together.

Several frustrating minutes later after Vilmos had smashed his fingers a few times, he gave up. He looked to Xith for a hint of approval or some sign to stop but Xith offered no response.

Vilmos didn't want to disappoint the shaman. He snarled back a frown and returned to pounding the rocks together. After smashing two more fingers, Vilmos cast the stones against the cavern wall. "I give up, I simply can't do it."

Xith stood and moved toward Vilmos. "You're not trying hard enough."

"That's it," Vilmos said, "I've had it!"

"*Calm down,*" said Xith, "listen to me closely. All right?"

Vilmos nodded.

"You are going about this in the wrong manner. I said, 'use your natural talents.' Magic is one of your greatest talents, Vilmos."

"But I don't know how to use it that way."

"*Try,*" invoked Xith. "All you have to do is try. You have the ability."

Vilmos mulled over Xith's words for a moment. He was still afraid of his magic. Nothing good had ever come from using it. "I will not do it."

"Draw the energy into you slowly. Only build the power that you need," instructed Xith, watching the boy's face carefully. "Can you feel it?"

Vilmos did as told. He attempted to draw the power in slowly. "I feel nothing."

"*Focus* on the fire and turn the energy inside you onto it."

"H-how do I do that?" Vilmos was confused.

"Do not think about the how," said Xith, "just do. *Focus* the energy on the fire, think about lighting it."

Vilmos thought, "Enough already, I'll do it." For an instant afterward a spark lit the room but Vilmos could not tap into the power afterward no matter how hard he tried. He became frustrated. "I can't!"

Xith removed his boots and placed them next to the unlit wood, stretching out his short, stubby toes as if waiting for the fire to warm them. "You mean you won't do it. You block the energy flow. You know you can do something simply because you can. Do not worry that you won't be able. Follow my instructions closely. Are you ready, Vilmos?"

Vilmos shrugged.

"Take a deep breath. *Breathe* it in slowly."

Vilmos inhaled a deep breath as Xith had instructed; his lungs filled with air.

"Feel the air inside your lungs," Xith said. "Feel it; it is there."

Vilmos took another deep breath.

"Now exhale, continue to breathe deeply, feel the air flow in and out. Feel the power within you."

Vilmos did as he was instructed.

"Continue to breathe, clear your mind." Xith's eyes glowed. More stirred within the boy than magic alone.

"I'm trying."

Xith opened his pack and pulled out some foodstuffs, splitting the last of the supply of bread and cheese between the two of them, offering the largest share to Vilmos. "Now *listen,*" commanded Xith, smiling reassuringly. "Clear your mind. *Concentrate* only on breathing."

Vilmos cleared his mind until his only thoughts were of his breathing. He continued breathing deeply as he attacked the food vigorously. Within minutes he had gobbled down his share and was staring intently toward Xith's, which the shaman had barely nibbled at.

"Go ahead, Vilmos, take it. You are a growing boy. Eat."

Vilmos raised his eyebrows. "Are you sure?" His expression read.

Xith nodded and then said, "It is time now. Focus the energy…Concentrate…Gather it in slowly."

Xith waited.

Vilmos leaned back and patted an excessively full belly. Feelings of comfort brought relaxation to his mind, and as he relaxed he found he could feel the power in the air all around him, and then he found he could bring it into him just as Xith had stated.

Xith smiled again. "Find your center…Draw upon the power around you, drink it in—but only a small amount. Focus the energy…*Use it now!*"

Vilmos did as Xith stated. The energy was there and he was able to focus it. Suddenly a brilliant, blue-white flame burst amidst the wood. Vilmos' eyes went wide with amazement as he exclaimed, "I did it!"

Secretly Xith helped the spark grow so that it was strong enough to flare and burn. Within a few seconds, the kindling was burning brightly and shortly afterward the fire was roaring to life. He waited until the fire was warming his outstretched toes and Vilmos had gloated long enough and then said, "Next time try not to waste so much energy."

Missing the false sarcasm in Xith's voice, Vilmos elected to ignore Xith's comment and enjoy the fire. It was, after all, warm and did offer some cheer to the otherwise dank cavern. He removed his boots and placed them next to the fire, stretching out his legs alongside the shaman's. He smiled then, looking over at Xith.

"Tomorrow is another day," Xith told him. "*Sleep* now."

"But Xith," Vilmos protested, "I'm not really tired."

Xith eyed Vilmos. "Yes, you are, now *sleep.*"

Xith waited, interested in the response and the apparent rejection of the guiles of Voice. Vilmos started to say something and Xith quickly said, "No more questions, go to *sleep!*"

Vilmos stretched out next to the fire and with eyes almost closed, he feigned sleep. Bodily tired but with a mind too full of unanswered questions to sleep, he eventually turned frank eyes cautiously to the place where Xith sat, eyes wide, feet stretched out, hands happily stroking a long wooden stick, whittling it away with a short tooling knife.

"Xith?" Vilmos called out with a hint of boldness.

"Save your strength, you will need it," Xith said, not looking up. "Tomorrow will be a long day in Vangar Forest."

Vilmos sat up, his eyes filled with sincerity. "But why was it safe to use the magic now and not before? Are the dreams gone? And why did Midori have to go?"

Xith set aside his knife and stick, and then waved a hand over the fire. The flames sprang back, seemingly into the wood, until only a few tiny tongues of red-white fire remained. "A great many things will be explained at a time when I know you are ready to hear them. Too much waits in the days ahead for me to properly begin your education. You have chosen to accept the way of the Magus; as such you must know that nothing is ever simply revealed all at once, rather in bits and pieces.

"Your use of magic alone didn't bring me to you, it was also your dreams. Once I sensed them, I sent Midori to watch over you until it was time. When the time was near, I came."

Xith waved his hand over the fire again. The flames turned brilliant white and Vilmos saw images playing amidst them. He leaned forward, his eyebrows knotting together as at first he became confused then alarmed.

"Pieces of your dreams," Xith said. "All those who have special gifts are troubled by such dreams. They are the playing out of good and evil. They are the reason magic is forbidden, for during the dismal centuries before and after the Race Wars the unwary so easily succumbed to the destructive nature of dark magic that in the end it became more prudent to destroy would-be mages than to try to save them from themselves.

"The Watchers were born of this period and we took it upon ourselves to save those we could for we knew what peril lay in a world without magic." Xith's tone became melancholy. "That I am the last of the Watchers, there is little doubt. Should I breathe my last breath this night, there will be no more watch wardens and magic could fade from the land forever."

Xith picked up the staff he had been working on, and then he reached back into his pack and pulled out another. Although the flames were now pale as a pink rose, Vilmos could see the second staff was the one Xith normally used.

Xith moved the staff he had been whittling toward Vilmos but didn't let him touch it. "When I finish this, I will give it to you. On that day, you will know your education is truly beginning."

Vilmos grinned, then frowned. "But what of the dreams, are they gone?"

Xith regarded Vilmos for a time. "To any other, I would say yes. To you, I say we will have to wait and see. You, Vilmos, are special."

Vilmos blinked and suddenly thin streaks of fire lit a night sky. There was no moon, no stars, just the boundless lines of scarlet cutting into the ebony of the heavens.

At his feet was a dirt road and ahead beyond a crossroads was a forest of dark trees. The dark trees, glowing with an eerie purple radiance, called to him. Vilmos clutched his arms about his chest and started to follow the dirt road, a voice from behind him startling him as he did so.

Vilmos turned around. A strange woman took his hand, her touch soothing, her skin soft, her smile friendly.

"I am to accompany you to Arr," she said, "hurry now." She raced off, pulling Vilmos behind her.

Vilmos stopped. "Who are you?"

"I am Erravane, a friend. I am to take you to Ril Akh Arr. Come with me to the temple."

A voice raced through Vilmos' mind. It said, "Within dwell the shape-changing beasts of the night that worship Arr. Be forewarned, they come for you."

Vilmos fought to pull his hand away from the woman's numbing grip, noticing now that her face, although it seemed human-like, was not a human face at all.

"No," Vilmos shouted, "I will not go with you!" At the words and the resistance, Vilmos suddenly found he was back in the cave with Xith, staring at the flames.

Xith looked Vilmos directly in the eye. "You can almost feel it, the presence of evil upon the wind. They await us in Vangar Forest, I am sure of this now. The fourth comes, and she is enraged."

Chapter Eleven

"Adrina?" Emel screamed, his mind filling with dread.

Hastily, Emel dismounted. Panic mandating his every move, he began a frantic search. He shouted over and over, "Adrina, where are you?"

For an instant he felt a breath of air on his neck—perhaps the wind from beyond the forest. Then a hand clasped firmly to his mouth. Another hand removed his sword from its scabbard.

"Do not scream. I will not harm you," whispered a dark figure, whirling him around so he was left staring into heavy gray eyes. "We bring word from land and people."

The figure led Emel deep into the forest. Emel counted the others lurking in the shadows as he was led passed them. There were twelve in all. He soon found himself in the midst of a circle of dark-robed figures. The hoods were secured, masking their faces. Princess Adrina sat in the middle of the circle beside a tall light-haired woman. Dark skin said the woman was surely a southerner, but her pale hair, blonde, almost white, was out of place.

"Who is your friend?" asked the woman of Adrina, not turning to look at Emel.

Adrina replied, "He is the son of the captain of the Imtal guard."

"Sit, Emel Brodstson," the woman said, beckoning with her hand. Then to Adrina she said, "We do not have long, the power of my enchantment fades from the land, soon clouded thoughts will become clear and there will be those that realize what has occurred."

Emel watched Adrina nod several times as though she was listening to the woman talk, though he heard nothing save soft rain and perhaps wind.

"Travel not to Alderan by the sea. The ship from Wellison will not arrive. You are in grave danger princess. A great evil has put its mark upon you. It is good you have someone who can cut the veil with his care for your welfare. You would be wise to care as much for yourself."

Adrina glanced at Emel, then asked, "Why me?"

"The struggle is long and many are its pawns. The journey you have embarked upon is but the first step along the path. The evil has chosen you because of your position of influence and because of the emptiness within you."

"Can I not rid myself of this mark?" Adrina asked.

The woman began speaking more swiftly now. "Look to two strangers for aid, for fate brings them to you. Beware those that are not what they seem and the traitor. A traitor among you will insist that you continue to Alderan when it seems you should not. Remember, only death awaits in Alderan."

Adrina regarded the woman and started to say something but Emel cut her off. "What is so important about this ship from Wellison? Why should we even listen to you? You should flee before the garrison soldiers find you and run you through."

The woman paused, apparently surprised to hear Emel's words. "Speak not words in haste, oft you may regret the reply. Yet if this is what you truly wish to know, I will tell you. Know there is a heavy price. Once a thing is known you may not so easily turn away." The woman paused and stared into Emel's eyes. Then seemingly pleased with what she saw, she continued. "The ship from Wellison has a most precious cargo, the heir to the throne of Sever. At this very moment King Charles lies dying in his bed. An assassin's poison is slowly eating away at him. Alas there is no cure, a terrible poison it is.

"He whose name I dare not speak uses King Jarom's lust for power just as it uses you and many others. Jarom sees himself seated in the throne room of Imtal Palace. To be sure, he will use the death of Charles and the fears of the heir to his own ends."

Adrina started to speak. The woman didn't allow her to.

The woman said to Emel, "Go to your watch fire. The soldiers are near. I would speak to Adrina alone."

Emel hesitantly turned away, his pace just slow enough to hear their continued whispers.

"He brings the change you so wished for. It has found a home in the emptiness of your heart. You care too little for those around you. You see not the servants who toil for you, workers on their hands and knees with the whip at their backs, drudges scouring the floors."

"I am not heartless," protested Adrina.

"Did I say heartless?" the woman asked. "Tell me, what is the name of the servant girl who cares so much for you that she remains awake through the night to re-stoke your hearth only to feel the lashings of a whip at her back the next day for laziness?"

Adrina fumbled for a name.

"Myrial," whispered Emel as he faded into the shadows.

"Queen Alexandria, your mother, would have shed tears at the hearing. Your position has made you forget there are others in the land who suffer. Your father is not the strong and caring king he once was. Fault him not, there are those who use his grief to their own ends and the years of war have not treated him well. You must open your eyes and truly see the world as it is."

Adrina tried to raise an objection.

The lady continued, "Go now. Look for the two strangers, find the son of Charles, beware the traitor and those that are not what they seem."

"But what can I do? I cannot rouse the southern garrisons to arms."

"I did not say to rouse the garrisons." The woman paused and stared into the shadows. "Emel Brodstson, if you have heard enough, continue on your way. Remember, there is always a heavy price."

***

Water, dark and icy cold, surrounded Seth. He groped for the surface, his lungs hot and ready to explode. His head stung, his vision clouded. Pain and darkness sought to overcome him. Then just when he thought his lungs would explode, he broke the surface and gasped for air.

Despair filled his mind as turbulent waters pulled him under again. Wildly, he grabbed at the surface, both arms flailing frantically. His hand found something wet and rough. He latched onto it. Coughing and choking, he held on.

The night above the water, nearly as dark as the world beneath the water, offered him little relief. Seth cursed his foolhardiness: He hadn't expected an ambush so soon after departing Kapital and somehow Seth knew he should have. He remembered little of how he had come to be in the water. One minute he had been standing on the deck of the Lady L, Sailmaster Cagan at his side, preparing to make one last desperate stand. The next, a sharp sudden pain in his legs and then the long plunge into cold deep water.

Seth suddenly realized he had no idea if anyone else had survived. He lashed out with his mind, *Sailmaster Cagan? Galan?*

Seth felt something pass underneath him and then touch his legs. Fatigue, disorientation and panic overwhelmed him. Sailmaster Cagan had told him about dark beasts beneath the waters, creatures called krens that fed on all manner of beast alike. His left arm had caught a blade and his right leg was gouged from thigh to calf.

Seth kicked out with his feet and slapped the water with his free hand. He lost his grip and again slipped beneath the dark waters. He reached for the surface and the handhold. The piece of wreckage had to be there; it just had to be.

Seth broke the surface, only for an instant, only long enough to fill his lungs with air and calm the red-hot fire in his chest, then storm-tossed seas pulled him under again.

Great Father, I cannot fail. My need is great! he called out in despair.

Seth? called out a voice weak in his mind. *Seth?*

His thoughts spun. He reached out, a hand found his. *Bryan?*

Kick harder, I'll need your help. I can't do this alone. Grab on, hold on, don't let go... Just a little more... Just a little more... Seth, you must help me.

With Bryan's help, Seth crawled onto the small section of wreckage. He lay on his back panting for many long minutes. Exhaustion nearly carried him away to sleep, but he fought to maintain consciousness. *Did anyone else survive?*

I'm not sure, I saw you get knocked into the sea as the mast crumbled, and I panicked. Everything after that is a blur. The ships are all gone. Fire and water took them.

What about Sailmaster Cagan?

Seth, I don't know... It seems he went down with the Lady L. Bryan paused, his mind filled with obvious anguish. *How did they know we had begun the journey? There were so many, so many...*

Seth found sudden resolve. *We survived, Bryan. We have not failed yet... Wait. Did you feel that?... The anguish, the sadness.*

Seth, I'm sorry, I'll shield my thoughts if...

No, someone is out there... Seth turned his thoughts inward and sought to concentrate his will. Then he groped outward with his mind, straining to maintain his strength while he searched. *Galan?*

Seth pressed his weight against tired arms and sat. He stared into the inky darkness of a largely overcast night sky. He saw little, his mind filled in the pieces. *Someone else is with her... She's holding Everrelle afloat... Galan won't last much longer. She's exhausted.*

Frantically, Bryan and Seth paddled with their hands through choppy waters. It seemed with waves slapping against the makeshift raft they barely moved at all. Then suddenly, two dark shapes appeared out of the gloom. Everrelle, barely conscious, was near death and brave Galan was utterly exhausted from the struggle to keep two afloat in turbulent waters.

Chapter Twelve

The plains beyond Imtal Palace, the rolling foothills of the Braddabaggon and the green of the forest were all far behind Adrina now. The day before they had passed through a quiet village with an inn; the brief reprieve from the outdoors had felt good. Early this morning the column had crossed into Mellack proper.

Surprisingly, the new day brought a beautiful, clear sky. Adrina's mood became cheerful despite her saddle-sore backside and her heavy thoughts. The southern road, though still muddied, was readily traversable and the column was able to travel at a remarkably good pace considering their rate the previous days. Adrina had seen very few passersby this day—only a few merchants, who Captain Brodst had sent immediately away to peddle their wares elsewhere, and the infrequent travelers who hurried along on independent missions.

Over the past days Adrina had thought of little else other than the words of the mysterious lady and the heir to the throne of Sever, Prince William. She had only met the prince once, but that had been three long years ago at her mother's funeral. She remembered little of her distant cousin, only that he had the bluest eyes she'd ever seen.

Adrina watched everything and everyone she passed, thinking every pair of peddlers would be the two strangers or that every guardsman that came near her was the traitor. "You must open your eyes," the lady had told her, and Adrina was trying.

Emel stayed as close to Adrina as his duties allowed. The two had discussed several plans of action but nothing they came up with seemed appropriate. The lady had told them to tell no one of their conversation, but how could they do otherwise? They had to tell someone—for how could they stop the column from proceeding onward to Alderan—but who?

A sounding of the horns signaled a slackening of the pace and as Adrina looked up she saw Emel racing back to the middle of the column. Hours ago he had been sent out to lead a scouting party.

Adrina nodded her head as he passed her. She noticed he looked nervous and knew he would return as soon as he reported the group's findings. Captain Brodst had been sending out scouting parties at regular intervals ever since they had crossed into Mellack Proper. Adrina guessed that this was because Mellack Proper was a king's holding without a garrison. The citizens of Mellack looked to the Duchy of Ispeth that bordered it to the southeast and to Imtal to the north for its defense.

She didn't have to wait long, though; Emel was reining Ebony Lightning in beside her a short while later.

"Did you see something?" she excitedly asked him.

Emel looked away from Adrina's eyes. "Nothing but fields as far as the eye can see."

"Why are you sweating so? And you look peaked. What is wrong?"

Emel turned a grimace into a smile. "Ebony wanted to race, so I pressed the group hard. I saw no harm in it. We are nearly upon the borders of Ispeth now."

"Isn't much to Mellack Proper, is there?"

The expression on Emel's face grew grim. He lowered his voice to a whisper as he began to speak. "Did you know that tomorrow a detachment will break from the main company?"

Adrina turned frank eyes upon Emel. "Have you thought of what I said earlier?"

"I've thought of little else." Tension was evident in Emel's voice. "Do you really think it is wise?"

"Do we have any other choice?"

Ebony nickered. Emel stroked the stallion's mane. "I need more time. Besides, my father wants me at the fore of the column. We can talk again later. Agreed?"

Concern in her eyes, Adrina watched Emel ride off. Afterward her thoughts turned back to the road. An afternoon sun was just starting its descent and passing clouds brought dark shadows to the land. She hoped it wouldn't rain again, and as time passed and rain did not come she counted herself fortunate.

She listened to the clatter-clatter of hooves and heels along the hardening ground. The company had returned to a four-abreast formation with one squadron of Horse soldiers to the fore of her position, the Foot directly behind the middle ranks, and a final squadron of Horse to the rear. The palace guardsmen and the distinguished guests made up the middle of the formation with protective files set up along both sides of them.

Great Kingdom had few bandits in its heartland but Adrina knew Captain Brodst thought one could never be overcautious. As she looked on, the captain surveyed his group from end to end. He was conferring with the three commanders. From his especially grave scowl, Adrina guessed it wasn't pleasant words he spoke to them. Of the three, Captain Adylton, Captain Ghenson and Captain Trendmore, it was only Captain Trendmore that she thought warranted closer attention. Trendmore was an ambitious and manipulative man, or so Adrina had once heard during a session of her father's court.

Adrina chased after Emel in her thoughts now and, preoccupied with this, didn't notice the keeper's presence beside her, nor did she hear his words of inquiry until he spoke louder. She started at the voice, jumped in the saddle and had to rein in her mount to curb its excitement, which matched her own.

"What troubles the mind of one so young?" Keeper Martin asked.

Recovering her senses, Adrina said, "Beautiful day, keeper."

Martin mumbled something inaudible.

"Have you decided if you will continue to Alderan with us or not, keeper?"

"The East-West crossroads are but a day away. I may yet change my mind and go south with the party to Quashan', dear." Gray-haired Martin paused. "In truth, I am awaiting response to the message I sent to Keeper Q'yer. If all goes well I should receive it this night."

"Tonight?" she asked.

"Keeper Q'yer has had his week to recuperate from the last sending."

Adrina turned frank eyes on the keeper. "A dream message?"

The keeper smiled knowingly but didn't say anything immediately. Adrina knew little about the mysterious Lore Keepers, who in recent years had detached themselves from palace proceedings yet still seemed to know everything that went on in Imtal. She knew the keeper to be a man who preferred his records and his tomes to human companionship—at least that is what she had heard.

"You have careful ears, dear," Keeper Martin said, "Where did you hear such a thing?"

It was a check for honesty; Adrina knew, among his other duties as Head Keeper, Martin tracked the history of the royal family. At the age of consent, it would be time to draft a new tome, one with Adrina's name inscribed upon its leather binding. "Why from your own lips, keeper."

"A dream message is a form of communication," Martin said, his words sounding like an oration, "A keeper can deliver a message to another keeper in the form of a message that enters his or her awareness and takes the form of a dream."

"But how is such a thing possible?"

"Very simply, actually. The real difficulty lies in the proper use of your will. To begin you must clear all thoughts from your mind and reach into the center of your being. A spark of power lies there that is your soul. You reach out with that power until you touch the consciousness of the one you wish to communicate with. You speak through images and feelings that you create in your consciousness and pass... Boring you, dear? I am sorry, I tend to babble."

Adrina tried to remain focused on her goal, which was to find out what the keeper knew of their destination, but she was caught in the interest of the ideas he presented to her and this perplexed her. "Keeper Martin, you're not boring me. Can anyone do this? How come you can't use words?"

"Slow down, dear," Martin said with equal enthusiasm. "Only a few know how to properly utilize their consciousness to create a message. It is part of the knowledge passed down from Great Father to us alone, the Keepers of the Lore. Throughout time there have been others who learned to use this power. Unfortunately, though, only the keepers retain this knowledge now."

"I don't understand. How can you comprehend the dream if you do not use words?"

"I did not say words could not be used." Martin paused, adding extra meaning to the statement. "It takes an extremely powerful center to create a vision in the form of thoughts that enter another's awareness as audible words. The simpler form is to use images and feelings."

Adrina was excited now and did little to hide it. "Keeper, can you teach me, I mean... can you teach me how to use the dream message?"

The keeper sighed with lament. "I can teach you the theory but I am afraid it is a moot undertaking."

Adrina thought about his words for a moment. She still wanted to know what he knew about their destination but she *was* genuinely intrigued. She also hoped this would give her a chance to talk to the keeper alone. She had made her choice, she would tell the keeper of her troubles. She had only to tell Emel this now. "I do not mind. If you do not mind imparting your wisdom to me, of course?"

The keeper's eyes gleamed as he said, "Of course I don't mind. In fact, I'll take great pleasure in it. We'll start this evening."

Adrina grinned. Just then her mare nickered and as she stroked the nervous animal's mane, she thought of Emel at the fore of the column, and as she looked to Keeper Martin, she noticed he too was stroking his horse's mane.

***

The night passed with eerie swiftness. Seth awoke to find a midday sun. Images from the previous day seemed a crazed blur, but the ache of his body told him it had all been real. For an instant Seth felt sure he was alone, then he saw the others. They were the last survivors. Frazzled and haggard from battle and exposure to the sea, only four lingered in life, only these four that had escaped. Now faith in their service would take them to safety or deliver them from life.

Still exhausted, Bryan and Galan slept. Everrelle, weak from blood loss, slipped in and out of delirium. Seth turned bleary eyes to the sun, its warmth on his face felt good. He remembered now that during the night he had prayed for the day to end the bitter cold. He removed his cloak, which was still mostly wet, and allowed the sun to chase away any remnants of the night's chill. He then worked to bind the already festering wounds from the battle.

Each of his companions had many injuries—bruises, scrapes, lacerations—which proved to him how desperate the battle had really been and how miraculous it was that anyone survived. Everrelle was by far in the worst condition. Her right hand was missing four fingers. Seth was sure she must have reached out to block a blow and instead met the steel of a blade. Using strips of cloth from his robe, he did the best he could to wrap her hand, hoping it would help stay the infection. He turned to Galan next, Bryan afterward. His own wounds he bound last.

Scattered debris from the great ships that the dark, deep waters had claimed during the night was all around them. Seth worked against fate to gather what he could. As he worked, he thought of Cagan standing defiantly at the helm of the Lady L. He told himself that was how he wanted to remember the kind sailmaster and all the others that had perished with him. In the end, his search turned up an invaluable prize, a water bag. Half full but still a water bag. He put it beside the one Bryan had managed to escape the Lady L with, and thanked Great Father for their good fortune.

The day grew long. The utter exhaustion that held the others found Seth. Unwillingly, he slipped into delirium.

Days passed. Everrelle's condition worsened. Seth, Galan and Bryan took turns at the healing art, but weak from battle and hunger, they could offer little. Unbelievably, the raft, held together with prayers and pieces of cloth, had kept them afloat through those endless days.

Seth had held the hope that land was just over the next crest of the rolling waves or just beyond the next horizon. Bryan and Galan had also been hopeful. Days of nothing save dark waters had tainted that hope and the possibility of safe landfall waned. Now Seth could only lie idle with all his energy drained. Only his training kept his mind semi-clear and his thoughts open. *I am Brother Seth of the Red, First of that order, Queen's Protector*, he repeated many times in his mind.

He sought to cleanse his mind of questions he didn't want to answer. Nonetheless, the questions came. The ambush set by King Mark had been too well planned. How could anyone have known their plans so precisely? Was there a traitor among them? Had there been a traitor on the Lady L leading the enemy to them?

The thought of a traitor having been among them was too painful for Seth to consider. Brother did not betray brother. *No, I must focus.* Seth returned to the cleansing meditation.

Seth? came the whisper into his mind.

I am Brother Seth of the Red, First of that order, Queen's Protector. I must maintain clear thoughts…

Seth? came the whisper into his mind again.

It was Galan. Seth was glad to hear her voice in his mind. *Yes, my brother, I am still here.*

Seth, what will it be like in this land of Men? asked Galan.

Still lost in his meditation, it took Seth a moment to slip back into reality, a task accomplished only after Galan repeated her question. Seth replied slowly, thoughtfully, *It will be different, far different from anything we have ever seen that is for sure. Long ago our people often journeyed to their villages and cities. Our lands and cultures were close together then. It had been a peaceful time, but then came the Great Wars. The last and most devastating treacheries were the Race Wars during which Man drove all their distant cousins away. Into the far corners of the world we fled and never in over five hundred years have we ventured back into their lands.*

Seth felt Galan fight to remain coherent. Galan asked, *What did you learn during those many weeks you studied them? Do you really think they will help us? Or will it all be for nothing.*

Her faith was waning and Seth knew this. *Once we explain what is taking place, it will be their cause as it is ours. They must aid us. However, it could take a long time to explain. These Men*—Seth said the word with distaste—*prefer to stay out of the affairs of others until they are sure they have a marked interest in what is taking place. They often wait until it is too late.*

Seth, began Galan, there was a serious note in the unspoken voice, *there is something I should tell you that I haven't, something I overheard*—

—*I do not wish to know thoughts that I was not meant to. Some things are best left unknown.*

Like why you prepared for a journey to the lands of Man even before Queen Mother consulted High Council. Moreover, why your lessons began even before we learned of the return.

Seth was unsure whether he should voice the truth or not, but what did it really matter anyway? *There is much more in peril than our homes and lands. Queen Mother knows this.*

I must rest. Will you play the image Brother Liyan gave to you, the image of the forest? I wish to dream…

***

Captain Brodst called the column to a halt near the borders of Ispeth. "Eat well. Rest your feet and your mounts," he advised. "If the good weather holds we will try to make up the distance we lost to rains the days before. The earlier we reach the crossroads tomorrow, the better."

Adrina dismounted and led her mount to the top of a small rise where the commanders and the guests would have their midday meal. Mostly she wanted to listen in on their conversations but she was also very hungry.

From atop the hill she could look down on the whole of the extensive company. Ridesmen were tending to their mounts. Foot soldiers were resting tired feet. Obviously unhappy guards were posted around the perimeter. The attendant beside her was having a difficult time steadying Adrina's mare.

Not far off Adrina saw Emel and the small band of young ridesmen that had survived the encounter of the Braddabaggon. Little of their conversation rose to her ears, but she could tell the foul weather hadn't dampened their high spirits. To them, the journey to Alderan was still high adventure. Adrina wasn't so sure anymore, though she still longed to feel hot sands between her toes and taste the salty spray of wind-blown seas.

True to his word, Emel found Adrina shortly after Captain Brodst called the column to movement. Before she could say anything of her conversation with Keeper Martin, Emel spoke his mind. "I have given it much thought," he said furrowing his eyebrows and borrowing his father's scowl, "I truly do not know Father Jacob or Keeper Martin. I am sure they are both men of honor but I cannot vouch for their word. My father, the captain, on the other hand is a man who lives by his sense of honor and I can vouch for his word. He has never knowingly broken a trust."

Adrina didn't know what to say. She had tried to interrupt Emel but he hadn't let her. Just as she was about to say something, her mare whinnied. She ran her hands along the animal's withers and the base of the mane and scratched. The mare was fond of Emel's Ebony, but something was bothering her.

"There, there girl," Adrina whispered. Then turning to Emel she said, "What of Keeper Martin? He is by far the wisest man in the kingdom."

Emel scowled. "See, there you go. I make a choice and you don't like it."

Adrina was quick to explain about her earlier conversation with the keeper. "So you see," she concluded, "isn't Keeper Martin the best choice?"

Emel signaled agreement and for a time afterward no words passed between them. It seemed Emel's thoughts were elsewhere, and more than once Adrina had seen his eyes nervously darting about.

It was not long before the company crossed into the Duchy of Ispeth, replacing the quiet fields of Mellack Proper with groves of fruit trees that lined the road. The apples of Duke Ispeth were the best in the land and often graced the king's table.

As it was nearly autumn, many of the trees were laden with fruit and the sweet scent of apples, heavy in the air, was mouth watering. Adrina saw more than a few soldiers climbing trees and filling bags. No doubt, they were claiming the apples in the name of King Andrew.

Barely an hour after crossing into the Duchy of Ispeth, a vanguard of the Duke's small army was already on its way toward them. Adrina watched Emel and the riders around her grow agitated at the show of force. She didn't know why, though, because the soldiers of the column outnumbered the small group of Ispeth knights a hundred to one.

Captain Brodst commanded the column to a halt, and saying, "Stand at ease. Two runners. Banners high. Forward," dispatched messengers carrying the king's banner to greet the approaching riders.

"There's Duke Ispeth himself," Emel said unhappily.

Adrina maneuvered her mare closer to Emel's Ebony. "You've met him?"

"I *was* a king's messenger. Crossing into Ispeth uninvited isn't wise."

Emel made no further comment on the matter even when Adrina pressed him. She imagined that he'd met the duke before. She'd heard about the eccentric duke and seen him on several occasions, though he rarely attended the king's court.

"What are they doing now?" Adrina asked. "Are they setting up a tent?"

Emel didn't need to respond. Apparently, the duke ordered that two tents be built and workers were busily staking out the lines for the tarps. After the tents were erected, Duke Ispeth and Captain Brodst met in conference. Keeper Martin, Father Jacob and the three commanders were summarily summoned.

Garrison soldiers milled about, anxiously. Adrina stayed close to Emel, her eyes on the Duke's tent. Finally, she said, "What's going on?"

"Duke Ispeth is not the most trusting of men. I've had the pleasure of his company on several occasions, I know. If he sees plots and spies in the passage of a mere messenger across Ispeth who knows what he thinks seeing this mob... We'll not be traveling any more this day."

"At least we may get the chance to talk to Keeper Martin earlier than we planned..." Adrina's voice trailed off. Emel's eyes were scanning the horizon. "What is it, what has been bothering you all day?"

Emel said nothing, his eyes darting nervously away.

Chapter Thirteen

Three hours after dawn Xith and Vilmos entered Vangar Forest. Almost immediately Vilmos felt the crawl of unseen eyes upon him, but he did not really start to worry until the sun disappeared, blocked out by the forest canopy.

Despite ever thickening undergrowth, Xith maintained a steady pace, trying to stay directed north. At times it seemed as if the forest had a will of its own. Sprawling rows of brambles seemed to close any gaps as they approached, and the two would have to travel either west or east until they finally chanced upon a break. Sometimes this distance was only a hundred yards. More than once it seemed as if the brambles had stretched on for miles.

"Stay close," Xith advised for the second time.

"I still don't understand why we didn't use the road the soldiers cut through the forest," complained Vilmos. "Surely it went directly north."

"*Silence,*" commanded Xith.

Vilmos turned as the shaman had and saw movement out of the corner of his eye. His heart started pounding in his ears and a lump swelled up in his throat.

"*Run,*" shouted Xith, pushing Vilmos. "No matter what happens do not look back. Do you understand?"

Vilmos said nothing. Xith twisted him around and stared into his eyes. "Do you understand?"

Vilmos nodded.

The two ran in a flat out race. Trees became black blurs. They no longer turned at brambles; instead they plowed through them. Xith pushed Vilmos ever forward.

Cuts and scrapes on his hands, face, and arms and bruises on his knees, Vilmos ran on. He ran as fast as he could.

Every now and again he saw black shapes out of the corner of his eye that he was sure were not trees. It was only when he heard the first tormented howl that he became certain he was running for his very life.

Soon the tormented cries of the unknown beasts came from many directions, then gradually the howls grew closer and closer. Xith pushed Vilmos faster and faster, surprising the boy with his seemingly endless endurance.

Nervously, Vilmos glanced to his left and to the rear. His feet lead him to the right—there were no cries coming from the right.

Suddenly Xith stopped and Vilmos only heard the sound of his own running. He stopped, turned around, ran back to where the Shaman stood. His eyes grew wide with terror and his heart pounded so loudly in his ears that he couldn't hear what the shaman was saying. He only knew the shaman was staring into the shadows.

"They are leading us," Xith said, "do not let your feet stray."

The two started running again. Terror helped Vilmos find his second wind and soon he was outpacing Xith.

Coming down a ravine, Vilmos stumbled and fell. Xith picked him up by the scruff of his collar and lead him on. They breached a hill, crossed a stream, ran on in soggy boots; on and on they raced.

Vilmos was running to the pace of his heart, which was still pounding in his ears. He stretched his small body to its limits, again surprised at the shaman's seemingly boundless stamina. More than once he doubled over in pain and fought to catch his breath, and more than once the shaman forced him into movement. Sometimes dragging him by the arm or the collar. Sometimes pushing him. Sometimes just his wild stare was enough to force Vilmos to find his next wind.

Suddenly they burst into a clearing. A midday sun shining overhead told Vilmos they were safe, they were out of the dark forest. A sigh of relief escaped his lips.

Just as Vilmos paused to catch his breath, Xith directed his gaze to the other side of the clearing. The forest stretched on endlessly, the trunks of trees fading into the gloomy shadows.

Vilmos tried desperately to catch his breath. "Can we rest, please?"

"Not long," cautioned Xith, "those beasts aren't far behind us."

"What are they?" Vilmos asked.

"Some things are best left unnamed. To be sure, their masters are the reason the animals of the forest are angry." Xith's eyes darted to the shadows. "Run now, run as if your life depends on it, because it does."

"I need... more rest," said Vilmos, panting, "can you not use your magic on them?"

"For every one I could send back to the pits where they spawned, two more would come. No, we run." Xith pushed Vilmos forcefully with both hands, launching him into a mad dash for freedom.

***

Long after Adrina had bedded down the previous night Captain Brodst and the others had been in Duke Ispeth's tent. What they had talked about during those many hours Adrina didn't know, she only knew her hopes of talking to Keeper Martin had faded hour by hour.

"Emel," called out Adrina, flagging him down with her hands as he rode past. She attempted to make conversation with him as she had tried earlier. Again, he cut her off and rode on ahead. It didn't seem intentional, though, because he seemed worried about something. She thought it possibly related to the conversation the captain had had with the sergeant before they broke camp. She hadn't been able to discern their whispers, but the conversation had seemed rather one-sided with Emel doing most of the listening.

Aggravated she wrapped the reins tight in her hands and spurred her mare on. "Oh no you don't, Emel Brodstson!" she screamed after him.

Emel reined Ebony in and wheeled about to face Adrina. He didn't say a word. He didn't need to. His stare was angry and cold.

"Did I do something?" asked Adrina near tears. "Or does this have something to do with what happened yesterday?"

"It has nothing to do with what happened yesterday and everything to do with what happened yesterday."

"What's that supposed to mean?"

Emel cast a glum stare toward the rear of the column. Adrina could only guess that it was directed at the captain.

"I am sorry, Adrina," Emel said, turning away and chiding Ebony into movement, "I tried, I really did."

Adrina kicked her mare faster and faster, racing alongside Emel's Ebony. "Slow down, talk to me."

Emel's reply was curt, "My group has forward position throughout the morning."

"You don't have to protect me at all times. I saw you relieve the central guard again last night. You can't keep standing watch all night and riding all day. You'll drop out of the saddle."

"The Duchy of Ispeth is not all sweet-smelling orchards you know. At one time this was swamp as far as the eye could see. That is, before Ispeth River and its tributaries dried up, or so it is said. The farther south you go, the wetter the climate becomes. In a few days, you'll reach the swamps and if you are lucky the company will skirt them, if you're not you'll take the Kingdom road through them.

"Since you have to keep pace with the column, it'll take you a week to skirt the swamp, or at the very least three days by the King's road. Ebony and I cut through the Bottoms *once*. There are things in there without names, but they'll try to take you just the same. They don't call it the bottom of the world for nothing.

"Fog rolls in so thick by mid-afternoon that you can't see your hand in front of your face. I dropped my torch, *my torch*, and nearly lost it. It was the longest twelve hours alone of my life. I nearly lost my wits. It's a good thing Ebony was with me. Just before sunrise we went in, and an hour past sunset we came out."

A proud smile came to Adrina's lips. "I am not afraid," she said, "I have Emel Brodstson to guard me."

Emel's next words were drowned out by the sounds of the column.

Adrina shrugged.

"I am to go south with the detachment to Quashan'," Emel said, in a soft voice. Afterward he spurred Ebony on and didn't look back.

Adrina returned to her place in the column, the elite guardsmen tightening their circle around her. A dull pain in the pit of her stomach told her of emotions she sought to hold in. No tears ran down her cheeks though several times she fought them back as they welled up in her eyes. Emel was the only one who shared her secret. What would she do without him?

Anger and disillusionment found her. Hadn't the lady in the forest said Emel was now a part of that secret? Didn't that mean he should remain with her at least until they decided what to do? They hadn't decided anything, except to talk to Keeper Martin, which they hadn't been able to do.

She listened to the clatter-clatter of hooves and heels for a long time afterward. Only the far off angry calls of birds from amidst the apple orchards aroused her to the world. Apple pickers were chasing the birds from the trees.

As she turned to watch a flock of black birds rise from the trees, Adrina caught sight of Keeper Martin and Father Jacob coming from the rear of the column. Suddenly resolved to talk to the keeper, she slowed her mare and allowed them to overtake her. Determination in her eye, she said, "Beautiful day, Keeper Martin, Father Jacob. We will reach the crossroads in a few hours. Keeper, what news of the dream message?"

Gray-haired Martin grinned sheepishly. "I did not hold to my word did I, Young Highness. I am truly sorry. Duke Ispeth is both persistent and long winded. He would have rambled on and on through the night if Captain Brodst hadn't put an end to it when he did. And yes, Keeper Q'yer's message arrived."

Adrina flashed her eyes at the keeper. Well? They asked.

"Indeed," Martin said, tugging on his unkempt beard and turning to Father Jacob.

Jacob who had been nibbling on an apple, cast the core away. Adrina caught sight of the great swirling white circles that decorated the sleeves of his otherwise black robe. The circles that had once been bright white were now dull and dirty, coated with the dust of the road.

"I have given it much thought," said the priest, pausing to sigh. "You are right. I can sense it too. It is all around us."

"Then you have considered what we discussed?" asked Keeper Martin.

"I have, but I do not think this is the right time to discuss this."

"Indeed," said Martin, scratching at his beard again.

Adrina didn't say a word. She hoped the two would forget she was even there.

"Please forgive us, dear," said Martin turning to her. "Our thoughts are on other things at the moment. Perhaps it would be best if we talked later."

"Then you will be continuing with us?"

The Lore Keeper turned to Father Jacob then said, "Yes, I believe I will."

***

Vilmos stumbled, fell, came up on his feet again. For a moment in his confusion he thought Xith wasn't with him anymore, but then he caught a glimpse of the shaman's brown robe. Exhausted, Vilmos no longer ran. He simply plodded along, forcing himself to put one foot in front of the other.

Time progressed slowly. Most of the tormented howls faded to distant echoes and now it seemed only one of the strange beasts followed them. Vilmos heard its high-pitched howl sound off to his left.

By now they had gone so far and so deep into the forest and strayed off course so many times that Vilmos thought surely even the shaman had lost his way long ago. The beasts *were* leading them, forcing them to take an increasingly easterly course.

Vilmos could no longer determine shapes in the shadows. Everything was shadows and dull grays slowly turned black. Night was surely near.

The touch of a hand to his shoulder caused Vilmos to start. He jumped and nearly screamed. Xith whispered in a low voice, "Tie this rope around your waist. It will keep us from being separated."

Vilmos took the offered rope and began tying it about his waist.

"Follow where I lead you," said Xith. "Keep your hands out in front of your face protectively."

Vilmos finished securing the rope. He caught sight of a soft glow from the shaman's eyes. They were glistening silver once more. "Do your eyes allow you to see in the dark?"

Xith grinned. "It is the gift of Oread to her people."

Vilmos stretched his sore muscles, and eased the fire away from aching legs, then finally asked the question that had been bothering him for what seemed hours. "Are we lost?"

"The sense of direction of the peoples of Under-Earth is keen. Do not worry. Soon we will leave the Forest of Vangar and all of this will be behind us for a time." Xith said nothing more, except that they should begin moving again.

For an instant Vilmos saw thin streaks of fire lighting a night sky, then he blinked and he was back under the raven folds of Vangar's canopy. Vilmos stood and hurried after Xith, following the tug of the rope at his waist.

Chapter Fourteen

The column reached the East-West Road late in the day and here they stopped. The great road stood barren before them, its wide span thick with mud and seemingly sullen. A settlement had been here once but all that remained now were dilapidated and decaying buildings.

West along the sea lay the Barony of Klaive; across the swamps to the great sea lay the Twin Sonnets, the Free Cities of Mir and Veter. East, a great distance along the great road lay the end of Great Kingdom and the beginning of the Western Territories. Here the land was shrouded in ancient woodlands, a forest as deep and rich as the whole of the Territories, Eastern and Western. Directly to their south lay South Province and its capital Quashan'. To the north, Imtal awaited their return.

From here, a small complement of ridesmen, two detachments and the sergeant at arms, Emel Brodstson, would continue south. The remainder of the great company would follow the gradual westward slope of the road for a few more hours.

Adrina watched as the detachment rode away to the south and she rode westward. Decidedly, she would miss Emel. She wanted to chase him down and wish him a safe journey or maybe mumble through an apology, but held back.

She would have continued riding west and never spoken the good-bye she was harboring if a few moments of hesitation hadn't changed her mind. She wrapped the leather straps tightly in her hands and pulled them sharply to one side to turn the mare quickly. A swift kick to the hindquarters sent the animal charging. Her sworn protectors hurried to catch her, having been earnestly chastised for letting her out of their sight on previous occasions.

Not sure what she wanted to tell him, she was slow to call out to him. She wanted to tell him that it wasn't his fault. She wanted to tell him what she felt for him in her heart. She wanted to tell him that she would miss him.

As he turned to look at her, she lost her resolve. "Please give my regards to Prince Valam. Tell my brother I can't wait until his visit next summer," she said, saying what was safe and not what was in her heart.

Emel stopped Ebony momentarily and told her frankly, "Someone is shadowing the column, Adrina. Watch your every step."

***

Vilmos followed where the pull of the rope lead him, the world around him was now so black that he couldn't discern anything from the darkness. Not knowing when they would come to a rut, a hill, a ravine, he placed each foot down softly and uncertainly. He tried to keep his thoughts from wandering and think only of placing one foot in front of the other. This was a difficult chore as he fought exhaustion.

The single hunter continued to follow them, howling out at regular intervals, perhaps telling companions that followed silently that the hunt was still on.

Staring into the darkness and not being able to see anything was at times overwhelming, and during those times, Vilmos felt utterly helpless. He could only follow the tugs at the rope and hope that the person tied to the other end was still Xith—for exhaustion made him doubt even that.

His thoughts did wander, though, even as he fought to keep them focused on putting one foot in front of the other. He thought of home, the villagers, Lillath and Vil. Surely if the powerful shaman feared the creatures that chased them, the three villages were in danger. Yes, days of forests separated them, but how far did these creatures roam?

Vilmos groped his way around a tree that seemed to suddenly sprout in front of him. The ground beneath his feet was damp now. Vilmos knew this because of the thick mud clinging to his boots, making heavy feet that much heavier. Far off he heard the sound of running water as if a stream lay somewhere ahead. For a time his thoughts filled with a longing to drink of its cool waters.

They were coming down a long steep hill when suddenly the rope went slack. Vilmos' mind filled with alarm. Xith normally signaled with a double pull on the rope when he was going to stop.

Vilmos groped with his hands about his waist until he found where the knot in the rope began. Then he began to take up the slack in the line. When he had pulled in about five feet without the line going taut, he stopped. He was almost afraid to keep pulling. His hands way ahead of his thoughts kept working though and Vilmos soon found the end of the line in his hands.

Vilmos tried to rationalize. He told himself Xith must have untied the rope from around his waist. Perhaps the stream was just ahead and Xith wanted to tell him this. The running water did sound awfully close.

Bravely, Vilmos took a step forward into the darkness, then another, and a few more. The stream was there all right. He found it by stepping into it with a slosh. The water was cold.

"Xith," Vilmos whispered, "Where are you?"

No answer came.

Vilmos whispered in a slightly louder voice, "Xith?"

Vilmos heard movement behind him and spun about, nearly losing his balance. He saw the dull glow of a pair of eyes about halfway up the steep, forest-covered hill but the glow wasn't soft silver.

He stood deadly still. He heard growling now and then a howl, joined by many more. Confusion, exhaustion and panic mandated his actions.

Instinct and human nature took over his thoughts. The will to survive became his only objective. Blue sparks danced across his fingers tips without him even realizing it.

The light only served to fill in the images missing from his mind's eye. Halfway up the hill he saw them, a pack of the creatures that though they looked like wolves he knew they weren't. No wolf he'd ever seen had two heads. No wolf he'd ever seen was as large as a bear.

Vilmos slowly backed into the stream. The creatures inched forward. He inched backward.

When the waters swirling around him were knee deep, Vilmos stopped. The lead creature, the largest one of the whole pack, stood no farther than ten feet away from him now. Vilmos was suddenly sure this was the beast that had hunted and howled after them while the others in the pack had hunted silently at its side. It seemed to signal to the others to wait as it approached.

Instinct and the will to survive still at the forefront of his thoughts, blue sparks continued to dance across Vilmos' fingertips. He waited, staring down the strange two-headed creature, wondering why it did not attack him, wondering if it could lunge ten feet in a single, swift move using the powerful legs he saw.

Vilmos began to back up again, and the creature continued to approach. Each took one small step at a time, and stared the other down. Vilmos' two eyes matched against the creature's four, each daring the other to make a move.

The water about his legs was now only ankle deep, but Vilmos gave it little thought. He dared not waver his eyes from the position they held locked to the creature's. Soon Vilmos found that he was no longer sloshing backward through water. He had come to the far bank. The strange beast waited on the opposite bank, only a few precious feet away.

In the soft blue light, the creature's double set of fangs glistened white-blue. Two heads meant two mouths filled with up- and down-turned canine fangs. Vilmos and the creature stared each other down, seemingly to find out whose will power was stronger.

Something brushed against his shoulder. Vilmos let out a scream that echoed long into the night. He whirled about, fists poised ready to fend off the unseen attacker, only to find soft gray eyes fixed on his.

"Xith!" Vilmos shrieked, "Thank the Father!"

"Do not thank him yet," Xith said, "Back up slowly now. The Wolmerrelle will not normally leave an area they are protecting, but let's not give them any reason to think they should."

"Wolmerrelle?"

"Suffice it to say that beasts from different realms were not meant to mate, for when they do, the result is not for the greater good."

"Where did you go?" Vilmos asked as he inched backward.

Xith held out something in his hand that the boy didn't dare to look at. "They were leading us all right. Another pack was shadowing us, waiting until they had us cornered."

Xith put a heavy hand on Vilmos' shoulder, indicating they should stop. Vilmos noticed there were no trees around them. He stood in tall grass that stretched to his chest. The lead Wolmerrelle was still staring them down, but now it was a good twenty to thirty feet away. Vilmos groaned and put his hands to his face to rub bleary eyes. As Vilmos did this, Xith lost the support he had been using to keep upright. He staggered and fell.

Vilmos grabbed Xith's waist to help the shaman to his feet. He felt moisture against his hand. Xith's robe was saturated from his neck down.

"Do not worry." Xith's voice was weak. He coughed. "Most of it is not mine."

Vilmos knew then that it was blood he touched. For a moment, a small sliver of the moon shined down upon them as it broke through heavy clouds. Vilmos saw the shaman's prize. It was a head of one of the beasts, up close it was far larger and even more frightening than he had imagined.

Vilmos tended to Xith's wounds. He did as the shaman instructed and cleaned the wounds against infection then touched the stones of the river to them. "The stream is a tributary to the distant river Trollbridge that divides the Free Cities of Mir and Veter. It runs a long way from Rain Mountain in the center of the forest to where it joins the Trollbridge and helps feed the swamps. Its stones are healing in their own way," Xith had said, and Vilmos did not question that they were.

For the next several hours, Vilmos lay at Xith's side, afraid to let sleep take him. Several times as he stared through gaps in the tall grasses to the far side of the stream, he saw the strange creatures Xith had called Wolmerrelle. Xith had been right about one thing—they were best left unnamed. Putting a name to the horror he saw only aided their terrifying grip on his mind. Somehow he was sure that one day he would return to Vangar Forest and when he did the Wolmerrelle would be waiting for him.

Next time Vilmos knew he would not be so lucky. He would not escape as easily.

***

Captain Brodst called the company to a halt. The low road that lead down into the murky lowlands, aptly dubbed the Bottoms by both those few who dwelled there and by those who frequented these southerly lands, lay before them.

He cast a glance heavenward; the sun was well past its zenith and the storm clouds of morning were gone. His customary frown lengthened. He reconsidered his alternatives, to take the king's road or to skirt the mire. He had discussed these choices with Keeper Martin, Father Jacob and the other captains the previous day. The obvious choice was to take the shortcut through the swamp. They were already behind schedule, yet something Duke Ispeth had told him the night before last was bothering him now.

"Not a single messenger—and few travelers—have come north for more than a week," the duke had said, "tis a strange occurrence indeed."

At the time Captain Brodst hadn't given it much thought, he had been tired and angry. Duke Ispeth could be a stubborn man when he wanted to be. Captain Brodst remembered that just after the duke had said that he'd scratched his head and said, "It's probably nothing. In another week or so, I'll probably find that the roads were washed out again… Damned rainy season approaching, you know."

Something in the way the old duke had said it told Captain Brodst he didn't really believe what he'd just said. It was true Duke Ispeth was eccentric and suspicious of everyone; even so, Captain Brodst had never seen anyone as agitated as he'd seen the duke that night. He had ranted and raved for hours. He had told them about reports of strange travelers passing through his lands at night, peasants complaining that whole crops were disappearing and many other things.

Captain Brodst took in a deep breath. If the weather had been better, surely they would have been ahead of schedule and he could have opted to skirt the swamps. He had discussed this route with King Andrew because they both feared the closeness of the rainy season. Captain Brodst found it ironic that since the rainy season had arrived early he now seemed forced to make a completely wrong choice in an attempt to save time.

None of this worrying will save time, he told himself. They were at least one day behind schedule and needed to make up the lost time. The only way to do it would be to turn south. He gave the signal, pointed to the southernmost road and then spurred his mount on. In a few hours Captain Brodst planned to call a halt for the evening and, by mid-morning of the second day along this route, they should enter the outer mires.

Chapter Fifteen

A full day had passed before Xith felt strong enough to continue the journey northward, but in the three days since he and Vilmos had made excellent progress. They were now in the land known as South Province, a holding of Great Kingdom. The wounds Xith had suffered at the hands of the Wolmerrelle were healing nicely and now he looked to the days ahead.

The evil presence that had been with them those many days seemed to be gone—gone with Vangar Forest. Xith knew that all too soon the gentle wind-blown plains of this section of South Province would be gone. Their journey was taking them north to Great Kingdom and west to the great sea.

Soon it would be time to again work on awakening the power within the boy. Xith knew he must do this slowly and cautiously. To prepare Vilmos for the task ahead, Xith must make the boy face his fears. In the end, there would be nowhere left to run from, only places to run to.

***

The passage along the rolling hills that gradually sloped down into the Bottoms was moderately paced. Unfortunately, the seasonal rains returned with vigorous fury, forcing a deficient, sluggish rate upon the travelers. Fortunately, however, after several hours of intense storms, high winds carried the storm front away to leave the skies clear and the grounds muddied though passable.

The group escaped from the confines of heavy cloaks, dropping hoods and loosening the ties about their necks as the air grew warm. Adrina had been in a pensive mood all through the morning. Her thoughts were with Emel. She felt so alone without him and what made this even worse was that everyone around her seemed to notice it, especially Keeper Martin and Father Jacob.

Adrina's unease began to grow as they moved ever closer to the Bottoms and not only because the thought of traveling through such a place filled her mind with dread. She had been counting on the extra days the longer route around the mires would have provided. The road through the Bottoms would only hasten them to Alderan, and this more than anything else filled her mind with alarm.

Keeper Martin, who had been keeping a watchful eye on her and not letting her out of his sight, spoke, "There is nothing to fear, dear, the passage through the mires will be swift and we'll be smelling sea breezes before you know it."

Adrina expressed a sour grimace in response. Keeper Martin may have an intuitive wisdom, but she knew better than to think there was nothing out there. The putrid smell of rotting vegetation that the wind carried had to be hiding something.

Father Jacob added to the keeper's words, his voice trembling with emotion, "He is right, Princess Adrina. Tonight we will stay at a palace of such great beauty that it rivals that of Imtal's. And Baron Fraddylwicke is a most excellent host."

"Imtal is hardly beautiful," returned Adrina.

Father Jacob said cheerfully, "The palace once belonged to King Jarom the First of Vostok before he lost the lands to the Kingdom long, long ago. At one time, it was the gateway into the whole of the South. The Lord and Lady Fraddylwicke await us…"

His voice trailed off, but Adrina thought she had heard him finish with, "or so I do fear."

Captain Brodst, adding melancholy to the cheer by saying, "And it has only fallen into the mire three times since then."

Surprised at the Captain's joining in, Adrina said nothing.

"A trivial fact, I assure you," said Keeper Martin, "it was rebuilt each time with increasing care and magnificence."

Adrina smiled and responded, "I can't wait to see it. It sounds wonderful." She added for the keeper's benefit, "Full of history."

Her thoughts took a turn toward expectations and away from disappointment and unease. She was again surprised that Captain Brodst had spoken to her. "His scowl is his shield," she whispered to herself.

Adrina relaxed in her saddle and soaked up some of the warm air. She undid the ties on her cloak and removed it. However, the warmth that had fed their momentary good spirits came to a quick and not-at-all-subtle end. The ground seemed to readily suck up the warmth and the chill returned.

***

Vilmos had never been beyond the limits of the secret place he traveled to in his dreams, the confines of which he had been content to live in and *would* have been content to live in for the rest of his life. Suddenly a new world was opening to him. In it, he discovered new definitions of the boundaries around him and a thirst for knowledge of the outside world. The great windswept plains of South Province were truly beautiful and a far stretch from the lands of desolation described in the Great Book.

Vilmos listened intently to the shaman's words. This gave him something to focus on, which made it easier to forget all that was behind him.

"The element of fire is the easiest of the arcane elements to grasp initially. It is also the trickiest to control because of the tremendous raw power it taps," Xith had warned him and Vilmos had taken this to heart. After only his third attempt at producing a spark to ignite wood, he had performed "well" as the shaman had put it, "magnificently" as he put it.

He had mastered his first incantation—the first incantation of the element fire. He could now touch delicate power to wood with apparent ease and produce a soft red-orange blaze. Vilmos looked forward to the next lesson, which Xith promised he would teach him soon.

Now it was time for a reprieve from the heavy cares of the world. Before they moved on to the next lesson, Xith had told Vilmos he intended to take them to a place where they could rest for a time.

Ahead in the distance lay a rustic trade center. It was built along the eastern bank of a river, near a ford. Its three small buildings in various stages of decay stood at the fore of the road huddled around a two-story clapboarded building on which hung a tiny sign that read simply Inn, All Welcome. Other than this sign the settlement was void of all appearances of habitation. Closer inspection of the small inn showed that although it was in an equal state of disrepair as the buildings surrounding it, it was a relatively new structure.

Xith paused momentarily in the middle of the path and turned to look at Vilmos, then raised the hood of his cloak up over his head and pulled it forward to hide his face in the shadows it created. He motioned for Vilmos to do likewise. The sense of caution in Xith's features told Vilmos to act without hesitation.

The interior of the inn was as untidy and unsightly as the exterior. An open, dimly lit chamber that contained several tables and many chairs that were twisted and broken largely dominated the ground floor. Near an elongated staircase that led to the second floor sat a portly man upon a lonely unbroken chair. In front of him was the sole upright table.

The obese man, whom Vilmos surmised to be the inn keep, had a rather unpleasant odor about him. He didn't budge until he heard the sound of coinage dropping onto his tabletop and even then his only action was to point to the stairs, then raise three of his chubby fingers to indicate the respective room number.

Without a word, the weary travelers climbed the stairs and went to room number three. They closed and bolted the door behind them. Though it was only midday they found sleep came very easily, and it was not until many hours later that either stirred.

Vilmos awoke to find Xith staring at him.

"No dreams," Vilmos whispered reverently, as he had each day upon awaking since joining Xith. Then he turned frank eyes to Xith. "Where are we?"

"We have reached the edge of the disputed lands."

"The Borderlands," exclaimed Vilmos. "Bandit Kings and Hunter Clan!"

"No, not the Borderlands of the North, but—"

Vilmos cut Xith short, "Then the stories are true?"

"Those times are no more," said Xith, a twinge of sadness or perhaps longing in his voice—Vilmos could not tell which. "We are nearing the disputed lands of the South. Here only brigands and a few traders remain. We are only going to skirt the edge of this area. It is the fastest way to the sea."

Vilmos had never seen the sea, and in his wildest aspirations he had never thought he would. "The sea, really the sea?"

"We are at a last stopping place before we enter what was once the Alder's Kingdom but is now mostly ruins, except for Alderan."

"Tell me more, please." Vilmos was babbling excitedly.

"There isn't all that much to tell. Besides, your version of the truth would vary greatly from mine. You will see soon enough. We must turn our attention to other things first though," Xith said, a far off look in his eyes. "*Are you there?*" he called out in a scarcely audible tone.

"What do you mean?" asked Vilmos, responding not to the question but to the previous statement.

"Nothing. Rest," said Xith, relief in his voice, "we have a long trip ahead of us in the morning."

Vilmos sensed something was wrong, but whatever it was it

seemed out of his grasp. He leaned back, touched head to pillow and closed his tired eyes once again. Images of the day's adventure danced before his sealed lids—the most profound of which was the image of the burly looking innkeeper whose figure played ominously in his thoughts, with his fat hands raised, pointing at him, provoking him, warning him.

After what seemed hours of restless tossing and turning, Vilmos opened his eyes in frustration and sat up in bed. The last light of day still had not given way to the darkness of night and as Vilmos peered about the room, he was shocked to find himself alone. Xith was gone.

Vilmos was puzzled. Would Xith leave him? Maybe he went to relieve himself or something, Vilmos thought. He ran into the hall, but finding only greetings of darkness he quickly returned to the room.

Frustrated he sat back on the bed, curled his feet up tight and wrapped his hands around his legs. He sat that way for hours, watching the sun slowly disappear behind the neighboring building. Periodically he looked toward the closed door.

The shadows in the room began to take on an eerie perspective, casting odd thoughts into his impressionable young mind. A half-burnt stub of a candle lay atop the stand beside the bed. Vilmos reached out and grabbed it. He thrust it back into the pricket it had been removed from, with the apparent intent of replacing it though the new one had never been brought and the old one had never been discarded.

With a flick of absent thought, Vilmos sparked the candle to life. The brilliant orange of the flame danced in front of his eyes as if it played out a song to him. Vilmos was captivated and motivated by it. Yet a heavy breath unwittingly extinguished its fragile flame, forcing him to re-ignite it. It had been quite accidental but Vilmos was amused by it. He took to blowing the candle out and then lighting it again and again with his mind. He laughed a soft, silent chuckle to himself as he did this.

He played with the candle for a time, flicking it off and on, the light of the fire reflecting off his face in the otherwise dark chamber.

Mesmerized by the candlelight, following its on and off blink, eventually, quite accidentally and without even realizing it, Vilmos learned to gingerly manipulate the flame with his mind. He could put it out and then touch it again with his power to relight it, which was quite an accomplishment if only he would have realized it.

With a sudden twist the doorknob turned and the door opened. Vilmos heard voices from the hall.

"I'm sorry I couldn't be of much help old friend. I'm sure you are right; Alderan is the key. They'll surely travel along the coastal highway."

"Goodnight, Misha. I am glad your other guests decided to depart ahead of schedule," Xith said. He laughed as he slipped into the room, and then took a sip of the drink in his cupped hand. "We will have to do this again sometime." He turned to look at someone Vilmos couldn't see. "Goodnight to you too, dearest. Thank you, you have again done well. I truly did not expect to see you so soon. Guard well the final two scrolls. I will not see you again until after all this is behind us." Xith whispered the last in a voice barely audible, and then took another swig from the half-empty mug he cradled almost tenderly. He waved and then closed the door, trying only now to be quiet.

The scene was quite comical when Xith turned around and prepared to creep to his bed. Vilmos was waiting, and Xith could only smile as if a child caught in the act of doing something he knows he's not supposed to be doing. Without a word Xith crossed to the bed opposite Vilmos, sat upon it, blew out the candle Vilmos held and then lay back and closed his eyes.

***

The long file entered the outer mire. The coolness of the air entwined with the warmth of the ground caused wisps of mist to swirl underfoot even in the early hours of afternoon, giving the area an eerie haze. Adrina felt her body begin to shiver uncontrollably at the cool touch, a touch similar to the play of cold fingers along the exposed areas of her skin.

She pulled her cloak tightly about her and brought its hood up stout, retreating far into the recesses of the cowl as she had that morning. Although the cloak was still moist from the rain, it did manage to provide a bit of extra warmth. She was thankful for its touch of comfort and hopeful that they would reach the castle soon for she was growing very weary. She sank languidly into the leathers of a saturated, irritating saddle.

Torches were mustered from the supplies and spread through the long line as insurance that, should the mists turn to fog, the group would not get lost. Captain Brodst, using his flint and steel and a few pieces of his precious stock of dry kindling—some of the torches had gotten damp—lit the initial torch, which he passed to the sentinel to bear at the front of the column. For the present, this was the only one to be lit. The others were not yet needed.

The sun's rays were soon lost in a shroud of haze and the hours appeared to drag by. Dampness was so thick in the air that moisture sank into the very souls of those present. Adrina was caught up in deep feelings of portentous dread and she petted her mare's mane to soothe it—or so she told herself. It was really herself that she sought to calm.

She tried to think pleasant thoughts. She didn't like the swamp they traversed and she liked the dense fog even less. The combination of the two elements overwhelmed her mind and only the thought of the castle that lay somewhere ahead in the distance turned her woes toward eventual ease.

She could imagine the Lord and Lady of the castle: him dressed in a purple overcoat and a blue silk shirt, his court best, and her in the long flowing gown of the day properly coordinated with the purple and blues of the Lord Fraddylwicke, her attendants forever at her side. She imagined their greeting a grand affair at the great castle gates. The castle walls were not a dead and dreary gray but cheerful silver.

The column marched farther and farther into the mire. It seemed as if they had suddenly passed under a great thick blanket of endless gray. Captain Brodst was forced to call another halt. The double file with which they had begun the gradual descent into the mire was dispensed and a long drawn-out single file unfolded into the shadows.

Torches were ignited from the sentinel's and though this would have been reassuring under most circumstances, it only assisted the uncanny veil's pervasion of their thoughts.

Progress through the ever-thickening sheets of fog materialized as a feeble inching forward. The cries of the cricket and the frog, the buzzing of insects and the stirrings of other smaller beasts stopped. Only the sloshing of the horses' hooves and boots on the soggy trail remained and it was as if nature itself had paused, waiting for the next puff of freshness and life.

Adrina witnessed the line of lights assemble in front of and behind her. Then as she watched, the former disappeared one by one into the veil ahead. Those behind she didn't turn to look at.

Carefully following the movements of those ahead when it was her turn, she coaxed her mount by gently slapping it with the reins to start it moving at a relaxed gait. Still she stroked the animal's mane with her free hand. Briefly she looked back now to ensure that the rider behind her noted her passage and followed her lead.

She gazed intently ahead and tried to maintain a bearing on the dim glow of the torch Keeper Martin carried in front of her. The fog seemed to swallow any hint of the flame, leaving only a slight trace of its glow to guide her movements. The pace appeared to quicken instantly to a slow gallop and then decrease suddenly to a slow trot, making it extremely difficult for her to preserve the integrity of the file. She wondered how the rider behind her faired in her wake. She hoped that the other could sustain a bearing on her torch. For now she dared not look back for fear of losing sight of the elusive glow in front of her.

The cold mire air grew steadily damp and stagnant as the last remaining hints of the earlier wind disappeared. Adrina began to shiver uncontrollably once more. It was as if the unseen hands groped their way across her skin and the touch was cold and sinewy.

She tried to find warmth and security in her heavy hooded cloak but she found none. Just when she thought she could tolerate no more, it was as if those same unseen hands had reached out and grasped her throat, squeezing down with slow, firm pressure.

Suddenly she was afraid to move. What if she raised her hands to her neck and really did find an unseen hand gripped about her throat?

She wanted to scream out for help, to lash out at the unseen specter, to cry out to the dead land that she did not want it to claim her. She began to whimper and plea with the unseen hands to release her but this only caused a flood of suppressed emotions—three years of pain and anguish, sorrow and denial—to descend upon her. The dead, gray walls of Imtal were around her, looming up dark and deadly before her—like in her dreams—and all the land was dead and she, Adrina, was dead.

The specter was there with her—like in her dreams—to take her away but now she didn't want the specter to take her away. The prune-faced man with his twisted wooden staff had saved her before, but he wasn't there now and this wasn't a dream. She began to scream. Frantically she kicked her mount and pulled on the reins sharply. Her shrill scream cut short by a rationalization that came too late.

The horse beneath her confused by the mixture of opposing signs given it, reared upward. To regain a tight grip on the reins, Adrina twisted the leathers in her hands. This again sent misleading signals to the confounded and uneasy animal beneath her. It reared again.

A second pull on the reins caused the mare to shift sideways as it landed. The steed stumbled, then faltered as it lost its footing on the uneven roadside. Adrina's tumultuous, wanton eyes spun around as she tumbled.

No longer a participant, Adrina became an observer. The

torchlight seemed to dance around in circles before her as she felt herself falling to the ground. Her head was still spinning and her thoughts yet dazed as she landed with a splash into the murky waters and mud of the mire.

In a blur of frenzied thought, she felt herself sinking downward. A split second passed and she relived the fall into the water, eyes wide, cheeks puffed gasping at air, hands flailing, the light of the torch spinning wildly before her and then dying the instant it hit the dark waters with a sizzle.

A scramble to free feet from stirrups ended as she felt the movement of her body come to a sudden stop. Had she hit bottom? Was this it?

She held all the time in the world in the palm of her hands and she released a sigh of thankfulness, cut short by the horse landing on top of her with a horrific crunch. Adrina's pain was sudden, excruciating and vividly real as her world careened to darkness.

Chapter Sixteen

Seth looked to Galan who was still sleeping and wondered if dreams of the forest still swept through her mind. He knew little of the sea and winds, but unlike Bryan and Galan, he had been on the canals of Kapital with Sailmaster Cagan. He used a makeshift hook and tied bits of colored cloth to it, then cast out his line, a length of string from his robe. Over these past days, he had enjoyed no luck and while it truly seemed there was no life in the deep sea, he was not about to give up.

A hazy dawn eventually gave way to day as the sun made its inevitable climb. With irony, Seth remembered now that he had once prayed for the day's arrival to end the bitter cold of night. But the night didn't steal precious moisture from his weary body, the sun did.

The day gradually grew hot and dry. Seth found that his thoughts were beginning to wander. He maintained consciousness, only barely so, while he cast the line out and pulled it in slowly, as he had once been shown.

At one point out of the corner of his eye, Seth saw Bryan moving about the raft, but inevitably as the sun beat down upon him, thirst and hunger took over. His thoughts began to wander and shift despite his best efforts. He attempted to clear his thoughts, but this required a complete conscious effort, which under the torment of the blistering sun, with strength draining from his body little by little, he could not give it. He could only mourn the loss he could do nothing to regain. He perceived himself as a hapless child. He, First of the Red, with all his knowledge and skills could not resolve their dilemma.

Seth soon found himself drifting back to sleep and it was then that the warning from Bryan came. *We're in danger, krens!*

Seth came alert in an instant. It seemed he had just closed his eyes, but then he took note of the light of a virgining day on the horizon. Suddenly Bryan's warning registered in his mind. He called out *By the Father, Galan, Everrelle!... Everrelle?*

Galan awoke. Everrelle didn't. For some reason one of the great gray beasts began attacking the bottom of the raft. Bryan pulled in the fishing line. Seth noticed there was something on it. Seth asked, *You caught something?*

Bryan started to reply, *In a way—*

Bryan's voice was drowned out by Galan's scream. *Dear Father! Everrelle, Everrelle?*

Galan directed thoughts to Seth. *The infection, it's worse...* Then she turned back to Everrelle. *Stay with me, stay with us, don't go. 'We'll survive the journey together,' you said. Hold on, promise me you'll hold on...*

Another of the gray beasts that lurked just beneath the surface of the water nudged the raft as Bryan told them *Get Everrelle away from the edge!*

Days without food meant exhaustion. Galan too was exhausted, and the exhaustion only magnified her alarm and her panic. Seth could see it in her eyes. He directed Bryan to crawl to the other side of the raft and help Galan with Everrelle. He concentrated on angry thoughts and sent them into the minds of the dark shapes beneath the water.

The raft shook as it was buffeted by tail and fin. Angrily and relentlessly, Seth, Galan and Bryan beat at the dark shapes until the raft shook no more. The three stood quietly, huddled together, and stared into the dark waters.

One by one, fatigue overwhelmed them. Bryan was the first to collapse, Seth the last. Silence followed.

Galan broke the long silence with a very soft whisper, *Everrelle is gone... She promised she'd hold on, she promised.*

Seth didn't answer immediately. Sleep was trying to lull him. He felt Everrelle's passing but could do nothing more than wish her a safe journey.

After a few minutes, he directed a response to Galan, *Sleep, my brother, save your strength.*

***

Vilmos scrutinized the small kitchen. He could have sworn he had heard more than two voices last night.

"Beautiful morning, Mish'!" Xith exclaimed. He walked over to the large man and patted him on the back.

The innkeeper smiled and tossed Vilmos a wink, and then he showed the two to a table that was tucked cleanly away in one of the kitchen's many corners. While they ate, Misha stuffed several satchels with fresh baked breads, smoked meats and an assortment of various other foodstuffs. The aromas wafted through the air to the place where Vilmos and Xith sat and mingled with the pleasant smells already present, creating a feast for the senses of a king.

Not long after breakfast, Xith and Vilmos departed the inn. Misha had graciously offered them his wagon, and although old, worn and lead by a pair of jades, the wagon was comfortable and proved a very great respite from walking.

Vilmos thought Xith had been rather rude for not introducing him to his apparently good friend. He tossed Xith a snarled grimace but then turned to other subjects, visions of what lay ahead. Although he had never been to the Alder's Kingdom, he knew much about its lore from the Great Book. The Alder had been a very wise king. In signing the treaty with the southern kingdoms, he had ended the longest and bloodiest war in the history of all the lands.

The Race Wars, as those few who had survived later called them, had lasted generations. During that time whole peoples and nations had perished.

A nearly forgotten lesson echoed in Vilmos' mind. He thought of the once great kingdoms of the North. Lycya, mightiest of the kingdoms, swallowed by barren desert. Queen of Elves and all her people washed into West Deep. North Reach and the clans over-mountain consumed by the twenty-year snow.

Xith drove the pair of jades faster than they seemed to want to go.

Vilmos knew without doubt the rest was over. Something dread lay ahead, but what it was he did not know. He started to shiver and though he wrapped his cloak close about him, he could not chase away the cold.

***

Hot, it's so damned hot…

Endless waiting played heavily on Seth's faith. He knew it was faith that he must maintain, for there was nothing else. Only Mother-Earth would carry them to safety or deliver them from life.

Ah, please… please… make the sun go away… make it end…

A full-day sun blossomed overhead. The struggle to keep eyes open was borne. Once closed under the beating sun, blisters would return and with them infection, and then eyes might open no more. The ruinous combination of sun and salt water had already desiccated and blistered his body, yet it was his eyes that seemed his most sacred pride.

Seth struggled to his knees. He tested the strength of the pieces of ropes and tattered clothing that held the raft together. Salt water despoiled them. Still, they held well. *Thank you…*

A sudden tremor in his mind sent Seth's thoughts careening outward. *Bryan!* Seth called out.

He perceived no return response, though he could feel the other's anguish.

Oh please… please, hold on…

Seth carefully removed the cap from the last water bag they possessed and put a single droplet to his own parched lips.

Give me strength... He wanted more; he wanted every drop the bottle contained. *Give me strength...*

The water's caress as it moistened his lips caused a shiver throughout his body. The yearning for more increased, yet he could not, *would not,* allow himself to partake of it.

His hands were shaking. *Give me strength...* He implored.

Seth lowered the water bag. He reached over to where Bryan lay, and cradled his companion's head upward. Slowly and painstakingly, he dropped the precious liquid to Bryan's lips, savoring every drop as if it touched his own lips. He continued to drop the water to Bryan's lips, drop by precious drop, until the brother could swallow. Afterward, he did the same for Galan.

Bryan and Galan's faces were covered with sun blisters, as was his own. His thoughts were only for his fellows. *Two must survive no matter the cost,* he whispered to himself, *two must survive.* Those were Queen Mother's last words of warning.

Delirium enveloped his thoughts and the words echoed through his mind. Somehow he must shield them; somehow they must all survive.

***

The day ended and early night settled in. Vilmos and Xith set up camp in the safety of a clearing within a small woodland oasis. The rather large stand, an oddity this far south, was a hearty growth of fine northern fir, whose clipped boughs served as an excellent mattress upon which to rest. Lying upon these soft, scented pine boughs, arms crossed and head propped atop, their tired eyes stared up at the star-filled night sky with a gently shining liquid moon.

It was an autumn moon, a moon that was not quite full and loomed low in the sky with the distant, unseen sun casting a cool orange luminescence upon its face. In other times Xith would have called it a blooded moon and the portent would have been one of ominous foreboding, but under the current circumstances it merely moved him into a somber introspective mood.

While he didn't give the omen much thought, he did not cast it away either. Rather it hung there in the back of his mind while he floated off to sleep and later invaded his few moments of private dreams.

Chapter Seventeen

More long hours under the burning sun did little for Seth's clarity of mind. He was nearing total delirium. The only thought that kept him near sanity was the one single thought that had kept him through these final hours.

Two must survive, two must survive no matter the cost, went the echo in his mind. Surely some time ago he had ceased thinking it, yet the echo still clung to his mind.

With great persistence, Seth moved from a sitting position to a kneeling position—waves shifting the raft and his fatigue made the small accomplishment a difficult chore. He held there motionless for a moment and tried to recall why he had risen to his knees. After a lengthy pause, he sank back down to his haunches. There must have been something he had wanted to do, but what, he couldn't recall.

Two must survive, he whispered.

Weary, Seth slumped down onto his side. He closed and shielded tired eyes, using the tattered shards of a once magnificent cloak to mask his face. For what seemed hours, the ceaseless up and down swaying of the raft lulled him. By luck or fate, or perhaps a little help from Great Father, Seth managed to focus his will, though only for an instant. He reached outward with his mind trying desperately to reach a knowing consciousness. He found none.

The momentary clarity of mind also allowed him to concentrate. Surely there was an answer to their dilemma. He pondered this. Something had gone wrong from the start, but what had it been. Had there been a traitor among them? Was there a traitor among them now? Was it Bryan or Galan?

Seth dismissed the idea of a traitor. No one of the Brotherhood would ever betray Queen Mother—*King Mark,* whispered his conscience. *No, King Mark betrayed all. Survival is keyed to the past. The answer is there, if only I can find it.*

Exhausted, Seth started to drift off to sleep and was quickly lost to his dreams, dreams in which he could replay events that had unfolded against them.

No longer was he in his beloved homeland, surrounded by the peace and serenity of Queen Mother. Now he was thrust out into the strange and cruel world, into an unknown fate. Only Great Father knew how the long struggle would end.

His mind wandered further. He floated through delirium to mixed conscious thought. He began to think back, back to the time before they had left their homeland. At first in this mixed up delusion that to him seemed real, Seth heard only the voices, his and hers. As his thoughts cleared and he entered a deeper dream-state, he pieced together disconnected thoughts without much detail.

It was to this at first colorless world of dream with only the voices that he fled.

***

"Isador, I saw him. I saw him!" screamed Adrina, as she roused from a feverish state. "He is hurting. He needs our help!"

"Princess, it was only a dream," said an alarmed Father Jacob. The sound of Adrina's voice had startled him. He took the moist towel from her brow, dipped it into the cold water of the basin beside him and then reapplied it to her forehead. The fever must have finally broken, he thought.

"We must hurry," continued Adrina heatedly.

"It was only a dream," repeated Father Jacob. He patiently dabbed the girl's forehead with the cold towel.

"His eyes were the bluest blue. He spoke to me in the dream." Adrina lurched up in bed, and then after putting her feet to floor she stood. She looked around the unfamiliar room and stopped. A puzzled frown crossed her face. "Where am I and how did I get here?"

The room started to swirl around her, twisting and turning round and round. Adrina began to lose her balance. She fought to steady herself. Father Jacob caught her and ferried her back into bed. She looked up at him, her eyes wide and imploring, and said, "We must leave now. I know where he is. Just as the lady said, the ship did not reach Alderan."

Father Jacob was sure Adrina was talking gibberish again. She had said many things in her fevered state. "Child you must rest. Tomorrow will bring a new day. The others will return soon enough."

"You don't understand, Father Jacob. Get Keeper Martin. He understands; he will listen to me."

"I am afraid they have already departed. You have been asleep for quite some time. Now please get some rest, my child," said Jacob. He pulled heavy blankets up around Adrina to keep the girl warm.

Adrina wanted to say something else but Jacob silenced her and again bade her to sleep. As Jacob turned away, Adrina grabbed his arm and squeezed as hard as she could to gain his attention. She didn't want to sleep—at least, not yet. Once she had his attention, she stared straight into his eyes and stated in a calm, portentous manner, "When did they leave? We must go now before it is *too* late."

Father Jacob was taken aback by her words, something told him to listen to her. "Slow down, Princess. I am afraid I don't understand. Tell me of the dream."

After a brief moment of silence, Adrina said, "It was in my dreams, father. I saw Prince William and he spoke to me. I know where he is and he urgently needs our help... There is something wrong."

"You are full of fever. Prince William is in Alderan. No harm could have befallen him there."

Adrina closed her eyes for a moment though she did not let go of Jacob's arm. "No, the ship from Wellison did not complete the journey. The voices, the message, Father Jacob, it was all *real...* You must believe me. If only Keeper Martin were here. He *would* understand."

"I believe you young princess," said Father Jacob, "but you are in no condition to travel."

Adrina regarded Father Jacob with serious eyes. "Are you patronizing me?"

"You close your eyes and rest now. I'll see if I can arrange travel accommodations." Jacob nodded his head wearily. He wasn't convinced it was a good idea to leave Fraddylwicke Castle. He departed Adrina's chamber with troubled thoughts filling his mind. His hope was that the girl would be fast asleep when he returned.

***

Waves beneath the raft shifted it and just as his thoughts were coming to a clear, full focus, Seth was jolted from his slumber. He opened bleary eyes to a night sky. He did not marvel at the arrival of darkness. The night sky only meant cruel heat was gone and bitter cold had replaced it.

He was thankful though that Bryan and Galan were soundly sleeping. They had survived yet another day beneath the untiring fury of the day sky.

He opened the water skin and put several droplets to his lips. He could have easily finished that last bit of water in the container. It would have only taken a second more. He reveled in the fantasy of it slipping coolly down his throat. The fact that his throat was swollen and every such swallow would have brought sure pain did not taint the longing.

Give me strength, he implored.

Only as he raised the container back to his lips did he find restraint. *Thank you...*

Two must survive, went the ceaseless echo in his mind. He turned his eyes back to the dark waters and a thought from the dream found him. *The mind shield.* The mind shield could resist his probing thoughts. Anyone could be lurking out there in the darkness, waiting just beyond the next crest or trough.

High Hall, why High Hall? Seth thought suddenly, though he didn't dwell on this long. He was elated. Keys beyond the confusion in his mind could be found. *Bryan, Galan!*

He had considered the others a moment ago, though the thought had slipped away before he had a chance to focus on it. *Galan, Bryan?* he called out again.

Neither stirred.

A panicked probing assured him they were alive, although he didn't like the weakness that had come from Bryan and it worried him. Convinced that in order to survive the journey he must lose no more of his companions, Seth was prepared to go to any length to ensure their survival. He would have slashed his own wrists and fed them from the blood that oozed from the open gash if he could have. In the *very* real delirium of his mind, this notion was suddenly appealing until he realized it would quicken his own passage from life. And life, especially one's own, was sacred.

Suddenly he wished he had learned more about the sea. He knew little of the creatures that lurked beneath the dark waters, only that at night he saw them, the ones called krens with the high dorsal fins, circling round and round their tiny raft. When he had been stronger, he had chased them away by sending harsh emotions into their underdeveloped brains. Now he was too weak to attempt this and nearly too weak to care at all.

Somewhere in the convoluted corners of his mind he made a connection between the circling predator and Bryan. Suddenly he remembered the water bag still clutched in his upturned hand. He awoke Bryan and forced the brother to drink a few precious drops.

Do not waste brother, you need this more than I. You must live… came the shallow whisper into his mind, the voice was Bryan's.

Drink, I will not tolerate nonsense.

Afterward Seth gave Galan an equal portion of the water. *Drink, drink,* he told Galan. *The supply of water is almost spent and soon we will all be without its life giving essence…*

Although his teachings and his faith told him otherwise, he felt completely responsible for the fate of his two companions. If he had but one wish, he would be able to do something, anything that would ease their suffering.

It is time you saved your strength, imparted Galan.

Surprised by the voice, for he had been sure his thoughts were sealed, Seth apologized. *I am sorry Brother Galan. I did not mean to trouble you with open thought.*

Seth, you know better than that. Our fate is predestined, you cannot alter it. You cannot stop the inevitable any more than you can hold back the winds or the looming hands of fate…

Seth listened to her words yet he did not accept them. The weight of guilt had already scarred him.

Sleep well my Galan, he told her, although he doubted Galan had heard him for she was already gathered in a heavy sleep. The presence of the Father faintly came to Seth, as he too slipped quickly back to sleep and delirium. His dreams of remembrance grew surprisingly richer.

Two must survive, echoed once more in his thoughts, just before the dreams gathered full force.

***

Adrina gathered her strength and sat up. She stretched her arms and her sore back with a hefty, stretching yawn. A few minutes passed without movement as she attempted to shake dizziness away. Eventually the room did stop moving. She slipped over to the side of the bed and placed her feet on the floor.

Carefully she reached out, grasped her boots, then slipped her feet into them. A bit wobbly, she stood and looked about the chamber. Bright daylight pouring in through a terraced doorway instantly caught her attention. She walked out onto the balcony and squinted at the bright orange of the sun, which to her astonishment was midway in the sky.

She rushed back into a chamber that seemed suddenly dark. She stumbled. She had moved too fast. She pressed up against the frame of the door and held herself there for several long breaths while her eyes slowly readjusted to the dimness of the interior.

After a quick scan for belongings in the unfamiliar room, she prepared to leave. Instinctively she checked her hair in the large mirror that stood beside the door on her way out. Her hair was a mess. She ran her fingers through it to straighten it. Abruptly she stopped what she was doing and stared at her reflection. Something wasn't right. It took her a moment to realize she was wearing a nightgown. To have put her boots on while she still wore bed clothes—whatever was she thinking?

She wasn't thinking—and she knew this.

Her head ached on one side—a dull throbbing that numbed her awareness—as if she had been kicked and a large swollen area on the right side of her skull attested to this fact. She touched it gingerly and winced.

Think clearly, she told herself. She tensed and took a couple of deep breaths, trying to concentrate.

It took her a moment to remember what she was doing and only after staring into the mirror again did she finally realize what she needed to do next.

"Riding clothes, riding clothes," she muttered to herself.

At the opposite end of the large chamber was a partial wall-divider, which she finally realized was where the dressing area must be.

Adrina touched the lump on the side of her head. She screamed out. Her brain was there—in pain.

It was a slow methodical shuffle to the divider and even slower changing into her riding clothes, which were clean and thankfully dry. She recalled now that they had been wet, that she had been wet.

A dull thump sounded at the door as she was dressing and Adrina shouted, "Just a moment," her head throbbing with pain as she did so.

It took a few more careful minutes before she finished dressing and walked over to open the door. She opened it to find Father Jacob standing solemnly, a deep-set frown on his face.

"I was hoping you would be fast asleep when I returned," he said, as he stepped into the chamber. "You are still flushed with fever. A day's delay will cause little harm. I am concerned about your health, child, more than anything else. That was a nasty fall. You need to rest."

"There will be plenty of time to rest later, Father Jacob." Father Jacob started to reply. Adrina reached out and took his hand in hers. "I must do this, Father Jacob." She spoke with sincerity.

Adrina started to lead Jacob into the hall and as he stepped back into the corridor he stopped. "Wait a minute, am I crazy? I didn't want to do this, but if I have to... Get back into that bed this instant, you will sleep!"

Adrina stepped deftly passed Father Jacob. "This will not wait, father. He is dying, I know it." Hesitant, Adrina stopped herself from saying anything more.

Jacob took a step toward her. "Go on," he said.

"It was only the voice at first, calling out, but then I started to see things. It was as if I were traveling a great distance. There was so much I know I saw that I cannot recollect, so much, Father Jacob... The vision first led me out to sea, then to the southern coast."

"Did you?" asked Jacob, "No, of course you didn't, did you?"

"Did I what, Father Jacob?"

"At any rate, we cannot leave until Captain Brodst recovers. I would not hear the last of it if I left him in Fraddylwicke Castle with the Baron and Baroness."

Adrina nearly fell as the words hit her. Father Jacob fought to ferry her back to bed but she wouldn't let him. "Who leads the column to Alderan?"

"The second in command *was* Captain Trendmore. He assumed command after Captain Brodst's unfortunate accident. He waited until late this morning, but couldn't wait any longer. With Prince Valam's arrival in Alderan in three days, he had to leave. It will take a miracle—" Jacob glanced heavenward. "—for them to make that march in three days. I am sure Captain Brodst said it would take at least five."

Adrina's face turned deathly pale. Now she understood why the detachment had turned south for Quashan'. Now she understood why so much was at stake in Alderan. "Prince Valam is to meet the ship from Wellison, the ship carrying Prince William?"

The lady's words flooded into Adrina's mind and piece-by-piece she started to put the puzzle together. A voice whispered in her mind, "The ship from Wellison has a most precious cargo, the heir to the throne of Sever. At this very moment King Charles lies dying in his bed... King Jarom sees himself seated in the throne room of Imtal Palace. To be sure, he will use the death of Charles and the fears of the heir to his own ends."

Adrina decided right then to confide in Father Jacob. She recounted the meetings with the strange lady. She told him of the first meeting in the palace tower at Imtal and the second meeting in the forest on the night of the heavy rains.

As Adrina watched, it was clear a flood of awareness swept over Father Jacob. He was silent for a time then he mumbled words Adrina barely understood. "This is the very message Great Father sent—the message I have puzzled over these long past days."

"Father Jacob, are you all right? Is there something I can do for you?"

"Just let me stand here a moment, child." Father Jacob paused, took a deep breath then added, "On second thought, let's sit. Perhaps over on the bed…" Father Jacob regarded Adrina with marvel. "I told no one about the voices and the portentous messages that brought me to Imtal Palace on a dark night what seemed so long ago. I did not even tell the cunning Keeper Martin."

Chapter Eighteen

The first shafts of light from an early morning sun shot over the horizon. The light touched the haze of Seth's mind and caused him to rub his burning eyes. A dry yawn issued from his mouth, and then with one partially unclenched eye, he squinted toward the brightness.

It will be a clear day.

Seth both welcomed the sun's warmth to end the night's cold and feared its erosion of their bodies. For Seth, the days were longer than the nights and, upon reflection, he did indeed prefer the night despite the often-bitter cold.

Time passed. The sun seemed to wither and weaken Seth even more this day. The dryness and excruciating pain of his throat aroused him to its swelling—it was nearly swollen shut. He attempted to squeeze down a lump of dry, pasty spittle, and cried out in a muffled whimper as he did this.

So much water around me and none to drink.

Their small supply of fresh water was nearly exhausted and this was now the only concern in his frazzled mind. Sea water, it was all around him and he could drink none of it.

Why can it not rain, Father?

Still unconcerned for himself, Seth first touched a few precious drops of moisture to Galan's lips then covered her face and arms again with the tatters of his robe. He drank then, a little more than he should have, barely getting the drops to slide down his aching throat. He gave Bryan the last few drops the water bag contained.

Is it all for nothing, Father?

The day turned to night and back again to day. Seth felt the vitality within him ebb. His consciousness fell to total decay. He could no longer focus his will to maintain him, which frustrated him utterly. The forces of nature were all around him, yet he, Seth, First of the Red, could not touch them. He was losing himself and his center. Soon he would slip away to a peaceful bliss that he would have welcomed only a few short days ago.

He had struggled too long to give in, fought too hard to give up. *Great Father, is that you? Have you come to gather me home? What did I do wrong?... I do not wish to go... I could not have stopped the ambush... I cannot fail. I must think. I must focus...*

***

Adrina approached the low portcullis that separated thick walls midway along the castle's southerly bastion. She continued past it to the stables where a stately wagon was being prepared. The Lord and Lady Fraddylwicke had chased after her every step of the way from the inner courtyard to the wall, but neither the baroness' "Your Highness, please, the tea is ready," or the baron's "The wagon would have been ready in another hour," would slow her down.

Yesterday it had been the baron who had convinced Father Jacob that they should not leave the castle until this morning. It was true that by the time preparations had been made and they were ready to leave it was late afternoon, but there still had been a few hours of daylight left. What harm would a night in the swamp have brought?

This morning, the baroness was dead set on having tea after breakfast. Who drinks tea at daybreak?

Adrina cast a glum stare behind her. Father Jacob hurried along beside the baron and Adrina heard him again speaking an apology. "It seems we must leave at once on an urgent matter," Father Jacob was saying. "Please give the message I left for Captain Brodst as soon as he wakes. You have been most gracious hosts. His Majesty will surely hear of this."

"Raise the portcullis," Adrina screamed to the guards inside the gatehouse.

"The wagon is most splendid," Jacob said, seemingly to drown out Adrina's words.

No doubt, Lord Fraddylwicke had chosen the stately wagon with its four-horse team with clear purpose. Adrina knew this was meant as a symbol both of his wealth and of his generosity, which he hoped would be relayed to King Andrew. She didn't find it odd that she could so intensely dislike a man who she had only met yesterday evening.

Behind her, Adrina heard men shouting, she looked back to the outer courtyard to see a small contingent of foot soldiers mustering. Adrina stopped and whirled about to face the baron. "A gaggle of foot soldiers will only slow us down. We need the wagon and the provisions you promised, nothing more. Tell them to return to their duties."

"Your Highness, I must object," Baron Fraddylwicke said. "I must see to your protection. The swamp is no place for a lady such as yourself to be alone."

Adrina started respond, but Father Jacob spoke first. "He is right, Princess Adrina. It would be best to have an escort."

"Fine, if they are to come along, have them mount up. They can ride, yes?"

"I am afraid—" Adrina held her breath. The baron was fond of those three words. "—that the scant few animals that remain are ill-fit for riding. Your Captain Trendmore took every horse in Fraddylwicke. I told him I needed mounts for the King's messengers—you see, usually we trade out on a one-for-one basis—but he said he wanted them all and would keep his. Even sent men about the countryside. He left nary one behind. It is only by the grace of Great Father that my personal team remains."

Adrina started to say something but then realized that it was fortunate the baron had hidden the animals away. Her irritation with the pompous baron decreased. She bit her cheek. "That was a wise decision," she said, "my father, the King, will surely hear how you have helped me, for I will tell him personally. The foot soldiers stay here, however."

Baron Fraddylwicke's face suddenly seemed to glow and the baroness touched her kerchief to her eye. "As you wish," the baron said.

Father Jacob nodded approval and helped Adrina climb into the wagon.

***

The sun was midway in the sky before Seth finally came back from the endless world of gray delirium and dream. Visions of ships sinking into the dark, waiting waters that surrounded him even now, slowly fell from his eyes. It seems so much needless loss.

A light breeze played soothingly across Seth's tormented skin. Hidden behind a murky cloudbank a pale sun looked so distant and harmless, yet its ill effects had whittled away his body and his strength slowly and effectively.

Rain may come, Seth mused. If rain came, it may just save them. Then again, the storm unleashed with the rains could drown them just as easily.

Hours diminished to the slow pace of the passing of minutes as time slowly plodded on in agonizing increments of seconds and heartbeats. Ignoring the hunger pains in his clenched and swollen stomach, the brittle dryness of his lips, and the tremendous aching of his brutalized body, Seth attempted to center his thoughts.

He knew somewhere in his teachings there must be an answer to their dilemma. He searched the indexes of his mind. A wish sprang to the fore, a wish that he had learned more about seamanship from Cagan, the crafty sea captain whom he had known since childhood and who since his childhood had commanded the Queen's own fleet. Such learning would have proven a worthwhile investment, yet then he had not had time for such foolish endeavors.

Seth felt a faint prick of pain in his mind. He strained to focus his thoughts. As he did this, sadness swept over him and in an unexplainable way Seth knew something was wrong. *Is someone in my thoughts?*

A gentle whisper entered Seth's mind.

Yes? he answered.

If I told you I was afraid, what would you say? asked Galan.

Seth reached out for Galan's hand and took it in his. *We all have our fears, Brother Galan. It is not wrong to fear what we do not know.*

I fear death, returned Galan sending feelings of hopelessness along with the words. *I fear in death I will find only longing and emptiness.*

*Great Father will not forsake—*Seth felt another prick of pain in his mind. *Is that you, Brother Galan?*

The voice nearly inaudible in their minds and edged with bitterness was Bryan's. *You are wrong. For those who have failed, there can be no joy in the next life.*

Seth disagreed. *While blood courses through your veins it tells you that you live.*

I died long ago, returned Bryan.

Bryan's sadness flowed strongly to Seth. It encompassed him and the whole of their bantam raft. Seth felt pain again. *What are you doing in my thoughts?*

I'm dying Seth.

Dying? Seth wheeled about the raft wildly. Frantically he searched for the precious water bag. His aim was to pour its every drop down Bryan's throat in the desperate hope that it alone would keep him. It was then Seth remembered they had no more water. He had used the last of it.

No Brother, said Seth. *It is not time, it is not your time! You must hold strong. You cannot desert us. We need you. I need you. There is so much, so very much...*

Bryan didn't or couldn't answer.

Seth's eyes flashed to his wrists. The blood coursing through his veins gave him life; it would give Bryan life.

Go ahead Seth, whispered the voice, Bryan's voice in his mind. *Two must live. It is your fault I die. You owe me your life. You bring shame and dishonor to our kind.*

Paralyzing anguish shot through Seth's mind. Galan told him *No, Seth, it is his time. Our time is yet to be destined.*

Galan cried out in pain. Hands suddenly gripped Seth's throat. *Bryan, what are you doing? Remember, you pulled me from the water; you saved my life. Galan, he's choking... me. Bryan, are you mad?*

Bryan squeezed harder. *You still don't understand.*

The hands still at his throat, Seth struggled wildly to his knees. Galan made her move and hit Bryan from the side.

Seth found Bryan unexpectedly strong and only with Galan's help was he able to break the hands from his throat. Together, wobbly and barely able to keep their feet, Seth and Galan fended off Bryan's blows. Seth ducked to dodge a blow. Galan lunged at Bryan, and knocked him off his feet. Together they fell into the sea.

Seth let out a high-pitched cry of anguish. He scrambled to the edge of the raft.

Galan and Bryan broke the surface. They were still struggling. On his belly now, Seth reached out to Galan. He felt the tip of her fingers touch his.

Bryan pulled Galan under with him for what seemed the final time. Seth lay still. He stared into the dark waters through red and burning eyes. Despair ravaged his heart.

Chapter Nineteen

The four-horse team eagerly responded to Jacob's guiding hands. At first the gentle countryside that encompassed Fraddylwicke Castle greeted them, but this was a short-enjoyed oasis in the midst of surrounding mires, and after only an hour of riding the roads began to slope gradually downward to be reclaimed by the wetlands.

Instantly Adrina and Jacob felt moisture in the air and smelled pungent odors of stagnant waters. Fortunately the roads leading away from the castle in this section of the lowlands were well reinforced. The main road was built up a full three feet above the waiting waters. Adrina marveled at the feat of ingenuity and determination it had taken to build such an access way.

A dreary haze hung over the mire, giving it unparalleled uncanniness. This when added to the sense of foreboding Adrina felt, put her at considerable unease. She puzzled over a great many things, especially how Prince Valam fit into all this. To be sure, they must reach Alderan before her brother's arrival. They also needed to catch up to the column and warn them, but what would they tell them to watch out for and what of Prince William? If his ship had not arrived in Alderan, why had no messages been sent north?

As she tried to think about all this, Adrina's head began to throb, the pain becoming so intense that all her thoughts eventually fell away. Ahead in the distance lay disparate crossroads, which led to tiny villages whose buildings dotted the landscape. Mounted on top of tiny cross-sections of land that were barely habitable, the villages seemed much like the swamp's scattered weeping willow trees, waiting to be reclaimed someday by the dank surrounding waters.

Hoping to rid herself of a throbbing headache and troubled thoughts, Adrina turned to Father Jacob. Although he seemed deep in his own concerns, she endeavored to spark a conversation with him. "It all looks so lonely, does it not, Father Jacob?" said Adrina, her voice mixing in with the thump-roll, thump-roll of the wagon's wheels. "I'm curious about Lord Fraddylwicke, such a grand castle in the middle of all this waste. Everything so well maintained. These roads as well. The villages we pass are impoverished. With tithing to the temples there can be little wealth left to tax. Does the Baron tax in blood?"

Jacob was slow to reply, but it seemed clear as he began that he grasped Adrina's intent, which was to rid their minds of troubled thoughts for a time. "I find these lands curious as well. Only the southern portion of the mire remains populated, you know. During the Great Wars the castle was a major strategic point for King Jarom the First, but now it serves no useful purpose. Other safeguarded passages to the southlands are available."

Adrina listened to Father Jacob talk as the thump-roll of the wagon's wheels lulled her.

Father Jacob took a drink from a water bag and then continued, "In a way I pity them and not only because the desolation and isolation they endure seem overbearing. Generations of war and life in such a place left behind a bitter and superstitious people. Their ancestors were King Jarom's Blood Soldiers. Too brutal and uncivilized for the civilized world that emerged after the Great Wars and too many to exterminate, they are all but forgotten about by both the kingdom that gave them birth and the kingdom that conquered them."

"Blood Soldiers, why have I never heard about them?" Adrina asked.

Father Jacob whipped the reins held tightly in his hands. "You won't find anything I've just told you in any book in Imtal, this I assure you, though Keeper Martin would verify the history. It is perhaps best they remain forgotten."

Weariness swept over Adrina like a storm. Her face turned pale and though she fought to stay awake, sleep came.

The wagon continued to speed along the trail. Jacob's thoughts were on the wagon and the trail ahead. It took great care to hold the trail steadily at the increased speed. He was so engrossed in his concentration that he did not notice Adrina's state. He only heard the horses' hooves thundering along the trail.

The sky above grew overcast as the winds began to pick up. An ill feeling intensified in Father Jacob's gut. His intuition told him a heavy storm was approaching. He cast silent prayers to Great Father to protect them from the rains and to allow them to complete their journey unscathed.

A losing affray was being conducted against the squall in the good priest's mind. The clouds overhead turned dark and callous quickly. Jacob felt their presence as an evil spirit invading his privacy.

The air turned cold. The first droplets of rain fell. Jacob beat at the reins with increasing ferocity matched by the increasing fury of the wind. Sprinkles of rain thrashed against them, then the downpour began.

Jacob secured the top button of his cloak and turned up the high collar. "There are extra blankets in the rear." Jacob stopped cold, the words frozen on his lips. Suddenly he saw Adrina, her face colorless, deathly pale, and fear entered his thoughts and took control. He commanded the horses to halt.

With trembling hands, he reached out and touched Adrina's face. It was cold, sticky wet with perspiration and rain. He removed the extra blankets from the rear of the wagon and bundled Adrina in them. He drove the horses onward then, faster and faster. Somewhere ahead he hoped to find a crossroads that would lead to a village.

Anxiety swept over him as they sped along the road. He chastised himself in his mind. Rain began to fall in mighty torrents as the storm engulfed them. Wind, rain and diminished visibility made the road treacherous but Jacob did not slow the horses. He continued to push the wagon to its limits.

Lost to the frenzy of the moment, his mind stressed and incapable of clear thought, Jacob panicked. Frantically he scanned ahead, his thoughts running in a hundred different directions and many times he glanced worriedly at Adrina.

Jacob drove the team on, urging the animals still faster. The dirt trail quickly turned to mud and it was only the high sides of the road, thankfully packed in a precisely built wall of rock on either side, that held the mud in place. The horses raced through this muck, kicking up a splatter of mud and small stones. The droning thunder of hooves and the racing of wheels rose above the clamor of falling rain and mounting winds.

Soon Father Jacob gave up hope of finding a village ahead. Recalling the villages behind them, he now sought a place to turn the wagon around. Again and again his eyes darted to Adrina's still form. A relieved sigh came as he finally reached a spot with an adjacent path where he could turn the four-horse team and wagon around in a tight circle.

Jacob reined the team in and with a pair of leathers in each hand, guided the horses quickly through the twist. A sudden creaking of the wagon's wheels whining above the sound of rain and wind startled him. He pulled the reins in the opposite direction. The team turned back, but his reaction came too late. The axle was surely cracked. The left front wheel was out of kilter and it would only be a short time before the wheel broke free.

Jacob shook with dread. Still, he forced himself to think through the situation. Alone he couldn't fix the wheel should it snap. He would have to seek shelter from the storm and attempt to repair the damage later. He didn't move for what seemed a long time. He just sat there, eyes wide, searching. He wanted to see a village along the horizon. The last village they had passed was quite a distance behind them. Perhaps he could reach it if the axle held long enough.

The air around him, which was already cold, grew icy as the storm raged on. Father Jacob wanted to curse, wished his vocation would allow him to curse. To scream aloud just once would have satisfied all his pent up frustration. Instead he found the wisdom of his faith and prayed to Great Father for guidance. Briefly afterward, the will of the Father flowed strongly through him, but then it was as if the storm sucked away the renewed vitality as readily as rain and wind beat down upon him.

A portent of evil filled his mind like a sickness, yet even in this Jacob attempted to find good. The will of the Father had found him even in this hellish squall. Faith maintained, he continued his scan of the area, his eyes wandering along the adjacent trail while the heavy downpour obscured his vision.

Abruptly he stopped. He squinted, and strained to fix his gaze ahead in the distance where he thought he saw the outline of some low structures. Were they dwellings or was he imagining them?

At a careful gallop, ensuring his pace did not upset the wagon too much, Jacob ushered the four-horse team on. The tiny road was no more than a raised path but it did appear to lead toward a village of sorts. Jacob held his breath with each bump, and prayed the axle would hold, and each time it did, he released it in a heavy sigh.

The mighty structures he envisioned were no more than a collection of thatched huts clumped atop a mound of dirt, but in his mind Jacob was sure he and Adrina would find warmth inside.

The ailing axle finally gave way with a resonant crack and the wagon slid to an awkward halt. Jacob held Adrina tightly as the wagon toppled to one side. Clinging to his faith, he wiped hopelessness from his face, and then picked up Adrina in his arms. Great Father would not let him fail. He would carry her the remaining distance. Relief was only a few steps away.

The next hundred yards seemed liked miles to Jacob. Step by step he sloshed through the mud. His back ached and his arms were tired, but he did not stop. A wooden door loomed in the distance and eventually he came to stand before it. He cried out into the stormy sky a solemn thanks to Great Father. With a heavy fist, he rapped on the door of the hut.

The dull echo of his blows was the only response. In desperation Jacob tried to force the door open but apparently it was barred.

"Go away!" said a meek voice from behind him, "Go away!"

Jacob turned around wearily, his face expressionless as he looked upon the small boy in front of him. Jacob said, "We need your help."

A middle-aged man appeared from out of the gloom. He approached the boy and put his hand on the boy's shoulder. "You must leave, we cannot help you."

Jacob didn't move.

The man urged, "Please go, you must go."

"I am Father Jacob, First Minister to the King. I need your help."

"So," said the boy.

The man hushed the boy, and said, "You must go and if you truly be the First Minister to the King, you will know what peril it is to accept strangers during such an evil storm." With that, the man took the boy's hand and hurried away.

Chapter Twenty

Vilmos was the first to wake. Wet droplets of morning dew were the first things to greet him. He didn't want to leave the warmth of his blankets or the soft gentle fir bed to enter the cold uncaring air. A foot, an arm, a leg, slowly probed and eventually Vilmos slipped from comfort into the cold.

As he stood there not moving, adjusting, the only thought in his mind was to find some dry wood. With it, he'd make a fire to take the chill away. After a long gradual coaxing, he set himself to the task.

Xith awoke a short while later to the pleasant crackling sounds of a blazing fire, the warmth of which felt good against his face and hands. He sat up and edged his body closer to the fire, surprised that he hadn't even felt the energy expenditure Vilmos had used to start the healthy blaze. Perhaps, Xith thought to himself, the boy was ready for the next lesson after all.

"Well good morning," Xith said.

Vilmos returned the shaman's warm greeting with one of his own and went in search of the food supplies, which had been left in the wagon. He grabbed a little of this and of that, items that appeared most desirable to his sense of smell.

The jades were still loosely tied to a low hanging branch next to the wagon. Thankfully they had not gotten free. Vilmos stroked one of the mares, which was agitated for some reason, until she calmed, then walked back to the fire and sat across from Xith. He offered the shaman a small portion of the carefully selected prizes he had brought back with him.

Gingerly he picked at the food before him, those selections he had not given away to Xith, hard pressed to decide which to eat first because too many arousing scents arose from the stores Misha had prepared.

Vilmos ate a honey cake first and then nibbled on a bit of spiced beef, salted pork and finally a tiny mincemeat pie. He washed it all down with several long swigs from a water bag filled with a sweet drink that tasted of grapes.

When Xith finished, he stood. "Are you ready?" he asked, patting Vilmos on the shoulder, a subdued deviousness was mixed over with half-warm tones.

"Sure," said Vilmos. He stood and crossed to the wagon. He started to climb onto the wagon's running board and stopped abruptly as something hard hit him in the back with a resonant thud.

Vilmos whirled around.

Xith laughed and threw another rock at Vilmos, forcing him to dodge it. "You should always be prepared for the unexpected. This is the next lesson, our second lesson. You have learned well the forces of fire. Now you shall learn those of air…" so saying, Xith hurled two more rocks at Vilmos.

The first Vilmos had expected and dodged successfully, but the second hit him in the back of the hand. Angry, frustrated and not understanding the point Xith was trying to make, Vilmos climbed into the wagon.

"Pick up this rock with your mind." Xith pointed to the small stone in his hand.

"I can't, I don't know how."

Xith threw the stone at Vilmos. After waiting a moment, he then picked up another and did the same. "Yes, you do. Midori told me all about your magical pranks. Why do you think I came when I did? I came because I thought you were ready. You have done this before. *Think!*"

Vilmos stood, unmoving and unyielding, not knowing what to do.

"Stop the rocks from hitting you! *Do it now!*" said Xith in the Voice, which shook Vilmos' mind and stirred his thoughts, but his response was still, "I can't. I don't know how."

"*Think!* It is a very simple process if you have already mastered the forces of levitation. Remember when you were at home and often you circled things around you? How did you do it? Do you remember?"

Vilmos knew well the pranks he had used to drive tutors away, but he didn't understand how it related to a rock being thrown at him.

"Levitation is the process in which you use the element of air to carry an object. Remember flying, floating above your valley?"

Vilmos' thoughts returned for the first time in a long time to his special place, which he had thought lost to him, and understanding followed. "That is easy, but I don't—"

"*Silence, listen!*" Xith commanded, slipping again into the compelling voice to grab Vilmos' attention. "Instead of using a positive force to lift the object, exert the force out as a wall and repel the object away from you. This is the first lesson regarding air; it is the easiest way to repel an object from you. The second lesson is a little trickier and requires a great deal more energy. *Watch!*"

Purposefully sluggish as he overemphasized the strain and the concentration, Xith called the rocks from the ground. One at a time, he methodically lifted the stones and pebbles around them until the air was filled with rocks of all sizes floating through the air. With a summons and a wave of the hand, Xith stirred them to movement as one would a swarm of angry bees. He hurled them through the air, and then turned them around, directing the swarm at himself. An instant later they were reflected harmlessly off an invisible barrier. "Now, do you see?"

Vilmos replied, "If someone is throwing rocks at you, I guess so."

An immediate pained expression crossed Xith's face, it was clear he was upset. One by one the rocks took flight again, yet this time they were volleyed at Vilmos. Several hit him before he collected his thoughts, his hand hurt, his legs hurt and he was really getting angry.

It took a stone hitting him square in the face, knocking him to the ground, before he decided this was no longer a game. Vilmos had sudden flashbacks to a barren ridge and raging winds. Vilmos stood and brushed the dust and dirt from his clothes. For a moment, he paid no attention to the debris flying around him.

He collected energy into himself, slowly as Xith had taught him, pulling the energies of creation inside. His only problem was that he didn't know how to properly release it. The energy welled within him until he let it ebb and subside. He cast infuriated eyes upon Xith, saying haughtily, "Continue."

Xith smiled an eager smile and slowed the rate of the barrage to a steady, constant attack with fair interval between each wave. "Push them away, Vilmos."

Again Xith paused and waited for Vilmos to gather his thoughts. A single pebble at a time started moving again in slow motion.

One stone was on its way toward him. Vilmos pushed out with his energy. It wavered and fell to the ground.

"Yes!" Vilmos cried out. He had successfully repelled it. The wall wasn't yet in place around him, but it was building. In one side with the new and out with the old, he thought to himself. His concentration was building as well and so was his confidence.

"Very good," said Xith, "try two."

Two rocks launched at Vilmos at a steady pace. He managed to stop one, but the second one hit him and broke his concentration. He threw his hands up in the air as a sign he wanted to quit. His head ached; he had enough for one day. "Can't we continue another day?"

"*Try again! You can do it!*" The use of Voice made it mandatory.

As always Xith's words of praise inspired Vilmos. He knew this time he would not fail. Two stones fell away harmlessly, successfully repelled, but he wasn't prepared for the third that hit him from behind.

"Build the wall," Xith said. "Try again."

Especially goaded on by Xith's perky smirk as the last rock had hit him, Vilmos grew angry. He was not going to let Xith or anyone else get the best of him. He stopped one, two, three, four, five and even a sixth stone.

Xith picked up the tempo and changed the directions from which the stones came. Two and three pebbles in groups homed in like beacons on Vilmos from different directions, but again he successfully warded them off.

Sweat dripped off Vilmos' brow. He was tired but Xith would not stop. The air was filled, a clutter of tiny objects, launched at Vilmos. Vilmos cast Xith a lopsided smile, equal to Xith's own menacing grimace. He had built his invisible wall and nothing would get through.

"Nothing will get through," Vilmos whispered to himself. He was nearly exhausted.

Xith did not let up and neither would Vilmos yield though he was past exhaustion and moving toward delirium.

"You waste too much energy; learn to conserve it. *Shape your power,* use it to your advantage."

"I can't do all that at once!" shouted Vilmos, breaking his concentration for an instant.

Xith answered with an increased volley. "*Concentrate!* Do as you did before. Use part of your consciousness toward the task of building the wall and another toward shaping it. Try to release the spent energy. From this lesson stems the basis for your magical shield, the shield that will protect and keep you in dangerous times."

A part of Vilmos digested the words Xith had just spoken while the rest of him set to the task of building the repelling wall. It was so much easier to do before when he had not fully realized what the shaman was trying to teach him through the seemingly simplistic lesson of repelling rocks—*A magical shield, wow!*

Again Vilmos let the wall slip, only for an instant, and was smartly answered with a rock hitting him. The shock cleared his thoughts and jolted his mind into action. He strove to perform the feat and this time succeeded. He could feel the energy flow within him.

Xith told him, "*Control,* always stay in control. You must control the energy; don't let it control you."

Vilmos had forgotten to exercise control in his momentary lapse. The energy was flowing through him like a tidal wave, flooding his mind. Concentrate, Vilmos thought to himself, I must hold it steady. Gradually, he gripped the energy and regulated it. The power flowed but did not flood over him.

The assault continued minute after exhausting minute for almost an hour. Xith pushed and pushed until he felt Vilmos had reached his limit, and then he purposefully pushed him beyond it.

Vilmos learned fast to control the energy flow and maintain the wall. Soon it became easy, requiring less energy, less thought to maintain. He found his center. He knew exactly how much energy he could build and how to shape it. He was in control. He even thought Xith looked pleased.

An idea came to Vilmos, a plan that seemed easy. Devious thoughts spilled over into this plan. He gathered a small reserve in his energy flow, a slight store inside him. The energy caressed him and Vilmos bathed in it. He split his thinking into three parts, one for the wall, one to keep the flow and one to begin to conserve the energy for his little scheme.

Vilmos' shield totally fell as he first attempted this feat. Vilmos thought Xith was clearly displeased, but Xith took it as a sign to end the lesson—Vilmos was progressing well.

"No, I want more," Vilmos demanded.

"I think you've had enough for today. You should rest. You have already discovered that from the simple stems the difficult, this is true with all things."

"Just a little more," pleaded Vilmos.

Xith waved his hand and began the assault.

A reorganization of his thoughts enabled Vilmos to build a reserve slowly. The wall didn't flicker and he attempted his ploy. Instead of just letting the rocks bounce off his shield, he hurled them away. It took great concentration to keep up all three—the flow, the wall, the casting away—but he managed and now maintained the energy flow and the shield and was successfully repelling the stones.

Xith didn't appear to notice the subtle change and Vilmos was pleased. At first, he could repel only one rock at a time in a given direction, but later with practice he achieved two and then three. He settled there, while he adapted to the strain and soon this too became easy.

Vilmos stared at Xith with a wide grin. He was certain Xith didn't know what he was up to. He continued until he could deflect an entire barrage at one time and then he went back to throwing them in a few select directions. Although difficult at first, Vilmos succeeded and abruptly he was passing the rocks Xith's way.

Xith was taken completely by surprise. He hadn't even expected such a twist. He was pleased as he allowed the first rock to hit him, very pleased.

"That is a very difficult feat to attempt when just starting," Xith said as he lashed out with his magic and lay to rest all movement around him. "Enough for today. You need to rest. The lesson is ended."

Vilmos was beaming; he had done it. He had surprised the shaman if only once. Xith fixed Vilmos with a long hard stare and without a word, began to harness the jades.

Vilmos climbed onto the wagon's running board, then moved to the seat. He watched as Xith finished harnessing the jades.

"Can I take the reins?" Vilmos asked as Xith climbed into the seat beside him. Xith handed him the leathers. The animals lurched forward under unskilled hands.

"I'm sorry, shaman!" said Vilmos turning to Xith.

"No apology is necessary. You performed excellently. You've learned a great deal more today than I had expected. I had hoped… but then you did. You have learned one of the hardest lessons there is to teach."

"I did?"

Wordlessly Xith took the reins from Vilmos' hands. "Yes, you have. You have learned to control your energy while your mind is occupied with other tasks, but most importantly you have learned to assimilate your thinking. By grouping the way you think into sections. That is a very great deed in itself.

"It may sound easy, but under duress it is often the hardest thing ever imagined to try. The more you can do at one time the better you will be. If eventually you can do many things without even thinking about them, you will truly be one to be respected.

"You will find the talent very useful. Now maybe you are ready to learn how to control and channel your energy while you sleep. I think, however, we will save that lesson for another time."

Xith drove the jades on. For a time the grasslands seemed to spread endlessly before them, and then rolling hills returned. As they reached the summit of the last in a long string of green-covered hills, Xith reined in the jades.

"There," Xith said. He reached out with his hand and pointed. "The great sea, West Deep…"

For a few long minutes they sat quietly and stared down at deep blue waters, and then Xith coaxed the jades into slow gait. He steered them to a course parallel to the great sea, before whipping at the reins with heavy hands. As he did this, he nervously glanced skyward. The sun was hours past midday.

Chapter Twenty One

"Good Father Jacob, can you hear me?" a soft voice called out. "The dawn has come and gone, and still you sleep…"

Jacob stirred. A battered old man was standing over him. Jacob said, "Where am I? How did I get here?"

The old man didn't reply. Jacob heard the unpleasant sounds of hammering now, which suddenly sounded to him as if someone was driving a spike into his head. Still half in a daze, he opened his eyes. He looked about the room. He was lying supine on a cot opposite the hut's only bed. His eyes flashed with surprise as he realized the bed was empty. "Where is Princess Adrina? Have you done something to her?"

The old man batted his eyes at Father Jacob as if the priest had just stung him. "That one is full of wind and fire. She's been directing my sons' efforts all this morning, fixing the wheel on that wagon of yours."

Jacob moved sluggishly to a sitting position. "And you are?"

"I am Master T'aver," said the old man. He scratched his long white beard. "You came upon my home during the devil's own squall yestereve. You truly are First Minister to the King. You performed a miracle last night that never in all my years have I seen."

Jacob cocked his head and looked out the window. "The banging has stopped."

"Yes, it is near midmorning. Some hours now my sons have labored at that wheel. It must be fixed. You should eat now and with godspeed you'll be on your way."

Jacob started to stand; T'aver put a halting hand to his shoulder. "Wait. The food will come. We should first talk. There are things you must know if you are to continue your journey."

"What can *you* possible know of my journey?" Jacob asked. Again he moved to stand. The fog in his mind was clearing now. He was worried about the young princess. Adrina was just strong-minded enough to be out and about while still very ill.

T'aver moved a chair to Jacob's cot. "Five days after the last full moon, I received a portentous message from an old friend. The message was in the form of a scroll, sealed magically."

Jacob's eyes went wide at the mention of the forbidden craft—it was one thing to use prayers and gifts from Father and Mother, quite another to tap into the fabric of the world.

Master T'aver continued, "Meant only for my eyes. It told me things I didn't want to believe—not that I doubted the word of the Watcher."

Again Jacob's eyes grew wide with astonishment.

"I truly did not believe until your arrival yestereve. Trust the girl's instincts Father Jacob. She walks under a charm…" T'aver seemed about to say something more, but just then the door opened and an old woman carrying a tray of food entered the hut. Master T'aver bade Jacob eat and said no more.

***

The four-horse team seemed strangely unresponsive as Father Jacob directed it back to the main thruway. Overhead the sky was clear and deep blue. While Adrina was hopeful it would remain that way, she couldn't deny the ill feeling building up from within. She cast Father Jacob a concerned glance and wondered at his silence. He had said little to her since awaking and nothing of his conversation with T'aver.

At a quiet, unbroken pace the journey continued, with the musty and pungent odor of the swamp eventually replaced by a fresh, cool breeze that promised of the coast and the sea ahead. Adrina watched Jacob guide the wagon repeatedly, chiding the horses to swifter and swifter speeds. She was sure they would arrive in Alderan too late to stop whatever was taking place, also sure Father Jacob felt the same thing.

That night they camped only when it became too hazardous to continue along the shrouded road. Adrina slept bundled in many blankets in the back of the wagon. Jacob slept on the ground beside a meager fire.

Adrina came awake before dawn and, as the false dawn gathered, Father Jacob and Adrina began their race again. The sea soon came into view and a wonderful sensory explosion of salt air and sea life followed. In the distance seagulls speckled the air and dotted the landscape of a rocky coastline, their calls reaching the approaching two on gentle breezes.

Adrina's face flushed with sudden color, turning from the ashen pale it had held to a rosy alabaster as sea breezes blew against her cheeks. A smile touched her lips and she touched her hand to Jacob's and momentarily held it tight. The sun and the breeze felt good. For a brief moment, she thought of Lady Isador. Lady Isador who longed for southern breezes and tall grasses.

"I made it to the sea," she said glumly, her voice so soft and shallow that it blended into and was lost in the sounds of wind rushing past her ears and birds in the sky overhead. Her eyes fixed on a point out along the horizon and out across the waters of the sea ahead. Somewhere out there was Prince William. Adrina was sure of that now. She saw his blue, blue eyes staring up at her again.

Adrina prepared herself to ask Father Jacob a question that had been in the back of her mind for some time. She was already sure what Jacob's answer would be, but felt she had to ask anyway. Either Jacob would confirm her fears or—and this is the reason Adrina felt compelled to speak—he would tell her that things were not as bad as they seemed. She took in a deep breath, laced her fingers together and then spoke. "Father Jacob…"

Jacob cast her a sidelong glance.

"Do you believe King Jarom would try to kill my brother?" There, she said it, but she didn't feel any better for the saying. She took another deep breath and braced herself for Jacob's response.

Jacob seemed to sense her anguish. He put the reins for the team in one hand and with his free hand touched hers. "That is a question I have asked myself. The fact is that King Jarom murdered King Charles and that obviously he wants to stop Prince William from reaching the North to bring word of this terrible deed to King Andrew."

"What could King Jarom possibly have gained from killing Charles?" asked Adrina.

"It could be that he wishes to restore Vostok to its former glory."

Adrina's eyes widened. She recalled something Keeper Martin had told her before they had entered the swamps. "If King Jarom took Sever, what would be next? Would he go beyond the disputed lands?"

Jacob's expression betrayed his thoughts. Adrina had never seen him at a loss. It was clear he hadn't considered this.

"The lady in the forest told me that King Jarom sees himself seated on Imtal's throne. Was Vostok once that vast?"

"Never that vast, but at the end of the Race Wars when only the five sons of the Alder remained in power, King Jarom the First controlled nearly all the lands from Neadde to Ispeth. It was his Blood Soldiers that pushed the enemy back to the sea near the mouth of the Opyl River and it was he with his own bare hands that committed patricide and started the last Great War."

Adrina felt suddenly sick and sorry she had spoken at all. She said nothing more, and neither did Father Jacob.

Upon reaching the rocky coast, Father Jacob turned the wagon in a wide semi-circle and took the southerly route. Alderan was now only a half-day's ride away. With luck, they would reach the city before dusk. Another question neither Adrina nor Jacob wanted to answer was whether it would be too late to stop what was already set in motion.

***

The section of the coastline they traveled along became a series of rocky crags with sharp, jutting spurts that jumped out into the yearning sea. Rough hewn, carved by the forces of nature that acted upon the waters and enveloped them at times, the crags seemed somehow alive.

The wind, a steady gale with mixed patches of warm and cool, often carried with it a soft salty spray as waves crashed into the shore. When the afternoon sun gathered full in the sky, the day still held the promise of clear, cloudless skies. Adrina sat silently, her hands clasped tightly together. She reflected on earlier thoughts, letting her gaze wander as the wagon twisted and turned.

The breezes became cooler as the sun began to settle toward the glossy blue waters of the sea and the cool air felt good against Adrina's skin. Still, Father Jacob stopped the wagon for a moment to retrieve two blankets from the rear. He searched through the satchels of foodstuffs and came up with a rounded loaf of black bread and a dark yellow cheese.

The meal was a hurried affair. Soon after finishing, Father Jacob drove the horses onward. It was a quick start, followed by an unwholesome lull that hung in the air. Even the sea breezes seemed to be aware of it as they softened. Then the pleasant sounds of the great West Deep disappeared altogether. The calls of the gulls died out. The splashing of the waves became subdued. Even the rolling of the wagon's wheels became secondary to the great quiet that was all around them.

Father Jacob slowed the horses to a sedate pace. His eyes searched.

Adrina remained silent, her thoughts mostly idle and insubstantial now, though she could not shake the voice of the lady from her mind. It unnerved her. It called out to her and the fact that it grew stronger the farther along the coast they rode did not make her feel any easier.

A sudden change in the air around them came as a single, dark cloud passed in front of the sun, momentarily creating an eerie shadow across the land. With the momentary darkness came a spontaneous downward shift in temperature. Jacob and Adrina clutched the woolen blankets more tightly and subconsciously shivered to ease the sudden chill.

The horses cast frightened whinnies into the air, their sixth sense warning that danger lurked near. Adrina's heart seemed to stop beating in a temporary lapse until the sun's brightness and warmth once more covered her. But even with the warmth's return, the chill was not so readily cast away. Rather it lingered much, much longer. It was as if an evil hand reached out and stroked her, telling her, bragging to her, that it was near.

Adrina cast a glance heavenward. The sky was as clear as it had been a short while ago. The dark cloud was gone, vanished, as if it had simply evaporated after it had passed. As her eyes returned to the horizon, she grasped Jacob's hand and pointed to an object far in the distance. Jacob followed the direction her outstretched hand, which led him out along the coast and into the dark waters. Yet what Adrina directed him to wasn't out amidst the darkening waters but across them, back along the serpentine coastline. A cloud of dust arose and it seemed a large group of riders rapidly approached.

"Father Jacob," said Adrina, "I don't have a good feeling about this."

Father Jacob seemed to still be shaking off the previous chill. He made a quick scan of the area, apparently looking for a place to hide, before he replied, "Rocks and squat grasses don't offer much cover, child. This wagon is too slow and awkward to maneuver in this rough terrain…"

Jacob paused in thought, Adrina cut in, "Perhaps, we could

unhook the team and proceed on horseback."

"By the time we did that it would already be too late." As he spoke, it seemed an idea came to Jacob. He had Adrina pull her long black hair back and tie it up in her scarf. Afterward he pulled the blanket around her so that it partially concealed her face and then he did likewise. The air was chilly and it wouldn't have been all that unusual for them to be bundled against the cold and the spray from the sea.

Jacob didn't stop the horses as he had thought to do, but instead proceeded at a slow pace. The riders steadily approached. Adrina's gaze grew gradually downcast until she was practically staring only at the dirt in front of her. The riders slowed as they passed for a cursory inspection, but quickly increased their pace and sped away.

Not raising her downward gaze, Adrina saw only the riders' mounts, a blur of hindquarters and forelegs, as they passed. She closed her eyes and nearly fell asleep until Jacob nudged her to tell her everything was all right.

Adrina lowered the blanket, but still kept it about her shoulders. The danger was gone, or so it seemed. She cast a nervous glance over her shoulder at the group of riders and then watched as Father Jacob flicked the reins to hasten the team.

They continued to wind their way along the serpentine coast, and Adrina cast her fears away. The trail became steadily rock-strewn, making passage over it rough and often very difficult. Large boulders that had to be circumnavigated sprang up in the middle of the trail and the width of the coastal road became steadily narrower.

Adrina followed and wandered among the empty waters, breaking the coastline with her eyes, searching for that which was not there. The voice in her mind had grown sullen and quiet, and now her thoughts wandered free with the waves, rolling and sinking with each as they turned under, rising as each new wave was born, racing as they crashed into the rocky shore.

The emptiness was still present however, and the sounds of life still void. This lifelessness played heavily on Adrina's thoughts. With each new curve she wondered what lay on the other side. The coastal highway they rode along wasn't usually a bustling thoroughfare, so she didn't think it was odd not to see any other passersby. It wasn't that she really wanted to see any, actually, but she wouldn't have minded seeing a friendly face—she didn't consider Jacob's pensive stare friendly or comforting.

Her thoughts slowly turned to the encroaching night. The sky was still clear but Father Jacob had told her storms here usually came suddenly and frequently.

Adrina cocked her head and listened to a sound carried by the wind. "Father Jacob?" asked Adrina with a timid voice. "What is that?"

"What is what?" replied Jacob.

"Can't you hear it?" Adrina asked.

Jacob pulled the reins taut and the horses slowed to a halt. "Can I hear what?"

"The singing."

"Singing?" Jacob tossed her an odd glance then put his hand to her forehead. "Stick out your tongue child?"

"Father Jacob, listen…"

A puzzled frown crossed Jacob's lips. "Maybe I do hear something, then again it doesn't sound like singing." A distant low rumbling came from behind them now. "It is only thunder, child."

It took both a moment to realize that the thunder they heard was the plodding of hooves against the rocky ground. Frantically they spun around and stared back down the trail behind them. A clump of dots trailing dust slowly became visible. The band of riders was returning.

"That's not what I hear, Father Jacob," Adrina said.

Jacob strained to listen then, gasping as he heard something. "By the Father, I do hear something."

Adrina grabbed the reins from Jacob's lap and whipped them. The horses took off at a gallop, causing the wagon to jolt wildly. Adrina glanced behind them. She could make out single objects now, horses and riders. The group was gaining on them. "They'll catch us before we can get away," she said.

Apparently feeling suddenly inspired, Jacob shouted, "Give me the reins, child! We'll give them a run for it!"

Adrina didn't give Jacob the reins, the strong presence of evil had returned. She didn't know whether it was from behind her or ahead, but she knew it was there. She strained her tired eyes, trying to see what was ahead in the distance. A small sandy inlet settled where the ridgeline sloped down to the sea, forming a cove of sorts. This was the first place she'd seen where the road ran directly along the waters. The section appeared to have been washed away by the recent heavy rains and the inlet thus formed.

"There!" she shouted. Adrina didn't have to point to the object in the sand now. She knew Jacob saw it too.

"Halt!" sounded a loud, masculine voice that appeared drastically close.

Both Adrina and Jacob skewed their eyes left to see a rider that seemed to suddenly appear beside them. As a reflex Adrina halted the wagon. Her mind was filled with sudden panic. Why now when they were so close? She wanted to cry. Her eyes swelled with tears, which slowly began to roll down her cheeks.

The face that loomed over her, angry and fierce, seemed to lunge at her as the rider stepped from the horse to the wagon's deck. Just as the rider reached his hands out to grab Adrina, Jacob snatched the reins from Adrina's hands and whipped them as hard as he could.

The four horses dashed responsively forward and the rider, who had been struggling to maintain his balance as the wagon sprang forward, tumbled to the ground. A crunching sound an instant later said he struck the hard ground fatally. Adrina regained the reins from Father Jacob and a chase commenced with Adrina's only goal being the sandy inlet not far ahead. She was certain something was there, but exactly what she didn't know.

Jacob shouted to her, "Look, there is another group of them ahead of us… Give me those controls back… We can't outdistance them, we have to think through this logically."

"No," shrieked Adrina. She slapped Jacob's hands away.

The wagon shook and rattled as it raced along the rough trail. Heedless, Adrina urged the horses on until the back end of the wagon was bouncing into the air. Jacob tossed nervous glances behind. It was clear he was more concerned about those that loomed up from behind than those that were ahead of them. The riders behind them were chasing them while from what Adrina could see, the group ahead wasn't moving at all. "What are they waiting for?"

"I wish I knew," Jacob said. "Wait a minute, are those Kingdom standards?"

Adrina quickly replied, "So what if they are?"

Jacob stared long. "Great Father, they are! It must be the column. We're safe, Adrina, we're safe."

Those were Jacob's last words as a mailed hand cuffed him in the side of the head. His head struck the wagon's deck below Adrina's feet with a crunch that sent chills up Adrina's back. Her terror-filled shriek was cut short as she fought off hands that sought to grab the controls from her. Panic gripped her mind. Her screams became wild and shrill. The strong hands snatched the controls away from her and the wagon was brought to an abrupt halt.

The same strong hands twisted Adrina and wrenched her from the wagon's seat, throwing her roughly to the ground. Momentarily everything went black as the wind was knocked out of her.

Adrina scrambled backwards on the ground as the angry man swept down upon her. He picked her up again a moment later and began to shake her violently. Adrina's head bobbed and her teeth rattled. Her thoughts stifled by fright. Even when the man stopped shaking her, still she trembled uncontrollably.

"Treacherous murderer!" shouted the angry voice of the man whose strong hands squeezed into Adrina's shoulders.

Frustration and despair lead Adrina to tears, but anger and pain soon took over. She clawed and kicked her captor, raking him across the face.

With one hand the large man roughly pulled back her long hair as she struggled to break free, while his other hand groped for something, Adrina didn't know what.

Out of the corner of her eye, she caught a glint of something shiny. She swallowed a heart-sized lump in her throat as a short, fine blade was applied to her upturned neck.

"A-dri-na?" came a distant voice.

Upon hearing her name, the terror-filled fog in Adrina's mind cleared. Adrina stopped kicking and clawing her captor. She turned. The first face she saw was familiar to her.

"Emel!" she cried. She wiped the tears from her face, and reached her hands out to embrace him. Still she shook uncontrollably. "But you were... that was... you then... Where is my brother? Has he already reached Alderan? Is it too late to stop him?"

The large dark-skinned southerner holding Adrina did not let her go. Instead he returned the blade to her throat. "By the Father, her blood *will* stain this blade."

"Hush. Let her go, what are you doing you fool?"

"But they killed Wrennyl!" The southerner spun Adrina around and stared at her.

Adrina saw fury in his eyes. "It was a mistake, a mistake. We didn't know who you were and it was an accident that... that... he... fell, an accident."

Emel snatched Adrina away from the angry man. His free hand went to his sword in its sheath. "I said, back off, back off..."

Menacingly the large southerner took a step toward Adrina. His blade poised ready to strike, he spoke, "Lord Valam will surely hear off this... Wrennyl was a good man!"

"I trust he will," said Emel, "especially since this is *the* Princess Adrina."

Chapter Twenty Two

A single figure lay washed onto the beach, folded into the area where the recent storms had formed a sandy hollow. Wreckage lay scattered on the shore around him. Adrina ran to him. She knelt in the wet sand beside him and touched a hand to his cheek. She expected him to greet her with his warm blue eyes, but to her horror and shock, his skin was cold, cold and stiff with death.

"He is dead," Adrina said, "we are too late… Alderan? How far are we from Alderan?" Adrina grabbed Emel about the shoulders. "Where is Prince Valam?"

"Our party from Quashan' circled north around Alderan only a few hours ago. We expected to meet the column on the north side of the city, but we found nothing. His Highness sent our detachment north and another east to find the encampment. His aim was to proceed to the city outpost. Why aren't you with the column? Did something happen?"

Adrina explained as best she could what happened after Emel had left the column.

Emel swept Adrina up in his arms. Caught up in the reassurance of his touch and the warmth of his embrace, Adrina pressed her lips against Emel's. For a moment Emel returned the passion of her kiss, then he stood stiffly and turned away from her.

"No doubt Captain Trendmore is our traitor," Emel said, "and more likely than not, he ordered the column to turn north at the sea instead of south. I never should have left you… This is all my fault. I didn't listen to what the lady said and look what has happened."

"It wasn't your fault."

"What about my father's accident?"

"Emel, I don't think you could've stopped it even if you had been there. Now is not the time to dwell on the could-have-beens."

"Indeed," said a voice from behind Adrina. Startled, she turned to see a strange small man and a boy. They were seated in the shaded part of the rocks behind her, and she had not seen either before.

Emel immediately drew his blade and stepped between Adrina and the stranger. "Proceed with caution friend, I'd just as soon run you through as not. What are you doing here?"

"Same as you," said the strange short man as he stood. "We were drawn here."

"Stay where you are," warned Emel.

The stranger took a step toward Emel. His hands were raised and it seemed to Adrina he was unarmed. "Here is where the paths cross. The many become one for a short time," so saying, the man reached out his hand to Emel.

Emel lunged forward, his blade arched high, and then it plunged deep into the man's side. Adrina's scream came too late.

***

Vilmos stepped protectively across Xith's prone form and waited for the assailant to make his next move. He was angry and magic raged unchecked through him.

"We are friends, not enemies," Vilmos said, eyeing the two. He had seen the young woman somewhere before but couldn't place where. The face, the hair, the green eyes like jewels were all familiar.

The man raised his sword defensively. Vilmos felt himself losing control of the magic.

"Put away your weapon," Vilmos said.

"Emel!" yelled the man's companion. To which he responded, "Stay out of this, Adrina. I will let no one harm you." Emel turned back to Vilmos. "Tell your companion to get up none too quickly. Or I'll run him through again."

"*Trust* is a two-way path. *Put away your weapon,*" said Xith, using the Voice to calm. Then he grabbed Vilmos' hand and said, "*Control!* Remember that anger and that hatred for another time…*"

Xith gasped for breath. "The stones… in my bag, you'll find a sack with five stones, bring… it to me…"

Vilmos brought the small bag of stones but never looked away from the one who had attacked Xith.

"You are… swift… with a blade," Xith said through gasps, "we may soon… have need… of your skills."

Voices called out from the road now, "Emel, are you all right? We heard shouting? Do you need help?"

"*Answer* them. Tell them you are fine. *Tell them you will be along presently…*"

"We are fine," Emel shouted. "We will be along presently."

"There isn't much time. Gather round, gather round. You too, young princess." Xith winced from pain. "Vilmos, the stones."

"Are you dying?" Vilmos asked with the utmost seriousness.

"Your apprenticeship is hardly at an end. He barely grazed my side."

Vilmos looked down at the shaman's saturated robe.

"Even small wounds bleed and the pain is not in my side, it is in my head. Our friend there has had quite a trial. I shouldn't have attempted to connect to his mind without blocking the flow of feelings. Never have I been so overwhelmed by anything…" Xith winced again. "I needed to find out what he knew. Just as I needed to know about you, Princess Adrina."

"You heard everything we said before?" Adrina asked.

Vilmos turned to regard the young woman. Momentarily he was caught up in her great brown eyes.

"Seated there in the shadows, it was hard not to. Do not worry, your secrets are safe with me. As I said, and as my companion, Vilmos, said, we are friends. We were drawn to this place for a reason. Each of us has a part in changing the many paths, for here the paths converge."

"How do we know we can trust you?" Emel asked.

Adrina asked, "What of Prince William? Is that him?"

"Emel Brodstson, even the lady of the night knew the way of your heart," replied Xith.

Emel's face flushed red.

"No," Xith said turning to Adrina, "that is not Prince William... If I probed correctly, our friend's name is Seth. He traveled here across the West Deep from a place called East Reach... They were ambushed and only a few survived."

Xith adjusted Vilmos' hands and moved the healing stones. "The rest of his memory was rather disjointed, but as the other there is human and he isn't, I can only assume that some sort of struggle took place on this very beach, and here he lost his only other companion. We will know more when he regains consciousness, but for now we have more important things to concern ourselves with."

"What do you mean not human?" Emel exclaimed.

Adrina put her hand on Emel's shoulder, but he brushed it away. Xith said nothing. He only stared.

"By the Father, it is you!" called out a voice from behind them.

Vilmos turned to see an aged man dressed in a dirty black robe. One side of the man's face was swollen and bruised.

"How long has it been, ten... no twelve years." The man's expression became sullen. "Returned from under-mountain just as you said. I didn't want to believe it when I heard it yesterday morning."

Xith regarded the elder for a moment and then said, "You, Jacob, do not look well, and here I'd heard you were now King's First Minister."

Jacob said, "I should have known I'd find you at the heart of all this."

Xith smiled now, apparently at the other's expense. "I am merely one of the fools on the board. I hope I know my part and move accordingly."

"Father Jacob, you know him?" asked Adrina.

"Of course I know the…" Xith put a silencing hand to his lips and Jacob spoke no more.

"Do you wish to inquire about my lineage now?" asked Xith of Emel who still had his sword drawn, "Or do you wish to know of the fall of Alderan?"

Princess Adrina's eyes went wide. She turned to Emel and glared at him. "Fall?" she asked.

Father Jacob waved Emel's weapon away. Emel sheathed the sword then said, "All is well in Alderan."

"All *appears* well in Alderan, because that is what was meant. Do we argue now, or do we ride for Alderan?"

"We ride," said Adrina.

Chapter Twenty Three

The group waited in the forested hills to the east of Alderan. Father Jacob sat beside Xith. "Yes, we will listen."

Vilmos, Emel and Adrina sat likewise. They formed a loose circle around the shaman.

Xith cleared his throat, turned his eyes around the circle, and then said, "The Alliance of Kingdoms is all but broken. King Jarom has been flooding the upper southlands with men loyal to his cause for many months. Where he doesn't have soldiers, he has spies. His spies are everywhere and his reach is long. He has also been paying the bandit kings to maintain their campaign in the North."

Father Jacob and Adrina nodded fast agreement.

Xith continued. "In all but name, Jarom *is* the absolute ruler of the four kingdoms of the south. Only King Charles was brave enough to oppose him and while this was true up until a few short weeks ago, it is no longer true. The Kingdom of Sever is now without king and its heir, its heir—"

Adrina interrupted, "What of my brother?"

Xith regarded Adrina and then continued, "King Jarom fully expected King Andrew to answer King Charles' call for aid and for the safekeeping of Charles' son, Prince William. King Jarom may be quite surprised to find only a prince, but then again, Prince Valam's death—" Adrina's face flushed white. She began to tremble and Xith expected her to say something or to burst into tears, but she didn't. "—will allow him to usurp *all* lands south of the Trollbridge, all the lands of the South. Already troops march on Quashan'. With the cities' commander gone and the garrison sent north, the city will easily fall. If it does all the lands of Man will be under his rule in short order."

"I was just in Quashan'," Emel said. "The whole of the garrison was in company."

Xith turned frank eyes on the untrusting young guardsman. "If King Jarom can pay off a Chief-Captain of Imtal Garrison right under the king's nose, surely he can likewise persuade a Quashan' garrison commander or one of his captain's or even one of his under-captains to relay an incorrect order."

"What can we do?" asked Father Jacob. "A great force must have laid siege to Alderan. We have no more than forty riders."

"Fifty six," Emel said.

Princess Adrina's downtrodden expression turned upward briefly.

"I suspect Alderan was taken without a fight from the inside," Xith said. "For all we know, they marched straight into the city under Kingdom standards and the citizens greeted them openly."

Xith took a long swig from a water bag. His throat was dry and overworked. The ride to Alderan had gone smoothly, but not quietly. "Once Prince Valam is dealt with the forces in the city will turn their sights on joining the march on Quashan'. This is what we *must* count on."

***

"Are your men ready?" Xith asked.

Emel nodded. Xith joined Father Jacob deeper in the midst of the trees and there the two spoke in hushed tones.

Fifty-six ridesmen anxiously waited near the edge of the forest for the dusk shadows to deepen. They had been waiting in the trees for several hours now.

Adrina scratched absently at the mosquito bites on her arms, hands and face. The City of Alderan seemed deceptively quiet. Emel's closeness to her was reassuring, but she was still ill at ease. She glanced to the strange wise man that had told her to stop calling him Watcher. "My name is Xith," he had told her.

The conversations with Xith had left Adrina filled with dread, especially his seemingly casualness about the fact that Prince Valam would most probably be dead when and if they found him. Adrina hadn't burst into tears then, though it had taken considerable effort not to. Now she could only remember fond thoughts of her only brother—big as a bear and with a heart twice any normal man's. It was in Valam's shadow that she used to walk the streets of Imtal and his dreams of seeing the world that filled her young mind with thoughts of fantastic adventures.

"Are you all right?" whispered Emel in Adrina's ear.

Adrina nodded snapping out of her reverie.

"Good. You and Father Jacob will wait here until we return. If we're not back by sunup, leave. Make progress north as fast as you—"

Adrina cut Emel off with a hiss. "I'll not stay here and worry through the night. Where you go, I go. Remember the words of the lady?"

"Only death awaits in Alderan," returned Emel.

Adrina glared at him. "You expect me to turn away when every hand counts? I am as good with a blade as you are, perhaps better."

"Besting me on the practice field is not the same thing, Adrina," Emel said coldly.

Xith returned. "Keep your voices to a whisper," he said.

Adrina started to speak. Xith raised a silencing hand. He wavered his gazed, his eyes shining as he stared out into the darkening land. "Everyone back and stay down," he said, "not a sound anyone…"

Soon figures carrying shielded lanterns appeared from the dark shroud. Behind them came horses and riders. Behind the riders, heavily laden wagons. Behind the wagons, more horses, more men.

From her vantage point, Adrina began counting them as they passed. She stopped as the numbers swelled over two hundred.

Adrina found it unsettling that she heard only the occasional squeaking of wagon wheels to mark the group's passage. Riders were leading their mounts whose hooves were apparently padded. The weapons and armor of the soldiers she saw were also apparently padded, for as they passed, the normal clink-clink of metal scraping metal was absent. The group was traveling southeast, southeast to Quashan' just as Xith had said they would.

The southeastward passage continued for more than an hour, and then for an hour afterward nothing. No shielded lights pierced the darkness and no sounds pierced the uncanny silence.

Out of the corner of her eye, Adrina saw Xith raise his hand and suddenly the press of bodies around her was absent. The small band of Kingdom ridesmen was suddenly sweeping toward Alderan City. Split into three tiny groups, they would strike the city from the north, east and south. The intent was to make the enemy remaining in the city think they were under attack by a large force. Adrina didn't know exactly what Xith hoped to accomplish by this, for surely the defenders would discover very quickly that only a few dozen men were carrying out the attack.

Adrina felt a hand on her shoulder. She spun around surprised to find it was Emel. She stared at him in momentary disbelief. "You didn't go with the others?"

"Xith asked that I remain, and I have." Emel didn't seem happy about the prospect, but Adrina was—Emel wouldn't die with the others.

Adrina's smile faded when she saw Xith's glowing eyes upon her.

"Vilmos, Adrina and Emel you'll ride into the city with me," Xith said, in a quiet voice. "Only Father Jacob is to remain behind. He'll watch our new companion, and he knows what to do should we not return. To your mounts, our route into the city should be wide open soon. Hurry now, there is no time to waste."

The Kingdom ridesmen attacked the city's watchtowers from three directions. Xith, Adrina, Emel and Vilmos made their way to the city from the south.

Adrina was surprised to hear the sounds of a raging battle coming from the northern sectors of the city now. One thing she had neglected to consider, as Emel had pointed out, was that Alderan was a Kingdom city and had been a united city even before there had been a Kingdom. Apparently, those in the city thought the King's army had come to liberate them. No true Kingdomer would sit idly if they thought the King's army was storming the city.

Under this shroud of confusion, the four crept into Alderan. After they had safely passed the city gates, Xith signaled them to stop and gather round.

"We make for the city center." Xith spoke very softly. "Even now all routes to the keep will be guarded. If for some reason anyone gets separated, watch your way with care, but head for the keep at once. Remember, all through streets are set up like the spoke of a wheel. They all lead to the center hub, and the keep."

Xith paused, then looked to Adrina. "To get into and around the inner keep unseen, we'll need your help."

Adrina stared blankly at Xith.

Speaking for Adrina, Emel said, "She's never been to Alderan."

"Down to the last detail, Imtal Palace was fashioned after Alderan's keep," Xith explained. "Only the old sections of the palace though. The maze of passageways used by the King's family should all be unguarded. Surely you've walked them a thousand times..." Xith's voice trailed off.

Adrina smiled, she could walk those passageways in her sleep. Then she frowned. "But—" she began.

Xith cut her off saying, "Once safely inside and set upon the path, you and Vilmos will remain behind. Emel and I will proceed from there. Do not worry, if the prince lives, we *will* find him. Getting out of the city will be the problem..."

As anticipated, the southern sectors of the city were nearly deserted. The four, now on foot, blended into the shadows of cobbled streets as best they could. Emel clearly had not wanted to leave Ebony behind, but eventually he had. Twice they had made their way past patrols without mishap. Fortunately both patrols had been racing north where the battle for the city raged.

Intermittently Adrina's eyes flashed on the small form of the boy, Vilmos, who walked beside her. He seemed a likeable lad, but a bit young and surely inexperienced. She could see open terror mirrored in his eyes and more than once he had reached out his hand to hers to find comfort. Adrina too found comfort in his touch and in the rapier still in its sheath, which she clutched with her right hand.

Emel had the lead, and at about ten paces ahead, Adrina could only glimpse his form as he passed the infrequent lights of the darkened city. Somewhere behind them Adrina knew Xith lurked. Many times Xith had disappeared down a side street to reappear beside them at the next intersection or the one after that.

Adrina gulped for air and her heart skipped as Emel suddenly appeared out of the darkness.

"Patrol," he hissed, "they head south, not north."

Emel flashed his eyes at Xith. Xith waved them into a nearby alleyway.

Huddled in the shadows of the alleyway they waited. Soon, Adrina heard heavy footfalls, and then she saw torchlight and shadowed faces. The patrol stopped at the intersection of the street and the alley, directly in front of the horrified onlookers. Adrina heard harsh whispers and angry voices. The members of the patrol were obviously displeased about being sent to watch the city's southern gate while the battle raged elsewhere.

From her vantage point in the shadows, Adrina could see much more than the outlines of faces. Light from their torches reflected dully off their armor and the swords withdrawn from their sheaths. The angry man who seemed the leader of the patrol was bearded and though rather gaunt, just from the tone of his voice and the way he stood, Adrina was sure he was capable with a blade and hardhearted. He was arguing with another man who wanted to return to the north. Both men's words were becoming increasingly belligerent.

To Adrina's horror, the leader of the patrol set upon the other man. In one swift move, he brought the point of his blade to the other's throat and plunged it inward. Adrina screamed, which would have brought sure discovery, if Emel hadn't clasped a hand to her mouth just prior. As it was, her muffled scream mixed with the horrible gurgling sounds of the dying man as he sought to speak a few last words.

The leader removed his sword from the other's throat as he fell, and without another word, the members of his patrol continued south.

Emel removed his hand from Adrina's mouth and put his hands on her shoulders. "Are you all right, Adrina?" he whispered.

Adrina couldn't answer. She felt numb and sick.

"It will pass, Adrina," Emel said. "As I said, this is not the practice field. This is real. Are you all right with that?"

Adrina still couldn't answer. Emel shook her.

"Adrina will be all right in a moment," Xith said. "Give her some breathing room."

Xith took Adrina's hand.

"We near the city center," whispered Xith. "Once past the last line of buildings there will be no cover. On my signal move quickly, without stopping across the square to the walls of the keep. Emel, you'll go first. Then Vilmos. Then you, Adrina. Once at the wall, speak not a word. Await my signal to continue."

**

At a flatout run, Adrina raced across the square. Her heart was pounding in her ears. Vilmos and Emel had already made it safely across the open hundred yards to the shadowed wall and were excitedly watching her run. Adrina glanced from Emel to the archers on the walls. Only one of them needed to spot her and it would all be for nothing.

Halfway across, Adrina no longer held back her smile. The run was strangely exhilarating after the tension of creeping through the besieged city. She glanced back once to look for Xith. She knew he waited somewhere out of sight behind her to make the last mad dash across the square.

When Adrina glanced back, her foot caught one of the square's cobblestones. She tumbled and fell, her face striking cold stones.

Disoriented, she looked up. Emel was edging away from the safety of the wall. She waved him away.

Her eyes rose to the top of the wall, a single figure stood looking down over the square now, seemingly his eyes looked straight at her. Breathless, Adrina waited for him to raise an alarm or notch an arrow to the string of his bow.

Unmoving, Adrina waited, and waited. The archer stood still. He stared down into the darkness of the square. For an instant, it seemed their eyes locked. The archer raised one of his arms—surely he was about to reach into the quiver at his side for an arrow.

Adrina's heart stopped and the whole of the world seemingly collapsed in around her. Adrina stifled a moan, held her breath and waited.

The archer turned away and continued his march along the battlements of the wall. Adrina thanked Great Father for smiling down upon her and launched herself into a run.

Hastened by her fright, she crossed the remaining distance to the wall in a surprising burst of speed. Emel caught her in his arms and held her for a moment before both turned to look back across the square. Immediate shock registered on their faces, Xith stood in plain sight in the middle of the square.

Adrina heard Vilmos whisper, "Run, run." He began waving his arms wildly to the shaman. Heedless, Xith waved them on. "*Go now,*" he said in a voice that was strangely compelling and seemed to carry across the square on the wind, *"Do what you must..."*

A cry went up from the wall and suddenly a number of voices were echoing an alarm. Almost immediately afterward, Adrina heard the twang of bows and the hiss of arrows. She squeezed her eyes tight. Fool, she thought to herself, sacrificing himself for no gain.

"Quickly now," said the boy, Vilmos, seeming suddenly resolved to action. "Pray my master's diversion buys our way into the inner keep..." His words fell away, and as if in response to his voice, a blue-white streak raced through the air to the wall. Disquieting screams followed.

One of the archers fell from atop the wall and smacked the cobblestones not more than five feet from where Adrina stood. The man's face was twisted oddly toward her. A certain emptiness in his eyes and the unnatural twist of his body told Adrina the fall had been fatal.

More blue-white streaks raced to the wall. Another soldier fell to his death. Adrina saw no trace of the blue-flighted arrows that had claimed either man. Emel grabbed Adrina's hand and pulled her after him.

The minutes that followed were crazed and everything for a time afterward passed in a blur. Adrina found herself racing alongside Emel and Vilmos. She remembered remarking that the buildings of the inner keep truly did resemble the old wings of Imtal Palace and that true to Xith's word, the King's entryway into the main building was unguarded. She lead them along unlit passageways that were familiar to her feet even in darkness, yet she knew they only seemed that way.

It wasn't until many uncertain minutes later that Adrina halted abruptly. She realized she no longer heard voices and that the footsteps she was running away from were her own and that of her companions. When she stopped, first Vilmos and then Emel slammed into her.

"What's wrong?" asked Emel.

"Nothing," Adrina said in a hiss. She turned to Vilmos. "Did Xith tell either of you where they would hold my brother?"

Even in muted darkness, Adrina could see the boy shrug.

"I thought he told you," Emel said.

After a long silence, Vilmos spoke. "Xith said it would be easy and that getting out of the city would be the hard part. Your instinct is what led you here in the first place. Where were you going?"

Another period of silence followed then Adrina said, "My father never liked these passageways and doesn't use them. It is true that very few even know they exist." It was the first time in a long time that she had thought of her father-king and now her thoughts were of Imtal. If Alderan had fallen and Quashan' was next, what of Imtal. Had Imtal already fallen?

"Where were you going?" repeated Vilmos.

Adrina closed her eyes in thought for a moment, and then lead them on their way. After ascending a flight of stairs and after a few twists and turns in the passageway, the three found themselves standing before a door. Only Adrina knew for certain what was beyond the door, the others could only guess. She slid the door open, expecting to find her room.

She was about to step into the room, when Emel swept past her, a short blade cupped in his right hand. A rather large man stood hunched over with his back to the door only a few feet away. Emel stealthily crept up on him and plied the blade to his throat. He spun the man around.

As Adrina sought to speak, no words came forth. Her eyes were wild and Emel stared at her for a moment in apparent confusion.

"Adrina, what is it?" Emel asked her.

"Valam," Adrina said. "By the Mother, you live." Adrina was crying now and she ran to embrace her brother.

Shocked, Emel lowered the blade from the prince's throat. "Dear Father, Your Highness, forgive me. I had no idea."

Valam embraced Adrina in a great bear hug and swept her from her feet. His joy was short-lived, his expression grew suddenly grim and he let Adrina go. "It is not safe here, you must go."

"We are here to rescue you," she proclaimed.

The prince put a finger to his sister's lips. "There are things occurring here that you cannot hope to understand. You must leave at once."

"What is wrong with you, Valam? Come quickly." No sooner had Adrina said this than someone off to the side of the room cleared his throat. Adrina turned and from an adjacent doorway, great blue eyes greeted her. Adrina asked, "Prince William?"

The other nodded and grinned evilly.

"Run, Adrina, run," Valam said. He flung Adrina toward the passageway and barreled at the prince.

Complete pandemonium followed. Confused, Emel and Vilmos stood their ground. Adrina recovered her feet and stared in wonder at the struggle between her brother and Prince William. Valam had a firm grip on the other's throat. William was straining to reach a short blade in his belt.

Adrina watched in mute horror as Prince William broke free of her brother's grasp and whirled about to face him. Prince Valam was nearly the largest man in the Kingdom. With bare fists he could take any man, but where Prince Valam had only his fists, the other had a long, curved blade made for close-quarters fighting.

Two guards rushed into the room. Again Adrina tried to scream but no words came forth. Seeing the guards, Emel sprang forward and engaged both.

Undaunted by the menacing blade, Valam circled defensively, waiting to attack. William it seemed was also waiting for the right moment to strike. The end came quick and clean, Prince William sliced in with his blade, Valam countered and then planted a solid blow to the side of the other's unprotected skull. Prince William went down, his knees crumbling, his body collapsing beneath him.

More guards swept upon them from the open doorway. Emel screamed wildly and pointed to the passageway. Vilmos remained deathly still, apparently gripped by fear. Adrina turned. Soldiers were streaming out of the tunnel behind her. Before she could get free, one had her arm and twisted it back forcefully; a burning pain shot up to her elbow.

Prince Valam descended upon the attackers like a hungry demon, his eyes unfocused and angry. He grabbed the man that held Adrina by the throat, lifted him off the floor and flung him to the wall. Without stopping, Valam slapped Emel's blade away and backed Adrina, Vilmos and Emel into the corner. He stood guardedly in front of them.

With the aid of two guards, Prince William regained his feet. He rubbed the side of his head and directed a vengeful stare at Valam.

Valam maintained the faceoff against the many guards in the room and directed his eyes at William. "Tell them to back off," Valam shouted, "we'll submit!"

"Enough, enough," William said. He clapped his hands together and the soldiers backed away. "Stay your ground. Let's shed no more blood than we need to for now. We have what we wanted and a prize or two to boot."

Chapter Twenty Four

Through the night Father Jacob watched the strange one, the one called Seth. As the shaman had asked, Jacob placed the healing stones one by one to Seth's forehead. He had seen such stones before in the Temple of the Mother, but never had he witnessed their ability to heal. When first held, the strange stones hummed and glowed bright yellow; touched to Seth's forehead, the color slowly drained from them until they were left dull, black and empty.

Two hours before dawn Seth had opened his eyes and spoken. "Where is my companion?" he had asked, his words in the old language.

The old language, being the language of priests and priestesses, hadn't surprised Jacob. He had answered without thought in the same tongue. "I do not know; I am sorry." It was only now that Father Jacob was deep in conversation with Seth that he realized Seth spoke in the old tongue, the language that had once been universal to all peoples when trading goods and now is preserved only by those of the Mother and Father.

"Myth and lore would have most Kingdomers believe that your kind are akin to fairies, pixies and sprites."

Seth smiled and regarded Jacob with his blue eyes. He seemed to know Jacob was joking.

Jacob continued. "You must meet a friend of mine. Keeper Martin would write entire tomes filled with your words. There would be a definite gleam in his eyes as he wrote: elf of the gold and green forest, most fair and generous."

Yes Jacob, I am very much mortal, just as you, Seth said, answering the question that had been on Jacob's mind for some time. *Many of my companions journeyed to Great Father so that I could be here and it fills my heart with sorrow to know it was all for nothing…*

"You will have counsel before King Andrew, friend Seth, this I promise you."

You do not understand, without my companion, Brother Galan, I have failed. My fate is here… She was needed to return to my homeland, the land of East Reach.

"There is something you must know, Brother Seth," Jacob said, borrowing the title, as it seemed appropriate. "The one who found you said something that was strange. On the beach where you were found, it appeared there had been a struggle of some sort. One dead man attested to this. Unless there was a man in your party?"

There were no Men. Seth's voice sounded suddenly distant. His eyes flashed, his expression became one of puzzled remembrance. *Yes, yes there it is.* Seth sent surprise and hope into Jacob's mind along with the words.

For the first time Father Jacob realized Seth spoke in thoughts and not aloud. *Do you walk in my thoughts?* He asked himself.

It is the way of my people. I took open thought as a sign that you wanted me to enter your mind. I am sorry if I have offended you.

"Nothing of the sort, Brother Seth," Jacob said, "You continue to surprise me is all. There really are poor records of the four peoples after the Race Wars."

Tell me of this other, the one who found me and the one you are thinking of now. He is of the four peoples, is he not?

"Xith, last of the Watchers. I first met him thirteen years ago. He came to me in a time of great need. He promised he would return one day when the need was again great, and he has. The heart of darkness itself is consuming Great Kingdom. I fear our fates are intertwined, my friend."

More, I am afraid. I remember some of it now. At the last, I called out with my mind in desperation. The call, I fear, lead more than just those who wished to aid me. I fear I summoned your enemy as well. Seth attempted to stand and did so only with Jacob's help. *I would help you. What must I do?*

"For now, there is little we can do. If Xith has not returned to camp shortly after sunrise, we journey north and return with the King's army marshaled before us." Jacob looked to the East where dawn was forming on the horizon. "To war," he whispered. "For now we can only wait and hope against hope… I truly fear the worst."

***

It was the morning of the second day since their capture and still Vilmos cursed himself. Xith had told him to do what he must and he had done nothing. To him this was unacceptable, and as he marched with his hands tied painfully tight behind his back, he hung his head in shame. It seemed of small consequence to know that Prince William and his henchmen had fled Alderan out of fear they might not be able to control the city any longer.

Vilmos knew little of the Prince of the North, Valam, but he was sure there had been tears in his eyes when William of Sever had ordered the city set ablaze and that no building should be left standing. That night, even from miles and miles away, they had seen the unearthly glow of the burning city. Vilmos had seen rage and naked hatred in the Prince's eyes then.

They had been moving since daybreak without respite. The first day they had stayed near the coast, traveling south, but this day they traveled more east than south. Vilmos knew this because the sun shined almost directly in his eyes, making the world around him bleached and hazy. He knew only that Princess Adrina was to his right and that if he didn't maintain a correct pace, he stepped on the heels of the guardsman, Emel.

Sweat dripping down from his forehead ran into his eyes and with his hands tied behind his back, Vilmos couldn't wipe it away. Exhaustion sought to overcome him and he fought to stay alert. He still held hope that Xith would somehow rescue them.

An abrupt kick from behind sent Vilmos sprawling. Screaming, he hit the hard ground face first. He spun around angrily and spat out dirt.

"Rest," said the voice of the figure towering above him.

With his back now to the sun, Vilmos found the haze in front of his eyes slowly clearing. He stared up at the shadowed figure, which hovered over him for a moment more before turning away.

"Are you all right?" Adrina asked.

Vilmos said, "I think so." His backside was a little sore but he'd recover. His pride was hurt more than anything. He had done nothing to provoke William's men yet it seemed they had singled him out. More than anyone else, he bore the brunt of their resentment and anger. He was the one who was forced to watch while the others ate, albeit meagerly. He was the one who was denied water or forced to drink from a bowl like an animal. He was the one who was pushed and kicked.

The brooding prince also regarded him. "You are tougher than you look, my young friend, I am glad." Prince Valam was silent for a moment, and then continued. "It seems you have been singled out because you are the smallest and the youngest. Their aim is to break you and thus break us all. Know that I *will* give repayment for every such mistreatment. Know also, that many a man would have already yielded."

Emel seemed to agree. He winked at Vilmos and said quietly, "Hang in there, we will surely make them pay."

Vilmos whispered back, "May Queen Elthia turn over in her grave so that she does not have to see the harvest her son seeks." Prince Valam turned a puzzled frown to Vilmos. "My father's words," Vilmos explained.

"It seems we were never properly introduced, my young friend. You look of royal blood and you speak like one well educated and Kingdom borne. Yet I have never seen you in any of the southern courts beside your father."

Vilmos' face flushed red. "I am hardly of royal blood, my father is a village counselor." Vilmos paused, his tongue growing flustered. "In truth, I am ill at ease in your company..." His voice trailed off momentarily.

"Yours too, Princess," Vilmos said, turning to Adrina briefly before turning back to Prince Valam. "In truth, I am not as tough as you might think. I was more afraid of crying in your presence than of my lost pride. Even William of Sever's men respect you."

"Respect and fear are two different things, Vilmos. They fear me only as long as we remain on Kingdom soil. Matters will change when we reach Sever." Prince Valam turned at the sound of approaching footsteps. "Water," he shouted at the guard. "Water for everyone!"

***

For two days Captain Trendmore drove the column north along the coast of the great sea. On smooth terrain the foot soldiers maintained a steady pace and made good progress. Keeper Martin was hopeful that by afternoon the walls and spires of the Free Cities would be in sight.

Doubt had grown in the Lore Keeper from the moment the column had turned north instead of south, but Martin had no definite proof to act on his feelings. He couldn't act on hunches and doubts. For all he knew, Captain Trendmore was indeed following Captain Brodst's orders. Then again, if he didn't take action soon, who would?

Keeper Martin cast a sidelong glance at the close-mouthed rider to his left, then lowered the hood of his cloak and looked to the sea. A strong breeze out of the north carried with it a salty spray. "On such a hot day," Martin said, "the moisture and the breeze are refreshing. Don't you think so, captain?"

Captain Adylton replied, "The sun near midday is hot here, Lore

Keeper, you would do well to keep that hood about your head."

Martin eyed the tall, dark-skinned southerner who had removed his cloak about an hour into the ride and rode with short leggings that exposed calves and knees.

Captain Adylton quickly added, "Playing in the surf and lying by the sea is about all I did in my youth. My father was a fisher..."

Keeper Martin smiled—a mischievous smile. In a voice that barely carried above the plodding of his mount's hooves, he asked, "Did you sail these waters often with your father then?"

"More often than I cared to."

Martin noted Captain Adylton's annoyance and his apparent wish to end the conversation. "Would an autumn storm have driven your sails north or south?"

"I see," Adylton said, "that troubles you too."

Martin nodded. "I have sailed to High Province close to winter season many times. Always I felt the breezes upon my face when I stood at the bow."

"Aye, the winds change with the ending of summer. Autumn and winter bring cold breezes out the north."

"Captain Trendmore wasn't a fisher's son was he?" Martin asked.

"Hardly, his father was a tanner or was it a smithy—at any rate, no, I'm sure he's never sailed."

"I have known Captain Brodst for many years, yet I cannot recall his father's trade?"

Captain Adylton gave Keeper Martin a stern look. "You know as well as I that..." The captain's voice trailed off. He looked again at Martin, suddenly seeming to realize where Martin was going with his questions. "You are right. The storms would have blown the ship south if it strayed off course at all. Any experienced captain would have had little trouble in those storms. They were early autumn storms, full of malice yes, but not violent like the storms of winter."

Keeper Martin looked Captain Adylton straight in the eye. "Do you have loyal men in your squadron?"

Captain Adylton stared back at Martin. "They are loyal men all, and they follow all lawful orders of their commanding officers. None would turn against the other, if that is your hope."

"What of unlawful orders given by a man who is no longer loyal to his country or his countrymen?" Keeper Martin asked.

Captain Adylton reined in his steed, nearly coming to a halt. "Proving such a thing, Keeper." His changing the pace brought mayhem to those in the column behind him. A wagon driver's team nearly drove over him. Captain Adylton shrugged off the man's curses and spurred his mount. "How do you propose to do that?"

Keeper Martin judged the captain's receptiveness to the truth by the unease in his eyes. "There is news I have not shared with you, captain. The situation is much graver than you are aware of. It was not just the upcoming departure of a ship from the port city of Wellison that brought me to Imtal Palace to disturb King Andrew's rest in the middle of the night. Prior to this, I had been in the Far South for many months. Secretly.

"At first it was personal matters that brought me to Sever more than anything else. After, much more. It was fortunate that only Keeper Q'yer of Quashan' knew my whereabouts. Also fortunate that my last visit to Sever had been some years before.

"When I arrived in Gregortonn, all seemed well. The affairs in the capital were running smoothly. This all changed quickly. King Charles ordered the city sealed. The city garrison turned to the streets. Hundreds were arrested. Dozens killed in clashes. For a full day afterward the city was quiet. Only the flags removed from their poles upon the walls attested to turmoil. Just before dawn of the second day, the searches began. More arrests, more fighting. Luckily I was able to find reliable accommodations, which did not come without a price.

"Two weeks I was in hiding, plotting my escape. Then one afternoon while moving to a new safe house, I made a most unexpected discovery. Soldiers loyal to King Charles were no longer in control of the city. An agent of King Jarom had usurped power… Everything I'd seen suddenly made sense.

"Soon after I arrived in the new safe house one of my benefactors discovered my true identity. I don't know how, but it was a fortunate turn of events, for it was then that men loyal to Charles approached me. They spoke of a bold plan to retake the city and of a plan to smuggle the heir to the throne from the city to safety. It was with their help that I eventually made my way back to Great Kingdom."

Keeper Martin took a long swig from a wineskin, and then cleared his throat. "You know as well as I that King Charles' voice was the only vote of dissension in the Minors when King Jarom last sued for war and the dissolution of the Kingdom Alliance. His aim is to rule Great Kingdom, there can be no doubt."

Again disrupting the pace of the group, Captain Adylton reined in his mount and stared at Keeper Martin. The wagon driver behind the captain screamed angrily this time.

"Is there something wrong?" came an excited voice from behind them. A rider raced toward them. Both Martin and Adylton recognized the voice and the rider, Captain Trendmore.

"We must act, are we agreed on that, Captain Adylton?" Martin asked as he raised the hood of his cloak.

Captain Adylton signaled agreement and urged his mount onward.

"Is there something wrong here?" Captain Trendmore repeated when he came abreast of the two.

"I was just explaining to the good keeper that if he kept his face to the sun for another hour on a day like today, he would be as bright as a one of Duke Ispeth's apples before nightfall. I think it took him by surprise."

"Yes, yes indeed," Captain Trendmore said, a crooked smile coming to his lips.

Chapter Twenty Five

With the new day came rain, a ceaseless downpouring that made everything all the drearier. To make matters worse, the soft breeze out of the North that had been with them for days was by midday a steady gale. It brought with it a hint of winter's chill. To Vilmos it didn't matter that winter was still months away, he was chilled to the bone all the same. He longed for his hooded cloak, a place next to a warm and cheerful fire, and a bowl of winter stew.

The only good thing about this day was that his hands were free and although Prince Valam said it was yet another sign that William and his men were becoming increasingly bold and less and less afraid, Vilmos didn't care. He only knew how good it felt to have the restraints off his wrists.

Apparently seeing Vilmos' peaked appearance, Prince Valam handed Vilmos his overtunic. Vilmos was hesitant to take it.

Vilmos said, "You'll catch your death of cold, Your Highness."

"Snows in High Province are already knee-deep, and in winter they are so deep a man cannot walk across them. Take it, Vilmos, to me it will make little difference. The hide is specially treated and rain will not soak it. It will keep you from catching a cold. When the time for action comes we'll need everyone at their best."

Vilmos accepted the tunic and wrapped it about him. The Prince's overtunic was so big in fact that Vilmos was able to wear it like he would have his hooded cloak. He didn't put his hands into the sleeves. Instead, he pulled the collar up over his head and peered out through a space between the two middle ties.

They trudged on. Hours passed. Afternoon came. Still rain poured down upon them. Then just when Vilmos thought the day would end much as it had begun, his deepest fears were realized. The green of forest came into sight.

It was then, in a softly whispered voice that Vilmos told the prince, the princess and the guardsman of his previous travels in the Vangar. He also told them of the soldiers in the valley, and of the Wolmerrelle. All the while he spoke, an uncontrollable trembling and dread flooded over him.

"Thank you, Vilmos," Prince Valam said. For a time he was obviously deep in thought, then Valam said, "Be that as it may, we must address other matters. Once we cross the boundaries of the Kingdom into the Minors, our captor will have little use for you and Emel.

"I know not why he has allowed Emel to live, but I am sure now why you live. He is using you to keep me in check. He knew I would brood over the injustices he has given you and think not of other things like escape. His advisors whisper well in his ear. My mind is clouded no more. Tomorrow in the forest," Valam said, "we *will* make our move. To die fighting is honorable. To die with a blade in your back is quite another thing."

Emel seemed to agree. "Tomorrow," he whispered.

Vilmos started to say that Vangar Forest was no place for unarmed travelers, but Emel cut him off with a wave of his hand. Almost immediately afterward, Vilmos went sprawling face first into the muddy ground as he was booted from behind.

"Rest," said the now familiar voice. The guard, who apparently took great pleasure in his misdeed, turned away laughing as Vilmos spat and tried to wipe mud from his eyes.

Valam screamed at the guards, "Bring water."

None of the guards moved.

"Already they find bravery," Prince Valam whispered, "perhaps tonight in the forest would be even better."

"You give the word, Your Highness," Emel said, "and only death will keep me from your side."

"I do not think they will kill the two of you just yet. If you truly are Minor-born, Vilmos," Valam said, turning as he spoke, "William may just give you your life. Use that chance, Vilmos, use it for all it's worth. Go back to Tabborrath Village and leave the affairs of men to men."

Emel waved a hand under his chin. The conversation stopped. Vilmos turned and saw a guard approaching.

"To your feet!" shouted a gruff voice, signifying an end to the brief rest. Apparently their captors were eager for the feeling of safety that being within the borders of Sever would provide.

***

Like thieves in the night the enemy army had stolen upon Quashan'. From atop the city's fortified walls, Chancellor Van'te stared out at the enemy host. In the two days since their arrival, they had staged no attacks against the city and though they barred all travel into or out of the city, they harassed its residents in no other way.

Chancellor Van'te turned to the young sergeant at arms beside him. "How many do you estimate today?"

Sergeant Danyel' grimaced. "A few hundred more arrived in the night. Still, nearly the same as yesterday, around ten thousand."

"That is my estimate also." Van'te looked glumly to the young recruits on the wall. "How many were you able to rouse to the city defenses?"

"Two hundred more," Danyel' said proudly. "I told them nothing of the garrison's absence. None would have believed me anyway. Who would believe the entire garrison, save for the handful which includes me, is gone?"

The chancellor scrutinized the sergeant, and then said in a soft voice, "You think me the true fool to allow such an order to pass, don't you?"

"The seal was genuine, and what man can refuse a summons by his King. Perhaps Imtal has indeed fallen."

Chancellor Van'te wasn't able to respond. "Runner!" came the cry from the west wall.

Chancellor Van'te grinned; he knew if he were persistent enough one of his messengers would get through. "Give the man some help!" Van'te shouted to the archers on the walls. As archers began firing wildly at the enemy line out of their range, the chancellor moved to leave the wall. "Sergeant Danyel'," he said, "lead me from the wall."

The two hurriedly made their way to the courtyard where they hoped to find good news. It was a short walk. Still Chancellor Van'te, well advanced in his years, found he was wheezing and puffing by the walk's end.

When Van'te and Danyel' reached the courtyard, they found the runner winded and hunched over after his sprint across the field. Still without delay the runner handed Chancellor Van'te the scroll and in earnest the chancellor began to read its contents. "By the Father," Van'te muttered to himself, "it is from Prince Valam." His voice trailed off and shock registered on his face.

Chancellor Yi turned to say something to the runner and found the man gone, as if he had vanished. "Sergeant Danyel'," Van'te screamed in a high-pitched nasal tone as only he could, "I want that runner found!"

Danyel' signaled to the two soldiers beside him. They hurried off. Danyel' asked, "What does it say? Is the message truly from His Highness?"

Chancellor Van'te showed the scroll to Danyel'. A mute minute passed, then the sergeant said, "Are you sure this is truly Prince Valam's writing? Couldn't this be an elaborate hoax to make us quit the city?"

A pained expression crossed Van'te's face. He blamed himself for what had transpired. He felt suddenly tired and old. "I have schooled His Highness all the years of his life. Surely by now, I should be able to recognize his scrawl... See the loops above the I's, the double slashes on the T's and the way he stops to make an L?"

Danyel' nodded.

"Done that since he was a boy first learning to write, just to annoy me. Yes, I am sure it is his handwriting."

"Do you really believe that if we opened the gates of the city, the army surrounding Quashan' would guarantee safe passage for all who wished to leave?"

"Prince Valam didn't," the chancellor said quietly.

Danyel' seemed confused. "What do you mean?"

Chancellor Van'te flattened out the scroll and pointed to the last few lines.

Danyel said, "I still don't understand."

"The handwriting switched here... Can you see the darkening of the strokes?" Danyel' shook his head. "Never mind, never mind. Only a foolish old man or a young boy such as you would think five hundred could defend a city from ten thousand."

"You, Chancellor Van'te, are no fool," Danyel' said. He patted the chancellor on the back. "If any can save Quashan', it is you. Tell us what you would have us do, and we will do it."

Chancellor Van'te scratched at his chin. "At any rate, there is little we can do now. Soon enough they'll know we do not intend to quit the city, the attack will begin then..."

***

Prince Valam turned to Emel. "How many men are stationed around the periphery of the camp?"

"You mean, is there hope for escape this night?" Emel said, leaning close to Valam then and whispering something that Adrina couldn't hear. From the expression on her brother's face, it wasn't good news.

Adrina returned to her muddled thoughts. Since their capture, her thoughts had been ever jumbled and never clear.

A day of trudging along overgrown paths had left her exhausted and in tears. Mostly she was distraught because she had always considered herself capable of doing anything a man could do, yet every day now she saw how much she depended on Emel and Valam to make it through the day, especially this last day. Here she had found a bitter truth: until now her life had been a pampered and sheltered life.

Adrina was also agitated because it seemed Valam and Emel left her out of their plans for escape. Disappointed, she remembered a conversation she had with Emel days ago, just before Alderan. She had told him, "I am as good with a blade as you are, perhaps better."

Emel had replied, "Besting me on the practice field is not the same thing, Adrina." She remembered how coldly Emel had said it, and how bitter the truth of it was now that she understood what he had meant.

She heard the words of the mysterious lady in her ears. *"The evil brings the change you so wished for. It has found a home in the emptiness of your heart. You care too little for those around you. You see not the servants who toil for you, workers in the fields on their hands and knees with the whip at their backs, drudges scouring the kitchen floors... You must open your eyes!"*

Adrina thought back to another time and when she closed her eyes she saw the quiet fields of Mellack Proper—it was then only two days after she met the mysterious lady and her journey was only beginning. Lying there on the cold ground, her body sore, her stomach rumbling, the fields of Mellack Proper, the orchards of Duke Ispeth, the hills of the Braddabaggon and even the mires of Lord Fraddylwicke all seemed desperately far away.

Adrina rubbed painfully blistered feet. "My eyes are open, *truly* open," she whispered to the wind. Opening her eyes meant much more than simply seeing the things around her. It meant looking for and finding understanding in the world around her, looking not only with her eyes but also with her heart, mind and soul, and then finding resolve to action. It meant being a participant instead of an onlooker.

"Adrina!" hissed Emel in her ear, breaking Adrina from her thoughts.

Adrina started, Emel clasped a hand over her mouth, noticing then that the camp seemed suddenly shrouded in darkness. Beneath the forest canopy, no stars were visible. Even the central fire seemed muted by the stark darkness. She noted that the logs on the fire were all but fiery ashes. Apparently many hours had passed in what to her had seemed minutes.

Emel squeezed her hand, causing Adrina to notice the ropes that had been tied around her feet and hands were gone. Before she could speak her thoughts Emel nodded his head as if he were reading them. Her eyes went wide. Adrina tried to speak again. Emel put a silencing finger to her lips.

Valam gripped her shoulder and turned Adrina to face him. He showed her four fingers and then pointing to Emel, he lowered three. With two fingers raised, he pointed to her. Three to Vilmos, whose eyes were as wide as saucers. Four, Valam pointed to himself.

He then turned her head to look around the camp. In the distance Adrina saw the immense trunks of the great southern trees whose intertwined boughs formed the clearing they were in. At the far edge of the camp, a number of watch fires were set, but they also burned low. Only a handful of guards still stood their watch. Valam pointed out two of them. In the dim light Adrina watched them. One kept slapping both hands to his face, apparently trying to erase sleep from his tired eyes. The other was leaning up against a tree and, to some degree, faced their direction.

A long period of complete silence passed as they waited, for what Adrina wasn't entirely sure. Then without preface, Valam raised a single finger and Emel slipped away. For an instant afterward, Adrina saw Emel's silhouette against light cast by the fading fires and then he disappeared into the darkness of the forest.

Adrina held her breath as Valam gripped her shoulder. Unexpectedly he embraced her, and for a moment Adrina was smothered in his great embrace, then just as suddenly, he ushered her into the gloom after Emel. Her thoughts swam, Adrina didn't move. Valam gave her a push and suddenly she was racing along the ground on her hands and knees.

Many times she cast nervous sidelong glances to the center of the camp and to the nearest two guards at the perimeter. Any minute she expected someone to shout an alarm and the camp to burst into frenzied activity. As fear and anxiety sought to overwhelm her, Adrina fought to hold them in check.

She knew she had finally reached the edge of the camp when the trunk of one of the great trees appeared in front of her. The next thing Adrina knew, friendly hands were gripping her waist and pulling her to her feet. She didn't pull away from Emel's embrace. Instead, she hugged him fiercely. His warmth was the only reassuring thing she had known for days and now it was even more reassuring.

Silently Emel and Adrina waited. The next face Adrina hoped to see was that of the boy, Vilmos. Slowly over the five days of their captivity, Adrina had come to know Vilmos. To her it seemed a strange darkness lurked behind his eyes and also that his thoughts were ever distant and he was distant. She found this oddly alluring, for in him she saw a bit of herself.

Thinking she saw movement in the gloom, Adrina leaned forward. She knew at once the burly figure she saw wasn't Vilmos. Panic entered her mind and momentarily, the urge to flee. She pushed back against Emel's warmth, her body growing tense.

Abruptly Emel grabbed Adrina and roughly pulled her back and down. Huddled against the ground they lay together. Adrina saw a figure outlined against the murky pale of the dying lights in the camp. Soon afterward, a second shadowed form joined the first.

"Erravane?" hissed the first. Adrina held deathly still.

The other responded with, "Yes." From the voice alone, Adrina couldn't tell if the second figure was a man or a woman, though the first she thought a man. Among Prince William's soldiers, only a dozen of the several hundred were women. Although they were few, it seemed that they held high positions. Valam had suggested that perhaps they served as William's personal bodyguards, though he had been honestly unsure of this estimation since several of them came and went seemingly at their own leisure.

A long period of silence followed. Adrina couldn't see what transpired, though she knew both figures still stood only a few feet away. With a sudden heave, both were on the ground and for a time they rolled around in the leaves. Afterward, again silence. Adrina knew only that Emel's presence beside her was a powerful comfort.

Adrina heard muffled laughter and again the whispered voices.

"Quit, you'll alert the camp," hissed the first.

"Not likely."

"What do you mean?" the first sounded at the end of his patience. "Why are you here, Erravane?"

Behind her Adrina heard Emel's barely audible gasp. He had recognized the first voice at nearly the same time as she.

"One question at a time my sweet." Adrina was sure now, the second *was* a woman. Her name was Erravane, and the first *was* Prince William. "I have found what you sought."

"And the traitor?"

"Oh yes, a present for you." Erravane rose to her knees, and then dumped something onto the ground. She cackled madly, and then said, "His head."

William jumped to his feet. "I trust the other is alive?"

"The southern encampments have proceeded north as planned. The bulk of your army is spread out through the forest. Your commanders will join you here, tomorrow."

"What of King Jarom's army?...Wait a minute, what of the—"

Erravane cut William off, "You are ever impatient. She is well. I believe the deceased—" Erravane kicked the head and it rolled past

Adrina. Only Emel's firm and comforting grip around her waist kept Adrina from screaming. "—was tricked. Though I am not sure how. These creatures have strange powers."

"Then you were right?"

Erravane cooed. "Yes, my sweet."

"Where is she?"

"I was afraid you'd prefer her to me. What of this princess? I've heard tell she is quite striking."

William said, "She is a child."

"She is the enemy. Have you so soon forgotten the empty stare in your father's eyes?"

William said coldly, "I never will." He began to move back to the camp. "No games this time, Erravane, no games... Dawn is only a few hours away. I trust your pets will harry my men no longer?"

"My dear William, they take only what they need. The disappearance of one or two in the night is of little consequence. Would you rather have them turn on me?"

For the first time as he turned back to Erravane, Adrina saw Prince William's face clearly outlined in the pale light. "Perhaps it would not be such a—"

Erravane put a finger to William's lips. "You still need me, William of Sever. Do not say a thing you will later regret." With that, Prince William strode away, and soon afterward, Erravane. Both went in separate directions.

Emel helped Adrina to her feet. Finally she took a deep releasing breath. Before she had been nearly afraid to breathe and had done so only sporadically. Erravane and William had been so close.

Adrina heard movement in the leaves behind her. She turned, sighed, knowing at once it was Valam.

"I circled around," Valam explained. "The boy?"

Adrina shrugged.

Emel, who had been staring intently toward the camp, said, "There on the far side, do you see?"

Adrina and Valam turned and stared. On the opposite side of the camp, reflected in the light of the dying embers of a perimeter fire, was a mostly shadowed boyish face. Undoubtedly, it belonged to Vilmos.

"Were you listening?" Emel asked. Valam nodded and Emel continued. "The time to make our escape is now or never."

"No," Adrina hissed angrily. "Vilmos is one of us."

Valam took Adrina's hand. "We can do little now. We would waste precious time if we tried to circle the camp. There is too much at stake. You heard as well as I, the forest is full of William's men... Perhaps it is for the best. He should fare well and, should his instincts continue to lead him south, he will find safety quickly. On the other hand, we will not be so fortunate. Our duty takes us north. We will have the whole of an army at our heels until we either reach Quashan' or die trying." Valam paused, took a deep breath, then added, "Quickly now..."

Chapter Twenty Six

Vilmos watched his companions turn away and disappear into the gloom. Disbelief and dread flooded his thoughts. He had no idea how he had ended up on the opposite side of the camp, but the *one* thing he was sure of now was that he was on his own.

Anger quickly replaced disbelief and dread. Valam, Emel and Adrina had deserted him. Vilmos knew dawn was near and that he must act or surely he would be recaptured, but where would he run to? If he made a wide circle around the camp and tried to follow the others, could he find their trail? Did he want to find their trail? After all, they had forsaken him.

Vilmos caught movement out of the corner of his eye. He didn't wait to find out what it was he saw. He ran away fast as he could. Unsure which direction to flee, he ran aimlessly. His fear drove him on and only his instinct and the flora of the forest controlled his direction.

As dawn lifted darkness from the forest leaving only shadows, Vilmos stopped running. Tired, hungry and feeling desperately alone, he slumped on a moss-covered stump. He stared up through a break in the canopy where a ray of soft white light radiated down to the forest floor.

Vilmos moved to the spot bathed by the warm ray and found a

sense of security in it. He thought about Prince Valam, Princess Adrina and Guardsman Emel. He heard the prince's words in his ears, "... Use that chance, Vilmos, use it for all it's worth. Go back to Tabborrath Village and leave the affairs of men to men."

Suddenly Vilmos was homesick. It seemed forever since he had joined Xith and left Tabborrath Village. He lay back, crossed his arms behind his head and closed tired eyes. For a time he forgot about the dangers. He forgot that he was lost and alone in Vangar Forest. He knew only that images of home played before his closed lids.

***

The first shafts of golden light from a new day were just breaking the horizon far to the east. A wet spray blew in off the sea, and Keeper Martin shivered. He had awoken early and only he and the mid-watchmen greeted the new day.

A troubled dream had disturbed his few hours of precious sleep. Keeper Q'yer's response to his earlier dream message had been grimmer than he ever imagined it could be. Quashan' was under siege; how five hundred defenders held the city was beyond his imagining. More distressful tidings had been in the dream, and this Martin didn't even want to think about.

The sound of footsteps caused Martin to turn. He eyed Captain Adylton, who looked as frazzled as he felt. "You did not sleep well this night?"

"I did not sleep," answered the captain as he stared out across the dark waters.

Martin asked pointedly, "How many days to Quashan' without the Foot?"

Captain Adylton raised an eyebrow. "Two days of hard riding, and only if we can get enough fresh horses in Alderan City. Otherwise, three at best."

"How long would it take for the Foot to catch up?"

"Foot soldiers move like sand caught in those waves," Adylton said, eyeing the frothy surf breaking against the rocks. "Depending on the weather, I'd say seven days."

"At best?" Keeper Martin probed.

"Six, maybe five. They'd arrive spent and—" Captain Adylton broke off, apparently he heard the footsteps as Martin did. Both men turned to see who was approaching.

"Mid-watchman," Keeper Martin said. "He's been hawking me since I stepped out here."

Captain Adylton regarded the watchman, and then tossed Martin a wink. "My man… My men," he said, waving his hand in a sweeping gesture around the camp.

"And Trendmore's?"

"I gave his watchmen liberty. Told them to enjoy the Free Cities."

Keeper Martin tightened his cloak about him. "Then you've gone ahead. Are you ready?"

"Nearly so. It should all go smoothly. Better than half of his most loyal men are on liberty and he isn't the wiser… Have you received word from Alderan or has something happened in Quashan'?"

"You, Captain Adylton, are very perceptive." Martin explained about the dream message and the situation in Quashan'. Adylton grimaced. "So you see," Keeper Martin concluded, "there is precious little time to waste."

"What of Alderan? You didn't say. Did the ship arrive safely?"

Keeper Martin fixed eyes filled with distress on the captain. "Alderan is no more."

"Surely you don't mean," Adylton began. Martin nodded solemnly. "What of Prince Valam?"

Martin said nothing.

Martin was sure Captain Adylton was going to collapse. The captain's knees bowed and his face became ashen. Martin grabbed the captain's shoulders to steady him.

Captain Adylton turned to face the salty spray of the breaking waves. He was silent for a long time. It was clear he was slowly recovering his wits as anger and finally resolve seemed to replace disbelief. "What of the sea?" Captain Adytlon asked. "We could send the foot soldiers by ship down the coast... Or better still, up River Trollbridge. In autumn, the rivers run high. No deep-hulled ships, but still, with the right winds and heavy oars, they could land within a day's march from Quashan'."

An incomplete smile eased Martin's downtrodden expression. "You, my friend, have never bargained with free traders. It'll take a king's ransom to pay for passage. Still, the plan is not without merit."

***

With Emel leading the way and Valam pulling her, Adrina raced faster and faster. At first, she gave her sore and blistered feet little thought. She flitted along, and kept pace just behind Emel.

Soon Valam was pulling her more than she moved under her own power. Soon afterward, she was limping.

Seemingly without thought or hesitation, Valam picked Adrina up and with her cast over his shoulder, continued. For a time, all was well.

Between her brother's gasps as he heavily sucked at the air, Adrina heard shouts from far off. Valam and Emel apparently heard them too and panic urged them to new speeds.

They raced on. The voices grew near intermittently and then again distant. Dawn was at hand, and gloom began to lift from the forest.

"Their trackers are worse... than those of... South Province," Emel said between breaths, "but still, what I wouldn't give for Ebony about now... He'd get the three of us... out of this accursed forest... in no time."

Valam started to laugh or so it appeared, then suddenly he doubled over and dropped Adrina.

"It is a good time to rest," Emel said, as he slumped to the ground.

Adrina forced herself to stand on tender feet. "Are they far behind?"

"We'll know soon enough," Emel said. "Do you think you can

ഇന്ദ 235 ഇന്ദ

continue on your own?"

"If you two can, I must…" Adrina was about to let her words trail off, then she decided to voice her thoughts. "Do you really think Vilmos escaped too?"

Valam stood, then turned and stared in the direction they had just come from. "Let us hope so," he said. He ripped long strips of cloth from his shirt and gave these to Adrina to wrap around her feet.

Adrina's face lit with worry and showed her fears to the contrary. Emel took her hand and said, "I think he did, but now is not the time to dwell on things we cannot change."

Shortly afterward, the three began running again. Adrina moved as swiftly as she could. Valam and Emel did their best to help her keep up with them. Shouts came from off to their left now and their feet lead them right.

As they stumbled into a clearing, Adrina tripped over a bound and gagged figure that was lying in the grass at the clearing's edge.

Run, said a faint voice in their minds. *Forget me. I am lost. It is a trap.*

Emel grabbed one of Adrina's hands, Valam the other. They started to race away. A circle of dark shapes with glowing eyes emerged from hiding. A voice asked, "Where are our guests going?"

Adrina recognized the voice of the speaker. "Erravane?"

Deftly the speaker stepped forward, grabbed Adrina's chin in her hand and turned her face to the pale light. "You *are* a pretty one."

Valam grabbed Erravane's arm and twisted it back as hard as he could, which brought the woman to her knees. Pain was met with sick laughter.

"Do you mock me?" Valam screamed as he twisted the arm back farther still, fully expecting to hear the snap of breaking bones.

The arm began to bend and change in Valam's hand, growing thicker and shorter. Valam let go and pulled Adrina back, confusion and perhaps bewilderment showed on his face.

"If you move again," Erravane said, her voice changed as her body changed, "they will kill you."

"Close your eyes, Adrina. This is no thing for you to see," Valam shouted. "Of all the beasts of hell…"

Adrina couldn't close her eyes, she felt compelled to watch the metamorphosis. Erravane's eyes were glowing now, fangs filled her mouth, a mouth that was twisting and contorting, growing wider and longer as Adrina look on in fascinated horror.

Valam stepped in front of Adrina protectively. "If I had my sword," Valam said, "I would run you through and send you back to the icy pits you ascended from."

Erravane snapped her head and locked powerful, wolflike jaws around Valam's hand. Screaming in agony, Valam dropped to his knees. Adrina closed her eyes and squeezed them together as tight as she could. She waited for the screaming to stop and when it did, she felt compelled to open her eyes. She was just as surprised as Valam obviously was to find he still had a hand.

Erravane, clearly no longer human, spoke with an otherworldly voice. "I said, no movement." Erravane licked her front paw.

Valam spoke again, but took care not to move. "What do you hope to gain from this? Prince William will kill the lot of you as soon as he has no need for you."

"Ah, but I ensure that he continues to need me until I have all that I want. Now I have you, his precious little bargaining pieces. He will grovel on his knees to get you back."

Chapter Twenty Seven

"Well met, Keeper Q'yer. What brings you to the walls?" asked Sergeant Danyel'.

"A dream," responded the keeper, his voice distant, his eyes searching the horizon.

Sergeant Danyel' turned about on his heel and looked out at the campfires that dotted the landscape like a swarm of lightning bugs. "At dawn they will come again. They attack alternately from the south, east and west, leaving only the north wall alone. They toy with us and keep us occupied, though I know not why. Perhaps Great Father truly smiles upon us, for if they ever once attacked in full force, we would be swept away." Danyel's voice became soft. "What I would not give for a spy among them."

Keeper Q'yer seemed to only half listen to Danyel' as he stared; then as he turned away he asked, "What of Chancellor Van'te?"

"He sleeps awaiting the attack. I beg you not to disturb him if it is your plan. It is the first he's slept in days. We need his direction when the new day comes."

"I bring good news," said Keeper Q'yer, "I think he would approve."

Danyel' regarded the keeper's troubled eyes. "You don't look like a man bearing good news."

"With the good there is always the bad. Will I find the chancellor in his quarters?"

"No, he has taken up residence elsewhere. I will take you to him if I must."

"You must, this is important, a dream message from Keeper Martin."

***

"Let me untie her. You must untie her," pleaded Adrina, "she is in obvious pain."

Do not worry unnecessarily, whispered the pleasant feminine voice in Adrina's mind. *I will journey to Great Father, but it will not be at the hands of the likes of this.*

"Enough," snapped Erravane. "My patience is at an end. You *will* now tell me where the boy is."

The first rays of a new day pierced the thick canopy overhead, casting odd shadows about the forest floor. Erravane turned toward the light.

Suddenly and swiftly, Valam lunged at Erravane, but just as swiftly, one of Erravane's beasts leapt upon him and knocked him to the ground. Afterward, it stood defiantly upon Valam's chest, staring down at him, a deep rumbling growl escaping its throat. Adrina shuddered and edged closer to Emel.

"My pets are hungry." Erravane reverted to human form as she spoke, her voice losing its otherworldly hue. "Do they feast on a boy or one of you? The decision is yours, but do not take too long to decide." There was anger on her face, mirrored in her eyes. She walked in a wide circle around Valam, staring down at him.

"Which will talk?" Erravane asked, pointing her finger at each of the three in turn.

Valam, Emel and Adrina were silent.

"Which will die?" Erravane asked. When no answer was forthcoming, Erravane said, "If you do not choose, then I will choose." With a lightning fast snap of her wrists, Erravane wrapped her hands around Adrina's throat. "I choose the princess."

Adrina recoiled, the hands tensed around her throat until it seemed she could not breathe. Terrified, Adrina stared wildly at Erravane. Beside her Valam and Emel attempted to gain to their feet, but one of the Wolmerrelle had likewise leapt upon Emel.

"Why do you care so about a boy?" Adrina asked, her words coming out through a strained gasp. "Vilmos is long gone."

"His *name*," Erravane said sinisterly. "Thank you. Now, where did he go?"

"Home for all we know," Adrina said.

Erravane tightened her grip on Adrina's throat. Her long, sharp fingernails pierced the skin and drew blood. "That is not the answer I want. I tire of this, and I too hunger for a feast."

Straining ineffectively to raise his chest under the weight of the Wolmerrelle, Emel craned his head upward. "Let Adrina go! I will die in her stead."

Erravane started to laugh, a deep demented cackle. "So noble, so very noble. What about you Prince of the North? Would you die for her too?"

Valam said, "Let them both go and I will do whatever it is you ask."

"Is that a promise?" Erravane asked.

"Stop!" shouted a voice vaguely familiar to Adrina. "You do not know what it is you do. Make no promises to her kind." Xith emerged from the shadows and stood with his hands extended before Erravane.

"Watcher," Erravane said, no surprise in her voice. "Age takes your stealth. You clomp around like a Man. I wondered what it would take to make you reveal yourself, and now I know."

"This is *no game*. What is occurring is of *no concern* to you." Xith's eyes glowed as he regarded Adrina momentarily. Adrina saw strange emotions on his face and there was a quality in his voice that escaped her ears. "*Return to Ril Akh Arr and Under-Earth.*"

Erravane hissed, then attacked Xith. She knocked him down and stood over him. Xith made no move to defend himself.

"Attempt your guile of Voice on me again," Erravane said, "and I will kill you."

"Then kill me, Erravane, I grow weary."

Erravane hissed again and released Xith's throat. "You sicken me. All of you sicken me. So willing to die. So willing to sacrifice. Is the will to survive in any of you?"

Erravane cocked her head as if listening to the wind. "You are too late Watcher. The hunt is joined. Oh, they are joyous!"

"Vilmos did not kill Rake. It was I who took his head."

Erravane laughed again, the same sickly cackle. "I know, which is why I will enjoy their feast all the more."

Xith regarded Erravane for a time, then said, "Return to your forests. Nothing that happens here concerns your kind. You tamper with forces you do not understand."

"I will leave in good time, once I have what I came for."

"And what is that?" Xith asked.

Adrina shouted, "Prince William!"

Xith jumped to his feet. "Is that it, Erravane? Your appetite has changed."

"I already have his child in my womb."

Xith laughed. "If you had so precious a cargo you would have returned to Ril Akh Arr... A half-breed child of royal blood no less..." Xith added the Voice at the last, "*Let Vilmos go. You do not need him.*"

Erravane pounced on Xith and slashed his face with her fingernails. "I warned you, Watcher. I *will* kill the boy now."

As if stung, Xith reeled away from Erravane. "If he kills your pets, what then?"

"He will not," Erravane said quickly.

"What if?" Xith probed, "Would you no longer meddle in affairs that do not concern you?"

Erravane was obviously irritated at the course of the conversation. "Yes," she shot back at Xith.

"Is that a promise?" Xith asked.

"And if the boy dies, what then?"

Xith said simply, "I will surrender to your will."

"I would have you surrender regardless."

"You are far from our realm, farther still from the forest temple of Arr. Attempt a test of wills here and you will lose." Erravane slashed Xith across the face again. Xith held his ground. "If Vilmos survives, you will return to Under-Earth. If he dies, I will do as you bid. I would even help you birth the child if that is your wish."

Erravane's eyes widened greedily. "You would birth an abomination?"

Xith nodded purposefully.

Erravane grinned. "Your faith in a human child will be your undoing."

***

Quite sure what had awoken him, Vilmos stirred. He had been dreaming of Tabborrath Village but thoughts and dreams all spun away.

His eyes were wide, his mind in shock. From not far off came another long wailing cry, joined by more, which were still distant. He had sudden flashbacks to another time in Vangar Forest. He knew with certainty the Wolmerrelle hunted him.

He cast aside the prince's overtunic. The oversized garment had kept him warm during these past dreary days and chilly nights. Now he needed speed and not warmth.

As he started to flee, he caught a bit of an old memory. Perhaps he could trick the Wolmerrelle just as he knew he could the hounds of Tabborrath's huntmaster. Without delay, he retrieved the tunic. He dragged it along the ground, then scrambled up into a nearby tree and left the tunic there.

He ran then. He had no idea where he ran to, only that he ran away from the howls. The boughs of trees passed as dark blurs around him and as he ran, he imagined that Xith was beside him and that the shaman urged him to race faster and faster.

"They lead us," whispered an old voice in his mind. He nodded in understanding. He veered right instead of left where the unnerving calls sought to lead him.

His race became a race of desperation. He ran to escape, only to escape. On and on he raced.

He used his hands to ward off branches that seemed to reach out to grab him as he passed. He mounted a rise and started down its backside as he found his second wind.

The path muddied at the bottom of the rise. He came to a stream, kneeled briefly to drink of its cool waters and then hurried on. The calls were never far off.

Completely winded, he stopped. Clutching his chest, panting for air, he hunched over. His face, cold despite the perspiration that dripped from his brow, stung where branches had caught his cheeks. He fought to get his breathing under control and bit back the pain of sore muscles.

Gradually the splotches before his eyes cleared and he brought his breathing under control. He straightened up and looked around, noticing then that the forest seemed suddenly too quiet. His face blank and expressionless, he panned his eyes slowly from left to right.

Like slow death closing in upon him, he perceived the purple glow of the canopy overhead, and through a small break between tree boughs, he saw thin streaks of fire lighting a night sky.

Out of the corner of his eye, he caught movement and, perhaps, a flash of white. Suddenly, the voice of the past was in his mind again, "From this lesson stems the basis of your magical shield, the shield that will protect and keep you in dangerous times…"

He conjured the magical shield now, just as he had then. Out of the corner of his eye, he watched a great black blur sweep toward him. A yelp followed as the creature struck the invisible barrier. Still its momentum carried him to the ground with it.

Disoriented, he shook his head and inhaled. The force of the blow had knocked the wind out of him.

For an instant, it was as if he didn't think at all. All his bewildered thoughts stopped, the magical shield fell away, and then the beast howled and struck again.

He struck back with his fists. He clubbed the side of one of the Wolmerrelle's two heads. The creature wheeled back. He crabcrawled backward as fast as he could. Only his back slamming against the trunk of a tree stopped his crazed retreat.

Without Vilmos even realizing what he was doing, a trace of blue-white light danced across his fingertips. The bolt raced outward, and caught the Wolmerrelle full in the torso. Howling madly, it staggered backward.

He pressed his back against the tree trunk, and using his knees, inched up to a standing position. He was terrified and his every thought screamed out to him, "Escape!"

Again magic raced from his hands and struck the howling Wolmerrelle. The smell of singed fur and flesh choked the air. The creature charged, but managed only a single stride before collapsing.

For the longest time he didn't move. He sat wide-eyed, his thoughts still racing, still screaming, "Run! Escape! Get away!" But the Wolmerrelle was no longer moving.

Cautiously, he crept forward. He reached out with his foot and nudged the beast. He jumped back as it convulsed. Afterward it moved no more.

He was elated, tired from his flight and drained from the brief fight. He collapsed to his haunches but was given little time to recover.

A glimmer of movement out of the corner of his vision caught his eye. Suddenly he knew more of the creatures lurked just beyond his view in the shadows. He raised the magical shield. Again, it saved him. Only this time the great beast did not carry him to the ground with it, and this time he maintained the shield.

They came at him then, one by one in a great wave. He struggled to maintain the shield and keep his feet. Magic surged wildly through him as he drew in more and more energy. Consumed by it, he turned wild eyes on the five Wolmerrelle that circled him, waiting to pounce.

Again his thoughts were propelled to the past. In his mind, as he poised for the attack and turned in a tight circle, it was the great black bear that he saw. Reared up on its hind legs, it towered over him, a mountain of black fur and dark eyes.

He was no longer gripped by terror as he stared up at it. The voice in his mind no longer screamed, Run! It was chastising him. "Control, always stay in control," it said.

He fought to gain control of the rampant energies within him. Perhaps sensing a moment of weakness, the Wolmerrelle charged.

His shield held the creatures at bay and the charge served to focus his thoughts. Suddenly he realized something. Xith had traveled through Vangar Forest to reach the clearing beyond his village. He had all but admitted it. He had arrived on horseback and no horse could have descended into the valley from anywhere within many miles of that clearing. That night when Midori had left the camp, she had taken the horse with her, for the animal hadn't been there the next morning.

His own voice rang in his ears, "You weren't expecting hunters and trackers were you? Who were you expecting, shaman?"

"There is no need to trouble over the could-have-beens," returned Xith's voice, and Vilmos was now sure that a bear hadn't mauled and killed the girl from Olex Village. The bear hadn't attacked him during that fateful encounter and it probably wouldn't have. Perhaps it—she—was protecting him. Evident anger in his eyes and on his face, Vilmos turned to face the first of the great two-headed beasts.

"Do what you must..." rang Xith's voice in his ears.

The urge to let the magic flow unchecked through him was suddenly strong. He controlled it and instead channeled that strength carefully to his hands. Bolts of blue-white lightening sprang forth and struck one of the beasts. The creature died.

His magical shield fell as the remaining four attacked and overwhelmed him. White-hot fire shot through his right leg as a pair of powerful jaws clamped down on it. He let out a scream that rang through the forest.

Pain flooded his thoughts; panic took over. Wildly Vilmos lashed out again and again, wielding his magic, punching, even kicking when necessary to fend off the beasts.

Everything became a blur for a time. The beasts came at him singly, in pairs, all at once. He drove them off using every bit of strength he could muster.

One fell, didn't rise; another followed. Two remained. He could barely move his arms. There was a great gash across his chest. He felt cold and numb, the chill of death. He started to run, but as he was nearly exhausted he staggered more than he ran.

After what seemed hours, he found himself with his back to the trunk of one of the great trees of the forest. The last of the great beasts stared him down. He could barely stand now, and only the tree at his back kept him on his feet. Too weary to focus, too weary to find his center, he knew only that the magic was gone now, gone with his rage.

He didn't think it odd that this beast had only one head, though he did take note of it. This Wolmerrelle was smaller than the others, still somehow more powerful. Its eyes, glowing even in the light of the new day, regarded him in an almost human way. Though badly wounded, it dragged its hind legs, howled a tormented wail up at the heavens and then came at him.

In an attempt to flee, he stumbled and fell. The injured leg that had held him while his fervor raged, collapsed under his weight. His face slapped the hard earth first, his hands were too slow to brace against the fall.

With his face pressed against wet earth, muddied with blood surely his own as well as the fallen beasts, he lay where he fell, too drained to move.

A shadow blocked out the daylight filtering in through the forest canopy. He rolled his eyes up to see the Wolmerrelle standing over him. He shielded his face with his arms as it set upon him. The creature latched onto the arm and shook its head wildly.

He groped frantically with his free hand and kicked at the beast's head with his one good leg. His hand found only leaves and dirt, but there was something on the ground just outside his reach. He could feel the edge of it. "Shape your power, use it to your advantage! Concentrate, control, focus!" screamed the voice in his mind. He squeezed his eyes tight, fighting the pain, fighting to concentrate.

He focused on the object just out of his reach. It was the clubbed end of broken branch. He could feel it now vibrating on the ground. It wanted to inch forward into his grasp and then it did. With the branch in his hand, he began bludgeoning the beast.

The weakened Wolmerrelle howled and hissed. Repeatedly, it raked his chest with its forepaws. For an instant as he beat with all his might on the creature's head, he swore he saw a human face—his weary mind and body were surely playing tricks on him. He mustered the strength to deliver a last desperate blow and then dealt it, putting every bit of himself into the blow. The crunching sound of bone and wood followed. The branch broke. The beast collapsed.

Just as suddenly as the attack had come, it was over. Blood covered his face. His hands. His arms. He knew not whether it was his own. He didn't care. He had won.

"I did it," he whispered to the voice in his mind.

"You performed excellently," the voice whispered back.

He managed a smile, and then weak from blood loss and battle, he collapsed.

Chapter Twenty Eight

"If you strike," Xith said, regarding the clawed hand raised to his throat, "know that our arrangement is void. Moreover, if you do not kill me with that single blow, know that I *will* kill you. Know also that the boy's powers pale in comparison to my own and that my memory is as long as time itself. One day I *will* return to Under-Earth. It is in your hands whether I make my life's last work the siege of Ril Akh Arr or other matters…"

Deftly Erravane swept back her hand. "This is far from over." She said it evilly. She was hiding something and apparently Xith knew it.

"If you have designs on Prince William, think again. I need him alive," Xith told her.

"So do I," hissed Erravane.

"It is over, Erravane!" Xith grabbed Erravane's throat with a mystical force that Adrina couldn't see but knew was there. Erravane's beasts raced to her aid but crashed against an invisible barrier. Viciously they attacked the unseen wall but couldn't break through.

"Do not dismiss me," hissed Erravane despite the pressure of the phantom's grasp on her throat. A dozen more Wolmerrelle emerged from the shadows and suddenly the woods were full of long wailing cries. "You kill me and you will never leave the forest alive."

Xith pointed his finger at one of Erravane's beasts. He lowered the magic wall for an instant as a line of fire raced from his hand and engulfed the beast.

Adrina gasped. She realized the source of Xith's mysterious powers. "Forbidden magic," she whispered.

Erravane screamed a tortured wail, which matched the dying Wolmerrelle's. Her face twisted and contorted as she sought to change shapes, but no matter what she did, she couldn't break free of the phantom's grasp.

A figure emerged from the shadows. Deep blue eyes looked in Adrina's direction momentarily, and then suddenly the figure was moving with inhuman speed among the pack of Wolmerrelle. "Seth," whispered Adrina. The still figure whose head Adrina held answered, *Yes*, and there was evident relief in the tone.

Xith matched Seth's blows one for one with stinging magical flames and the Wolmerrelle fell all around them. Eyes bulging, Erravane clawed at the air. Before Emel and Prince Valam could gain their feet and join the fray, she cried out, "Enough, enough. Stop!"

Mid-blow Seth stopped, drew up to his full height and cast a sidelong glance at Erravane. The remaining Wolmerrelle made no move to attack him. Dumbfounded, Emel and Valam looked to Xith.

"It is over," Xith said. "If *you* leave here alive, Erravane, it will be up to you." Erravane hissed but ceased to struggle against the unseen phantom. Xith turned to Adrina then, "Ease your fears Princess, those creatures cannot break through."

Xith then turned to Seth. "You are bleeding."

It is only a scratch, Seth returned.

"As superficial as that single scratch may seem, it could kill you if not cleaned properly. Untreated, it will fester like nothing you've ever seen." He paused, and then turned back to Adrina, "I must apologize for waiting so long, but I had to be sure—"

"What of our deal?" interrupted Erravane, "You promised I'd go free."

"I made no such promise, though you did promise to return to Ril

Akh Arr and meddle no longer in affairs that do not concern you or your kind."

Adrina broke her trancelike gaze on Xith. She looked once more to pitiful Erravane, and then beckoned to Seth. "Sit beside me," she said, "let me clean your wound."

Xith smiled fondly at Adrina, as if remembering a thing from the past before he turned back to Erravane who had begun to howl.

"Let me go," Erravane hissed, "You have what you wanted."

Xith forced the phantom's grip. "Answer this question with care, your life depends on it. When will William meet King Jarom?"

"I do not know... You must let me go."

"She lies," Emel said. "Adrina and I overheard her speaking to Prince William. His commanders will join him at his camp tomorrow."

Erravane cringed and cowered away from Xith's stare. She began babbling. "His army is ready to march. The encampments are spread out all along the northern edge of the forest. William awaits the arrival of King Jarom's army before he strikes. King Jarom's advanced guard has already struck against Quashan'; they laid siege to the city days ago."

"Where is Jarom's army now?" questioned Xith. "Where is King Jarom?"

"Quashan', but the bulk of his army has just entered the southern edge of the Vangar. Even with the paths cut by William's pathforgers, days will pass before they arrive."

The unseen hand lifted Erravane off her feet. Xith asked, "William doesn't know this?"

"He knows only what I see fit to tell him."

Momentarily, Adrina saw surprise or perhaps glee cross Xith's face. Xith said, "The games end, Erravane. I would sooner cut out your tongue than listen to you speak. If you lie about King Jarom, I will kill you now and be done with it."

"He is an overzealous man who thinks he cannot lose. My beasts took great pleasure in harrying his soldiers… They are truly afraid of these forests now."

Xith seemed pleased with the answer. "You are free to go, Erravane. Know that I make no empty promises. If ever I see you again, I will kill you, and more… Return to Under-Earth for it is there that you belong, and not here."

The expression in Erravane's eyes as the unseen hand released her, matched that which had been in Xith's eyes moments earlier. Adrina and the others watched as Erravane and her beasts slipped away into the shadows. They took with them their fallen, leaving no trace of their presence.

As Adrina had finished cleaning his wound, Seth now saw to Galan's needs. He held a water bag to Galan's lips and she drank heavily from it.

Emel spoke first, voicing the thoughts also on Adrina's mind. "Do you really believe Erravane will do as you asked? I don't trust her."

Neither do I, sent Seth.

"Though eventually she will keep her promise, Erravane is hardly one to be taken at her word. She is strong willed and wants what it is she came for, this I am counting on." Xith turned to Galan and Seth, "Can she walk unaided?"

Brother Galan is weak from thirst and hunger…

Valam, who had been quietly regarding Galan's lithe figure, said, "I will carry her." Adrina had never seen such a look in her brother's eyes. Valam was smitten by Galan's angelic beauty, or so it appeared.

"Good, good," Xith said.

Adrina turned to Xith. "I must ask," she said. "Where have you been these many past days? Where is Father Jacob?"

"Know that this way matters have turned out better than they otherwise would have. I had very important matters to attend to, and I am truly sorry if you felt I abandoned you when you needed me the most."

Adrina persisted. "What of Father Jacob?"

"Jacob is well, but surely irritated," Xith said.

Adrina tried to speak again but Xith silenced her. "We must address other matters, gather round and listen closely." Xith said, waiting until everyone was listening. "You know the entirety of the second most powerful army in all the lands marches north and that Quashan' is under siege. What you do not know is that we have little more than this day and the next to set matters straight... We must first find Vilmos, and then—Adrina, Valam and Emel—you must sneak out of Vangar Forest, past William's army. You must return with help or all will be lost..."

***

"You want me to what?" screamed the galley's captain above the sound of pacekeeper's drums.

"I want you to continue up river," said Keeper Martin.

"Captain Adylton," said the galley's captain, "you claim to be a fisher's son, bring some sense to your companion."

Captain Adylton had been watching the rise and fall of the sweeps as they stroked the water and it took him a moment to respond. "If any of your ships are damaged, we'll pay you double its worth in gold from the King's treasury."

"Night is nigh at hand," complained the captain.

"Triple," said Adylton.

The ship captain still seemed hesitant.

Captain Adylton said, "Plus a year's wages for lost revenues during rebuilding."

"Lanterns!" shouted the galley captain, "Bow, starboard, port. Close watch! Drummer, mid beat! Relay the orders to the rest of the fleet!"

Keeper Martin nodded approval. He and Captain Adylton moved away from the helm so their voices wouldn't be within earshot of the galley's captain. With the noise of the drums, the grunts of the rowers and the splash of the sweeps, they didn't have to go far.

Keeper Martin said, "You learn the ways of free traders quickly."

"I didn't say I'd never bargained with free traders before my friend, what I said was I disliked free traders. I suppose there are worse ills in the world than a hunger for gold."

"Well said," returned Keeper Martin, "but how much is it going to cost to convince him to continue when one of his precious ships really hits bottom?"

Captain Adylton frowned. "Do you believe the river still so shallow, even with the recent rains?"

"If the Trollbridge was safely traversable at any time during the year, an enterprising captain, perhaps even our ship's captain, would have been sailing it long ago, and there would be ports up and down—"

"—I get the point," Captain Adylton said, shifting his stance as the boat swayed. "We will pray then that none of his ships run aground." Captain Adylton tried to change the topic of the conversation. "Did this Keeper Q'yer of yours receive your message yet?"

"The message entered Keeper Q'yer's dreams as I sent it, that is the way of the message. What I don't know is if he understood it, though we will surely find out soon enough."

One of the sailors called out, "White waters ahead!"

Keeper Q'yer and Captain Adylton raced to the bow.

***

Father Jacob eyed the grizzled commander who stood beside him. Reflecting the light of the new day, his green eyes shone with an uncanny luster. There was naked rage on his face, he was gritting his teeth and his hand on Jacob's shoulder was trying to crush bone.

His tone grim, Captain Mikhal said, "A costly attack at dawn it will be, but we must strike now. I cannot bare the sight of this."

Jacob peered out from his hiding place amidst the trees. From his vantage point, he saw most of Quashan' and the amassed army. The emblems on the enemy banners at this distance were hardly identifiable, though the colors were. They were not green and gold, but blue and black, the colors of King Jarom and the Kingdom of

Vostok. Jacob bowed his head wearily, but didn't respond.

The two stood there for a time, staring down at the army poised to strike the city as they obviously had in previous days. Quashan's walls were battered. The east wall, which they had the best view of, had large sections missing from its upper bulwarks. Thin trails of black smoke were streaming from the southern part of the city and a section of the nearby wall was charred.

Captain Mikhal turned and started to walk away. Father Jacob stopped him. "I too am nearly at the end of my patience. For days I have done nothing but wait, and while I grow tired of waiting, I made a promise to an old friend that I would wait when it seemed we must attack and he in turn made a promise to me."

"There are exceptions to any promise, and this is surely one, unless this friend of yours is His Royal Majesty or My Lord Prince."

Father Jacob looked directly at the captain. "Who he is is not important, that I trust him and would give my life for his *is* important. No, we must wait."

Captain Mikhal hissed and cursed in a low voice. He pointed, then spoke, "Look… Ridesman. Lancers. Hundreds."

"White and red," Jacob said quietly.

Captain Mikhal regarded Jacob. "It cannot be, it doesn't make sense."

Jacob sighed and bowed his head wearily. "Prince William's advance guard, his army comes."

"But, the Alliance?" asked the captain.

Father Jacob said, "The Alliance died with King Charles."

Captain Mikhal's nostrils flared. "That is as impossible as—"

"—an order sealed with King Andrew's seal rousing the whole of Quashan' garrison to Imtal being false?"

Before Captain Mikhal could respond, Father Jacob explained the last thing he had been holding back from the garrison commander. He spoke quickly and directly, telling Captain Mikhal a thing that he himself had not wanted to believe until he saw it with his own eyes.

"The Kingdom of Vostok and the Kingdom of Sever are united in their cause against Great Kingdom."

"If the Alliance is broken, what of Zapad and Yug? King Peter and King Alexas are marionettes and King Jarom is the puppeteer."

"We must give thanks to Mother-Earth and her divine providence," returned Father Jacob.

"Even the Stygian Palisades have passes, and there are certainly enough ships in the Far South..." Seeming to realize what he was saying, Captain Mikhal's voice trailed off.

Suddenly the call of dozens of trumpets broke the air.

Captain Mikhal's face was livid as he said, "They're preparing an assault. The time to strike is now while they muster. Nothing you say will make me change my mind. Nothing."

Father Jacob tried to bring reason to the stubborn captain. "Who will you serve by charging to your deaths? You must trust in—"

"—I've little faith, Father Jacob, I must confess this, for if you are going to tell me that I must trust in Great Father, you'll find me lacking."

Father Jacob raised a silencing hand. "I have faith for the both of us. I was about to say that you must trust in me."

Jacob paused and took a deep breath. He was about to speak when more trumpet calls broke the silence.

"The attack begins," said Captain Mikhal, his hand, returned to Jacob's shoulder, was again trying to crush bone. "My hand yearns for the hilt of my blade, can you know what it does to me to see this?"

Jacob winced. "Yes, I do know."

"We strike," Captain Mikhal said, "we strike."

Chapter Twenty Nine

In the middle of a circle of trees they sat, Seth beside Galan, Vilmos opposite Xith and the mysterious lady.

Vilmos listened carefully to the tall light-haired woman who he was sure had saved his life when no other could have. Mid-sentence she had turned to him and Vilmos knew she was now speaking to him. He wondered if she had read his thoughts.

"Like a tree with many limbs that branch out forever, with each new branch comes a choice and for right or wrong you follow one or the other." The lady paused, then stood. "Sometimes, two great boughs touch and for a time, their branches intertwine. Sometimes, the great trees form a circle such as this."

She gestured to the circle of trees. "For good or evil, they form an ever continuing chain. The evil that plays upon the hearts and minds of the disenchanted has its part in the chain. You cannot cleanse yourself of it forever though you can hold it in check. You, Vilmos, have found yourself. Do not lose or waste what you have gained."

The lady turned to Xith. "Go with my blessing. Remember, you will find help in a most unlikely source. To Quashan' you hasten." She looked at the others each in turn. "Galan, Seth, Vilmos, remember what I have told you. Sometimes it is best to remember our roots, for a tree without roots cannot grow."

She stood and Xith bowed his head. Seth and Galan did likewise and then Vilmos. Vilmos had only just looked down—for an instant, no more—but when he glanced up, the lady was gone. He flashed excited eyes to Xith, suddenly realizing something else. The trees were gone.

Vilmos felt emotions flood over him—first surprise, then alarm—a chill ran up his back. He looked to Galan and Seth—to him, their abilities were both strange and wonderful. He turned then to see what they saw. He was on a hillside; there was a walled city in the distance. The sun virgining in the East shrouded all detail in a golden haze. Faintly, he heard what could have been trumpet calls.

"There is much to be done before this day is finished," Xith said, waving for Vilmos, Seth and Galan to follow him. "I pray that we are not too late and that Father Jacob still waits."

***

Sergeant Danyel' burst into Chancellor Van'te's chamber. "The attack comes, we must hasten to the walls!"

Chancellor Van'te looked to Keeper Q'yer and when neither spoke, Danyel' repeated, "We must hasten to the walls."

Chancellor Van'te stood then and as he did, he again looked to Keeper Q'yer. Keeper Q'yer raised a hand to his lips. Instead of responding, Chancellor Van'te indicated Danyel' should lead the way.

As Danyel' turned to enter the hall, a runner, panting and out of breath, appeared in the doorway. "Hurry, the enemy…"

The runner paused to inhale and to wipe sweat from his forehead.

"We know," Danyel' said, wiping sweat and grime from his own brow.

Danyel' stumbled as he took a step toward the runner. Van'te grabbed his arm to steady him.

The runner continued, "No, you don't… understand."

Danyel' said, "Go on."

Chancellor Van'te looked to Keeper Q'yer again. He already knew what the runner would say but he listened nevertheless.

"They come from the south… the east, and the… west in a great swarm."

Sergeant Danyel's face turned ashen. Chancellor Van'te steadied him as he nearly fell, and then handed him off to Keeper Q'yer. "He is the one who has not slept since the siege began. Take care of him. I'll go do what I can. And keeper—" Chancellor Van'te stared directly into Keeper Q'yer's eyes. "—I pray that no more of what you've told me comes true."

***

From the direction of the city came the sounds of a raging battle. Vilmos saw Captain Mikhal glance toward the city then heavenward. It was midmorning, only two hours after they had found Father Jacob, and things looked surely grim for the defenders. Smoke was rising from the eastern part of the city as well as the southern part now.

"They'll come. *Patience*, Captain Mikhal," Xith said.

Captain Mikhal fixed eyes filled with rage on Xith. "Your promises are empty. For the life of me, I don't understand why I continue to listen."

"Please," Father Jacob said, "don't you see the folly in such a pointless attack? Only united with the soldiers of Imtal do we have a chance."

"I see only that the defenders will soon be overwhelmed. The Quashan' garrison isn't the largest in the Kingdom, isn't the strongest, isn't the best equipped, but we'll be damned if we stand by and watch our homes destroyed. Never underestimate the determination of men defending their homes. We'll fight. We'll fight like demons possessed."

"You should *relax*," Xith said.

Father Jacob said, "I pray that you will listen to reason."

"Save your prayers for the enemy when we drive them from our lands. The burning in my heart is matched two thousand fold by the burning in the hearts of my soldiers. We fight."

Before Jacob or Xith could respond, Captain Mikhal turned about on his heel in military fashion, and strode away.

Xith stopped Jacob from going after him. "Though you can slow the decision, you cannot change the minds of those who are already convinced to the contrary."

Captain Mikhal didn't waste any time, already he was barking orders to his men. While Vilmos didn't know military, it was clear Captain Mikhal did. Vilmos was about to speak when a masculine voice sounded in his mind. *He deems himself a failure. He will charge to his death if you let him.*

"I know," Xith said. "Can you ride?"

Seth sent an odd sensation of warmth that Vilmos had slowly come to realize meant a curt yes.

Xith motioned to an attendant and indicated the man should bring three horses. Xith said, "Brother Galan, watch well young Vilmos. He is an apt apprentice, and I shouldn't like to see him do anything that will sever our relationship prematurely."

At the hearing, Vilmos smiled. Xith had expressed genuine feelings for him. When he realized Xith aimed to race off without him, Vilmos frowned.

Before Vilmos could voice an objection, Xith said, "A very important task falls to you, Vilmos and Galan. You must go up into the highlands, then circle west until you can see Quashan's western gatehouse. If one of the three survived Vangar Forest and were able to find help and return, you must explain the situation as you know it." Xith looked directly at Vilmos. "Remember what I said about Erravane and pray, pray that Great Father is listening."

Xith paused and cast a sidelong glance to Captain Mikhal. A runner had just returned. "Captain," the runner said, "the sub-commander of the Foot awaits your orders."

Captain Mikhal nodded to the sub-commander of the Horse who was beside him. The sub-commander came to attention then departed. Captain Mikhal went off in the opposite direction.

Just then, attendants returned with the horses. Xith, Seth and Father Jacob mounted. It seemed Xith was going to say something more, but then Captain Mikhal ordered his foot soldiers to begin their advance. The three squadrons of foot soldiers, some fifteen hundred men, began their charge. They burst from the forest and raced down the slopes that they knew so well into the Quashan' valley basin, using the contours of the land to hide their movement as best as they could.

Meanwhile, the horse soldiers waited. Captain Mikhal had divided the Horse into two files. One would later sweep in along the northern flank of the Foot, the other the southern, but only when the time was right, for Captain Mikhal hoped the Foot would cover considerably more than half the distance to the city before the enemy would spot them and turn about to set up a rear defense. Only then would the Horse begin their charge.

Captain Mikhal's stallion pranced anxiously as the captain held the animal's reins taut. Xith, Seth and Father Jacob, on horseback, were beside him now. Captain Mikhal reached into his saddlebag and handed each a strip of green and gold cloth. "Field insignia," Vilmos heard the captain say, "tie it around your right arm. Do not lose it. It is the only thing that will identify you with the Kingdom forces in the mayhem to come. Father Jacob, stay close, I will do my best to protect you, for we will surely have need of your healing abilities."

"Would that I were a priestess," muttered Jacob.

From high overhead, Vilmos heard the call of an eagle. He looked up, and saw it circling above the city. He looked to Xith. The shaman's eyes were glossed over.

The Foot was nearly halfway across the valley floor. Vilmos expected at any time to see the enemy host turn to form a defense. But they didn't and the Foot continued their silent race.

Vilmos glanced to Xith again, and then back down the hillside. He looked beyond the Kingdom foot soldiers to the great walled city of Quashan'. He couldn't see the men upon the walls, though he knew they were there. They were the ones pushing back the breaching ladders and responding to the enemy's relentless charges with catapult volleys.

Suddenly the eagle dove from the heavens and just when it

seemed it would crash into the walls of the city, it disappeared. Xith came out of his trance and said something to Captain Mikhal that Vilmos couldn't hear. Captain Mikhal raised his sword arm high overhead, momentarily his broad-bladed sword glistened in the late morning sun, and then he thrust the blade forward. The charge began. More than five hundred riders spurred their mounts into a race.

Vilmos stood enthralled, unable to break his eyes away. The thunder of hooves blocked out the sounds of the distant battle. Galan at his side was silent as well. She too watched and listened. Eventually though, the thunder grew distant. The first excited shouts erupted from the enemy host and men scrambled to set up a frenzied rear defense.

Midway down the valley's slopes now, the Kingdom horse soldiers spurred their mounts, driving the animals as fast as they dared. Arrows from the Kingdom bowmen began to penetrate the enemy lines.

Suddenly, the first wave of foot soldiers struck the enemy's rear flank. Privately Vilmos cheered for the Kingdomers, but he was also torn between loyalties. Some of those on the field were from his homeland.

As Vilmos watched, Sever's Knights of the Lance, their red and white banners waving in the wind, rallied for a clash with the Kingdom riders. Instead of turning to engage them, Captain Mikhal's horse soldiers continued directly into the enemy ranks. Even from this distance, Vilmos heard the screams of despair, agony and panic that followed.

It is time, imparted Galan into Vilmos' mind. *We have a long walk ahead.*

Chapter Thirty

Captain Mikhal's mount reared up on its hind legs. All around the captain was the press of enemy soldiers. He removed his foot from the stirrup, kicked out an approaching soldier. The heel of his boot struck the side of the man's skull. Abruptly the soldier stopped, his knees crumbled under his weight.

Captain Mikhal didn't pause. He turned his mount, struck down with his long blade, and like a cleaver, it hew a defender before him. Captain Mikhal continued his charge.

Xith tried to stay close to Captain Mikhal. He defended himself as best as he could, relying largely on his magic shield while he concentrated on other matters. There was a breach midway along Quashan's east wall, and in just a few seconds as he watched dozens of attackers had pushed their way up onto the wall.

They were carving out an ever-growing section atop the wall. At the base of the wall, many more were preparing to raise breaching ladders, and behind them, hundreds waited to climb to the top of the wall.

Xith regarded Seth. The elf's prowess in battle was awe-inspiring. In the midst of the enemy ranks, Seth had leapt from his horse, seemingly undaunted by the fact that he had been surrounded. All around him lay the dead and the dying.

"I wish I had a hundred like him," shouted Captain Mikhal to Xith above the din of the battle.

"I wish there were a hundred like him," Xith said as he pointed to the breached section of the wall. "Do you think we can reach it?"

Captain Mikhal's eyes went wide; apparently he hadn't seen the breach until now. He raised his sword high and behind him a trumpeter's call rang out. He pointed his sword in the direction of the wall.

"To the wall," he shouted and charged.

The trumpeter's call rang out again, and while the bulk of the Kingdom forces were caught in attacks, hundreds rallied and raced after their commander.

Xith turned his mount about and charged in Seth's direction. Two bolts of lightning, cast first from his left hand then his right, cleared the way through the enemy ranks. He wheeled his mount in front of Seth. "Now is not your time to journey to Great Father, Brother Seth, they have need of your skills upon the walls. Climb on!"

Xith helped Seth onto his mount.

"Hold on tight," Xith said. He kicked his mount sharply.

They raced off.

***

Galan followed Seth in his thoughts, looking out through his eyes to the battlefield. She watched the green and gold of the Kingdom banners clash with the blue and black. For a time, it seemed those of the green and gold held a strategic advantage on the field, where the others held an advantage solely in numbers.

She lost contact with Seth's mind shortly afterward and knew only that he was caught up in the frenzy of battle. She was content to look down from her vantage point to the city below. The boy, Vilmos, walked silently at her side. She could sense conflicting emotions in him and a great urge to race to the field to join his master.

When they were directly north of the city, Galan and Vilmos began the long westward circle. Here they followed the rim of the valley. The sounds of the battle were reduced to a faint din in the distance and both the attackers and defenders were reduced to tiny figures moving about on the fields around the city's walls.

Galan lashed out with her thoughts, *Where are you, Seth?*

Galan felt Vilmos' subconscious shiver at the sound of the voice in his mind. *I am sorry. I should have directed the thoughts. I am ill accustomed to your ways, please forgive me.*

Vilmos asked, "Can you really talk across such a distance?"

Only if Brother Seth maintains the link and as long as we do not journey too much farther away from the— Galan broke off as Seth's vision filled her mind's eye with second sight. Seth was atop the east wall. The wind was blowing in his hair, and he was looking across the basin to the battlefield.

The green and gold were holding their own. With the Kingdom defenders back in control of the east and south walls, they could now lend considerable aid to the Kingdom soldiers in the field. Strange machines hurled rocks. Arrows from Kingdom archers rained down upon the enemy. The enemy still held a tremendous advantage. They outnumbered the Kingdom soldiers at least five to one.

Several large columns of the enemy army had fallen back to regroup. Three lines of shield bearers hundreds long amassed. Behind them, bowmen, preparing to fire on the move, would provide cover while swordsmen and pikemen waited to strike. The enemy commanders rallied them and then ordered the attack. The shield bearers, pikemen and swordsmen surged forward, a great moving wall that clashed with the first line of the Kingdom defense.

Enemy bowmen focused on the heart of Kingdom defenses. Pikemen used the shield bearers for cover, their long pole arms felling nearly all who came against them. Swordsmen filled in the gaps of those who fell and relentlessly the enemy wall surged forward. In short order, they cut off several groups of Kingdom soldiers from the main forces and gained control of the field.

Vilmos grabbed Galan's hand. "Look. They march, from the east!"

Seth, to the west, the forces west of the city are on the march. They aim to come up from the south. You must find a way to bolster—

***

—the forces upon the southern wall. I will pray for you and for reinforcements, sent Galan.

Seth severed the link and turned his attention to the defenders on the wall. One of them must be in command. He watched for a moment to see who was giving the orders, but there was so much chaos it was difficult to tell. He stopped a man rushing past.

Who leads?

A puzzled frown crossed the man's face. He turned and pointed, and then hurried off. Seth raced in the opposite direction.

Do you lead? Seth asked.

"I am Sergeant Danyel'." Sergeant Danyel' was also puzzled at the thoughts but was too exhausted to understand why.

Seth switched to spoken words. "From the west, the enemy comes. You must send reinforcements to the southern wall."

Sergeant Danyel' regarded the stranger wearing the green and gold. "There are no reinforcements. This is it. The Father must truly hate us."

Seth said aloud, "The enemy does not attack from the north. How many men do you have positioned there?"

Sergeant Danyel' wiped blood and grime from his brow. "Twenty. No, fifteen."

"You will have to bring more from the west and the east."

"I cannot bring any from the east or in the west I have more wounded than able." Sergeant Danyel' stopped abruptly, cocked his head, then reached for his sword. "Who are you? You wear Kingdom insignia, yet—"

There is not time to explain who I am; you must trust me, you simply must. I rode in from the east with Captain Mikhal. It was he who gave me this. Seth indicated the green and gold cloth tied around his right arm.

Sergeant Danyel' furrowed his brows momentarily, and then

grabbed one of the soldiers rushing by. "Send runners. Strip the north wall, any able-bodied men from the west wall and twenty from the east to the south wall."

"Sir, I go to the north wall. You know the enemy hasn't attacked at all from the north, Chancellor Van'te expects a strike there next."

"That was an order! I will deal with Chancellor Van'te if need be." Sergeant Danyel' stumbled, and Seth had to support him or else he would have collapsed.

The soldier held his ground, eyeing his sergeant and Seth.

Lead me to this Chancellor Van'te and I will talk to him, Seth told the soldier, then turning back to Danyel', he said, *You must rest, you are of little use in this condition.*

"No, I will go with you. Soldier, lead the way!"

Chapter Thirty One

Arrows poured down upon them like a ceaseless rain. Xith extended the radius of his magic shield to protect those around him, but could only extend its protective envelope so far. He was tired and his mind was on other things, mainly trying to pinpoint a weakness in the enemy lines through which they could escape back to the Kingdom lines.

While they had managed to push the attackers back from the walls, the enemy had only to regroup and come again. In the end, it had cost the Kingdom forces dearly. Of the hundreds of men that had rallied and raced after their commander to the base of the wall, fewer than one hundred remained. Most were foot soldiers; a scattered few were horse soldiers. While they were cut off from their lines and trapped in a sea of the enemy, they did not relent. They were determined to keep the enemy at bay.

Xith sat his mount beside Father Jacob and Captain Mikhal. The Kingdom commander was nearly exhausted, but remained tall in his saddle. There was defiant pride in his eyes. His soldiers guarded him with a fierceness rarely seen, and with their lives.

Xith wheeled his mount in a tight circle, continuing his search for a weakness in the enemy lines. He knew Captain Mikhal must survive, for in him lay the power to deliver the city from the hands of the enemy. The Kingdom forces were rapidly losing momentum. Without the leadership of their commander, and more importantly the strength he lent to his men, all would soon be forever lost. The time to act was now.

Xith's mount whinnied and reared. Xith fought to control it, and as he struggled with the animal, a flash of color waving not far off caught his eye. He steadied the horse. He stared; squinted, his eyes went wide as he realized what he saw was a royal banner. For an instant as the press of bodies around the King parted, Xith looked straight at King Jarom.

Xith wasn't the only one to see the banner. When Xith looked back to Captain Mikhal, he found that the captain had already raised his sword. Xith knew at once the captain was preparing for a direct charge against the monarch's defenses, a charge Xith had to stop before it was too late.

When their commander raised his blade high, the ten remaining horse soldiers around him did likewise. Before Xith could act, Captain Mikhal lowered his sword and spurred his mount. His men followed. The foot soldiers parted to let the riders through, and then took up position along the riders' flanks.

Xith held his ground for a moment, considering what to do. Again, he saw Vostok's royal banner fluttering in the wind, so close, yet so far. It was a hopeless charge. Xith knew it, but he also knew he could not stop it. He followed.

Abruptly the call of countless trumpets broke the air. Fighting on both sides broke off. Captain Mikhal and his men cut short their charge. All eyes turned southward. Poised along a ridge of the foothills was a line of horse soldiers a thousand across. The Kingdom forces began to whoop and cheer. Prince Valam and reinforcements had surely arrived.

A second time, trumpet calls broke the air. The riders began their charge, a great black wave racing downward. The Kingdomers continued to whoop and cheer.

Gradually their cries turned to murmurs of dismay, for behind this massive wave came a line of flag bearers. The banners they bore were bold red and stark white, and not Kingdom green and gold. Behind the flag bearers came long lines of foot soldiers. It was not Prince Valam at all, but the army of the Kingdom of Sever.

**

Vilmos' mouth fell open. He gawked at the red and white banners, and the force of thousands on the move to the battle around Quashan'. The Kingdom soldiers would soon be completely overwhelmed, and if there had been even the smallest of hopes for winning the battle before, it died with the arrival of the main host from Sever's forces.

Before he knew what he was doing, Vilmos found he was racing down the hillside.

Vilmos, stop, Galan called out, *you will only get yourself killed. We are to wait here and give instructions when reinforcements arrive.*

Vilmos paused only to turn back and regard Galan. Magic flowed through him like a tidal wave. His eyes, focused with rage, told her what he couldn't say. He cast off the voice in his mind that told him what he didn't want to hear and raced off.

Worriedly, he studied the distant battlefield. King Jarom's forces had fallen back to re-form and wait for the fresh troops. The Kingdom soldiers also regrouped, but they did not wait to attack afterward.

Vilmos, panting and straining for breath, forced himself to maintain a breakneck pace. Behind him, Galan with her longer strides was catching up to him. Vilmos fought to stay ahead of her but couldn't, and soon they were running side by side.

Galan persisted, attempting to change the boys mind. *Vilmos, what good will dying do? This is pointless.*

"I am a magic-user, just as Xith. I do what I must."

You are an apprentice.

Vilmos didn't answer, he pushed himself to race still faster. Sever's horsemen had already clashed with what remained of Quashan's garrison. The Kingdom soldiers fell back, tried frantically to re-form, but each time they formed a hasty shield wall it crumbled, forcing another retreat. Soon it became painfully clear that the Kingdom army was on the run.

Only a hundred yards to go now and Vilmos would be on the flat fields surrounding Quashan'. There he could stretch out his legs and there he was sure he would leave Galan behind. He ran to the pace of the thump-thump in his ears, which drowned out the cries of despair and anguish that the wind carried.

Once on the flat fields, Vilmos stretched out his legs, lengthening his strides. As he did this, his foot caught Galan's. Both stumbled and fell.

Vilmos was quick to regain his feet. He screamed at Galan, "You did that on purpose!"

Galan turned Vilmos about, so he was staring up at the valley's rim from the direction they had just come from. He had just started to protest when he saw them, a line of horse soldiers. The banners at the fore were green and gold. Prince Valam *had* come. He had found Keeper Martin and those of Imtal garrison.

Behind the horse soldiers came the foot soldiers, thousands of them, and far more than Vilmos or Galan had anticipated. Amidst the green and gold banners were banners bearing a blue circle on a field of white. Galan asked Vilmos without words and strangely with only emotions who the others were. Vilmos could only shrug. He didn't know.

Prince Valam, there! shouted Galan.

"Where?"

There! repeated Galan. She grabbed Vilmos' hand and pulled him to a start, and he chased after her.

***

It was now late afternoon. During the day the battle had taken many turns. The arrival of nearly ten thousand troops, Imtal soldiers and free men, had changed the tide of the battle for a time. Still, this had only made the field more even, not entirely equal.

Adrina was in the middle of relating the story of their journey and of how Keeper Martin and Captain Adylton had managed to persuade the free men of Mir and Veter to join the Kingdom's cause. "Most are oarsmen from the free city fleet, not soldiers, though still good with a blade," Adrina said. "Gold surely persuaded their loyalty, also a fear of losing their freedom, for after he had captured the whole of the South, King Jarom surely wouldn't have let the Free Cities remain outside his rule."

"Surely we cannot just sit here," Vilmos said, interrupting. "We must do something."

"I aim to do something, all right." Adrina grinned. "Tell me exactly what the lady told each of you. She did speak to each of you, right?"

Galan and Vilmos quickly told Adrina what they remembered of the conversation, though much of it seemed a blur.

"She spoke of choices being like the branches of trees and for right or wrong you follow one or the other, and of good and evil," concluded Vilmos.

Adrina asked, "Did she tell you to remember something?"

Vilmos was pacing. Adrina knew he was growing restless. She turned to Galan and found an unexpected expression in the elf's eyes. "What is it Galan, what do you see?"

Galan was staring off into the distance, her eyes unfocussed. *Seth upon the walls.*

"Really, you can see him from here?" asked Adrina.

Galan didn't answer. She was apparently lost in what she was seeing and Vilmos explained what little he knew of her gift, which he deemed akin to corporeal stasis.

It is not, Galan said, *it is a projecting of thoughts. I can project feelings and images too.*

"Like an image in a dream," Adrina said.

Galan didn't reply; she was again distracted by what she saw.

"Is there a way we can see as well?" Adrina asked.

Perhaps, returned Galan.

Suddenly, Adrina saw Seth standing atop the upper battlements along Quashan's southern wall. She could feel the wind blowing through his hair and the despair ravaging his heart. Seth's emotions flowed to Adrina, mixing with her own, and soon despair ravaged her heart as well. The enemy had breached the southern gates of the city and a wave of humanity was pouring in. Torches were being distributed and many buildings were already burning. Cries of panic rose; she heard women and children crying as they ran from the homes they fled.

When Galan broke the link, Adrina found she was trembling beyond her control and her cheeks were wet with tears. From their vantage point, they saw the billows of smoke, and eventually the flames as well.

Adrina asked, "Is there no hope?"

Neither Vilmos nor Galan replied.

Adrina turned to the group of guardsmen who Valam had insisted remain to see to her protection in case the worst happened. Their faces were racked with anguish and lament. She knew they wanted to join the fight, though it would surely cost them their lives.

She stood and wiped the tears from her eyes.

"I order you into battle!" Adrina shouted.

The ranking soldier said, "His Highness ordered us to remain."

Adrina glared. "And I am ordering you into battle! Now, mount your horses and go."

"We cannot," replied the ranking soldier.

"If Quashan' falls, I will have no need for fifty guards. I will have no need for guards at all." Adrina turned away from the speaker. "I will count to five, when I turn around you *will* be gone, and I will speak never a word about this. One... two..."

Adrina waited until the sound of hooves mixed in with the din of the battle before she turned back around. She was surprised to find that six guardsmen remained.

She glared at them, but they held their ground.

"We must stay," one of the men said. "If it comes to it, we will ensure you reach Imtal."

"If there is an Imtal," Adrina said coolly.

Vilmos seemed suddenly inspired by the sight of the retreating guardsmen and there was the same twinkle in his eye that Adrina had seen in her brother's eyes earlier. "Take my hand," Vilmos told Galan.

Vilmos' eyes glossed over, and it seemed he was in a trance. Adrina and Galan waited. Adrina was unsure what to expect.

After a time, Vilmos released Galan's hand. "In the foothills, the Wolmerrelle. Erravane." His voice betrayed dismay. "William of Sever, she certainly is seeking him out."

Galan's voice whispered in Adrina's mind, *You will find help in a most unlikely source.*

"To think, I once called him cousin," Adrina said, "If only we understood why he turned against Great Kingdom."

"Perhaps we do," said a voice from behind them.

The Kingdom soldiers rushed to protect Adrina. Adrina, Vilmos and Galan turned around and stared into the afternoon shadows. A man with gray hair and a distinctive salt-and-pepper colored beard slowly made his way from the shadows. Adrina said, "Keeper Martin."

Recognizing the lore keeper now, the soldiers backed down.

"You must excuse me," Keeper Martin said, "I have been listening to your conversation for some time. I circled back about an hour ago."

Keeper Martin walked toward them. Adrina saw that his face was drawn and pale, and then she saw the deep stain of blood on the right side of his cloak.

"An arrow." Keeper Martin said simply as he eased to a sitting position.

Adrina's eyes went wide.

"Yes, I will live." Martin motioned for them to sit. Adrina, Galan and Vilmos sat.

"I was in Gregortonn when King Charles was poisoned, and finally I understand why King William has joined with King Jarom."

"King? What—" Adrina began.

Jacob raised a silencing hand. "King Charles has passed on. The grippe took Phillip. William is heir. As you can see by the display in the field, there was no contest to his ascension. I am sure that it is with little pride and no love that the army of Sever sides with Vostok.

"The truth is that I myself did not understand what I had seen in Gregortonn until some hours ago, but by then I thought it too late to act on what I knew. I can see the error of that now and you are responsible for opening my eyes."

Adrina furrowed her eyebrows.

"Babbling, aren't I? Perhaps—" Keeper Martin coughed and gripped his side. "—it is the wound. Yet, I tend to do that normally. It is the green and the gold."

"Green and gold?" Adrina asked.

"All along I was sure agents of King Jarom had somehow seized power in Sever's capital, for you see, I saw through the disguises and when I saw banners of green and gold—Kingdom colors—to me such colors were not out of place, but those of Sever knew at once the colors were foreign."

Keeper Martin's face became extremely pale. He bit back pain, and then took a long drink from a winebag. "Do you understand?"

"I am beginning to," Adrina said.

"Brother Galan, as Lore Keeper of Great Kingdom, I know much more about your kind than the average Kingdomer, still your gifts are truly amazing. Can you truly project images into the minds of others?"

May I? asked Galan, suggesting she wanted to take a closer look at Martin's side. Keeper Martin nodded approval and then seemed not to notice Galan's hands probing the outside of the wound. *You did not remove the shaft of the arrow.*

"The shaft snapped."

Shock crossed Adrina's face as Galan's hand melted into Martin's side. Keeper Martin gave no indication of sudden pain. In fact, he seemed at ease. Adrina, torn between repulsion and attraction, watched.

The skin around Galan's wrist rippled as if fluid, and as if nothing was happening, Keeper Martin turned to Vilmos and said, "What little I know of the Watcher, through Father Jacob, leads me to believe that you are gifted with the forbidden as is he, and while I do not condone its use, I believe as does Father Jacob, exceptions must be allowed if they are for a greater good. You are also from Sever. Yes?"

"My home is Tabborrath Village," Vilmos said.

Martin said, "Your Highness, come here, let me look at you."

Adrina didn't move. Galan was withdrawing her hand and in it, she held the broken arrow.

"Your Highness," Martin repeated.

Adrina looked up. Martin looked into her eyes. "You are the image of your mother, and Queen Elthia as well. Can you braid your hair in a triple braid and let it flow over your right shoulder?"

Adrina caught a glimpse of a pink-yellow glow out of the corner of her eye. She looked back to Martin's wound to find it was gone, as if it had vanished. Adrina turned back to Martin and said, "I think you should rest, you are not thinking clearly."

"On the contrary, I have never thought more clearly." Keeper Martin waved one of the guardsmen over. He was a short, thin fellow. "Soldier, change clothes with the lad here. He will have need of your uniform."

Chapter Thirty Two

Xith kneeled beside Captain Mikhal and cradled the man's head in his hands. Most of the southern quarter of Quashan' was ablaze, and a full evacuation had begun. The Kingdom army was divided and they were now defending against two fronts. King Jarom's foot soldiers came from the west. The army of Sever pressed from the east. The horse soldiers of both kingdoms controlled the middle of the field.

It all seemed so utterly hopeless.

"Can you save him?" Xith asked Father Jacob, who also kneeled beside the fallen commander.

"The wound is grievous, I can only ease his suffering."

Xith said, "Do so, he has earned a peaceful passing from this life." Xith had been sore pressed to convince Captain Mikhal that his men needed his continued strength and guidance and that a single last rallying of his horse soldiers for a final charge would have been sheer folly. Xith found it a bittersweet irony that the commander had met the lethal blow while trying to return to the ranks of his soldiers a second time.

"He is gone," whispered Jacob.

"He was a brave man," Xith said.

Father Jacob bent his head for a moment of prayer and Xith did likewise.

Shouts erupted from not far off. "Fall back, fall back!" the voices screamed.

The former sub-commander beside them stood and urged them to retreat. Xith and Jacob stood and followed the new commander as his forces fell back to regroup.

***

Beside Adrina, Galan and Vilmos marched silently. Adrina could only vaguely see the silhouettes of the five soldiers who preceded them amidst the glare of the setting sun. Slowly though, more and more shadows shrouded the foothills and nightfall steadily approached.

Vilmos, dressed in the guardsman's uniform, held tightly the prize Keeper Martin had given him. He was their eyes. He kept watch from overhead—using the eagle form as Xith had used—and Galan at his side directed him. She read his thoughts, and thus they were able to steer clear of any patrols set up in anticipation of an ambush as the field became blurred.

Keeper Martin's plan had seemed bold as he had revealed it to them, but now as they moved ever closer to the ranks of Sever's army, it also seemed suddenly desperate and simple. They were to sneak into William's camp, find his tent and convince him that Great Kingdom had no part in his father's death.

The guardsmen disguised as Sever soldiers and the banner Vilmos held but did not display would help them on their way. Still, the most difficult part—moving through the camp, finding William and convincing him—would fall to Adrina, Vilmos and Galan alone, and mostly to Adrina.

***

Darkness fell, and still the battle for Quashan' raged.

Prince Valam conferred with his field commanders, the captains of the Imtal and Quashan' garrisons. Only a short time ago his forces had finally managed to break through the enemy lines to join with the soldiers of Quashan', and he had just now learned of the death of Quashan's commander.

Kingdom forces held the base of the southern and eastern walls of the city, yet the fire within the city still burned out of control. The enemy came at them along two fronts but fortunately could no longer attack from the rear or squeeze them into a killing zone. They had driven back the enemy horse soldiers and erected an inner and outer defensive line. In an ironic twist, they had taken control of the trenches dug by those that had besieged the city initially, and it was this that was helping them fend off the superior force.

"The attack slows, Your Highness," Captain Adylton said. He wiped fresh blood from his face and sheathed his blade. "I answered the call as soon as I could."

A soldier offered the captain water and he drank heavily. Captain Adylton continued, "It looks as if they'll soon fall back to their lines. The night comes."

Prince Valam said, "That is indeed news worth waiting for." Valam surveyed his commanders. "Has anyone seen Captain Berre?"

A sergeant with a soot-covered face answered. "He commands on the left flank, Your Highness. He sent me in his stead. He has the devil's own fury in his eyes. His home, a wife and three children, were along Cooper's Walk."

"Stand at ease sergeant." Valam looked to the burning city, and then to Captain Adylton. "What of the other Imtal commanders?"

The sergeant said, "Captain Ghenson's position was overrun. He was dragged from his mount, I believe he is dead."

Valam turned to the sergeant. "What news from the left flank?"

"Your Highness—"

Prince Valam interrupted, "Save the pleasantries for another place and time. Be frank and quick."

The sergeant spoke quickly then. "The line holds, the men are tired, hungry and thirsty. The wounded and the dying lie about the field. Their sappers are digging another trench line, and Captain Berre fears it is a sign they await reinforcements."

Valam gripped the sergeant's shoulder, and then turned to Father Jacob. "Father Jacob?" he said.

Father Jacob stood a little taller and nodded.

"At last, we have a stable position. Care of the wounded is in your hands. I want all wounded who can still walk, but cannot wield a sword, on relief brigade. Without food and water, soldiers cannot fight."

The soot-faced sergeant's downtrodden expression brightened.

Xith stepped forward. "May I speak?"

"Speak freely."

"Light skirmishes and raids will continue through the night, the enemy hopes to keep us expecting an attack that will not come and to wear us out. An all out attack will not come until just before dawn, but if we switch to a defensive and do not continue to press the attack, all will surely be lost come morning."

Valam was puzzled. "How can you possibly know this?"

Father Jacob said, "There are those who have divine gifts of sight, and Master Xith is one of them. You trusted him before; you must trust him again. Without him Quashan' would have already fallen, and none of us would be standing here now."

Valam extended his hand to Xith's shoulder. "I am sorry, it has been a trying day. You must know that you have my eternal gratitude and when this is all over, one way or another, I will repay you."

Xith said, "If you want to repay me, do what I say." He paused then and for a moment, it seemed as if he heard something far off. Valam heard it too, perhaps it was the call of an eagle from high overhead but he couldn't be sure. "Before moonrise, every available man must be mustered and assembled for an all out assault against Sever's army. At precisely moonrise, the attack must begin."

"We cannot desert the left flank," interrupted the sergeant. "There are two enemy armies—"

Valam raised a silencing hand and Xith continued. "Yes, it is very important that the enemy not know we have stripped our left flank. Moonrise is not for some hours and the night sky looks to be dark and clouded. We can use this to our advantage..."

Chapter Thirty Three

Vilmos unfurled Sever's banner. Adrina tried to imagine that she heard it flapping in the wind instead of pitiful moans and screams of agony. She forced herself to maintain a steady pace. Her heart pounded in her ears and she bit her cheek to remind herself to stay calm. Frantic thoughts flashed through her mind and more than once she almost cried out at the ghastly sight of the dead and the dying that littered William's camp from end to end.

For a moment, Adrina thought of Emel and wondered where he was amidst the fighting, and then the thought was gone. Ahead lay a tent with many guards posted around it. Adrina was sure it was William's. Expectantly, she inhaled a breath and held it, but when Galan continued past the tent without even turning an eye toward it, Adrina let the breath slip out.

"You passed his tent, is something wrong?" Adrina whispered.

There is nothing wrong, said Galan, carefully directing the thoughts.

After passing the last tent on the end, Galan paused. *This is William's tent. The other was meant to catch the eye of anyone bold enough to sneak into the camp.*

Galan did not hesitate long, instead she continued until she found a place with few campfires and no torches. *There were two guards just inside the entrance, but cleanly out of view. William sits at a table with his back to the guards. There was another in the tent, but he was preparing to leave.*

Vilmos tossed aside the banner. "You read their thoughts?"

In a way, yes, replied Galan curtly.

Adrina asked, "Is there a chance we can replace the guards with our own?"

One of the guardsmen stepped forward. "We will try. They are surely hungry or tired, or both. I can tell you there have been many times I wished for relief and would never have questioned it if it came."

Galan smiled, seemingly approving the show of bravery. She closed her eyes for a moment. *They are both hungry and tired. You are quite wise.*

"I am but a simple soldier who knows what it is to stand watch." The soldier broke off, his face showing concern.

"Go quickly," Adrina said, "may Great Father watch over you."

Two soldiers slipped away.

While they waited, Adrina took in the activity around them. Everywhere soldiers hurried about the camp, singly, in pairs, and in large groups. The camp was in a state of confused frenzy, but this was changing, order was being restored from chaos. The sound of the battle was fading. More and more fires were raised both along the camp's perimeter and its interior, and lines of torches were being put in place to mark hastily cleared paths.

Princess Adrina?

"What is it, Galan?" Adrina whispered.

They are inside.

Adrina saw two figures leave the tent. "Is it safe to proceed?"

Galan said, *It would seem so.*

Quietly the small group moved toward the tent.

"What would you have us do, Your Highness?" asked one of the three remaining guardsmen.

"When we reach the tent, we will go in, you three will continue past. Do not stray far though. We may have need of your sword arms.

Keep a close eye on the tent, and do not start a fight unless it is absolutely necessary. If an alarm is sounded, we will surely never leave this camp."

At the front of the tent, they stopped. Adrina signaled to the guardsmen to continue on their way. They did so reluctantly.

Adrina started toward the tent's entrance. Suddenly everything Keeper Martin had told Adrina flooded through her mind. She knew that in order to convince William of the truth, she must first find confidence in herself. Still, she didn't see how her resemblance to Queen Elthia would help anything. Or why it was important that Vilmos was a native Severian. Nor did she really understand how Galan was supposed to project Keeper Martin's memories of Gregortonn into William's mind when Keeper Martin wasn't even with them.

Galan grabbed Adrina's arm and pulled her back. *Wait, there is something wrong. I am not sure—No, I am sure, Erravane.*

"The Wolmerrelle," Vilmos said. He gasped. "We must act now or all this will be for nothing."

Galan stopped Vilmos from hastily running into the tent and indicated that they should move back in the direction they had just come from. *As unlikely as it seems Erravane's presence may actually help us. We should wait to see what occurs.*

"I agree," Adrina said, "we should—" From far off the sound of angry voices exploded into the air, followed by panic-filled screams. More shouting followed. Soon an alarm was sweeping through the camp.

Frenzy followed. The camp was in an uproar. Men were running about the camp screaming, "To battle! To battle! The enemy comes!" Then, Adrina heard shouting and screams from William's tent. She turned bewildered eyes to Vilmos and Galan. Together they rushed into William's tent.

The two guards lay face down in the dirt. Adrina did not doubt that they were dead. Apparently, Erravane had cut her way in through the back of the tent and aimed to go out the same way. In a half-human half-animal state, Erravane was dragging William out of the tent. Abruptly she changed directions and pushed her way back into the tent. Behind her came the three Kingdom guardsmen, their swords drawn.

Erravane spun around. Her eyes were wild. "Princess Adrina, you of all people should not stand in my way. William's disappearance will most certainly serve you."

William shouted, "She aims to kill me!"

"Hush, or I'll rip out your tongue. I will only kill you at the end and though you deserve much anguish for abandoning me, I will do it swiftly."

"Even William doesn't deserve to die," Adrina said, her voice strong and with no hint of the alarm that raged through her mind. "Release him, or you will never escape from this camp."

"If I do not escape, neither will you."

Vilmos pushed past Adrina. Blue-white fire danced around his hands. "Xith warned you not to meddle in affairs that do not concern you."

"It is you, the boy who killed—" Erravane was shocked. "No, it cannot be. You and the Watcher should be—"

"Not in the Vangar, we are here." As Vilmos spoke, he walked slowly toward Erravane, his hands poised menacingly. "Should he find you, he will most assuredly keep his promise."

Erravane howled and with inhuman strength hurled William at Vilmos. She turned to make an escape. The guards barred her way. Adrina knew for certain they'd be killed if they tried to stop her.

"No!" Adrina screamed. "Let her pass."

The guards stepped aside and Erravane fled into the night.

Vilmos and William were in a jumble on the ground. Galan and Adrina helped them to their feet. William's eyes were agape and shock was evident on his face. He started to say something, but before he could say anything, a soldier rushed into tent. Adrina turned about.

The Kingdom guardsmen began shouting and rushed forward to intercept the soldier who had drawn his sword and also had begun shouting.

The Kingdom guardsmen engaged the lone soldier of Sever.

Adrina began shouting, "No, no, Stop," but the combatants didn't.

The soldier lay dead on the dirt floor before other soldiers answering his call rushed into the tent. Soon the three Kingdom guardsmen were being pushed back by the sheer number of newcomers arrived to save their king.

Adrina turned to William. "Do something, make them stop!"

William seemed disoriented.

"Do something," Adrina repeated. She grabbed William about the shoulders and shook him.

"I am in no danger, I think, I mean—I need to sort this out." William paused, flustered. "Sergeant, soldiers, I order you to halt!"

The soldiers grudgingly broke off the attack. William pointed to two of them. "Find Commander Stenocco, tell him to come at once. Five more stand guard, the rest of you outside."

The soldiers didn't move.

"Throw down your weapons," Adrina told the Kingdom guardsmen. They hesitated. "Do it!"

The swords of the Kingdom guardsmen clanked as they hit the ground.

A puzzled frown returned to William's face as he turned to Adrina. "Why did you save me? I mean, Erravane was right, you should have rejoiced. Why are you in my camp in the first place, if it is not to kill me?"

"We came to talk." Adrina wanted to say more but she was trembling and there were tears in her eyes. Suddenly it seemed lead weights were around her shoulders and her legs wanted to collapse under the weight. "May I sit?"

"A chair," William said.

A soldier quickly brought a chair.

Adrina cleared her throat, and then looked to Vilmos and Galan in turn. She started speaking, determined to convince William using Keeper Martin's plan. Somehow things didn't come out the way she planned and instead she told him everything the plan entailed. She explained how they had come to the camp and sneaked through it intent on finding him, how they had planned to trick him and finally how they had planned to convince him of the truth. During the telling Sever's commander hurried into the tent but William ordered silence.

Adrina concluded by saying, "I tell you the truth when I say I harbor no hate in my heart for all you have done. I know what it is to grieve for one so dear it seems they are all you had in the world. I know what it is like to feel you are all alone. I know how such loss can cloud your mind and make you want to lash out at all the world, but if you loved your father, and I know you truly did, you will listen to reason. Great Kingdom had no part in your father's death. This you must believe."

Indignation crossed William's face. "How can you possibly know what I feel? How can you possibly know what it is like to lose a mother, father, and brother all in the space of a few years?" William's eyes turn wild. His tone became icy cold. "Kill them, kill them all!"

The Kingdom guardsmen raced for their swords. Adrina leapt from her chair and started screaming at William. Galan grabbed Adrina and pushed her back. Vilmos stepped in front of them both.

Commander Stenocco's eyes filled with joy as he withdrew his great sword from its sheath. He ordered his men to stand at ease. "Leave them to me," he said arrogantly, "I want them all."

The Kingdom guardsmen held their ground as the enemy commander advanced on them. When he was within striking distance, Commander Stenocco stopped and laughed, mocking the tension on the guardsmen's faces. He spat, and then with surprising speed, heaved his massive blade toward them. Adrina turned away and winced in anticipation of the sound of clashing blades. When she heard a dull thud instead, she turned back, expecting the worst.

However, the worst hadn't happened. Nothing had happened.

Commander Stenocco's eyes were wide and filled with rage. He lashed out with his sword yet the sword couldn't reach its mark. Repeatedly Adrina heard a dull thud. For a moment, the commander stood unmoving, a muscle in his cheek twitched nervously and then he cast aside his sword and began ramming the unseen barrier.

Adrina was as confused as the enemy commander was, she turned to Galan. Galan pointed to Vilmos.

"Princess," Vilmos said, "I cannot hold him back long. Do what you must!"

Adrina's thoughts spun inward. She turned back to William and felt suddenly sick to her stomach. She knew what she had to do—something she wished someone had done to her long ago. She struck William across the face with the back of her hand. "How dare you speak to me like that!" she screamed at him. With her eyes, she backed him into the chair behind him.

She continued, angry, "King Charles is gone; your self-pity will not bring him back! Great Kingdom and Sever have always been the strongest of allies. My father, King Andrew, has no desire to sit upon Sever's throne. That seat belongs to the line of Charles, to you… Think. Who stands to gain the most from such treachery? Think, and no longer let blind rage control your actions."

For a long time, William said nothing, and then he turned to the soldiers inside the tent and dismissed them all save for his commander. "It is no easy thing to stop what has already begun," William finally told Adrina, "I know you are sincere and though I want to believe you, I cannot. You spoke of proof. If you have proof that King Jarom was behind the poisoning of my father, I would hear it."

Commander Stenocco screamed, "This is a trick, their forces attack as we speak!"

William raised his hand, commanding silence. "You spoke of proof, I would hear it," he repeated.

Adrina turned to Galan. "Are you ready?"

Chapter Thirty Four

False dawn was on the horizon and still the battle raged. Seth looked down from atop the wall to the fields south of the city. The Kingdom forces were falling back to re-form for another charge, to the west Sever's army was also regrouping and to the east King Jarom's army was mustering for their first attack of the new day. Vostok's soldiers were fresh; few soldiers stood between them and the middle of Prince Valam's camp, as the bulk of the Kingdom army was engaged in the fighting to the west. Seth knew for certain that once the attack came the camp would be overrun.

Seth watched the men upon the walls prepare for the attack. Bowmen notched arrows. Soldiers loaded catapults. Others hunkered down behind the battlements and waited to counter the press of enemy siege ladders.

Trumpets chanted to the east. Vostok's army began to form in long lines. Shield bearers at the fore followed by pikemen, swordsmen and lastly archers. Horse soldiers in column formation waited with swords raised high.

The trumpets sounded again. Thousands of foot soldiers screamed and charged. Seth turned his eyes westward, expecting Sever's army to begin their charge. They had re-formed, but held their ground. Poised to strike to the west, the Kingdom army also waited.

Their rear ranks began to turn about and prepare a defensive, but did not move fearing a deception.

Perplexed, Seth watched the two unmoving armies. He gazed out into the distance, trying to see why neither attacked. Was there something on the field between them?

Galan? Seth called out, reestablishing the link between them.

Seth, came Galan's voice into his mind

What is happening?

Sever's army is quitting the field, Galan replied, and it was then that Seth saw the white flag and six figures moving toward the Kingdom lines.

Seth was puzzled. *To the east, the attack comes.*

By the Mother, I did not realize—you must find Prince Valam. William has decided to quit the field. Seth, he knows the truth. He also says he cannot fight against King Jarom.

Vostok's army came. The clash began. The Kingdom army seemed unsure of which direction to defend against. Seth started running along the top of the wall. He was sure disaster waited in this indecision. He tried reaching the prince's mind, but he had no idea where Prince Valam was among the mass of men in the frenzied camp below.

Sergeant Danyel'? Chancellor Van'te? Seth screamed.

Fatigue clouded Seth's mind, allowing panic and dread to flood over him. He raced faster and faster. As Sever's army began to quit the field, it became clear they were not just falling back and were actually retiring, a wave of cheers erupted from the mouths of the Kingdom soldiers. The men atop the walls also began to cheer.

Seth stopped running. The whole of the Kingdom army turned about, and weary or not, they began a driving charge. King Jarom's army hadn't anticipated such a massive counterstrike. Their shield wall was weak and it fell quickly.

In retaliation, Vostok's horse soldiers began their assault, but this came too late. The two armies were too intertwined and the enemy riders trampled their own soldiers as well as Kingdom soldiers. When the riders met the first solid Kingdom line, horses and men collided, lances met readied swords and pikes, and large numbers of riders were pulled from their mounts or had mounts cut out from beneath them.

The Kingdom army had its own horse soldiers and they were driving into the heart of the enemy army. Vostok's army, stunned and surprised, could only fall back, but without support from the other flank they no longer had superior numbers in the field. It was now they who were outnumbered.

One last time the army of Vostok tried to raise a defense so they could re-form, but this was shattered quickly and the Kingdom army made good their rout. The men upon the walls began cheering louder and louder. For days, their city had been besieged and now the enemy was on the run. They were elated and suddenly no longer weary.

Seth watched the Kingdom horse soldiers pursue the enemy army to the valley's rim and beyond. It was there that Seth lost sight of them. He too was joyous, and he joined in their cheers.

***

The fires in the city were at last extinguished and rebuilding would begin as soon as possible. Already priests and priestesses had arrived, answering Prince Valam's call for aid. The Priestesses of the Mother were caring for the hundreds wounded. The Priests of the Father were interring the dead upon the fields south of Quashan', and the former battlefields would forever more stand as grim reminders of the devastation wrought by even the briefest of wars. Great Kingdom's losses had been heavy.

Adrina's joy was tainted with sorrow. She felt so alone, even though Galan was beside her. Vilmos had gone off in search of Xith, and while Adrina was sure Galan would have rather sought out Seth, Galan had stayed with Adrina to comfort her. Emel had not been among the fit or the wounded, and she had searched through every one of the dozens of relief houses set up to care for the wounded. The only thing she could do now was to search among the dead for his body, a task that seemed too grim for her to bear alone, yet she was determined to find Emel and to say her goodbyes.

"Father Jacob," Adrina called out.

A very weary Father Jacob turned to greet her. He took her hand. "Your Highness, I have heard of your deed, you have done well, very well indeed." Jacob grinned, and a bit of fatigue lifted from his eyes. "I knew you would."

"Emel," Adrina said, "you haven't..."

"No, I have not seen Emel, yet I do not think you will find him here."

"I have looked everywhere but here, Father Jacob." Adrina was in tears. "He is nowhere to be found."

"I have lain to rest too many familiar faces, I remember each, and none was Emel's. Perhaps you searched the wrong places."

Adrina was convinced otherwise. "No, if Emel were alive, I would have found him or he would have found me."

Galan took Adrina's hand. *There are riders still in the field.*

Father Jacob sighed. "A few, yes. They help clear the fields. Most have returned to the city to join in the reparations. Emel is not among them."

A few, Galan said, sending disbelief along with the words, *I see hundreds.*

Father Jacob and Adrina followed Galan's gaze, a confused call going forth from the walls matched their surprise. That the large band of riders was a group of Kingdom horse soldiers there was no doubt, but the rout of the enemy army had been completed before the day had even begun, and now the day was nearly over.

The jubilant soldiers' swords and lances glistened in the late afternoon sun. They did not race their mounts; instead, they held them to a steady trot. The animals must have indeed been weary.

"Could it be?" Adrina asked.

Neither Galan nor Father Jacob had to respond to the question. At the fore of the group was a great black stallion. In Adrina's mind, there was no mistaking *Ebony Lightning*, Emel's beloved mount.

As the riders approached, their faces slowly became clear. Adrina knew for certain that it was Emel who rode Ebony. What's more, Emel wasn't just at the fore of the pack, he was leading it and behind him were over three hundred Kingdom riders. Their shouts and cheers rose to the walls of Quashan' and trumpets returned their jubilant cries with increasing vigor. Those in the streets of Quashan', curious as to what the commotion was, came to the field and soon thousands covered the near end of the field by the city's southern gate.

Father Jacob said, "His father would have indeed been proud of him this day."

"Indeed," said a voice from behind them. At once Adrina recognized the voice of her brother. Prince Valam put his hand on Adrina's shoulder. "Captain Brodst will surely hear of it, for I will tell him myself on the day I see his son is promoted to Fourth Captain, Imtal Garrison."

"Fourth Captain." Adrina replied, her thoughts in the distance.

Valam tightened his hand on her shoulder. "Imtal Garrison is without two of her captains, and who better to fill the place than one who has proven himself worthy."

Adrina pointed a finger at Valam. "You knew where he'd been all along didn't you." Adrina wiped tears from her cheeks. "And you let me worry and fret."

Valam turned her to face him, "I had a hunch but I wasn't certain."

Before Adrina could reply, Emel reined in *Ebony* beside them. He was grinning ear to ear. He leapt from the saddle.

Adrina ran to him and hugged him fiercely. "I thought you dead. Where have you been?"

Emel laughed then said. "Making sure Jarom's army never returns to South Province without giving precious thought to the consequences. We chased them so far, and they ran so fast, I'd be surprised if they weren't still running."

"You will make a good captain, Emel," Valam said.

Adrina was still hugging Emel fiercely, and now Emel's face was a bit red. "Captain?" Emel asked.

"Captain," Adrina said, and she kissed him on the cheek.

Valam cleared his throat. Adrina stepped back, and Valam gripped Emel's shoulder. "Fourth Captain, Imtal Garrison. Captain Ghenson was a good man, and I know you will lead well in his stead."

Chapter Thirty Five

Every day since the battle artisans had been hard at work rebuilding the city. The Master Stonecutter had seen to the walls and his laborers and masons had them nearly as strong as they once had been. Already the city's smiths had the ironwork of the southern gate and portcullis restored. The city's woodworkers had started construction on dozens of new homes. And the fact that there was already a shortage of nails, timber and bricks, proved how hard everyone was working toward the city's restoration.

Vilmos was growing restless. It wasn't so much that he was tired of life in Quashan's keep, but he was unaccustomed to people paying so much attention to him. Serving girls made him uneasy by catering to his needs and treating him as he imagined visiting royalty must be treated. The room he and Xith shared held riches beyond anything he had ever dreamed of. The mattresses on the beds were made of hundreds, maybe thousands, of goose down feathers, as were the magnificently plush pillows. He had never imagined a bed could be made out of anything other than straw covered over or that a night's sleep could be so restful and refreshing.

The sheets were soft and silky smooth. Servants would draw him a bath each evening and he used scented soaps to wash with. He had been given fine clothes, a jeweled dagger to put in the scabbard at his belt, and handsomely crafted leather boots that were custom tailored to his feet—no more ill fitting boots.

Oddly, it was the absence of his old and worn boots that made him yearn for home. He wondered how Lillath and Vil fared, and hoped that no harm had come to them. He had told Xith of his vow that one day he would return home, and Xith had said that perhaps one day he could go home, but that day was a long way off.

Vilmos looked at himself in the mirror again, made a face, and started to undress. Xith came into the room.

The shaman smiled, then said, "You look like a fine young man, come quickly. We cannot keep His Highness waiting."

Vilmos frowned, looked back into the mirror, then wordlessly followed Xith. He knew something special was planned for this evening, but what Xith hadn't told him.

They were descending the central stairs to the keep's great hall, when Vilmos asked, "Why all the secrecy? What is afoot?"

Xith stopped and faced Vilmos. "Enjoy yourself this evening. We will be leaving Quashan' in the morning. It is time to begin your education."

"Education?" Vilmos asked.

Xith didn't answer, instead he continued down the stairs. Vilmos heard playful laughter in his mind and before he followed Xith, he glanced to the top of the stairs. Galan and Seth stood at the top of the landing. Galan wore a deep blue dress befitting a princess and Seth wore princely clothes matched to Galan's dress.

We will leave in the morning also, Galan told them. Galan took Seth's hand as he offered it to her, and then led her down the stairs toward Vilmos. *Perhaps you will come with us to Imtal to speak to King Andrew.*

"I would like that," Vilmos said, "but I think Master Xith has other plans."

"Perhaps, perhaps not," Seth said. He spoke aloud. "I fear we are nearly late and should hurry."

Vilmos smiled at Seth's spoken speech. Seth was working hard on his Kingdom accent.

Galan laughed again, and Vilmos heard its echo in his mind as she prodded him to chase after Xith.

Vilmos raced off to the keep's great hall. Seth and Galan followed.

***

Hundreds of guests were seated at the many tables encircling the hall's main table. At the head of the main table sat Prince Valam. Seated to his left were Chancellor Van'te, Keeper Martin, Father Jacob, Sergeant Danyel', Captain Adylton of Imtal and Captain Berre of Quashan'. Princess Adrina, the soon-to-be captain Emel, Vilmos, Xith, Seth and Galan were seated to his right. Vilmos was glad to be surrounded by a few friendly faces, for most of the others in the enormous hall were strangers to him.

Wonderful aromas rose from the kitchen at the northern end of the hall and, nearly out of sight, attendants waited to bring food to the tables. Vilmos glanced to the four empty seats around the table and wondered who they were reserved for, then bowed his head as Father Jacob began the before meal prayer.

Father Jacob concluded the prayer as he had the past seven evenings, by giving thanks to Great Father for divine providence. Afterward, for a brief time, a discord of voices returned.

Vilmos looked about the hall.

Emel to his left said, "Still not used to it, are you?"

Vilmos replied, "To tell the truth, I would much rather eat somewhere more private."

"And miss all this?" asked Adrina. "Just wait till you see Imtal's hall."

Vilmos shrugged.

Emel whispered, "Me too."

Adrina asked Vilmos, "You will be coming with us to Imtal, won't you?" When Vilmos didn't answer immediately, Adrina glared, and then added, "You must."

Vilmos turned expectant eyes to Xith.

"Alas," Xith said, "it is time we were on our way. Vilmos and I have much to do. He has an education to begin."

Adrina made a face.

Xith said, "Do not fret Princess. Seth and Galan will accompany you to Imtal, yet, I suspect that you have not seen Vilmos and I for the last time."

Vilmos was about to say something when Lord Valam cleared his throat and then stood. A sudden hush spread throughout as Valam's gaze swept around the hall.

"On the eve of the seventh day of the cleansing of our home, we celebrate." Valam raised a golden goblet. "We commemorate those who have fallen in the defense of their kingdom and honor those who helped achieve victory...It is unfortunate that this hall cannot hold each and every soldier presently residing in Quashan', for down to the last man—" Adrina cleared her throat. "—and woman, they contributed to victory, and none more so than those of you seated here today. I, the citizens of Great Kingdom, and your king, thank you."

Valam raised the goblet above his head in salute, and then drank from it until it was empty. A cheer went up, and then everyone likewise honored the toast, Vilmos included, though he did not drink wine. Xith had warned him that he shouldn't and for good reason, because it was customary for each of the honored guests to likewise make a toast. Cheers followed every toast, empty wine bottles were hurled against the walls and attendants hurried about the room with new bottles.

When it came time for Vilmos to make a toast, he was so nervous that all he could manage to say was, "To Great Kingdom," and still the crowd cheered.

The last toast made, the cheers faded. Prince Valam stood. He raised his hand, signaling that it was time to eat. A cheer went up from the crowd and attendants hurried heavily laden plates to the tables. Keeper Q'yer sat at an empty place, and they were about to start eating when a page entered the hall. Valam took the roll of parchment the boy held. After reading the message, Valam whispered something to the page then the boy hurried off.

With his eyes, Vilmos followed the departing page until the boy disappeared into an adjacent corridor. A few seconds later, the page returned. Behind him were three men. One was a burly man dressed in a captain's uniform. The other two by their attire and poise seemed to be nobility, but their hair was fair and not dark as Adrina's or Valam's.

Vilmos turned back to regard Valam. Valam was grinning.

"One last thing," Valam said. "Please welcome, King's Knight Captain Brodst and the guests he brings from Klaive. The Baron of Klaive and his son, Rudden, conveyed a supply caravan of lumber from their hardwood forests and ore for nails from their mines to Quashan'."

"Greetings, My Lord Valam," said the Baron of Klaive and his son.

"Please join us," Valam said. He clapped his hands and attendants rushed forward to seat the newcomers.

Rudden was seated directly across from Adrina, and Vilmos was absolutely positive that she would at any moment slip under the table. She seemed to notice Emel, as Vilmos did just then. Emel was clearly jealous of the tall, good-looking southerner. Emel also seemed about ready to pull the arms off the high-backed chair he sat in.

"Let us eat!" Valam exclaimed. Everyone clapped. Adrina smiled. Valam shouted again, "Let us eat!"

And the meal began.

Chapter Thirty Six

Five weeks after departing Quashan' with Xith, Vilmos found himself in the seaside town of Eragol. There the shaman and apprentice enjoyed the kindness of the fishwives and fishers, but only until Xith secured passage on the Scarlet Hawk, a merchant ship destined for Jrenn.

The journey along River Krasnyj from Eragol to Jrenn lasted two wondrous days. And it was only during the first that Vilmos hovered over a bucket. Toward sunset on the second day, the Scarlet Hawk passed through the Mouth of the World, a natural river cave that cut under the Rift Range and whose Eastern bowels provided a port safe from harsh northern winds.

Vilmos and Xith departed Jrenn with a protected caravan bound for the Free City of Solntse. For days afterward, the unchanging sun beat down upon them. Xith's skin, unnaturally weathered and dark, proved to have better tolerance for this than Vilmos' fair skin, which was now sun and wind burned.

The sound of dozens of feet and hooves crunching the stones of Great Kingdom's High Road echoed in his ears. A steady gale coming out of the mountains to the north carried the dust of the Barrens across River Krasnyj to the travelers. The handkerchief tied around Vilmos' nose and mouth did little to keep out the dirt and as he ran his hand across his cheek, the gritty film made him long for a hot bath and clean clothes.

Sunset was near, and more than anything Vilmos wanted to hear the caravan master call out the final stop of the day. The ten garrison soldiers that protected the caravan were the only ones on horseback. While two stayed at the fore of the caravan and two to the rear, the others clustered near the carriage ferrying a lady of some standing in the Kingdom. Vilmos caught glimpses of her pale face from time to time through the carriage's white lace curtains.

Vilmos was surprised when the city of Solntse came into view and even more surprised when the caravan reached the city before nightfall. As they passed under the walled city's outer gatehouse Vilmos watched the gatekeepers who stood watch, certain that at any moment they would unloose volleys from their readied crossbows. But once they were safely within the city's protective walls, Vilmos' thoughts and attention turned to the grandeur of the streets and buildings spread out before him.

Xith had to hold Vilmos by the scruff of the collar to ensure Vilmos watched where he was going and ceased gawking, gripping the collar tighter suddenly to pull Vilmos away from a brightly clad female who was beckoning for him to follow her. Xith sighed, Vilmos didn't know that this was where his journey to the destiny that awaited him would truly begin.

Several times Vilmos had to step around men who just stopped dead in their tracks in front of him. Once he bumped into one, almost causing a ruckus, which Xith had to drag him quickly away from. Finally, Xith gave Vilmos an ultimatum, which was to follow him and only do what he did or, so Xith threatened, he would leave him in the street. Vilmos took the caution seriously and did exactly as Xith asked, so Xith relinquished the firm grip on the collar.

They passed through the central portion of the city with its high, three-story structures reaching into the sky, most of which were saloons, or rest houses as Xith called them. The heavy smell of whiskey and perfume often wafted out of these buildings to assault nostrils with their pungent odor. Along with these odors came the sounds of music and laughter, singing and even brawling, coming on a wafted puff of air as patrons would pass in or out of the buildings.

Vilmos would sneak a quick glance inside as the doors swung inward or outward; the sites within often amazed him. Men drinking tall tankards of ale or slugging down small glasses of this or that, Vilmos really couldn't tell what. Women sitting on men's laps or dancing happily to the sound of a flute or harp.

A large crowd gathered off one of the side streets they passed now. Shouts and the clashing of blades filtered to Xith and Vilmos' attentive ears. His mind filled with glee, Vilmos tried to dart toward the fracas. He would have made it cleanly away too, had Xith not snatched at his collar, latching onto a clump of hair instead. With a shriek, Vilmos stopped.

"Don't stray," stated Xith. "Perhaps tomorrow we can return."

"Tomorrow they will all be gone. The square will be empty. I've never seen a real brawl." Vilmos looked dejected. His eyes grew sullen.

"I assure you tomorrow they will be in that same courtyard from sunup until sunset. That is not a brawl."

"But…" began Vilmos.

"Quiet!" intoned Xith.

The avenues they strolled along gradually grew narrower and the saloons and shops became dingier and dirtier. Xith took on a slower, more aware gait as a feeling of unease filled his mind. Vilmos noticed this and instead of peering into the places he passed, he clung close to Xith and watched his surroundings with wide, wary eyes. Unconsciously he clinched his fists to the ready, not that he really knew how to use them, just that he felt more secure.

Xith stopped in front of a large, squat-looking inn and motioned Vilmos to follow him inside. Vilmos cast his eyes up and down the building's rough outer face, looking hard at the shattered windows and the dilapidated shutters; the run-down place had definitely seen better days. Xith told Vilmos it wasn't as bad on the inside and as much as Vilmos wanted to believe Xith, he couldn't.

When Vilmos stepped inside, he knew he had been right. The interior *was* in as poor a shape as the exterior. Vilmos was beginning to think that Xith liked to stay in dumps.

At least the last place they had stayed in had been somewhat pleasant inside, considered Vilmos, looking about unhappily.

"Don't worry," said Xith, "we'll just stay here long enough to get the supplies we need for the journey."

"Here?" stammered Vilmos in disbelief.

"Believe me there are worse places to stay. Besides, the rooms are actually nice."

Xith got them a room, which wasn't the greatest, but at least it was clean.

"See I told you to trust me," spoke Xith swatting Vilmos on the head. "Besides we can stay here cheaply and without drawing attention to ourselves."

"Why?" asked Vilmos, unable to resist the temptation.

In the midst of formulating a list of all the things they would need for the journey ahead—horses, ropes, saddle bags, water skins, rations—Xith didn't offer Vilmos an immediate response. Shortly afterward, he said, "Stay here, I have to attend to a few things. I'll be back."

***

Vilmos' thoughts began to wander and a cataclysm of images swam beneath closed lids. He saw the days he had spent with Xith and how dramatically his life had changed. He couldn't comprehend why this had happened to him. Everything was moving so fast, too fast. The little boy inside him was crying out to go back home to see his mother and father, but another voice within told him he could never go home, would never go home again.

With eyes unfocused and thoughts jumping to and fro, he stared blankly at a wall. Eventually this inward reflection slowed and fell

silent as he slipped into a light sleep. He awoke a short time later
when Xith returned muttering loudly to himself. Vilmos caught pieces
of what the shaman was jabbering and to him it sounded as if Xith
was having an argument with himself about money and thieves.

"What's wrong?" asked Vilmos excitedly, cueing in on thieves.

"Bloody street thievery I tell you," muttered Xith haughtily as he
abruptly stopped talking to himself.

"Prices for what?"

"Horses and a few miscellaneous things." The bags Xith was
carrying fell to the floor with a loud clank as he dropped them. He sat
down upon a bed on the opposite side of the room from Vilmos. He
pulled off his boots then and emptied their contents unceremoniously
onto the floor. Afterward, Xith lay back and closed his eyes, yawning a
heavy yawn.

Later that evening, Xith and Vilmos ventured out to the streets to
find something to eat. The streets after dark looked more ominous to
Vilmos. The people he passed, both male and female, appeared to be
in somber moods, and often were darkly clad with long flowing capes
or large collared cloaks. Flickers of light and the outlines of characters
that spoke in muffled voices loomed in the alleyways they passed.

Surprised to find the dreadful portent absent as they entered a
nearby pub, Vilmos sighed. The atmosphere of the small pub was
light and happy, and as they sat and waited for the hot gruel they had
ordered, Vilmos watched the patrons come and go. He studied the
clothes they wore and the weapons they carried; yet his main interest
was in catching pieces of what they were talking about as they passed.
All through dinner his attentions remained on a man who sat in the
corner, his back to the wall, opposite the most beautiful woman he
had ever seen.

The man, obviously a fighter of some sort, wore a roughly hewn
chain mail shirt with heavy leather underings and an odd brankened
collar around the neck. From time to time, Vilmos could see the man's
hands, which were covered in a mailed half-glove that left the thumbs

and forefingers exposed. Taking inventory of the man's weaponry as he had the others, Vilmos had seen the great sword slung crossways over the man's back, which even now he could glimpse the jeweled hilt of, and an auxiliary blade of considerably smaller size sheathed in the man's belt.

Of the woman, Vilmos could only see the long, black hair and sometimes he'd catch a glimpse of the side of her face. She had come in separately from the man and practically all eyes in the place had been cast upon her as she crossed the room, but when she had sat down with the broad-backed warrior everyone had returned to their own business, that is except Vilmos. He couldn't look away.

Cast of somber amber, the dress the woman wore was rather elegant. The dress had lace at the top that swelled around ample breasts, flowing down her arms in an open and obviously revealing fashion that had caused Vilmos to blush and avert his eyes until she had passed in front of him. She possessed no weapons, save for her infectious, cold gray eyes, which were down turned.

Vilmos watched the two as they sat still, neither uttering a word. The man from time to time would grind his teeth against the iron bit in his mouth or twist his mailed fist into the table. The woman sat there motionless, her head turned away, as if she was suspended in time. Vilmos pitied them, though he did not know exactly why.

As the pub's owner finally delivered their gruel and bread, Vilmos turned his eyes away from the couple, but as a fish to the lure, his gaze returned shortly afterward and he stared openly as he ate. He wondered what the couple's story could be and when finally he could no longer hold his tongue in check, he asked Xith about the man and woman. The only thing Xith said was that the warrior was an indentured man and the woman was of the street. Vilmos didn't think that though. He saw another story, especially in the man's eyes.

The meal finished, the drink consumed, Xith and Vilmos returned to their rented room. Vilmos was quiet for a long time, content to sit on the edge of the bed and stare at the wall. This puzzled Xith as he hadn't seen Vilmos like this before and he didn't know what could be wrong. He asked what was wrong several times, but Vilmos didn't respond.

"Are you sick?" asked Xith, "You haven't said a word since we ate. Usually you are teaming with a hundred different questions. *Forget* about the man and woman. We can't do anything for them."

The subtle directing of the Voice stimulated Vilmos' subconscious. Again, Xith knew of a secret yearning.

"But why?" persisted Vilmos, "What could make someone so miserable. I could see pain on both their faces."

"He is a debtor. Once caught in the cycle, it can never be broken." Knowing something else was wrong, Xith fixed Vilmos with a discerning eye. Vilmos was referring to more than what he was talking about. He was also talking about himself, though he was not fully aware of this. "Tell me what is really bothering you, Vilmos?"

Vilmos replied, "I just don't understand."

"Go on," said Xith with compassion.

Vilmos decided just to blurt out what troubled him, and so he did. "Why should I learn magic?"

"What?" exclaimed Xith taken aback, but also relieved. He hadn't expected this. He had thought this issue completely settled.

"Why should I learn magic? It is evil!"

"No," stated Xith, calming, gathering his wits, "Vilmos, you are very wrong. Magic is not evil."

"The Great Book says it destroys things and the book is what I studied all the years of my life."

"No Vilmos, you are wrong," said Xith, "The link you saw is correct: slavery is evil; selling yourself is evil; yet if you are forced into it, you are not evil. Similarly, magic can be evil if used in the wrong hands; so can all things. Money is the worst evil of all, but if used properly it can accomplish good. You learn magic for the purpose of good and not evil. I would think you would have accepted this now, particularly after Quashan'"

"Magic tears things apart, it destroys! It destroys everything!" persisted Vilmos.

"Wait, don't be so hasty in your judgment!" Xith was almost angry, he had to calm himself before he continued. "Magic is only evil if the person using it is evil. Those of weak mind are easily overcome by the greed for power, and too much power can be an evil thing. This is why you will learn to control the gifts you have been granted. This is why you must learn patience; great power in unskilled hands is useless."

Vilmos shook his head. He watched Xith, but in the back of his mind, he saw the warrior with his great blade poised and at the ready. The woman was crouched with her head tucked between her knees before him. Vilmos called to him in his mind, urging him on. The fighter raised the weapon to the ready and lunged at the dark figure, but at the last moment, he veered the blade and walked away. Vilmos shouted in a booming voice, "But he will return!"

"The dark one is a myth, a legend." Xith carefully applied the truth. "He is not real. He is real only in our imaginations. The legend was created long before the Blood Wars… Maybe he existed at one time, long, long ago. I don't know for sure, no one does, but I do know he does not exist now. Now his existence is only through lore and myth, perpetuated by those that wish to control. They are the true evil; they are what we should fear. For it is they who manipulate such things to their own ends, using it to justify all that they do."

"He is not real, you are free," Vilmos called out in his mind to the warrior whom he saw clearly again. The hulking figure shook his head, the weight of his plight evident in his slumped shoulders as he walked away. Vilmos watched as the man retreated and gradually faded from sight.

Xith continued, although Vilmos had stopped listening to the words. "During the time of the gathering they will try to destroy us to prevent the coming… Yet a few, a very select few, have used the myth for the good of all. They have turned it around. They use it to prepare us for what the future will bring and this is why we study the histories. We must learn from the past and when the time comes we must be ready."

Lost in another's dreams, thoughts trapped in the vision that played out before him, Vilmos waited.

Xith rambled on, speaking words he really should have never told to Vilmos, but for a reason unknown to him he said anyway. Vilmos half-listened but couldn't shake the images from his mind. The warrior stood, staring coldly at him with unyielding eyes. The woman did not move from where she lay crumpled on the floor. "Go, hurry now," Vilmos said, adding after a momentary pause, "but if magic is not evil, then why is it forbidden? Why do the Priests of the Dark Flame destroy magic?"

Xith collected his thoughts again, trying to hide the surprise the other's emergence had brought him. "It is to prevent the corruption the future will bring. You must learn to use your magic to its fullest. You must learn to master it before it masters you."

"What?" asked Vilmos not understanding; the vision had faded, leaving him confused.

"*Remember*," explained Xith through scrutinizing eyes, using the dominating nature of the Voice, "The fate of all the lands, including Great Kingdom and this great, great city, will one day rest in your hands. You must believe, Vilmos. Believe because you have to believe and because you want to believe. He does not exist. You must believe and remember only this. You must be ready for our journey to Under-Earth. Forget all else…"

Chapter Thirty Seven

Word of the recent battles had spread throughout Great Kingdom's farthest holdings and Kingdom supporters came from the far corners of the realm to enter the service of the garrisons. That Imtal had withstood that last desperate battle as the royal family set out for Alderan did not surprise King Andrew. He had expected nothing less from his men. That Quashan' had not fallen did not surprise King Andrew either. He had never doubted that Great Kingdom was too strong, too proud to fall into enemy hands.

"The treatise with Zashchita and Krepost' progresses well sire." The man speaking was Chancellor Volnej, a member of Great Kingdom's High Council. He looked nearly as haggard as his companion to his right, both having just returned from long journeys. "The timberlands are even greater than I ever imagined. They will yield finer masts than the Belyj, finer masts indeed!"

"Good, good," replied King Andrew obviously pleased. He shifted in his chair, and then turned fully to face the chancellor. "Another report in two weeks and no sudden changes like last time. We cannot protect the eastern tract of High Province as it stands now, and one more attack and they threaten to break away."

"High Province is Lord Serant's domain. Let him fret over it," rebuked Keeper Q'yer, a tall, thin man, young in years by most standards, whose face held a wasted appearance. He had just returned from High Province by sea, a two-week journey on the southerly run, and he was a man prone to seasickness.

"We will forgive you, keeper," countered King Andrew, who was full of terse words this day, as he had been ever since the stranger's arrival. His thoughts were taxed heavily by concerns over his youngest daughter, Princess Adrina, and the presence of more than one of the Lore Keepers at the council table put him slightly on edge. Imagine, juggling the seats on council to their satisfaction, he thought to himself. He was more than a little displeased. "Especially since we can see that you have not yet recovered your senses."

Father Francis voiced his opinions to the king and to the gathered council, "The Western Territories are our proclaimed lands. I do not see why we need cater to the whims of a group of ruffians."

King Andrew wasn't adapting well to the fact that the priesthood and the keepers had taken a sudden special interest in Kingdom affairs. He spoke his mind plainly, "The problem with you, Father Francis, is that you do not see at all, perhaps if you took a lengthy sabbatical you would recover your senses."

Father Francis blanched and shrank into his chair. He gulped for air, which he couldn't seem to find.

Coming to the aid of his fellow priest was mandatory, and Father Jacob did so only because of the obligation, "Father Francis has had a trying week, sire—"

"Haven't we all," snapped King Andrew unhappily. High Council should have been concentrating on other concerns—like the recent arrivals—and for the past several hours they had been discussing matters that the lower council should have been addressing.

"I motion to dismiss council until tomorrow," stated Keeper Martin, a hint of urgency in his voice. It had been a long morning.

"Accepted," muttered King Andrew, evident relief in his voice.

***

The soft falling of footsteps aroused Princess Adrina to conscious thoughts and she opened her eyes. She recognized the weathered, generous looking man approaching, knowing she owed him a debt she could never fully repay.

"Princess Adrina, hello, my child." Adrina no longer cringed at the mention of the hated word. Child was simply a word that expressed the way the gray-haired gentleman felt about her. "What troubles one so beautiful as you?"

"Oh, Father Jacob. I don't know," said Adrina, sounding exhausted, "I don't know what to do. I just don't know what to do…"

"Well my child, perhaps you should tell me. Mayhaps I could solve this quandary before you get wrinkles on your forehead and gray hairs to boot," chuckled Jacob.

Adrina laughed, a soft girlish laugh from the past. A moment later, she regained her composure, her newly found womanhood returned and the laughter fell away. She was confused and not confused. "Father Jacob, you always know what to say to make me smile or laugh. Thank you, but I think I have to solve this dilemma on my own."

"Really?" stated Jacob. "I don't think so. I can see another expression hidden on your face under the dark and grim one," continued Jacob.

"What would that be?" asked Adrina whimsically.

"I believe you know what it is already, my child," Father Jacob said, walking away.

Chancellor Yi had taken her aside just this morning and told her of King Andrew's wishes that she agree to the arranged marriage with Rudden Klaiveson. She didn't realize until her thoughts subsided that marriage was the very thing Father Jacob had come to talk to her about. How could he have known, she wondered, unless her father had put him up to it? A somber smile passed her lips as she thought of another who would also be forced to wed soon if her father, the king, had his way.

"King Jarom has a daughter of marrying age." Adrina had heard the chancellor whisper to her father during the previous evening's council. She hadn't heard everything said, just enough. "This would surely settle him into complacency... You must make a decision, sire... Look to the bonding of Princess Calyin and Lord Serant."

Once more, Adrina heard echoes of the only words of her father that had been audible. "There is no love between them. She has not even bore him a child yet..." Then she had heard only the chancellor's multiple replies again. "Sire, this will come in time. Surely, there must be a spark kindling... Sire, if it pleases you, I will send Volnej... Yes sire, he is reliable... At once, sire." She wondered if the chancellor ever tired of catering to her father's whims.

Adrina noticed how dark the sky had grown; the sun would be setting soon. As tomorrow promised to be a long day and she needed to retire early, she started to rise from her seat but stopped as she heard footsteps against the cobbled stones. The sound of an oaken cane striking the floor was all the announcement she needed to tell her who approached.

"Hello, Keeper," she said without turning to face Keeper Martin. A flicker of memory reminded her of the first time she had met Keeper Martin. It had been the day her mother passed away—it was odd how memories of that day returned to her now—a sorrowful day for all the Kingdom, especially for the royal family. A declaration of mourning had ensued and the entire populace had worn black the week that followed. Her mother had been well loved by all citizens of the Kingdom, earned through her own love and kindness to everyone around her.

Her mother had been so beautiful, Adrina suddenly recalled. Increasingly of late, she was reminded by others of how much she resembled her, though she didn't think so. Sometimes she could see the pain in her father's eyes when he looked at her. Adrina had grown to understand his pain very well, quickly discovering how to soothe it away, how to soothe all the troubles and cares around her away.

"Princess Adrina," repeated Keeper Martin for the third time.

"Yes?" said Adrina snapping from her reverie.

"Ahh, Your Highness, nice to have you with me," joked the keeper. He moved to take a seat opposite her. "I have been looking all over for you," he chided.

Adrina replied, "I'm sorry, Keeper Martin. You were saying that you have been looking for me. Correct?"

Keeper Martin leaned forward in the chair, watching her, ensuring he had her full attention. "Why yes, yes, I have. I understand that you have taken it upon yourself to take the outsiders before council."

Adrina told him frankly, "I have, Keeper Martin, and I will. There is a debt that I must repay."

"I know," said Keeper Martin, "but do you think this is wise? Few know the truth of the past and fewer still would be willing to help outsiders. The elves are thought to be enemies and if you go in open council and declare Seth and Galan to be elves, you will put their lives in great danger."

Adrina protested, "They were there to help save Quashan'. We couldn't have turned the tide of battle without them."

Keeper Martin eyed her closely then said, "A single deed does not undo a lifetime of teaching that points to the contrary. You must not do this thing until the time is right. Do you wish more harm to come to them?" So saying, Keeper Martin excused himself to go find Father Jacob.

She watched Keeper Martin as he went. He took a few steps, then rapped the ground mightily with his oaken cane. A flash followed and then the keeper was gone. Father Jacob had explained the process to her when Keeper Martin had performed the same feat departing in the middle of a council session, but she still didn't understand it.

"You see it is a skill acquired with greater knowledge of the world in which we live," Father Jacob had told her, "You exert your will and you wish yourself from one place to the next."

"But isn't that magic? And magic is…"

"Forbidden. Yes, it is, but that is not magic my child. Each person, each creature, that is born into this world has a force of will. Your will is the center of your being. Each is born with different amounts of will; some are strong, some weak. Will is what makes you want to survive, what makes you strong and many other things. Do you understand?"

"Kind of, maybe," she had said, "but how does it differ from magic? Do the Priests of the Flame tolerate such a thing?"

"Magic," Jacob had spit out the word with such distaste that Adrina even now recalled the expression glued momentarily to his features, "is said to be an evil thing. A truly evil thing. When one uses will they gather from the forces of nature and guide the energies through a focused center, your center being your level of will, of course. In this way, you simply channel the energies that already exist. You destroy nothing. The energy passes through you, you shape it to your needs, and when you are finished the energies are still there.

"Magic is a devouring force, it destroys. Instead of guiding the forces of will, it devours them. It draws upon the very threads of the universe. It steals the energies of creation and uses them. When a person uses magic, the energy they use is gone from our world, forever spent. It exists no longer and thus it leaves a void, an empty space, which only evil can fill. Now do you understand?"

Adrina hadn't understood, but she had claimed to.

"Princess Adrina!" screamed Father Jacob as he stood directly in front of her.

"What, what?" said Adrina dazedly, surprised to find Father Jacob standing in front of her and not the fading image of him from her daydream.

"Child, are you there?" asked Jacob sincerely. "How long have you been having these blank spells?"

"What are you doing here? I thought you left. Keeper Martin was looking for you."

Jacob offered the princess his arm. "Martin can wait. Let me escort you back to your room."

Willingly, Princess Adrina walked with Father Jacob. She was confused. She wasn't experiencing blank spells. "I know you already explained this to me once, but could you tell me one more time."

"Tell you what, child?"

"How does Keeper Martin jump from one place to the next. How does he use that cane to do it? I thought you told me that he used the power of will."

Father Jacob slowed his gait. "I think I know what you are asking, but please only one question at a time next time."

Adrina laughed and replied, "Well, how does he do it? And tell me the truth this time."

Jacob considered for a moment when the two had had such a conversation, and then it took him a while longer to recall what he had told her. He chuckled when he remembered. "Before, to be honest, I was trying to teach you a lesson. What I said about magic and will is true, very true, but I can see that you have given thought to what I said. So now you are ready to know the whole truth…"

"Well?" asked Adrina.

"The cane is an arcane device that is attuned to an instrument held at the High Council of Keepers."

Adrina exhaled. "Then it is magic?" Her eyes flashed.

"Well it is… and it isn't… to tell the truth, yet that is a story for another time."

"That's not fair," disputed Adrina.

Jacob turned the handle to Adrina's door, "Here we are. Get some rest; we can talk later."

Chapter Thirty Eight

Awaking to find himself alone and a cold breakfast on the table next to the window again didn't surprise Vilmos, the would-be apprentice was fairly confident of his master's whereabouts. The transition from bed to the little table beside the pleasant window filtering bright sunlight was made easily.

He brushed sleep from his eyes, finding no cheer in the new day or the bright sunshine. As he slowly scooped tasteless spoonfuls of thick, pasty gruel into his mouth, allowing it to slide slowly across his tongue and down his throat without chewing, he stared out the window. A blank expression was captivated on his face and for a long while, as he thought about the shaman, the city below cried out to him. It was his to explore if he dared—the whole of the largest city in all the lands, the whole of the Free City of Solntse, was his.

The early day sun shining steadily through the window brought out sudden bravery in him; no longer was he content to sit indoors and wait idly. Hurriedly, he gulped down the last of the cold gruel and slipped out of the cramped room.

The streets, though traversed by a number of early travelers, were still fairly deserted. After stepping out onto the dusty street, he veered left, moving at a half-run. He ambled around several long blocks before deciding which direction to proceed in. Passing some of the dingier establishments he recalled from the previous day, which were idle and empty, he quickened his pace, content to continue straight for a time. At the next intersection he paused, unsure whether he should turn left, right or proceed.

"Lost boy?" called out a gruff voice.

Vilmos rolled his eyes upward, taking in the tall figure in a single, gradual panning glance. "Not really."

"That's not much of a response," said the man, laughing.

Vilmos backed away warily, his eyes never straying from the sheathed, long blade at the other's side. "I have to go now."

"Wait," entreated the man, "perhaps, I can help you find the place you're looking for."

"There is a square near here," Vilmos hesitantly answered, "I must have passed it. Good day to you sir."

"Perhaps we're going to the same place. Describe the market you're looking for and maybe I can help."

Vilmos wanted to run, but didn't. "It's not a market. I'll find it, no need to worry." Vilmos ran from the outstretched hand.

"You wouldn't be looking for the competitions would you boy?" asked the tall stranger.

Vilmos' eyes lit up as if the man had just offered him a piece of candy. "Maybe," he squeaked in a small voice.

"Not too sure of anything are you? Do you have a name boy?"

Vilmos thought about the question; he didn't see any harm in answering it. "Vil… Vil… Vil-am, my name is Vilam."

"Don't worry, your secret is safe with me," said the man, grinning, as he tugged at the stubble on his chin. "I'm not supposed to be here either…"

Vilmos stepped into the street.

"If you are going to the competition, that is the wrong way. I could guide you there for a price," the man said.

"For a price?" asked Vilmos, confident he had finally discovered the man's ploy.

"For you my friend, a one time fee, good for all time. All I would ask is…" Vilmos took another step away. He had no money and he didn't know what the man would do to him if he refused the offer. "All I ask is a simple thing; you needn't be afraid of me. For you see, when I said I'm not supposed to be here either, what I was referring to…" The man switched to a low, whispering tone. "…is viewing the competition…"

The man switched back into a fuller speech. "Allow me to introduce myself. Bladesman S'tryil, a Ridesman by trade, a Bladesman out of necessity. But please don't call me by my name, as I said, I am not supposed to be here either. So, I will call you… Vilam… Is that correct?" Vilmos nodded. "You can call me, Greer. Do we have a deal?"

Vilmos nodded agreement again.

"You drive a hard bargain, Vilam. Come this way and you had better walk beside me. This is no place for a boy to be alone…" Vilmos glared at the man. "… If I were going to rob you, I would have done that a long time ago. I would not have even bothered talking to a boy. I would have just grabbed you by the ankles… just like this…"

The bladesman made a lunging motion with his right hand, reaching low and then flipping his gripped hand up. Vilmos flinched, imagining himself dangling upside down, both ankles gripped firmly in one burly hand.

"Held you upside down, until all the coinage dropped from your pockets… But you don't have anything in your pockets do you… Vilam?"

"Vilmos," corrected the boy.

"Vilmos, is it?" S'tryil offered the boy his hand to seal their pact. "Well, I shall stick with Vilam. Is that all right?"

Vilmos nodded. They continued down the block, across the next, then turned right at its end.

"Is this your first time at the competition?" S'tryil didn't wait for

Vilmos' response. "You see that long, high building there with the balcony? Good… that's City Garrison Central Post, that's where the competitions take place every year. Now if you can find that one building… for no others look like it, you're there… And look, here we are…"

Surprised, Vilmos looked away from his companion's face. The first bouts of the morning were already underway and a fair-sized crowd had already gathered. Vilmos pushed his way into the circle beside the man he would call Greer. He reminded himself of this fact.

"Here, stand in front of me, but don't take a step forward. You see that circle there… Good, don't brake it… and if someone comes lunging at you out of the circle, in the name of the Great Father, jump out of the way…"

Vilmos started again. "Who's going to attack me?" he cried.

"No one as long as you stick close. I was talking about the combatants. If they start to get too close back away, or you're liable to get a sharp blade stuck right where you don't want it." S'tryil motioned graphically with his hands again. "They've taken people away every day so far… They just don't want to move out of the way… So, mind my warning… Move, and move quick!"

"How many days does this go on?" asked Vilmos excitedly, swaying his small body to the reactions of the warrior to his right, the one he favored. Two men struggled with great battle swords, the kind Vilmos had seen yesterday.

"Weeks, until the final competitors are chosen," said S'tryil. Vilmos jumped back as the competitors battling in the circle came close. "And then those chosen will go on to train for many more weeks. There is a special grudge this year… Do you see the man seated up on the high balcony? He is Lord Geoffrey…"

"Is he dead?" exclaimed Vilmos, one of the fighters had just fallen.

The first match ended. The victor returned his great sword to the long scabbard strapped crossways upon his back, dipping the blade skillfully and quickly over his right shoulder down into the scabbard with a casual, fluid motion that made the great blade seem unencumbering. He raised both arms high over his head, waiting for the next challenger to enter the circle. The man on the balcony, the one Greer had called a lord, stood. A voice boomed out across the courtyard.

"Shalimar takes the first match. Who would challenge?"

A hush came over the crowd as the waiting began.

Vilmos pressed close to Greer and whispered, "Why is no one moving?"

"Stand still, and silent," hissed the bladesman.

Lord Geoffrey spoke again, "There is no challenger? Are there none worthy?"

"What's wrong?" asked Vilmos, "Why has the fight stopped? Is it over already? Did we miss it all?"

S'tryil snapped a hand to Vilmos' mouth. "Be still," he muttered.

"You there." A hand pointed and all eyes followed its path. "Do you take the challenge?"

S'tryil swallowed hard. "No my lord," he spoke in a gruff voice again, "I was just quieting my… m' son. Please forgive me."

All eyes turned back to the balcony as Geoffrey continued, "Then I declare, Shalimar the…"

"Hold on," cried out a man from the crowd, hastily appending, "My Lord."

The man clad initially in light mail, entered the ring, removing the heavy chain shirt as he did so. The next bout began and with its commencement, S'tryil removed the restraining hand.

"During relief, you must say nothing," chastised the bladesman, "that man there, is one of the best in the whole of the Free City. I may bout him one day, though not today."

"I am sorry," apologized Vilmos, "I didn't know. Why do you know so much about the competition? Yet you said yourself, you have never been here."

S'tryil replied, "Well that's not quite accurate, I said I'm not supposed to be here. I didn't say I've never been here."

The two combatants faced off. The winner of the first bout was clearly tired, but this did not slow down his attacks. A relentless heavy arm drove the challenger to the far side of the circle, nearly chasing him beyond the line, a disqualifying step for the challenger.

"Do you see now why no one wanted to enter the combat?" asked S'tryil.

Vilmos wavered his head, he understood.

"He will be chosen, if no others challenge him after this bout. He will join the others on the balcony..." Vilmos' eyes followed the gesturing hand up to the balcony. "I've seen him win five battles in one day; he is good, real good. Today should be his last day. Do you see the weariness in his eyes? He is fatigued. He will not last much longer, especially if there is another challenge."

Vilmos asked, "Will there be?"

"We'll have to wait..." The bladesman smiled.

"Those three..." Vilmos pointed to the men who stood behind the seated lord. "Did they go through the same... the same..." Vilmos was unsure what word to use.

"Yes, they did. Do you see the man standing in the middle? The broadest one?"

"Yes," said Vilmos quickly.

"He's the lord's son—"

"Then he was assured a spot." Vilmos cut in prematurely.

"I wish that were the case," muttered S'tryil, "I wish that were the case." After pausing momentarily to regard the sure victor in the contest, he continued. "The test of steel lasted six days for that one. A record I do believe. Many believed the same as you, and every year he teaches them the meaning of the word defeat. No, he is by far my biggest concern."

Vilmos was silent for a time. The match had ended. The one called Shalimar had won again; the challenger was carried out. Vilmos pursued no questions about the defeated man. He waited quietly, eyeing the dark, vaguely red stain that marred the hard dirt only a few steps away.

A new challenge never came. Vilmos saw glee in the jaded face that marched from the courtyard.

A ruckus erupted from the crowd amidst shouts of applause, two men were shaking a stout, fat man and behind them another pair faced off about to brawl.

"Stand close!" shouted the bladesman.

Unsure whether to remain silent or speak again, Vilmos clung close to S'tryil. "What is wrong?" he whispered.

"This always happens; someone doesn't want to pay their marker. He'll pay or suffer the consequences. Don't worry, the contest will continue. It always does." S'tryil turned his eyes back on the vacated circle. Vilmos did likewise. "One more," whispered the bladesman, not meaning Vilmos to hear him.

"What do you mean, one more?" Vilmos asked.

"Well, let's just say the matches after next are the ones I came to see…"

Vilmos, not knowing when to desist, asked, "What is that supposed to mean?"

"Don't worry, the next combatant is very skilled. So skilled in fact that I'm confident he'll go on with the others, but that'll be days from now…" explained S'tryil. "There, you see the one stepping into the circle… He is Shchander, quick and sharp. His attack is his best skill, not very good on the defense…"

"Do you know all the fighters?" asked Vilmos, an innocent enough question.

"Quick, aren't you," retorted the bladesman, "in a way, yes I do." He was beginning to take a liking to the boy.

"If he's not very good defending, how come you think he will be the victor?"

S'tryil grinned. "You're smart aren't you? Watch the way he jabs. He'll get two to three thrusts for every one of that man's, I guarantee you. That's why he'll win. He never tires; it's amazing. The sad thing is that most of the would-be challengers know this. No, they're waiting for the next... The strongest have been holding back; they want a taste of the best, especially after his lordship's defeat in Imtal last winter... They figure he's getting old. Gray if you know what I mean. Me, I don't think so. He's been the best for a decade now, and the Father willing, I think he'll make a come back this year..."

Vilmos nodded, which was a sign for the bladesman to keep mumbling on and on. It was strange that he told a boy things that he would not tell to any other.

"Beat by a captain of the palace guard. Can you imagine the thoughts that roamed through his mind in that moment of defeat? Now if you want to see a real test, a combat to the death, there is such a test of steel..."

"I think the boy has heard enough!" boomed a voice that Vilmos instantly recognized. He knew he was in trouble, though he didn't know how much.

"I beg your pardon," remarked S'tryil, "Do you know this man, Vilam?"

Vilmos replied, "yes," at the same time Xith asked, "Vil-am?"

Vilmos thanked Greer for allowing him to stand under his protection and then, after tossing hesitant glances at the match and Greer, he hurriedly followed the angry shaman.

Shortly afterward, Xith and Vilmos hastily departed Solntse. Most of the paths they crossed on the westward ride seemed familiar to Vilmos, as if they had been along them before, or at least the area seemed familiar.

Xith paused briefly, seemingly to check the air. He eyed the sky and then stared out across the horizon from north to south. Apparently satisfied, he continued onward.

As the light of a new day gathered, the horses were allowed a brief reprieve. The area of rocky crags and jagged, peaked hills they were in was indeed familiar to Vilmos. Xith pointed out that they were still in the hill country separating the Great Kingdom from the Borderlands, and from the vantage point atop one of the jagged hills they had come to, they could see most of the unofficial boundary that the hills formed.

It was there atop the jagged hill that Vilmos heard Xith speak the words, *"Eh tera mir dolzh formus tan!"* in rapid sequence and there that Vilmos felt the tremendous raw power of the untamed lands unleashed. A moment later, he and Xith were in the icy bounds of the Between—that place between worlds where the souls of the dead lingered before they passed beyond this life, that place without dimension that a mage could use to transition between realms.

The icy cold and darkness of the Between melted away to become something else, and in this place there was no moon or stars, only boundless lines of fire cutting into the ebony of the heavens. At Vilmos' feet lay a dirt road and ahead beyond a crossroads was a forest of dark trees. The dark trees, glowing with an eerie radiance, called to Vilmos, and it was in that instant that he knew he was in Under-Earth.

Chapter Thirty Nine

Adrina entered her room and was fast asleep soon after her head touched the pillow. When she heard Isador enter and push back her curtains, it seemed she had just gone to sleep. She wondered if the old nanny was going daft and she opened her eyes only after long hesitation, astonished to find it was already morning, late into the morning by the show of the sun.

"Good morning, princess," said Isador cheerfully, though she didn't feel cheerful today. "Remember today I leave for South Province, so I'll be departing shortly." Isador really didn't want to leave so soon, but winter promised to come early and she had so much to do before then. Her house had not been occupied for some time, and it stood much as she had left it decades ago. Oh, the house had its caretaker all right, appointed by the king. In fact, many caretakers had come and gone over the years, but the house had not weathered well under the well-meaning hands. She had much to do before winter snows covered the roads. "But, not a moment before I'm sure you've eaten a good breakfast. You haven't been eating well over these last several days—"

"Days?" cut in Adrina. The last thing she remembered was Father Jacob walking her back to her room. She had just gone to bed when Isador came in, or so she thought. Troubled and trying hard to think, to remember, she recalled only blackness. "Isador's leaving?" she thought, bewildered, saying aloud, "I'm sorry, Izzy. I must have forgotten… I've been so busy."

The nickname flooded the nanny with happy memories and she smiled. "Yes, that is why you will rest a bit and eat, understand?"

"Yes," Adrina said, quickly adding, "ma'am."

"I had a long talk with Father Jacob this morning. He is concerned about you, do you know that?"

Adrina responded quietly, "Yes."

"Now stay in bed, I'll return shortly with your breakfast," chastised Isador in her motherly tone. "I'm truly sorry, Adrina, but South Province can wait no longer for my return." It wasn't the truth. The truth was that Adrina had grown up, Andrew would have no more children, and she was no longer needed.

Hearing the ring of wonder and promise in Isador's voice as she said reverently the name of her home region of South Province reminded Adrina of her older brother, Valam. Knowing that her place was in Imtal and Isador's was now elsewhere, she said nothing.

Isador quickly returned, carting a tray piled high with food smelling of delicious and mouth-watering aromas. Servants followed in the nanny's wake, fluttering about the chamber, dusting and cleaning. The tray lovingly settled precariously onto the bed, a cloth napkin tucked into the brim of the blouse, fork and knife propped into hands, left and right respectively, Adrina was allowed to eat.

"Isador, will you send Valam my love?" Adrina asked.

"Of course I will, princess. Now, please eat this."

"I can't eat all this!" exclaimed Adrina looking down at the tray.

"You will, for I will not leave till you finish!" The sincerity in Isador's voice evident, Adrina began to eat vigorously. She was hungry after all, almost ravenous. "Good, good," whispered Isador to herself as she watched Adrina eat.

The breakfast finished, Adrina sadly took Isador's hand. Isador had practically been her mother these past several years and it saddened her deeply to think of the nanny's departure, perhaps the reason she had pushed the thoughts from her mind.

Adrina helped Isador pack the remainder of her belongings and then the two walked quietly to the waiting coach. Dourly she gave the old nanny one last hug, tears in her eyes, as the bags were being loaded. She would miss Isador very much.

"Good-bye, Izzy," she sadly whispered.

"Don't worry, princess, I will keep in touch, I promise. You are old enough to take care of yourself now. You don't need me holding you back any longer. I must return to my home and settle a score with the years and you must go on to lead your own life." Adrina promised she would and with that, Isador stepped into the carriage. "I must go, princess," spoke Isador with a heavy heart, "it has been so long since I last visited my home. You are welcome to come and visit any time you like."

Neither said any more after that; there wasn't much else to say. They regarded each other for a few more moments, and then Isador signaled the driver to proceed. Adrina watched the black back of the coach pull away, carrousel wheels spinning, spinning. She was sad, but also happy. It was time for Isador to return home. Adrina waved her hand until the coach disappeared from the courtyard, still seeing those two high carrousel wheels spinning, spinning.

As Adrina turned from the courtyard, she found her father standing not far removed from where she had said her good-byes. His shoulders drawn back taut and his eyes wide, the king stood sullenly. Though he knew her work here at the palace was finished and it was time for her to return home, he too would miss Isador. Adrina smiled, embraced her father warmly, then she took his hand and mounted the long alabaster stair that flowed upward to the entrance of the central audience hall.

Father Tenuus, the palace's only in-residence priest, stood rigid at the top of the stair, his best imitation of the stone warriors that embellished the upper deck of the alabaster stair. His gaze fixed on

Adrina as she and her father passed. She had been skipping evening meals and missing his invocatory prayers, and while he wanted to talk to her about this, he remained silent and statue-like. Father and daughter parted in the hall, with Adrina returning quickly to her chambers and Andrew ambling at a sedate pace toward his chambers.

Adrina pictured her father the way she had seen him once not long ago, in his bed robe and slippers shuffling to his private audience chambers—that had been the night Keeper Martin had arrived unexpectedly, followed by Father Jacob. Her thoughts quickly became lost and tangled again as she reminisced the days that had followed.

Upon reaching her chambers, she changed from the colorful housedress she had worn into colorless riding clothes. She chased off her attendant's every attempt to assist her and though she never made it to the stables, she wandered the halls, contented. Eventually she found herself standing before a familiar door, which she quietly opened.

***

Adrina sat beside him, dabbing a wet cloth to his forehead. She heard his question, but didn't know how to answer him. She didn't know if he could understand her thoughts as she could his. She felt responsible for the attack upon Seth and Galan. She, like the others, had underestimated the fear with which kingdomers and southerners alike regarded the two.

The company had barely left Quashan' when it happened, the attack coming in the middle of the night as they made their way north. The poison in the darts that hit them was the same poison that took King Charles. That they could fight its deadly affects this long was surprising. That Seth was winning against the poison and gaining strength every day was clear.

Seth probed Adrina's mind again for the words that eluded his memory. Slowly proceeding until he formulated words using her tongue, the Kingdom tongue, then rephrasing his earlier question, he asked, *Do you know where Galan is? Does she yet live?* But even as he asked, the answer to his question came to him.

Adrina answered, "Your companion lives, but we know not for how long. It is a miracle she has lasted this long. She is very weak but she has great will to live. She must be holding onto the last ounce of her life. Father Jacob is doing all he can to save her. I am truly sorry. I pray for her and you each night."

Seth knew Adrina's words to be true, he would not let go of the last thread of Galan's life. Defying the laws of natural order and the laws of the Brotherhood, he held it firmly in his grip, and he vowed he would never let it go. He reached out with his mind to Adrina now, again in the language of her people, *You must take me to her.* This time the words came easier and he didn't stumble over each. His memory grew clearer.

"No," said Adrina rigidly, "you must rest for a while yet, then I will take you to her. You must understand…" Adrina paused and her words turned to sobs of regret, "I am sorry. We have tried everything. We didn't think you'd live. But I hoped and prayed you would, and you have…"

I have rested too long. You must take me to her! I haven't the time to explain to you why, you just must!

The words thrust upon her mind like a hammer, Adrina winced from the sudden pain. She closed her eyes for a moment in a failed attempt to fight back the sting. Weariness swam through her body, fatigue sought to carry her into sleep, sleep she wouldn't allow. "Not just yet," Adrina chided to herself. She had heard the urgency of his plea, but held firm to her conviction. "Father Jacob is with her and so are many other priests. You can see her tomorrow."

Seth's short attempt at resistance ended as he collapsed back into the bed; he had made it to a seated position and no farther. Adrina leveled a spoonful of warm soup upon him, which he promptly refused. The soup didn't look appealing to him and it smelled rather odd.

Adrina raised a sharpened finger to him and waved it. "If you don't eat you will not regain your strength!" She thought she sounded rather like Isador, and perhaps she did.

Seth was about to argue that he wasn't hungry, but he decided to the contrary. He would eat first to appease her, and then he would argue his point. The broth did, however, taste good despite its odor, different from what he was used to, yet very good.

Adrina emptied spoonful after spoonful into his mouth, satisfied to see him eat and happy he appeared to be recovering. Her thoughts wandered after she watched sleep overcome him again. The power of his voice, the voice that could reach inside her mind and touch her, brought to her wonderment.

The sun shining brightly upon the long, wide window across from her created an orange glow on the glass panes and lit up the room with a spray of golden rays. Adrina drew out a lengthy yawn; the day was growing heavy on her and for a few fleeting moments she thought of Isador, whom she sincerely missed.

A light rapping came to the door and as it opened a moment later, Adrina recognized the familiar form of Keeper Martin. Her face lit up when she saw the old keeper and the sad thoughts vanished. She recounted for him the brief conversation with Seth and the fact that he was growing stronger.

This intrigued and puzzled Martin; perhaps Seth could save his companion where they could not. He remembered a lecture in the Book that spoke of the elves and the powers they were supposed to hold. He wondered if the tale could be true; all the research he had done told him yes, but still he had his reservations.

After they had talked in depth and only after Martin had promised he would remain until she returned, Adrina took a deserved reprieve. She went back to wandering the old section of the palace and the old halls that she revered, especially those that were well removed from normal travel. After a time she found herself in the kitchen, where despite the cooks and the scullions who were in the midst of preparing the evening meal, she made herself a light snack and then ambled out to the far terrace to watch the sunset.

As she walked, she looked about dourly for Father Tenuus. She whispered to herself, "Yes, Father Tenuus, I am going to miss the evening meal."

She expected to find the balcony vacant when she reached it and was surprised to find her father there, sitting alone, no aids or pages, or even Chancellor Yi who was habitually at his side, were present. Adrina knew her father well enough to know that if he was out here, he was remembering her mother and was best left alone. Quietly she turned and walked away, so as not to disturb him. She understood the need for recalling the past from time to time—the dreams, the hopes, and loved ones' faces.

Shortly after she backtracked across the garden and circled her way up the western tower, Adrina found herself watching the sunset from one of its uppermost stonework windows. From where she was perched, she could turn and look down below to see the gazebo and her father.

The changing colors of the setting sun sinking below the horizon dazzled her eye and captivated her heart for a time, and it wasn't until the sun had faded completely from sight and darkness enshrouded her perch that she turned to look down at the little white gazebo. It was also then that she felt the presence of someone standing behind her, lurking unseen in the growing shadows.

Adrina smiled as she turned to see the outline of an armored man standing stout against the stonework of the tower wall, knowing instantly it was Emel. He motioned her to follow as he moved to the door across from her and out onto the upper bulwarks. She heard the clanging of his heavy armor and the banging of his heavy staff as it struck the broad stones of the floor in front of him as he walked. And slowly, she followed.

The stave, the symbol of the watchman, was a thickly carved piece of hard wood about five feet in length, finely sharpened at one end and blunt on the other. The watchman tapped the stick onto the resonant stone floor as he walked to let those on the opposing walls know he was still there, and when he heard the returning taps, he knew his fellows were also still present. They walked at a stately pace and when in step, built up a rhythm that circled around the four walls, always starting from the East in the morning and during the day where the sun arose, and from the West in the evening and at night where the sun set. The ritual was an old one from times past.

Adrina grabbed Emel's hand and held it for a moment. "Wait," she cautioned.

"You know I can't," Emel replied.

"But you don't have to do this anymore, you are a garrison captain," argued Adrina, not letting go.

"I can't," Emel said, pulling away. His staff rapped at the ground as he marched, partially drowning out her words. " I must earn my men's respect through diligence and attention to detail. I am not my father."

"Nor should any expect you to be," said Adrina quickly. She reached out to touch his hand. "Only for a moment," she begged, throwing her words softly to him in an attempt to lull him into listening to her.

Emel smiled and walked away. He called back to her, "Follow me and we can talk."

Adrina ran to catch up with him now, his staff pounding the floor annoyed her and caused her sentences to come out broken as she attempted to talk between each tap. "Can you... stop... that infernal... noise... for a second."

"You know I can't!" shouted Emel.

Adrina stormed away, running back to the stairs and out of sight, before Emel could respond. He had been avoiding her since the return to Imtal and that cut into her heart more than anything.

***

"I know what occurred was unwarranted and not your fault. I was a fool not to take precautions," Seth said, speaking aloud. He smiled then and returned to Adrina feelings of warmth and happiness, adding afterward, "Take me to see Brother Galan, please. She needs me."

Adrina thought it ironic that Father Jacob had been waiting for the better part of the day at Seth's bedside and Seth awoke now only minutes after Jacob had left. Father Tenuus, Keeper Martin, Chancellor Yi and many others had all been coming in and out of the room all day and it had been all Adrina could do to keep them at bay.

She thought it also ironic that a girl of her years had to keep men several times her elders away from a sick man, but that is the way it was, and although she understood their impetuousness, she did not condone it. She had chased them each away as quickly as they had returned, with one exception being Father Jacob, without whose advice and wisdom, she wouldn't have had the strength or audacity to push them away. Jacob understood well how to be tactful—and now he had just missed Seth's awakening.

Brother Seth of the Red, corrected Seth to Adrina.

"Are you always there in my mind?" whispered Adrina in her thoughts.

Not always, but I am... I am sorry if it offends you...

"It does not offend," whispered Adrina in her thoughts.

You must take me to Galan!

The sense of urgency touched Adrina. She sensed the pain and she tried to explain to Seth that the council needed to talk with him first, but he refused. The vigor with which his emotions and thoughts hit her today, surprised her. And upon reflection, she didn't think just taking him to see his companion could hurt anything. The council could wait a little longer.

"I know of councils," called out Seth, "You are right, they can wait. I must attend to more urgent matters first, then I will surely sit before your illustrious council." *You could not keep me away...*

Adrina called out to the guards posted outside the door. They came bursting into the chamber, half prepared to do battle with the mysterious stranger and half prepared to vault away if there was indeed trouble.

You see, whispered Seth to Adrina alone, *where I come from all are friends and if someone were indeed your enemy, only then would you need such men...* He had searched Adrina's mind for the correct word for the two guardsmen, but the word guard didn't really seem fitting.

"Lower your weapons!" commanded Adrina, "Brother Seth and his companion are guests. They are not under house arrest."

The guards looked first to Adrina, then to the stranger. They would have sprung from the room if she had dismissed them. "We are truly sorry, Your Highness. We meant no affront."

"Give me assistance. We will take Brother Seth to his companion in the far wing," commanded Adrina.

"But... We are under orders to see that—"

Adrina cut the guardsman off, "Under whose orders?"

"Captain Brodst himself," replied both men at the same time.

"You heed a captain's order over mine? You are indeed fools!" screamed Adrina.

"I am all right," Seth sent to her mind alone, "I need no assistance."

"Quiet!" snapped Adrina, she had directed it to the guards, but it had been perfectly timed with Seth's statement. "Guards," she commanded, "to his side! Take his arms and follow..."

Really... I can walk on my own...

"Really, indeed," mocked Adrina.

The guards cast her odd glances. They were more concerned for her than the stranger, but they did as she requested.

The foursome traversed a long hall, descended a twisted stair, then ambled along another lengthy hall. They came next to the open courtyard, and here Seth asked them to pause. Momentarily captured by the beauty of the open air, the sunshine, the brightly colored flowers of the garden, and seeing the elegance of nature made Seth feel more at ease. It seemed so long since he had been this close to the earth, allowing the forces of the Mother and the touching hand of the

Father to flow more readily to prescient mind.

Release me, he thrust into the minds of the guardsmen, strength returning to his limbs.

The guards backed away warily. Again, they would have run if not for the cross look in Adrina's eye.

Galan's bedchamber was filled with a collection of clergy led by Father Jacob. They were whispering an ancient prayer, a healing prayer, one of the most powerful they could tap. The priests had gathered and were using Jacob as a focus through which their energies flowed.

So far, they had made little progress. Galan's face was still deathly pale and her heartbeat was still barely perceivable. As Seth entered the chamber, the focusing stopped, the prayer stopped, and as one the priests looked up—Seth's powerful will acted like a magnet upon their minds. A voice, captivating and melodic entered their thoughts, shocking them into bewildered frenzy. *I am very grateful for your effort, but I am afraid only I can save her.*

"No," shouted Adrina in response, "You need to save your strength!"

The chamber was absent of sound for a time. Father Jacob understood Adrina's concerns and honored her opinion. He furrowed his brow, cleared his throat several times, then repeated Adrina's words, but more tactfully, "Friend, save your strength. We will save your companion. The poison will work itself out, I promise."

Seth studied Jacob for a time before he offered a response. The man who stood before him, interested him, he had called him friend and Seth paused a moment to regard him. He could feel a sense of power in this one, power of a different sort, not of will per say, more of intellect or wisdom. And he smiled in polite form.

She is beyond your help, imparted Seth, in response to the anxiousness that flowed to him from the gathered priests. *Father Jacob would you ask your fellows to leave,* directed Seth.

"Perhaps we can do this together," responded Jacob, thinking but not saying that since they were all males it would be best to pool their healing powers. A muttered curse that ensued brought a smile to Seth's lips. Jacob had wondered if Seth would understand the absence of the priestesses and know they held no malevolence.

I understand, directed Seth into Jacob's mind, *my people too have their holy customs and, if you would honor them, I must do this alone…*

Again Jacob's expression grew wide with amazement, perhaps there was indeed more here than he understood. "Please leave us…" began Father Jacob. " Brother Seth wishes time alone with his companion." He stood a moment, staring at Seth. He would have to find Keeper Martin immediately; they must find all they could in the histories. The Great Book told little about Seth's kind, but perhaps if they delved deep enough into the ancient texts they could glean more. He also had to inform council they could call a General Assembly soon. "Lets go now… Father Tenuus, you coming?"

Father Tenuus nodded and followed Jacob from the room.

The room was empty now, save for Adrina, Seth and Galan. Adrina stepped quietly away from Seth's side, glancing at the last moment into his eyes. She stopped, reached out and touched his cheek. She was the only one who had seen the tears well up in his eyes and stream down his face, whether they were tears of joy at seeing his companion or tears of sadness she did not know. Sorrow filled her heart and, as she departed the room, tears glistened down her cheeks.

Father Jacob waited for her in the hallway and she saw him hazily through her tears. "Father Jacob?" she sobbed.

"Yes, princess," he replied.

"Do you think he can save her?"

Jacob took her hand and walked with her down the corridor, "If there is one in this world who can, I believe it is him, child. Never have I felt the will of any as strong as the one I felt when he entered the room."

The tears dried up and Adrina paused to stare out over the garden as Seth had; somehow to see bright sunshine and vibrant life made her feel better too. She kissed Jacob's hand in appreciation of his kindness, and as she did so, Jacob blushed a tiny shade of red. She knew he understood how she felt.

"He regained his strength quickly," spoke Jacob.

"This morning he awoke and ate well. By afternoon, it seemed most of his strength had returned, and now he seems to have almost fully recovered. Miraculous indeed!"

"Strong that one, I'll say. Come child, I will see that you sleep!" exclaimed Jacob dragging Adrina along behind him, "You look so very tired, you must get some rest… besides, there is nothing we can do now save pray. We must pray long and hard."

Adrina didn't attempt to refuse. She knew Jacob wouldn't have believed her and she wouldn't have been telling the truth if she had denied her exhaustion. Yet as fate would have it, the two chanced past Chancellor Yi, who was busily rushing past on his way to King Andrew's chambers. The council was awaiting the king's presence at the day's session, which he was late to again, but he was the king after all and therefore pardonable. Luckily for Adrina, Yi snatched Jacob away to the meeting and she was left on her own.

For a moment, Adrina considered Yi's face, the nose wasn't red anymore and the dark circles were gone from under the eyes. Adrina broke her stride. She had heard no sniffles as he approached or after he had passed. A touch of mirth lit her face. Imtal palace had been dead before, gnawing away at them a piece at a time, the chancellor especially, but no more.

She considered following the two to the council chambers and sitting in on the session, but quickly let the idea pass. She would rather be alone for a while and she almost walked to her room to lie down as she knew Jacob would have wanted her to do or as her body desired, but instead, she crossed back to stare silently at a closed chamber door, listening intently for any sound that might escape from within.

After hours of waiting and pacing back and forth alone, stirring her mind with frenzied thoughts, Father Jacob returned from the council meeting. He was somehow surprised and not surprised to find Adrina waiting there slumped against the wall half asleep. He muttered under his breath that he should have taken her back to her room first and then gone to the meeting, but now it was too late.

He shrugged his shoulders in a gesture to show the futility of arguing with her, and then joined her. A strong force of will emanating from within the chamber told Jacob Brother Seth was occupied in activities beyond anything he could comprehend. For many days, the priests had been changing off in the healing chant without success. It seemed they could do nothing to aid the dying one. Only today, they had decided to try the impossible, to breach the realm of their powers and combine their wills. At the time Jacob had thought it was the only solution, he was not so sure anymore.

All his thoughts of failure did not disappear so readily, however; he cursed the priestesses and their damnable rituals. An image of Jasmine, the High Priestess flashed through his mind. During the days before winter, a priestess was not to be found throughout the whole of the Kingdom. Sealed away in sanctuary, carrying out private worshipping, which although Jacob knew and understood he did not fully condone, the priestesses carried out the wishes of the Mother. His thoughts lingered on the face a moment longer, then he turned to careful, reverent prayer—the prayer he had promised before but had not had time yet to give.

Neither he nor Adrina said a word as they waited, slumped against the wall; interrupting the sanctimonious silence seemed somehow wrong. Despite the skirt she wore, Adrina sat on her haunches. The good father simply abided by pressing a weighted shoulder to the stonework of one of the hall's grand arches. Unconsciously between breaths, one or the other would pause to lend a cautious ear, hoping for a sound or a sign, anything at all to cast away the fears.

Beyond the door, inside the room, Seth sat engrossed in meticulous calculation, ensuring every detail in his mind down to the last minuscule item. Once all had left, he had raced to Galan's side and kissed her lightly on the cheek. His thoughts had run wild—the task that lay ahead, that which he must attempt, the sacrifice he must make, the denial he must send to the Father, all things he had to consider.

Oh Galan, my Galan… What have I done? He breathed in a deep breath to relax his mind and body, quickly pursuing it with another, waiting until his thoughts were absolutely clear before he delved into the long, tedious task ahead. The room, having served as a meditation chamber of sorts, would suit his purposes well. Slowly, methodically, he spread unlit candles around the bed in a full circle, chanting a prayer long forgotten, lost to all save his people; its pious message purposefully designed to begin the focusing of his will as well as to gather his thoughts. Curiously, the candles served only as symbols of faith to the Father, each representing a thing material, thus to remind the Father of times past, times of great need.

Seth's labor began with the channeling of a single thought, allowing it to occupy his consciousness. He maintained the chant fixing his will, refining it, until all else faded from his center—the last candle gently put in its place completed the circle. Seth crossed to the front of the bed and kneeled, cross-legged on the floor. Gradually he raised the level of his mental chant, reaching outward until it encompassed the entire chamber yet not beyond. The sound of his silent words of thought was so intense that if there were any others in the room of lesser will they would have been driven away.

He cast a wayward thought away from his mind and touched outward to the air around him, slowly lifting himself above the bed with a levitating force. He raised his hands, turning them palm up, fingers at first interlaced to channel the energy better. Moving each finger now, separately in an independent flicker, he touched the candles each with a different spark of energy, forcing them to light in the same instant as one. A cleansing of his inner self again allowed him to reflect his will only inward while he waited for it to build—the bright red-orange of the sun, the green, green pastures of open plains, the placid blue waters of a gentle lake and the serenity of life were his only thoughts.

The power of the world circled him and he had only to reach out to grasp its force. He could shape this will, bend it to his own desires, caress it with his touch. The will of nature, the will of the very air in which he floated, came to him and he focused it, channeling it ever so carefully within him while a pleasant calm passed over him. Suspended in time, touching its boundaries, he held the power of the world in his hands.

He called forth the wind.

A slight breeze, a warm soothing flutter, started to blow in a fine whisper across the chamber, increasing precariously in strength until it was a gale, then a gust. He touched the forces of will he held in his beckoning hands; the wind became a raging torrent of swirling force. The candles blazed, burning with such intensity as the wind gathered strength that the heat they emitted brought beads of sweat to his brow.

The peace of the earth surrounded him and took him in, and then it was time.

Seth yearned to cast his spirit to the place Galan's moribund soul was trying to flee—the moaning of wind escalated to a deafening roar. A metamorphosis settled upon the brightly burning flames, ten tiny suns sprang to life as Seth leapt beyond.

Everything stopped, deadly silent. The air was no longer warm to the touch, but cool, cool enough to drive a shiver into his heart.

Seth groped for the last unraveling strand of the diminishing life before him, not knowing if the strength within him was enough to sustain it. He felt the will of the Father. It was all around him.

The Father wanted to bring his daughter home, to end her suffering, to carry her away to a better place, but Seth was selfish and did not want to let her go. He had not held onto this, the last thread of her life, for so long to let it slip away wantonly between his fingers. He had not maintained her spirit through the long ordeal to let it fall away now when success was so near. *Two must survive,* went the whisper in his mind.

Father, I implore you! Seth cried out until he reached the very last ounce of his mighty will, *My need is great, please hear my call and listen to my words!*

His message fell as the crescent of a wave smashing against the shore in the dead of night, matching that of the land as it was rent and hopelessly twisted and his will became the soft grains of sand sucked out by the churning black waters.

Wallowing in the darkness and turmoil, Seth collapsed to the floor at the head of the bed. His journey ended.

Chapter Forty

Storm clouds that early morning had hinted of still loomed to the east, slowly progressing westward with the passing of the day, but it was not clouds that marred the sky and made the day seem drab. It was the dust, and the folded cloth wrapped around his face did little to help matters either.

The dust blew into Vilmos' eyes and made it painfully difficult to stay alert as Xith had asked, and it obscured what could have been a clear day—if you could call a blood red sky with eerie yellow clouds in the distance a clear day. Everything that grew along their path was stunted from the lack of light the eternal dust storms created. Strange blue grasses bunched up in large, thick clumps made the horses falter often. The wind carried with it the occasional tumbleweed, which in addition to the unbearable dust harassed them. Ahead in the distance, grew scattered groves of trees, which also appeared to be of the same unhealthy variety of plants as the grasses.

Progress across the windswept land was slow and it was nearly an hour before they wound their way to the first stand of trees, which as they passed through, struck Vilmos as oddities. The stunted trees had knotted trunks, thick at the base with sudden spurts of thin and thick in between their wide outreaching arches, and at the very tips of these wide outreaching boughs were sickly yellow-green leaves.

For a time, it seemed they jumped between the stunted clusters of trees, playing leapfrog with the dead land, then for a long time afterward, it seemed the dead land had swallowed them.

A large grove, formed from several smaller groves that many long years of persistent growth had matured, was ahead. In the center of this large grove was a small clearing formed from the odd felling of the largest tree, which had for a millennium served as the center piece of the grove, but now lay wasted, oddly smitten by the same elements that had spawned its growth.

"Can we stop here for a minute and catch our breaths?" asked Vilmos wearily, pulling the mask down as he did so.

"Only for a moment," replied Xith, "even though we're out of the open, it is best to be a mobile target."

"Target for what?" began Vilmos, just as several somethings dropped out of the trees around them.

Humanoid, or at least human-like, the creatures had tough, scaly, green skin, clawed hands and feet. Vilmos covered his nose with his hand as he breathed in their putrid stench. His stomach churned and it was all he could do to keep from throwing up.

Out of the corner of his eye, he saw the glimmer of white fangs flash and the next instant he smacked into the ground in pain. Xith glared at the creature perched on Vilmos' chest about to rake his head from his shoulders. A blue flame shot out from the shaman's hand, striking the creature full force, engulfing it in flames.

Vilmos tossed the screeching beast off him. It slumped to the ground and did not move again. Feeling helpless Vilmos looked worriedly to Xith, his body frozen to the ground, his mind not allowing him to move. He could only see the faces and watch. A tingling sensation surged through his arm, perhaps the letting of warm blood across cool skin.

"Come on Vilmos, snap to it!" yelled Xith as he dispatched another of the creatures. He called out with more words, but frantic howls snatched them from the air.

A creature dropped down beside Vilmos, its eyes moved to the ground where its companion lay and then it lunged. Instinctively, Vilmos threw up his shield, barely in time as the creature's claw struck the barrier and glanced off.

The raising of the shield was as the turning of a switch that brought awareness to Vilmos. He searched for Xith, only to find the shaman was gone. Three creatures circled him, watching his every move, waiting for the right instant to pounce.

In alarm, Vilmos cried out, but no answer came. He was afraid, something might have happened to Xith, though he didn't know what or how. He watched the beasts carefully as they came for him one by one, shivering increasingly with each successful reflection.

"Xith!" he shouted with all the strength of his voice. No answer again. "Xith, are you hurt?" he called out. Again, nothing.

Fear built up within him, if Xith was dead so was he. He couldn't possibly survive where Xith had failed. More of the creatures came. They surrounded him on all sides. Gradually they crept forward, their stench overwhelmed Vilmos' senses, the putrid odor of rotting flesh. "Xith couldn't be dead. He was the only real friend I ever had," thought Vilmos.

As if in response, a knifelike claw broke through his barrier and caught him in the shoulder. The pain was excruciating and filled him with anger and fear. His thoughts turned to Xith. He could feel the anguish Xith must have felt.

"For this you shall die!" rang his voice.

A flame sparked from outstretched hands, striking one of the beasts dead in the chest, and in a burst of flame the creature died. Surprised at the power that surged in him, Vilmos shouted in glee, a wicked smile touching his lips. He released the power within again and two more fell to the ground.

He whirled to face the last two. He didn't know how but he detected terror in their expressions as they started to flee. "You shall not run away from me foul creatures!" he boasted, with a loud booming voice, as flames bright and deadly sprang forth from outstretched hands.

The creatures' last sounds were agonized cries of pure pain. Vilmos almost pitied them.

As the frenzy in his mind passed, he stood shocked, simply amazed at what he had wrought for many long minutes. Tears rolled down his face and his words were drowned in sobs. He sank to the ground; he was alone. Xith was gone without a trace.

It took quite awhile, but finally Vilmos rose to his feet and wiped his tears away. The wound in his side and shoulder ached but luckily were not too deep. His thoughts returned to concerns about Xith's whereabouts. He thought perhaps the creatures had dragged the body off to feast upon the carcass and he began a search that took him well into the evening.

As night fell, exhausted, he set up camp within the grove and although he wasn't really hungry, he ate all of what little rations he had on his person. He made a bed amongst the boughs of the great fallen tree, unaware of the tiny seedling nestled within the tangles of the shattered trunk and once proud roots, nor was he aware that it was the spirit of the great tree itself that had bidden him to start the warding fire. He only knew the horses were gone, Xith was gone, and he was desperately alone in a place that was completely foreign to him.

Troubled sleep found Vilmos a short while later.

***

Instinctively, Adrina covered her ears, but it was to no avail, for she could not block thoughts from her mind. She touched her hand to Seth's and gripped it tightly, saying sternly, "Relax, Galan is fine. She is sleeping in the next bed, there…"

Across the room to the bed, Seth followed the line of her arm. He sighed upon seeing Galan's sleeping form, the Father had truly granted his wish. "How long have I slept?"

Adrina replied, "Since the day before yesterday."

"And Galan?"

"She started to recover almost immediately. She is growing stronger with each new day. She hasn't said very much and she would not leave your side."

Seth replied as he kissed her hand, "I owe you my life and among my people when one saves another's life it is theirs from then on."

"Hush, get some rest and you will be up on the 'morrow. The council wishes to speak with you then."

"What is wrong with now?" This was more of a statement than a question. Seth didn't see why he couldn't sit before it now. The power of speech didn't tax his weakened condition, he could still think and thus talk.

"Shh!" said Adrina thrusting out a restraining hand, "They will wait. Tomorrow is a better day."

Adrina soothed him until he drifted back to sleep, making him drink some broth along the course. She waited until he had passed into deep slumber before she left his side. She checked on Galan, surprised Seth's outburst hadn't awoken her.

Adrina's chambers were not far off and her aim was to steal several hours of much needed sleep. She wouldn't be allowed the luxury so soon. She only made it as far as the hall before running into Keeper Q'yer. "How could you, keeper?" demanded Adrina, knowing Keeper Q'yer's presence could mean only one thing, the council had come to the end to their patience.

"How could I what?" countered Q'yer.

"You know what I am talking about. We must wait."

"Princess, I must be frank with you, the council can wait no more. I see no reason to delay."

"Would you disturb a man on his deathbed?" demanded Adrina.

"He isn't dying," replied Keeper Q'yer, attempting to calm her.

"Does Father Jacob know you came here?" asked Adrina, further tempting the wrath of the man's office. A short time ago she wouldn't have had the nerve to put demands on a keeper, but things were different now.

"Under the circumstances, I elected to come to see the stranger. Father Jacob knows I am here." The keeper attempted to move past her. "I must know for myself."

"Couldn't it be prolonged just one extra day?" yelled Adrina after him, "I am sure by then he will be fully recovered. His companion should also be able to attend, then you can have them both."

Adrina followed Q'yer back into the room and then back into the hall. As she did so, she saw Father Jacob standing at the hall's far end—a torch in its iron bracket cast an orange glow behind him. He raised a finger to her lips, she was not to say anything about his presence; she didn't, she only continued her plea, using diplomacy where other tactics had failed. "I will go to my father if need be," she argued, using her last bargaining chip, "he will listen to reason."

The keeper eyed her. "I am afraid that will do no good. See that the strangers are ready for council by noon time tomorrow."

Adrina shouted to the departing keeper, "Their names are Seth and Galan. Brother Seth and Brother Galan... They are not strangers. They are friends."

"Don't be cross with me, I am only performing as told," yelled Keeper Q'yer back to her as he disappeared into the shadows of the hall, heading in the opposite direction from Father Jacob.

Adrina almost screamed another response to him, but a restraining hand to her lips stopped her short. Father Jacob had come up behind her and was now standing beside her. "I am sorry, Father Jacob, it is just..."

"What love will do to you," said Jacob.

"What?" said Adrina, losing her chain of thought. She laughed then.

"So which lucky, young lord is it? Your father has paraded them by all week and for the life of me, I don't know how you have the time for them and our guests. Is it Rudden Klaiveson at last?"

Adrina spoke her mind, her tongue racing, "The answer is rather simple, I don't. I send them away with such a parting that they will never return to Imtal Proper, though I always tell father I had a wonderful time with this one or that one. Rudden is the only on who keeps coming back. You wouldn't tell, would you, Father Jacob?"

Jacob smiled. "I must be going, child… so much to prepare. Good-bye."

"Wait a minute," she told him, "What about the meeting?"

"Didn't you listen to what Keeper Q'yer said, he said 'tomorrow at noon'—you won. I'll come back later. I have some more elixir for you to mix into the broth." Jacob smiled and strode off.

It wasn't until an instant later that she finally realized that Father Jacob had sent the keeper to her on purpose. She ran down the corridor after him, catching up to him just before he got safely away. Out of breath from running, she yelled, "You sent him to me, didn't you?"

Jacob replied simply, not breaking his stride, "I did."

"Why?" she demanded again.

"Don't fret so, he listened to you did he not?" replied Jacob.

"Yes," said Adrina.

"Well there you have it," said Jacob as he continued to walk away.

Chapter Forty One

"No word from South Province, sire," repeated the page, fraught with fear of possible retribution.

"What do you mean there is no word? Did you not deliver the message to Lord Valam?" returned Andrew, his voice weak and the vigor lost from his tone. It had been a long, trying day and he still had court audiences to look forward to.

"I delivered the message into the hands of his lordship, he read it, said nothing, then told me take my leave, sire, nothing else." The messenger, who had already been visibly nervous, trembled vigorously now.

"He told you to leave?"

"Yes, sire, he did, sire," insisted the page.

Andrew waved his hand to dismiss the page, but still struck with fear, the youngster didn't move. "You're dismissed," hissed Chancellor Yi, "leave before His Majesty directs his displeasure."

Chancellor Volnej gulped for air as King Andrew directed his gaze at him. He attempted to look away, setting his eyes on the retreating form of the frightened page, but this did no good.

"The report," stated Yi, putting the king's apparent will into words.

"Yes, the report," responded Chancellor Volnej, settling uneasily into his high-backed chair.

Just then, Keeper Q'yer was admitted to the council hall, and momentarily Volnej was forgotten. "Keeper Q'yer, what brings you to lower council?" asked Andrew, in his inquisitive tone, a bit of vigor returning to his tone at the expectation of good tidings.

"The two will be ready to sit before tomorrow's noon council, sire," said Keeper Q'yer.

Andrew's downtrodden eyes lifted slightly. "Good, very good." The king graciously motioned for the keeper to take a seat at the table—the invitation was more a following of etiquette than anything else; Keeper Q'yer now held a seat on the upper council and whatever was said of import in the lower council was always relayed to the upper. "Will you not stay with us, Lore Keeper?"

"I am afraid I cannot, Your Majesty, the Council of Keepers await my arrival," and with that, Keeper Q'yer departed the council chamber.

Soon afterward, Andrew turned his gaze back to the Chancellor Volnej.

"Sire," began Volnej, "I am afraid the news is not entirely what we had hoped for. They are savages sire, savages all." One of the council members cleared her throat. "Sorry, I know of your place of birth, but you know the point I was attempting to make."

"I know what you were implying," she replied.

"Proceed, chancellor." The voice was that of Yi. He knew how to keep the council session flowing, one of the reasons he was Andrew's primary adviser.

"Grant me two more weeks, sire. I can work miracles in two weeks," the words said, Chancellor Volnej gulped air again.

"So be it," said King Andrew, "Two weeks, no more. We have faith in you, chancellor, do not make us lose it."

With those words, a motion was made to dismiss the council and all agreed. As Chancellor Yi watched the council members file out of the chamber, he noticed that King Andrew had not stirred out of his great chair at the far end of the room. The king's eyes heavy with fatigue and his face pushed into his upturned hand, nearly asleep. "A word with you, sire," called out the chancellor, "you still haven't been sleeping have you? What of the tonic Father Jacob worked up, did it not work?"

Heavily, Andrew wavered his head. "It is on days like this that we need your help, old friend." Yi's long face lit up at the compliment. "You provide us with strength we would not otherwise have."

"Perhaps it would be best if you returned to your chambers and rested. The audiences can wait."

"No, chancellor, they can not," disputed Andrew. "If we are not in touch with our people, then we do not deserve to be their king. How else would we touch our people and know their cares and worries?"

"That is what the councils are for," protested Yi.

"Councils know nothing of people, chancellor. Never forget that—councils know nothing of people. The people are the land and the land, the people." The sudden glow in Andrew's eyes was matched by the deeply respectful look on the chancellor's face.

"Perhaps you could only see those of the greatest import—"

"—and which would those be, chancellor, can you honestly make the distinction?"

"There is one in particular, sire," began Yi, "but I believe most of the others could wait."

"You lead intentionally, don't you?" Andrew lifted his chin from his hand as more of the weariness eased away.

"Well, I had hoped to, sire." Yi slowly approached the far end of the table where Andrew sat as he spoke. "A huntsman from High Road Garrison rode through the night to get to Imtal to have audience with you. His mount collapsed from exhaustion at the palace gates, and from what I hear he tumbled from the animal and never looked back."

"Go on," urged Andrew.

"It seems two of his sons were taken prisoner when a group of

Border Bandits ambushed a caravan."

"Taken prisoner by whom?" cut in Andrew, a note of concern in his voice.

The chancellor smiled to himself now. He had peaked Andrew's interest, hopefully he could keep it and direct it away from the audience hall, but he had to proceed carefully. By hook or by crook, he would see that the king got the rest he deserved. "By Solntse Garrison guardsmen, it seems the two sons were part of the raiding party—or so it is said. The case is exceptionally strange. The father claims they were forced into it, and he claims to be an old acquaintance of yours, though I have never before heard the name."

"The father's name?" asked King Andrew.

"Ashwar, but—"

"And the names of the sons?"

"Let me see, he surely sobbed through them enough..." Yi stopped, reflecting. "Keille and Danyel', yes that's it, Keille and Danyel'. They have already been sentenced by the Free City Council; the punishment will be dealt tomorrow and the punishment for thievery in the Free City is—"

"Death," spoke Andrew grimly, "Describe this man called Ashwar."

"Tall, broad shoulders, high cheek bones, black hair, and he wears a gray—"

"—Cape." interrupted Andrew, "Correct?"

"Yes, you are, did I miss a detail, sire, is there something I don't know?"

"No, chancellor, you were thorough as always." Andrew shifted in his chair, his eyes becoming unfocused, as if he was far away. "He was once Chief Huntsman at High Road but he is no longer there... Do we have enough time to stay the execution?"

"It could be managed, if it is your will. Surely, thieves can not be let off easily?" The chancellor sought to keep the king's attention focused.

"Tell the Huntsman Ashwar we remember the day many handfuls of summers ago when he gave aid to a foolish boy, and we remember the debt owed." Chancellor Yi furrowed his brow. He had not expected this. "Scribe a message to Geoffrey of Solntse, the first son is to serve seven years in the royal guard. See that he does not serve near the border areas. Quashan' perhaps. The second son is to be fully pardoned after sixty days at hard labor."

"Yes sire, I will see to it at once. Will you rest now?"

"Yes chancellor, rest," said Andrew, his eyes clearly showing the weight of his office.

Chancellor Yi hid his elation.

***

"She is really quite remarkable," explained Jacob, "this was the first time I really got to talk with her."

"Yes she is," answered Adrina, "who is that with her?"

"Father Francis, he is here for the council session. He just wanted to help out."

Knowing the other's nature, Adrina asked sarcastically, "More so he couldn't wait to see our guests."

Jacob smiled and nodded. The two talked for a time, turning from conversation about Seth and Galan to various other subjects, chief of which was the council meeting tomorrow. Adrina was attempting to wedge herself into a seat in the chamber and as she talked to Jacob about it, she thought of ways to convince her father. She didn't want to miss anything that went on within those walls and if she had it her way, she wouldn't.

Eventually, Father Francis joined them in the hall and entered into their conversation. Adrina didn't know much about Francis, only what she had heard from others. She hated to prejudice someone, but his reputation preceded him. He did appear to be as inquisitive as she had heard, but other than that, she couldn't confirm the things she had heard about him. He seemed rather conservative and quite knowledgeable in the histories; perhaps, surmised Adrina, this was the reason Jacob had chosen Francis to accompany him at the meetings.

The three talked at length. Father Francis was curious about every detail Adrina could give him about Seth and Galan. He pondered her every word and she marveled at his great consideration. By the time the two priests departed, she had a totally different opinion of the pious Father Francis.

Adrina? Came a whisper into her mind, the voice was pleasant and feminine. Before she realized whose voice it was, Adrina looked about the vacant hall. *Princess Adrina, are you listening?*

"Yes," responded Adrina in kind with a whisper, although it was aloud and not a thought. "Can you hear me? I thought you were sleeping."

Not really. Come into the room. The door swung eerily open at Adrina's touch. Galan had been trying to sleep, but many thoughts clouded her mind, images of all sorts, pleasant and unpleasant.

"What is your home like?" asked Adrina, a thought she had considered but until now had been afraid to ask.

Galan answered with, *It is hard to explain. I do not know what to compare it with. I have not seen your world, your...* Galan borrowed the word from Adrina's mind, *Great Kingdom is unknown to me.*

Adrina frowned. She had hoped to find out something more about them, anything at all would have helped—this frustration readily filtered to Galan. Adrina had given her and Seth so much. She wanted to repay that debt in part, a token of some sort.

"Tomorrow at noon, the council will meet," spoke Adrina, "they wish you and Seth to attend. Do you think you will be able?"

Don't worry so, Princess Adrina. This is the reason we came across the great Western Sea. We must speak before your council, it is what we were destined to do. You can prolong fate only so long, replied Galan reading Adrina's innermost concerns. She almost asked Adrina about Seth, but she could feel his presence nearby now. Thoughts of Seth made her feel happy and think of home. In her mind, she saw the Queen Mother, the palace, and the beauty of her homeland. An idea came to her then and she knew how to let Adrina see her world. *Adrina,* she began. *I have an idea… I want you to relax and open your mind to me. I want to show you something…*

Adrina didn't quite understand what Galan meant, but she did relax and eventually Galan coaxed her into opening her mind. With warm, gentle feelings, Galan stroked Adrina's mind.

A warm breeze tantalized her skin and a picture began to form before her closed lids, fuzzy at first, then clearing slowly. An enormous palace loomed upward in front of the window of her mind. She stood at its foot.

Beautiful, spiraling towers reached up into the heavens. She could reach out and touch them. An essence of peace and happiness flowed to her, and overwhelmed her. She was free and happy.

Abruptly the image blanked and the flow of emotions ebbed. "What's wrong?" Adrina asked bewildered, blinking her eyes at the seeming sudden brightness of the chamber. "What's wrong? Are you all right, you don't look so good?"

Nothing, nothing, whispered Galan through tired eyes. She was glad her simple picture had brought Adrina joy. *I must rest a bit more that's all.*

Adrina watched as Galan drifted back to sleep. Soon her own eyes became heavy. As eyelids melted into place, she followed Galan into the land of dreams. The face before her eyes was Seth's and it lay frozen in the window of her mind against a backdrop of spiraling towers.

Chapter Forty Two

Vilmos awoke in a warm, soft bed. He peered around the room warily as a knock came to the door, soft and then hard, but Vilmos did not move to answer it. After a couple more raps, Vilmos heard the rattling of something being set onto the floor, then the sound of footsteps as someone walked away. He waited cautiously for the footsteps to fall away and then he opened the door slightly. On the floor he found a tray containing a bowl of murky looking soup and a large chunk of black bread covered with some sort of jam or honey. Also on the tray was a pair of candles, with one being lit and placed into a wooden candleholder of sorts.

Vilmos eagerly picked up the tray and carried it back into the room. He placed the candlestick onto the small table next to the bed and then sat down, preparing to eat. To his delight, the soup was a wonderful combination of beef and vegetable, and the jam on the black bread was mouth watering.

As he slurped the last bit of soup from the bowl and as he placed the bowl back onto the tray, he noticed something odd—a small object, a tiny wooden figure painted white with a crown adorning its head. Vilmos thought it odd, but without really thinking about it, he placed it onto the table next to the candle.

A warm, full gut brought the yearning to sleep but the aching of his shoulder and stomach did not go away. It was then he saw the bandages over his wounds and recalled the happenings of the previous day.

Some hours later, the last rays of the setting sun filtering in through the window awoke him. He crossed to the window, pressing his face against the cool, cheerless glass, and stared out into the growing darkness. As he watched, the sun disappeared below the horizon.

Some hours later, the glimmer of a dull, yellow light brought him to the window again. As he watched out the window, a large figure carrying a lantern completed the crossing of the narrow street below and disappeared into an adjacent building. A shadow of light could be seen through the opposite windows, meandering back and forth as the figure crossed to a staircase and faded from sight again, ascending into what must have been an attic since the structure had only one apparent floor.

He mused momentarily about sneaking out of his room to check the surroundings. Deciding to do just that, he opened the door slowly. Vilmos quickly realized he was in an inn. The upstairs of the inn, Vilmos discovered, held an odd number of rooms; there were three rooms on either side of the hall that were marked one through six and another room marked seven at the far end of the hall.

One by one, Vilmos listened at each door along the sides of the hallway for sounds of occupancy. Hearing none, he checked the door handles; all the rooms were locked. The room at the end of the hall appeared similarly empty, though a faint light shone under the door. Interested, he stooped down to peek through the door's keyhole; unable to see anyone in the room, he put an ear to the door again to listen for sounds of movement.

"May I help you?" said a burly voice from behind him.

Vilmos jumped up and smacked his head on the door handle. He winced from the pain while rubbing the top of his head. "Sorry, I dropped something," he said, quickly adding as he turned around to face the speaker, "well I had better be—"

Vilmos cut his words short as he stared in horror at the abhorrence before him. The creature was well over six feet tall and so large-boned that it scarcely fit into the hall. The skin was scaly and had a yellow-green tinge.

Vilmos tried to scamper back down the hall, but he couldn't quite squeeze past the portly figure fast enough. Caught by the scruff of his shirt, he struggled to break free.

"What's the matter, never seen a troant before? I'm not going to hurt you—I don't eat people. Human meat just doesn't taste as good as it used to." The creature smiled then, its teeth glistening yellow-brown in the torchlight.

Understanding the other was joking, Vilmos fixed his face in a half smile but didn't manage a response.

"So my father was a troll and my mother a giant, big deal. It's not that unusual. I'm the one who found and brought you here."

Vilmos replied weakly, "Thank you."

"My name is Edward, but you can call me Eddie—or Ed, which is even shorter—if you like it. How come you didn't return my invitation?"

"What invitation?" Vilmos asked.

"I gave you white," replied Edward. Vilmos still didn't know what Edward was talking about. "Haven't you ever played King's Mate before?"

Vilmos thought about it for a moment and replied, "No, is it fun?"

Edward put a hefty arm around Vilmos' shoulder. "Get the king piece I gave you and I'll teach you… It is more than fun."

Vilmos hurriedly retrieved the tiny king piece from the table where he had placed it and then the two made their way to the stairs. The large arm returned to Vilmos' shoulder as they did so, and for an instant, Vilmos thought he would collapse under the tremendous weight of the great arm.

The stairs creaked and moaned under Edward's weight as the two slowly descended to the first floor. The large open room below was pleasantly lit with numerous candles hung from the ceiling in raised candelabra. On the center table in a room filled with tables and chairs, lay a large wooden board with small, hand hewn squares etched into its surface and a number of tiny wooden playing pieces strewn haplessly about.

Edward ushered Vilmos into one of the chairs and turned the board to face them properly. "So you've never played before," said Edward checking Vilmos' eyes for honesty. Vilmos shook his head. "Well, I'm going to teach you, so listen closely."

Vilmos leaned forward.

"Look carefully at the board. You will see it is seven columns wide and nine rows deep. There are… Hold on just a moment, I forgot something." Edward rose from the table, a slow and careful feat. He poured a draught from a large wooden keg, setting the frothy mug onto the counter momentarily as he tapped a second keg. The second glass full, he handed it to Vilmos. A healthy swig left thick foam around the innkeeper's lips, which when clean licked roused a smile. "Go ahead try it. I just can't play without drink—and neither should you!"

Vilmos sniffed at the liquid in the mug, it had an unpleasantly strong odor. He raised the cup to his lips and stuck his tongue in for a taste. To his surprise, the drink held a sweet, tantalizing taste, somewhat like honey. "It is good!" he exclaimed.

"Why, of course it is," expressed Edward, jovially. "Now listen closely to what I have to say… All right, now where was I… Oh, yes. The board has seven raised areas, five of which are in its center, these form an 'X'. The remaining two are in the center of the last row on each end, the king goes there."

Edward began placing the pieces onto the board, explaining each as he did so. He told Vilmos to put his king onto the board. The white king had an oversized, jeweled crown on its head and a sheathed sword in its right hand. The black king wore a dark cape with a singlet for a crown and held a scepter in its left hand. Edward placed it onto the board.

The next piece was that of a knight with a sword raised high into the air; this piece was the swordmaster, one occupied a square on either side of the king. Placed beside it on the left was a priest, and on the right a priestess and lastly onto the ends went the keepers.

Into the next row, Edward put five figures, which represented the fools. They were placed onto the board in the first, second, forth, sixth and seventh columns, leaving an empty space in front of the swordmasters, because as Edward had told Vilmos, 'The swordmasters needed extra space to maneuver around the board.'

Intrigued by the game he had seen old men labor over for long hours though they had never offered to show him how to play, Vilmos listened to every word intently. He paused only to drink as Edward did.

Finishing off his cup, Edward went to pour himself another, deciding after he had already filled it just to pull the entire keg over next to him so that it would be within arm's reach. He also filled Vilmos' half empty mug, before he sat back down.

"Drink up, Vilmos. It is good for you," said Edward laughing. "Are you ready to begin again?"

Vilmos raised the cup to his lips and smiled indicating a yes.

Edward continued, "All the pieces move differently. It is easiest to remember the moves this way… The king can only move one space at a time, but in any direction. The swordmasters may move any number of spaces, but must always be adjacent to the king. They revolve around him and rotate around his moves, moving always in direct lines. One must always be in an adjacent square touching the king, and the other may be adjacent to the king or the other swordmaster. So you see, it is fairly tricky to move those three pieces around the board, as you can only move one piece per turn. So you have to really plan your moves. Are you following me or did I lose you?"

Vilmos shrugged in response. He understood the concept

somewhat. He would wait to play the game and hope he moved correctly.

As Edward wanted to clarify this point anyway, he went through a few practice moves with the black king and his swordmasters. He moved the leftmost swordmaster forward one square, indicating that it was still adjacent to the black king, and then he moved the rightmost swordmaster diagonally two squares, it now rested before the other swordmaster. Edward indicated why this was a valid move. He then moved the king piece forward one square. He followed through a number of these simple maneuvers until it seemed Vilmos had caught on.

"The priest and priestess move diagonally," Edward said, beginning again, "in one direction only, any number of spaces on a given turn. Similarly, the keepers may move vertically or horizontally any number of spaces. The fools can only move one space at a time, either forward or backward. That's how they move... Now you must just remember this one last, very important rule. Only the king or the swordmasters may pass through the raised squares or stop on them..."

Vilmos watched as Edward pointed out the locations of the seven raised squares again.

"With one exception—if the king occupies the center raised square, any of the pieces of his color may cross the raised squares, but only for as long as he remains on that space." Edward stopped to take a heavy swig again.

"You capture the pieces according to the direction that the capturing piece moves. Except for the fool, the fool only takes pieces that are diagonal to it. That is why he is called the fool, for he is the only piece that captures other pieces the opposite way that he moves. The king cannot be captured until both his swordmasters are taken from him... So you must take both the swordmasters first in order to capture the king and win... Do you understand?"

Vilmos thought about what Edward had just stated, confused by it. In his mind, he moved the pieces around the board. He understood that part of the game, but not how to capture another person's piece. "But how can you capture the king and win if you have to take the swordmasters first?"

"Through sacrifice, Vilmos… Nothing good is gained without sacrifice," laughed Edward with a touch of irony.

All the pieces in place now, the game progressed slowly, with Edward observing the defensive while Vilmos gradually learned the intricacies of the game. Vilmos was enjoying spending the evening in Edward's company. Edward's honest, open, goodhearted spirit was exactly what he needed to fill the empty spaces of his mind and heart.

After a short period of moving the pieces back and forth, neither gaining nor losing ground, Edward switched to an offensive posture and with great precision, not losing a piece, he stripped Vilmos of his five fools. Amazed at how sudden his pieces had been captured and taken away, for he thought he had been careful, Vilmos became inspired by the strategy involved in maneuvering the pieces. Before he had been reluctant to attack, yet after Edward's wave, Vilmos was left with no other choice.

Seeking to recoup some of the losses, he ended up sacrificing away his pieces. In an amazingly short time, he was down to only three pieces, a single swordmaster, a priestess and the white king, his king. A few moves later and the game was over. Edward's boisterous laughter momentarily filled the small inn, echoing long along its halls and through its many empty chambers.

The two played late into the evening, with Vilmos losing many games. Eventually his skills and strategies improved as the evening progressed and by the evening's end, he was providing ample challenge for the astute master of the game of King's Mate.

Chapter Forty Three

Ne, ehto ne dolzh byt, ehto ne dolzh byt… Ochen dol zhdal, i sechas…

"Galan, are you listening?" asked Adrina.

Yi tozh, tak ochen dol, nu… We must start to think like Men and practice vocalized speech, in their tongue, Brother Galan.

Pochem, yi ne…

They find it very strange when we speak with our minds. Their customs are very different from our own.

Adrina tilted her head back and dipped her long hair into the water of the bathing pool. "Galan, what's wrong? Did I do something?"

I know, yet perhaps it is best if they think us different. Was Galan's last remark to Seth. She broke the link and focused on Adrina. While churning up the waters of the bathing pool, she imparted, *It is nothing. I'm a little confused that's all… Tell me more about this council of yours. What is it like?*

"The Great Council, the High Council, is made up of the ten wisest of the Kingdom. They are chosen for their skill at making decisions and positions—"

Sounds very much like our own council in the Eastern Reaches, retorted Galan, reading Adrina's thoughts before she could put them fully into words and not meaning to cut her off. The hot water seeped into her body, soothing and invigorating.

All conversation ended as the two enjoyed the bath. Galan didn't restore the link with Seth, though he thrust thoughts into her mind two more times. Remembrance of the homeland that seemed so far away came to her, allowing her to think of little else.

When they finished bathing, they found a pair of silken dresses where their discarded gowns had been, put there by the invisible hands of the attendants. The same invisible hands that busily dried the princess, then fitted one of the dresses.

I cannot wear such as this, imparted Galan.

"I have given it to you, it is yours," said Adrina.

"I am sorry," began Galan, not realizing she spoke aloud. Her speech flowed with a broken pace, but other than that, it was Kingdom tongue with Kingdom accent—borrowed from Adrina's mind. "In my homeland… one of my office can't wear such as this. My robe of office is a subdued shade of red. I am only the second, Brother Seth is the first."

You are not in your homeland, Brother Galan.

"You must take it, the tailors made it especially for you, for the council meeting. I won't let you sit before our upper council in a house robe."

Seth, we are in a private conversation… Galan clipped the link forcefully, even though she had been the one to accidentally re-establish it. She hadn't known speaking aloud would affect her thoughts thus, and she had spoken aloud unintentionally.

You're still angry about our earlier conversation. Forget it, you owe me nothing. Nothing, remember that… We shall sit before the council, and you are to do as told, threw in Seth just before the link broke.

Adrina slipped the dress around Galan's shoulders before any further objections could be offered. The fit was perfect. Cool silk against her skin sent tingles through her body. She had never before worn silk.

"It is truly beautiful," she whispered, "thank you."

***

Seth, Galan and Adrina waited in the antechamber to the council hall. Adrina assured them the wait would only be a few minutes. Counting the time as it ticked by, the two waited patiently. Seth's mind flowed fluidly in and out of conscious thought while Adrina and Galan conversed. He remembered sitting in the antechamber of another hall, far far away.

Seth, called out Galan, *What do you think?* She hadn't considered that she would be interrupting his thoughts.

I'm going to probe their thoughts, Galan. I need to know their intentions before we go in. And I need to know if their—Seth touched Adrina's mind slightly,—*King Andrew is akin to our Queen Mother.*

You shouldn't, cautioned Galan, *Adrina's thoughts are open and she won't mind the intrusion.*

Don't worry, they can't detect it, and besides, her thoughts are prejudiced, King Andrew is her father.

Despite Galan's cautioning eye, Seth reached out to those within the hall, wandering in through the eyes of a broad-shouldered, broad-backed man, seated upon a high mounted chair. He gazed out through those eyes, regarding those that were gathered before him, seeing only the faces, nothing more. He heard their voices and followed their conversation, silently joining them.

"Out with it captain, have the rumors been confirmed or not?"

"No, Keeper Martin, they have not." The captain grimaced.

"Get on with it man," demanded the black robed priest.

"Father Tenuus, please contain yourself," said King Andrew.

"You must excuse me, sire. I am not well. I think I have the chancellor's cold," replied the priest.

A raucous laughter erupted from the chamber, audible even behind the closed doors.

"Then we should proceed as planned, sire," said another priest, the white ribbons of his office decorating the dark sleeves of his robe.

"Yes, Father Jacob," spoke King Andrew, "I should think so." He turned to regard the captain then, "Send word to the garrison. Keep the patrols light but keep them steady. We do not want any more incursions. We have the bandit kings on the run and we want to keep it that way."

The captain's frown broadened as he waited for the king to finish.

"This should be a matter you handle yourself." King Andrew paused regarding Captain Brodst. "Is there something wrong? Or should we find another who is more willing."

"Sire, there is none more willing to serve than I… You have my word and my oath of honor," quickly returned the captain as his eyes darted about the room. There was a look in his eye of pain as if he had been stung. "Sire, I mean no disrespect, but—"

"But what?" demanded Andrew.

"It is nothing, sire. By your leave, sire," said the captain excusing himself.

Silence followed for a moment, a set of doors opened, and then there was a pause. Seth saw a long, unhappy face stare back at the king from the doorway. The eyes were not quite angry, rather, openly displeased and the frown quickly shifted to a scowl.

The captain looked away then. His footsteps echoed across the chamber once more and the doors were closed behind him.

"Father Tenuus?" said King Andrew. "You know what to do. Correct?"

"Yes, sire," said the priest.

"Good, very good," mused Andrew. "And father, ensure that the poor captain doesn't discover our little ploy. The celebrations will commence on the Seventh day and carry forward to the next. Imtal has not forgotten the deed."

"Yes, sire," replied Father Tenuus smiling slyly. He regarded the king then and in his eyes, Seth saw admiration/adulation.

"Ensure the captain has an enjoyable time, but have Swordmaster Timmer keep a close eye on him. We want him fit. Remember, no swordplay other than the trials. And Chancellor Yi?" The chancellor turned to regard the king. "What of your sources in the Free City? What do they tell you?"

Chancellor Yi looked about the chamber, seemingly hesitant to speak.

"Out with it, what is the lay of it? Is it the same as we thought or not?" demanded King Andrew.

"Yes, sire, I believe it is," admitted Yi, a hint of submission in his voice.

"Good, send something special to our mutual benefactor in Solntse."

"I will at once, sire," replied the venerable chancellor. "Is this the end of the previous business? Are we then on to those waiting?"

King Andrew nodded, sitting straighter in his chair as he looked about the room.

Suddenly the antechamber doors sprang open. Seth's mind jumped for an instant back to the High Council of the Eastern Reaches. *I know what I must do Queen Mother*, he whispered, rising to his feat.

After his announcement into the hall, Seth said in the polite form of his people, "I am Brother Seth of the humble order of the Red."

"I am Brother Galan, also of the order of the Red," added Galan.

Both spoke aloud.

"Welcome unto the High Council of the Great Kingdom, please be seated," spoke Chancellor Yi. Father Jacob graciously indicated the two seats they were to occupy at one end of a long, triangular-shaped table.

Seth drank in the influence the hall held over the mind in one glance as he sat down. The high-vaulted ceiling, graciously accented by each cutting rib with its intricate tierceron design. The table massed in the direct center of the hall, following each diagonal cross-section of the vaulting above with three carefully placed groups of five chairs per side. And the enormous oaken pews leading out to the wings in three concentric rows. All lending a circular effect to the triangular countenance of the great hall. He thought the chamber a wise choice.

A group of gray-haired, stately looking men sat in two groups of five on either side of the table across from them. Directly behind them at the pivotal point on a plain, wooden throne sat a stone-faced man, who could only be King Andrew.

The chamber emanated a subtle power all its own. Perhaps it was the gathered knowledge of the men who sat within it or perhaps it was due to the design, Seth couldn't tell which, although both seemed very real possibilities to him and here, he felt at home. The hall reminded him of a different place that was so far away he could scarcely recall its beauty; that place too, held a far-reaching power.

Keeper Martin spoke first. As head of the Keepers of the Lore, he spoke the words best that King Andrew wished expressed. "Brother Seth, we of the council of ten have many questions about you and your people, as we are sure you have of ours. The first question we must direct to you pertains to the purpose of your journey. What has brought you on such an obviously costly endeavor to our lands? And why now?"

"I would gladly answer all your questions," said Seth closing his eyes, breathing in the profound air around him before he began again. "Our lands are under siege by an evil that is centuries old. If not defeated, this evil will spread to your lands. It will kill and enslave your kind as well as my own until it dominates the world, for this is its goal. Even as I speak armies gather, the war begins and such a war there hasn't been in generations of your kind."

"Why have you waited until now to return to our lands, only in time of need? Why did you not tell this to those who found you?"

Seth turned to the man, whom he had never seen before, who had blurted out the previous statement. He reached out with his hand and pointed a sinewy finger. "Chancellor," directed Seth. "As a member of the High Council, you know why we left your lands and why we haven't returned. Your kind drove us away… in the Race Wars all was destroyed."

Wide-eyed, the old chancellor sat back, leaning away from Seth's outstretched hand. He did not make further comment. Keeper Martin quickly stepped in again, saying wisely and simply, "Brother Seth, we understand."

"We are in a time where peace is almost at hand after many long years at war with the bandit kings and the near collapse of the Kingdom Alliance," said Andrew, regarding Seth closely. The silver of the elf's skin and the odd color of the eyes called to him.

Deliberately, Seth switched from talking aloud to speaking with his mind. A whisper of his thoughts met each person sitting around the table, touching King Andrew last. Then he spoke aloud with purpose, "I waited for this moment when I could sit before your council and address it as an equal. I wanted to know the thoughts in your minds, your concerns and most importantly your reactions. This is why I have waited. These words were meant for me to impart, not from a sick bed, and not to a ... lackey." *Lackey, wonder how that would translate?* He liked the word, having just borrowed it from one of the council members. He switched then to thought, sending words and emotions, *But standing before you. War will come to your door and when it does it will be too late. You must act now! Our kind needs your support, do not wait until it is too late.*

Directing his words to Andrew and the others he could see that they were confused. Father Jacob jumped into the conversation. "Do not be alarmed, as I have told you, Seth and Galan are telepathic, they can speak with their minds."

Brother Seth speaks the truth. Please, you must help us, the voice that touched their thoughts was Galan's sweet melody coated with urgency and desperation.

"Brother Seth, when you speak of support, what type of support do you mean?" A very direct question made by Chancellor Yi, who until now had been quietly listening.

Seth regarded the chancellor and answered openly. "Ships, men, supplies; all you can give to us."

The tide of the conversation flowed heavily back and forth, growing heated at times, stopping at other times. Seth carried on the debate with Galan acting as his support, going on long into the afternoon, with the council considering each point and counter-point carefully. As the meeting closed, Andrew bade them to return to the antechamber while the council deliberated.

***

As the two returned to the antechamber, Adrina asked them how things went without considering that things could go awry. Seth had read the minds of the men in the room as he had spoken with them, still he couldn't tell if they supported him, for the most part they seemed undecided.

Just like these Men, he imparted to Galan, it was almost a curse. *They lied, Brother Galan, they lied. The Kingdom is hardly returning to a state of peace... They fear their neighbor's every action. They greeted us with this same fear.*

Galan touched her hand to Seth's shoulder to reassure him, whispering into his mind alone, *We have done our best, they will listen. Do not worry. It is fated...*

Adrina, unable to hear their private thoughts, asked, "Do you want me to send for refreshments?" She was trying—in the only way she knew how—to be helpful.

Princess Adrina, we do not want any refreshments, shot back Seth, his thoughts angry.

He didn't mean that, Adrina. Did you Seth? Galan directed the thoughts now, *Seth, how could you? She did not deserve that. She is not the one you are angry with. Are we so far away from our beloved homeland that the Queen Mother's love cannot find and fill our hearts?*

Seth was worried. He had perceived the many turnings in the conversation. The decision could go either way and waiting helped nothing, it only further instilled his doubts.

Pretending she had not heard Seth's remark, Adrina tried again to spark up a conversation. Galan tried to join in light conversation at first, but after a time she too became quiet.

The hours drifted by, each falling into the next with slow persistence.

As her unease grew, Adrina had to restrain herself. She wanted to burst through the double doors into the chamber. The antechamber doors had been open before. She had heard most of the discussion. She didn't understand the need to delay or why they were deliberating. And she understood Seth's bitterness. She had been so driven once.

Determined to break the silence, she did so, directing a question to Galan, asking her if she was hungry. Galan admitted she was, as did Seth after Galan prodded him. Adrina found a servant and sent him to the kitchen to bring a light meal.

The servant had just returned with a small feast, when the great doors opened and both Seth and Galan were beckoned to come back to the triangular council table. Even before he sat, Seth read the thoughts of the council members.

He knew the choice of everyone in the room. He could only sit and listen to the resolution as Chancellor Yi spoke it.

"Brother Seth, in a determination such as this there can be no disharmony, thus we held up the council until the decision was entirely unanimous," he paused then for effect and Seth knew this. "We understand the hardship of your journey and regret the decision, but it is our decision that we can not support you in your endeavor. The meeting is concluded."

Chapter Forty Four

Two days came and went with Vilmos spending the majority of his time on opposite sides of a playing board from Edward. Although the break was enjoyable, Vilmos was growing increasingly anxious for Xith's return as the third day ended.

The inn was an unusually empty place with Edward and Vilmos being the sole occupants. In the three days not a single visitor or traveler had arrived. Vilmos would often glance out the window when he heard a noise, hoping it was Xith. Usually it was just the wind rattling the shutters. Edward had noticed this and often told Vilmos not to worry, and that his friend would find him soon enough. Vilmos fretted nonetheless.

Vilmos and Edward were in the midst of yet another game of King's Mate. So far, Vilmos had lost three of his fools and his keeper. Edward had not lost a single piece. Vilmos did, however, have his king in the center raised square, which meant for a time he controlled the board.

Cleverly, Vilmos swung his second swordmaster onto an adjacent raised square; now it could not be taken. Edward thought long and hard for his next move and only after careful calculation did he move his priestess diagonally forward to endanger Vilmos' first swordmaster. Vilmos rotated the piece around to take one of

Edward's fools, which left Vilmos in a sweet position to take either one of Edward's keepers or swordmasters the next turn. As Edward could not counter the move, he sought to gain by the loss. He moved his swordmaster into a vicarious position, hoping Vilmos would claim the keeper.

Vilmos studied the board prudently. The keeper was an easy piece to take, but the bold move was to take nothing and move his priest adjacent to Edward's king and swordmaster. Vilmos could not take the king while the swordmasters remained; he would wait until Edward tried to claim it. The piece was backed up by his own keeper, which in turn was further supported by the swordmaster, which could swing one space farther to the left if necessary. The latter play was tight and tricky but Vilmos attempted it.

Edward smiled at the move, which he considered amateurish, quickly devouring the boy's swordmaster with his priestess. A broad smirk was evident on his face, until in a series of quick and calculated maneuvers, Vilmos stripped four of Edward's pieces, the first priestess with which Edward had taken his swordmaster, the swordmaster which had been backed by the priestess, the keeper Edward could do nothing to protect, and lastly Edward's only remaining swordmaster. Now Edward's king was without protection.

Edward could do nothing to prevent Vilmos from taking the pieces, only sit back and watch with amazement. Wide eyes and a dropped mouth replaced the smile on his face. Edward couldn't maneuver his king out of the trap Vilmos had set; in another move it was check, and in one more, the game was over.

"Wow!" exclaimed Edward, "Where were you hiding those moves?"

Vilmos held the black king in his hand. The ebony from which it was carved was cold and though the piece itself was smooth, Vilmos felt as if the carved edges could slice into his fingers. "I just did as you said. I sacrificed the priest to gain the king."

"Vilmos," stated Edward, his face drawn and straight, "do you know in all the years I have been playing, that I have never been defeated. I have never lost until just now."

"You are the one who taught me, my friend," spoke Vilmos sounding wiser than his years. He held out the black king to Edward.

Edward took the king and started setting the rest of his pieces in their starting positions. "One more game and then we'll call it a night. Okay?"

Vilmos nodded agreement without hesitation and began setting his pieces in place.

Edward led with the first move. The game progressed from there with painstaking sluggishness.

Edward meticulously poured over every option with each movement of a piece, thinking several plays ahead. There was visible strain in the air around the quiet table as the hours passed.

Vilmos stretched out his arms and shifted frequently in his chair. His backside was getting very sore and numb from the long duration they had been sitting around the table. His weariness began to distract his attention away from the game, but he would not yield.

In the first hours of the game, not a piece had been taken or exchanged; the field was maintaining a careful balance of offensive and defensive postures. With movements in a seesaw motion back and forth, up and down the board, each probed the other's intentions.

Outside the windows of the inn, the gentle light of morning was forming on the horizon, though neither noticed. Nor did they take note of it when the darkness of night became void to the bright sunshine of a new day. The game continued, unabated.

Edward wiped a dew-like perspiration from his brow without taking his eyes from the board or moving his other hand, which rested on his king. Vilmos had forced him into a retreat. He cursed under his breath as he pulled his king from the center square.

Waiting for Vilmos to make his next move, Edward closely watched the board, estimating which pieces Vilmos would move where and how he could counter. When Vilmos made the move

Edward had surmised he would, another offensive push toward center, Edward was ready for the counter, but before yielding he checked the alternatives.

A smile formed on Vilmos' lips when he saw the move. Suddenly weariness and fatigue were replaced by a sense of elation, which he hoped was not false hope. Vilmos set in with a precise attack that he had been saving to throw at Edward.

The intensity of the game heated up as Vilmos claimed his stake on Edward's pieces. Vilmos pulled piece after precious piece from the board with Edward claiming one occasionally. Clearly on the run, Edward pulled his pieces back to defensive positions to prevent the capture of his king.

The wind outside picked up, though neither noticed; their attention was lost to the board, each carefully deducing the next move, the next counter. Vilmos was ready to make a claim for victory; soon he would push Edward into a corner he could not escape from. He grinned again and then purposefully stalled as he sipped from a near empty glass.

Slowly, he brought his hand to the board, perhaps toying with the expectant expression on Edward's face. He would move the white priestess diagonally up the board to put the black king in check once more. Vilmos eyed the dark king outfitted in a long ruffled cloak, holding a scepter in its left hand and the odd singlet crown upon its head, as he slowly brought the priestess across the board. He was lifting his fingers from the board and Edward was contemplating his next move when the wind outside surged and in a sudden sweeping crash, the windows of the inn were dashed to pieces.

Tattered shards still clattered to the floor as a voice rang out, a savage, eerie voice that slurred the words together into a fervent snarl. "Remain seated, or you'll both die!"

With a troubled expression on his face, Edward looked up from the board, perhaps angry at the disturbance. "Can you not see, we are in the middle of a game?" shouted Edward.

Three hair-covered beasts stood inside the inn, one at the door, the speaker, with a henchman to either side of him. Edward glared at the speaker, which he assumed was the leader. Each was heavily armored in the typical banded mail of their kind, with weapons at the ready.

Edward knew their kind well. He had seen them many times before, though he had never been a victim of their assault. They were the paid hunters of Under-Earth; the half-animal, half-human race disgusted him. He watched the leader for an instant, watching it closely, saliva dripped from its two upturned canine fangs as it licked its hair-covered face.

"What is it you seek?" asked Edward diplomatically as he stood, trying both to gain time to think and to place the oddly familiar voice.

"We wish no harm. We seek out the boy. Give him to us," hissed the beast through its hound-like mouth, saliva, dripping with each word, slapped the floor with a splash in a small pool readily forming at the beast's feet.

Edward hesitated a moment, carefully edging toward the group as he spoke, placing himself between them and Vilmos. "As I stated, you are disturbing our game. I have nothing against the Hunter Clan, nor does my companion." He stalled for more time.

Vilmos' thoughts spun, the Hunter Clan.

"Just do as ordered!" shouted the beast leader as he pointed his double-edged blade towards Edward.

"Can we not discuss this? I am sure we can come to an agreeable solution," said Edward, as he gripped the chair beside him tightly with his right hand, eyeing closely the two crossbows directed toward him. "Surely, you can lower your weapons. A mere boy and a fat troant can't hurt you…"

"Enough words, you die!" screamed the beast. "Kill!" he told his accomplices.

Edward belted the closest beast to him with the chair, knocking it to the ground; its arrow triggered, flew harmlessly into the ceiling. The other beast shot Edward cleanly in the leg with its crossbow bolt.

"Run, Vilmos run!" Edward shouted as he toppled the table over on its side.

Reacting to Edward's advice, Vilmos started toward the stairs. Luckily he shifted his gait slightly to the right and a quiver whizzed harmlessly by his head. Safely to the stairs, Vilmos stopped and peered over the rail at Edward. Only then did he consider the repercussions of his actions. How could he just leave Edward standing there? He had to do something to help, but what?

"Freeze!" shouted the beast, "Do not move further!"

"Run, Vilmos! Don't look back, go find the shaman!" shouted Edward.

Vilmos heard the desperation in Edward's voice; still he did not want to go, but he was scared, so he ran.

Edward launched toward the attackers. He had only taken one step forward toward the door when a bolt pierced his chest. The pain was immediate and excruciating, but Edward only winced slightly. He had been in worse places before and survived. He had given the shaman his sacred word he would watch over and protect Vilmos until he returned. Determination carried him another step.

"Up!" shouted the beast leader, as he dispensed his sword at the henchman sprawled out on the floor. The beast immediately scrambled to its feet and picked up its weapon. The second beast licked its furry mouth and reloaded its crossbow with another bolt. "You're finished. Quit while ahead and life in your veins," snarled the leader.

The pain was great, but it did not stop Edward. He shook a defiant fist at the attackers and took another step. His wounded leg was slow to respond to his wishes, as the first volley had cleanly pierced his leg at the knee, so rather than a step, it was an awkward limp.

He reached out and snapped a leg off one of the chairs that were littered around the inside of the inn. He bore it disobediently before him as a club and moved closer.

Two more quivers pierced Edward's body as he took another step. He slumped harshly and suddenly to the floor, his eyes wandered to the stairs that Vilmos had just topped. As he watched the boy disappear down the hall, life drained from his limbs. Then Edward died.

Chapter Forty Five

Seth had quietly listened to the words he knew the chancellor must speak, allowing his anger to burn until he could no longer control it. He hurled a wave of his will through the minds of the assembly that forced tears to their eyes. His anger was non-selective, so even Adrina, seated in the antechamber, felt its wrath upon her. Somehow she didn't succumb to its pressure, she understood it.

Seth, win through diplomacy, cried out Galan to Seth's mind alone, *use your knowledge. Hope is not lost.*

Gradually, Seth relinquished the power of his will, immediately searching for the ones he knew could comprehend what was at hand. His search settled first on Keeper Martin and he directed harsh words into the keeper's mind, playing upon the keeper's knowledge of Lore and the wisdom found within. Afterward Seth made an instinctive attack on Father Jacob. He knew Jacob understood the ways of the Mother and the Father.

Although some held mixed feelings both in support and against, Seth's quest ended there. He could find no others who truly supported his cause. *The decision was not a unanimous one. Some were coaxed into swaying the other direction,* directed Seth to Chancellor Yi.

Chancellor Yi stood, indignation on his face. "Brother Seth, we understand the way you feel, but the decision was unanimous. I am afraid we will hold no further discussion on this matter, and please no more outbursts."

Galan held firm a restraining hand on Seth's leg as she saw his temper swell. He returned her gesture by shooting an angry thought into her mind, *Fear and anger are emotions these Men heed to most often. Let them see anger and let them know fear.*

Seth, wait, have faith, my brother, returned Galan, *Look to Adrina...*

The council grew quiet and no further words were spoken. Galan had to squeeze her nails into Seth's leg to keep his words in check. She could see his emotions flare, about to erupt again.

Chancellor Yi stood and turned to face King Andrew, "The resolution stands; I move to dismiss the council." King Andrew nodded in agreement. "The meeting is at an end."

No, Seth, no! directed Galan to Seth, but her words of restraint could not stop him now. Just as Adrina passed into the chamber from the anteroom, Seth jumped from his chair and began to lash out with a fury unequaled. The council cowered back from him, truly afraid, while those around King Andrew moved protectively, instinctively between their king and Seth.

Adrina simply stared at Seth, and he stopped. Setting her eyes next on Father Jacob, she did not say a word, the look of disillusion on her face spoke for her. Her gaze forced Jacob to stand. He knew much more than he had said, much more.

"Perhaps a review is in order, Your Majesty," Father Jacob said then, "There are some things that I have not stated, things that—"

King Andrew glared at the priest.

"Yes, sire," said Keeper Martin, "I believe Father Jacob has a point; perhaps we have been overly forthright. Our own concerns are centered on the affairs of the South. Perhaps, our view is too narrow. I would second the motion for a review tomorrow. This is a decision best not made hastily." Keeper Martin nodded graciously to Seth then took his seat. He had known Father Jacob was holding back. The two had been friends too long not to know when the other was withholding something. The question was, what was Jacob withholding? He intended to find out before the day was out.

"That is the second motion. Are there any who would object?" asked Chancellor Yi.

Tomorrow? screamed Seth excitedly, angrily.

Seth, scolded Galan, directing the thoughts to him alone, *Faith.*

"Yes, I am very tired. Tomorrow will be a better day," agreed Seth, a small show of charisma as he spoke aloud.

Adrina cast an angry glare, which was directed momentarily about the chamber, and then escorted Galan and Seth outside. With feelings of disappointment flowing through her mind, she walked alongside the two. She didn't know why the keeper hadn't told the council what he had discovered through the dream messages, or why Jacob's observations about Great Father's presence were not mentioned. She only knew they had been silent when they otherwise wouldn't have been.

"Seth, Galan," she began, "I'm sorry. Maybe I could've—"

—*No,* returned Seth, *It is the will of the Father. We will try again tomorrow and this time we won't fail. I am truly sorry about my earlier behavior; there is no excuse for it. I hope you will be gracious enough to forgive me.*

"I know what it is to be so driven," whispered Adrina to herself, forgetting that the two could read minds.

Tomorrow then, imparted Seth, a hint of sadness in his voice.

"Then you have a plan?" asked Adrina candidly.

Seth shook his head, *I will find one though, and by tomorrow.*

"Can you not show them your world? Perhaps then they will understand," said Adrina without consideration for the impact of such words—Galan had been exhausted after the momentary image gifted to a single mind.

Show them my world, repeated Seth as he reached into her mind to perceive what she was referring to. He saw the image Galan had imparted upon her and an idea was birthed. *You are truly a good luck charm, Princess Adrina,* he called out to her, throwing excitement and enthusiasm into the voice, *I think, I know now what to do, what I should have done today. What I must do.*

"Well, what is it?" asked Adrina.

Seth didn't have to admit what it was that he was thinking or even open his closed thoughts to Galan, she knew and her face took on a shocked expression. *No, you must not. We will find another way. We just have to think that is all. Promise me you won't!*

Seth didn't respond in kind. He tightened the seal on his mind, which Galan perceived as a response and begged him again to reconsider.

***

Lost in thought, Seth leaned back onto the bed and stared up at the ceiling. Galan attempted sleep, but found none. Slowly her eyes came to rest on Seth. Admiration showed in those eyes for the strength and intellect she saw there. Knowing he would find a way to change the council's opinion if anyone could, she was content.

Temporarily, she stayed an urge to go to him and comfort him in his time of need. She did want to give him something though—she owed him so much—anything that could take away the pain she knew he was feeling, especially as he faced possible failure and disgrace.

The floor was cold as she touched bare feet to its hard surface. Her heart told her to go to him, and she did.

Lost in his plight, Seth didn't notice her approach. Only a few feet from his bed, she stood, looking down at him. A small part of her told her not to go to him, yet a larger voice urged her on. She took the next step toward him carefully and deliberately, knowing what it meant. Her conscious held her no more; there could be no turning back now. The soft, silken dress she wore hung loose about her shoulders as she sought to slip out of it.

As she did so, a light summons sounded at the door, and she started. Quickly, she retied the strands she held, fixing the dress into place, moving directly to the door before Seth broke from his reverie.

At the door, begging her forgiveness for the disturbance was

Father Jacob. He seemed disappointed to find Adrina absent, having wanted to speak to the three all at once. "Brother Seth, Brother Galan," began Jacob, "I wanted to speak to you personally about earlier. There are things that you don't—"

—*Save your tired words, good father. The fault rests on no one other than myself...* Seth's message was mingled with strong anguish. *Please leave us, Father Jacob. I have much to consider.*

Father Jacob regarded Seth, seeing the determination and anguish in the elf's eyes. "But Brother Seth, I must insist."

Latching onto the priest's hand, Galan led him from the chamber. *Go*, she whispered to his mind, *we will manage.*

She watched his retreating form until it mingled with the night shadows of the corridor. *Thank you*, she sent after him.

Seth returned to his thoughts, considering and reviewing every word the council had spoken that day. He searched for where he had gone wrong and looked for a way to convince them.

Galan closed and secured the portal. For a time, she stood quietly watching Seth. She would have turned away as intended, had the impulse to comfort him not returned.

Her silken dress fell to the floor as she stepped out of it. She crossed to the side of his bed and touched delicate fingers to his hand, crouching down in bed beside him and pressing her lips against his.

With the aid of her nimble fingers, Seth undressed. A circle of heat bathed the two forms pressed tightly one against the other. Galan redirected her will now, probing with emotion absent of thought. A single finger traced her supple curves, finding reassuring softness amidst the firm and briefly, Seth returned the passion that flowed to him.

He had to reach deep within himself to find restraint to push her away. Nevertheless, he did so because he could not indulge the temptation.

I am sorry, he sent to her mind with great sadness, *I cannot. We must not.*

Is this not what you've longed for? Galan asked him, tears in her eyes. *Brother Liyan told me of your heart before we left Kapital. He told me to understand the desire in your heart, even if those feelings did not find me. Such feelings are not lost on me. Seth, I need you beside me this night.*

Chapter Forty Six

For Seth the night had been long, the waiting only subsided to be replaced by anxiety as morning arrived. Through endless hours of darkness, he had formulated a plan, pouring over it step by step in his mind, and now he could only wait to carry it out. Shadows had shrouded the chamber most of that time, although occasionally the unseen clouds would pass allowing the somber light of a few soft stars to filter in. His eyes had been drawn to her then and he had looked upon her still form beside him; regret filled his heart. He could never tell her about the wild rousing she had given to him simply by her touch and purposefully, he tucked these thoughts deep within his mind, locking them away.

The mood throughout the morning, well after breakfast, remained tense. No one could break the silence, no one wanted to. Adrina had carried Galan away to the garden, leaving Seth alone with his thoughts, and now he sat in a chair turned to an open window, a place where he could feel a cool breeze blow upon his face. Nature flowed around him and through him better with the green of life before his eyes and concentration became easier. He was soon lost in a cleansing meditation. Mind, center, soul went the whisper in his mind.

The council was gathered and in full readiness as Seth, Galan and Adrina arrived. This day there was no way Adrina would not be present; she felt she had earned the right to sit beside the two, and she did.

Several hours earlier, King Andrew, Chancellor Yi and Keeper Martin had gathered to work out a group of questions for Brother Seth to answer. Father Jacob still had said nothing, and his whereabouts at present were unknown.

The monarch understood the plight of the elven people, but he also knew the Kingdom could not withstand another war now; the timing was wrong. They were on the verge of restoring the kingdom alliance and Great Kingdom needed to rebuild the things years of war with the bandit kings had destroyed. High Province under Princess Calyin and Lord Serant were prospering and had risen to respectable levels of civility. South Province under Lord Valam's steady hand was recovering from the siege on Quashan' and the burning of Alderan. The Western Territories remained as an area of concern, but with conservatism they would succeed there as they had elsewhere. The lands the Kingdom sought to reclaim in the North would be put in jeopardy if garrison troops were withdrawn, especially since the coming winter meant the sea route would be closed by winter storms and those returning to the North must pass through the Borderland region. The Free Cities held mercenaries for hire, but even their numbers weren't that remarkable and their pay was twice the rate of a normal soldier. The balance among the southern nations was too volatile now. They had their own concerns and each would have to be enlisted separately, if at all—an endeavor that could take a very long time. No, the timing definitely was not right, but how could he explain all this to Seth. Andrew did not know.

When Father Jacob arrived, the proceedings began. Seth was not in a civil mood today. From the moment he entered the council until the very instant he left, he planned to seize their attention. As he stepped into the council chamber, he offered the customary courtesies, being as gruff as possible though not obviously so. A heavy burden of duty pulled down upon him—failure meant disgrace, a yoke around his neck that he silently shouldered.

He waited for the correct moment to seize the floor and when it was right, he grabbed it readily. Circling his voice from right to left around the room, starting sadly with Galan, he touched the minds around him. *What I am about to do may take you by surprise, but when I am finished, I am confident you will have no more doubts concerning your obligations. It is an ancient gift among my people...* He sent along with his words, a sense of longing, yearning.

To focus his will, gather it and caress it until it flowed unhindered through his center, he closed his eyes and began a silent prayer. A glowing light, soft and pure, began to enshroud his body. The rhythm of the chant reached out to all, though few understood its words. Seth launched his spirit upward, spiraling, soaring.

Please condone my act Great Father, intoned Seth quietly.

With each word, Galan felt stabbing pain in her heart. She realized what Seth was attempting, and though she could have severed the link, she did not. In that instant, she understood why Seth had refused her at first and why regardless, the pain of loss struck her. She called out with her own hopeful prayer to the Great –Father, and despite her ability to separate her feelings, she burst into tears. *You promised you wouldn't,* she imparted to Seth alone.

Fading from whole to distorted to the point where he was no longer visible, Seth's features changed and for an instant, it was as if another stood in his place. His voice followed the changing flow of his body, shifting from the eerie to the captivating, and finally to a strange echoing rasp. Slowly his facial features changed, blended and melted away. A form, beautiful and feminine, filled the place where he had stood. Abruptly, the distortion ceased and the face of a woman began to embody itself upon Seth's, the voice became enchanting, almost delicate.

I am Queen Mother of the Eastern Reaches, first to convey the will of the Mother and the Father. I have been long in waiting for this day...

Shocked into a reverent silence, no one dared to respond.

Disbelief crossed many of the faces more than once and closely pursuing doubt came wonder, which quickly became speculation. Why did a people of such might want for anything? In the face of an army with such strengths, they mere men were no match. So why were they called upon and why were they needed at all?

Yes, it is true, do not disbelieve. The crossing of the minds is an ancient gift, but also a taxing gift. Our council had discussed at length how we could prove our need to our ancient kin. We had faith in Brother Seth's resourcefulness and knew he would choose this method, for only in this way could our point be proven beyond any doubt. Do not mourn Brother Seth, he has given his spirit and his life freely to the task. His spirit will soon rest without pain.

Adrina, who was sitting to Seth's left, gasped. She could see the expression hidden on Seth's face—the face she surmised only her and Galan could see beneath the Queen Mother's visage because of their proximity to Seth. She looked to Galan and upon seeing her tears, broke into powerful sobs. The anguish with which the words had been spoken was not lost to her as it was to the others, she felt the pain and anguish inside her. It sought to numb her and sweep over her.

Queen Mother regarded those in the hall for a few moments and then said, *Join hands all to complete the link... Quickly now.*

As one, the group joined hands around the table, completing the circle and the link. Suddenly it was as if they were in a different place, seeing through another's eyes. A strange and beautiful place wrapped in white came into view. The royal palace, seen through the eyes of a roaming hawk, soaring on puffs of hot air up into the sky, zooming in through an open window, coming to rest just inside the window, was magnificent.

The hawk cried out, a high piercing, mournful cry that echoed in the ears long after it passed, then it launched from its perch, bringing with it a light breeze that trickled around the room, blowing in a downward spiral—the same downward spiral it descended with. It landed upon a high-backed chair, calling out one final time, before the vantage point changed. They saw through another's eyes now, a view from the thrown through the eyes of the Queen Mother herself. Her eyes drew up, up to the window on high, waiting until the free-spirited hawk has passed without, then returning to the calm crystalline walls about her.

What you see before you is High Council Hall of the Eastern Reaches. The Queen Mother paused, continuing in a soothing whisper, *Chambers are chosen for specific reasons...* As the queen's whispers massaged their minds, the scene focused once more. The hall at first glance seemed cluttered, designed without purpose. Carved from a single piece of solid granite, every inch covered in strange patterns, the chamber had a mysticism about it that with slow eventuality caught the eye. A round oaken table of enormous proportions rested in the center of the hall, or grew, if that were possible, for it seemed a living entity. Forms appeared around the table, seeming to float in the air, perhaps upon the light breeze that flourished pleasantly. As the seconds passed, the purpose of the design started to unfold. The patterns in the walls took on shapes and images, depicting stories, adventures, telling the history of Seth's kind, ever growing, ever changing.

Keeper Martin held his breath, as the focus returned to the table.

Designed over a thousand years ago by someone very great, a genius even among our kind, yes it is a very great place. Great structures house tremendous power, a testimony I see you also understand. Everyone in the kingdom hall could feel Queen Mother's mood grow darker and more pensive. The business at hand is unpleasant, but it must be. Sathar has returned from the Dark Journey; even now his armies gather. Thousands flock to his banner. It is truly an evil thing. Already he has overrun his neighboring provinces; soon he will march his troops into the Eastern Reaches, our homes. In time, we will fall and then he will begin the slow, ceaseless invasion of your lands and by that time, nothing will be able to stand in his way.

The hall shook as the image began to fade, not a flutter or a falter but an emotion filled tremble.

Galan gasped, even before the vision focused. A murmur ensued, growing steadily loud and disquieted. Ripping winds swam across the chamber. Hands gripped a porous crag as eyes looked down from a lofty precipice. The wind was cool, the touch of the rock cold. The mountain trembled and shook. A great mass of soldiers could be seen in the fields below, spread out like ants, tiny specks of black moving by the thousands across the face of a plain. The earth shook to the beat of their march.

Behold! The great western plain… This mountain range marks the boundary between the Eastern and Western Reaches. The army on the western plain is the army of Sathar. Soon He will overrun our mountain outposts, pouring through the passes. He will not stop until our lands are his and then—

"Queen Mother," ventured King Andrew, "it will take time and many preparations must be made before we can offer any aid. Also, the council must decide whether we will offer any aid at all. We can see your need is great, but to send our people—"

Silence! Listen Man-Child, the Queen Mother commanded. *Listen to what will happen, this will be your future! When the cursed returns from the Dark Journey, all will flock to his banner or fall. Any who oppose his total domination, any who resist, will be enslaved or killed. During the time of the Gathering the earth shall be torn asunder and thus will the Coming begin. The tormented will cry out in anguish for their blindness. For at the very end of their existence they will discover their grave error, but it will be too late, they will cease to exist and their kind will be lost from the pages of the book of Life.*

The great army swarmed over the land, coming to rest before a small castle. The viewpoint was still the same, a far off rocky precipice. The rock was cold, as was the wind.

This is what happened to those who have already tried to oppose him.

Behind the vast army came thousands more, spreading across the horizon as they marched like a destructive wave. Houses looted and burned, smoldered. Amidst endless pillars of black smoke and red flames, fields burned. Dead lay scattered about the land and the living cried out in anguish. Hands clutched bitterly the cold, cold rock, while eyes swept toward a castle that stood defiantly, resisting thunderous blows upon its walls. The hollow knocking on the walls resounded in the ears and chased their thoughts.

A valiant few protected the walls, while the swarm gathered full. The thrashing grew. Walls that had held secure fell away.

The vision allowed much more than simple sight. It was as if the group at the council table was actually there. The air about them filled with smoke from the burning houses and land, dark smoke that brought tears to eyes made breathing difficult and darkened the chamber. The anger and fear of the fleeing, the agony and pain of the dying, the putrid stench of scorched flesh, all flowed to them.

Queen Mother did not hold back a single overwhelming emotion or sensation. Terror filled their hearts and minds, growing to the point where they just wanted it to stop so the pain would end. Almost believing that when it did end, it would take them with it, and even this they would have welcomed.

Brought to the threshold of life and survival, then to the brink of what lay beyond, the Queen Mother carried them swiftly back. Latched onto only the pain, making it linger upon them as the scene dissolved. A face, a face of untainted beauty, filled their minds. One could not stare into a countenance of such magnitude, so powerful and yet so very exquisite, for very long.

Galan whispered, *Oh, my Queen Mother. May they see your wisdom clearly.*

The Queen of the Elves shouted into their minds then, *I am sorry to be harsh with you, but it is the only way to emphasize what must be done! Severity sometimes breeds expedience.*

In an avalanche of silence, the pain ended, leaving most beyond the capacity for words, even the most capricious of the group. King Andrew regretted the words he had earlier spoken and now words were beyond his grasp.

Father Jacob took the initiative, "I think I speak for the council, Your Grace." He looked at each of the council members and they each in turn nodded approval, and lastly he looked to the king, who also nodded approval.

"Your Grace," began Father Jacob as King Andrew touched his hand and with his eyes, urged the priest to sit.

King Andrew had second thoughts. He found the courage of words in his heart. "We have heard your plea and we shall heed your warning. However, you must also know, action will take time. We wish politics were a simple thing, but they are not. Others will also be skeptical. The king's word is law, but we must have the backing of the alliance. Without this backing, our kingdom would fall before our army returns. We are convinced in the sincerity of your words. You have our sacred oath, we will do everything we can to aid your cause."

I trust in your word and your honor, King Andrew. A thanks to all of you gathered in council. I am afraid I must leave you now. The link has lasted overly long. My son's spirit yearns to journey to the Father. A long pause followed, then in words which issued from Seth's own lips, came the following message, *Do not let his sacrifice be for nothing.*

Chapter Forty Seven

Vilmos found himself running down a dusty plain without knowing how he had gotten there. The last thing he remembered was running up the stairs of the inn. Nervously he glanced over his shoulder, catching glimpses of the inn and its surrounding structures as he did so.

Fortunately, it seemed no one followed. Vilmos didn't know where he could go to find safety; of this area, he only knew the inn. He could run, but to where he did not know. He must somehow find Xith, but he didn't know where to start his search. Words echoed in his thoughts, "Find the shaman, run." Vilmos ran; he was running as fast as his legs could carry him. He stopped mid-stride as he caught a glimpse of something behind the inn. His thoughts spun and he started to dash away, then stopped again. *Horses!* He wondered if he could get to them before the hunter beasts found him. The horses seemed his only chance for escape now and this thought drew him in.

Warily, Vilmos came around the back of the inn where three black stallions were tethered. He approached cautiously, looking in all direction for signs of the attackers. The first horse he approached whinnied and reared up in the air to the bounds of its tethers.

Vilmos backed away, keeping a wary distance from it and

approached a different horse, one that did not shy away from him. Afraid of discovery, he swiftly untied the horse and climbed into the saddle. Perhaps it was the fear or the rush of adrenaline that surged through his small body that carried him away, but he had ridden for nearly an hour before he realized that he had never been on a horse before without someone alongside him to help him along.

He reigned in the horse to a frenzied, puzzled halt, tossing a long, hard look behind. He shrugged his shoulders and then whipped the horse on, without giving the idea further thought.

Driven by his subconscious back to the only place he knew, the only place where he might find safety, it wasn't until much later, after Vilmos had calmed down and his heart had stopped pounding in his ears, that he started to wonder why the hunter beasts had never followed him. Images of the gnarl-faced beasts still chilled his thoughts; he wondered what had become of Edward, momentarily refusing to accept that Edward might be dead.

He thought maybe Edward had killed the strange beasts and that is why they did not chase him. Yet the look on Edward's face as he had fallen to the ground—cold, callous death had been in those eyes—but still he denied it. He also wondered if maybe the bastards followed him and were waiting for him to rest and then they would pounce on him.

The horse of the beastmen was strangely resolute and powerful, galloping along at speeds that baffled Vilmos. The animal seemed to be driven on by the desires of its rider and was able to sustain high speeds for long periods without becoming fatigued. If Vilmos' sixth sense was urging the animal along, it was also guiding the animal along the trail back to a place he knew well. Soon he found himself at the magical gate he and Xith had used what seemed so long ago, his mind spinning so rapidly that he opened and triggered the gate without a second thought.

It could have been minutes, hours or days later that he found himself near the Trollbridge, the steady steed beneath him. The world faded to black after that, until he found himself near a cave on an open valley floor, the cave he and Xith had spent the night in. Here he stopped, both to rest the horse and to search the cave for signs, any sign, that Xith had been there again. He found nothing, only emptiness. The next day he continued on, driven by the insanity in his mind.

Vilmos soon perceived other agonies—hunger, thirst and weariness. He chanced on a small brook, the same brook he and Xith had stopped at many weeks previous, drinking from its cool clear waters until his thirst was quenched and his belly full. Seeing no signs of anyone near, he sat along the edge of the water and removed his shoes, sticking his sore, warm feet into the cool, soothing liquid. For some reason that perplexed him, his legs ached, which was partly because he didn't know how to ride and was leading with his lower body in a seesaw motion.

Several hours later as the sun sank low on the horizon, Vilmos was on the opposite side of a valley. It would have been a full day's trek by foot.

A sudden peace swept over him as he made the long climb from the valley floor out onto a rocky precipice; he felt as if he had come home and indeed he had. Vilmos looked back across the valley, amazed at how much ground he had covered. The strange, powerful horse of the beastmen showed its first signs of fatigue now, and its rider was utterly exhausted.

Vilmos let the horse cool down for a time, stroking its long, firm neck and mane to pacify and comfort it. Neither was able to stop for too long though; the strange compulsion that led Vilmos on seemed to flow to the horse and both were enthralled by it. He looked to the forest then and to the trail that led into it and through it. He knew that on the other side of it lay the thing that pulled him on. He had to know, needed to know, what had happened there.

On the back of the magnificent steed, Vilmos rode into the forest, low branches and thick growth along the sides of the trail eventually causing him to reconsider the treacherous ride. He cursed low under his breath as he dismounted, holding a grudge against the forest for forcing him to walk when he was so weary.

Grudgingly, he walked along the tangled trail that was becoming increasingly treacherous in the ever-diminishing light; the only thing that kept him moving was the thought of his home just ahead somewhere. His face and hands were scratched from the branches that caught his skin as he brushed against them, yet he trudged on.

The march along the now indiscernible trail seemed without end.

With one hand held out in front of him for safety, he charged through the thick undergrowth, pulling the hesitant horse thoughtlessly behind him with the other. He no longer recalled its momentous deed; he only knew that ahead lay his home and with its finding, warmth and safety. It wasn't until a low branch appearing from out of the darkness around him nearly poked out his eye that Vilmos stopped; jaded, he slumped his back against a nearby tree completely oblivious to the world around him. He didn't even know that where he had stopped was just a few yards from the forest's edge, but even if he had known, sleep still would have befallen him.

Morning came as a rush of frenzied thoughts as Vilmos awoke waving a stick wildly in the air before him, thwarting the attack of unseen hands. Perspiration dripped from his brow and into his eyes, blurring his already sleep-filled vision. He saw shapes looming before him, and he continued to wield the stick bravely.

"Who is it?" Vilmos shouted as he tried to wipe the sleep and sweat from his eyes. "Go away, leave me alone!" He didn't know that he yelled into empty air and that his illustrious assailants were but images left over from a dream—a dream filled with a hideous grinning face. To clear his mind, he shook his head from side to side, attempting to chase away the last of the night's chill as well as the vile spirits he perceived around him.

His senses returning, he looked around beside him for the magnificent horse, only now fully cognizant of its feat, but the beast was nowhere to be found. He was saddened by its disappearance, later thinking that he was just as well without it for he couldn't care for it, nor feed it. He couldn't even feed himself, he was starving or at least he thought he was.

A bright light sinking into the darkness from a clearing in the distance caught his attention. He walked toward it, amazed when he came abruptly to the forest's edge. Across a grassy field stood the white-bricked house he remembered so fondly. Smoke rose cheerfully from its chimney and there were no signs of anything amiss.

Vilmos took off toward the house at a race, wild thoughts spinning through his mind. He mounted the stairs, put his hand to the door and then stopped. He didn't know what to expect within. What if his parents were dead lying on the floor, or what if they were there and nothing was wrong, what would he tell them? Still considering these thoughts, he opened the door and went inside. He ran through the kitchen and into the pantry, which was full, as always, of fresh fruits and vegetables. The sight overwhelmed him and he started to eat ravenously, going no further until he had had his fill.

He found his room as he had left it.

"Was it a dream?" he asked himself, saying the words aloud to break the silence around him.

Next he ran into his parents' room, which was empty. The bed was made and the room was tidy, clean as his mother always left it. A brief search of the entire house revealed nothing out of the ordinary. The only thing wrong was that no one was home, but Vilmos was prepared to wait—maybe they had just gone into town. He knew they would return soon and everything would be fine.

Hours passed, but no one arrived. Vilmos grew hungry again and raided the pantry a second time. With a full midriff, he sauntered to his room and plopped onto the bed, patting his warm, full stomach.

Content, he lay still, staring up at the ceiling. A short while later, he propped his pillow up against the wall, removed his shoes and leaned up against the pillow. In his mind he went over past events, everything he had experienced had seemed so real. He could see Xith's face in his mind. He could see Edward and the beasts. He could see Valam and Adrina. He could see Seth and Galan.

A familiar place called him and so he went, he had not been there in what seemed ages. He stood above the majestic, peaceful valley on his personal precipice—the valley that had its mirror in the realm of the real as well as the imagined. He felt so soothed by the vision that he followed the mighty eagle into the sky. Lazily, he swooped and turned.

Hours passed, floating on the breezes churning up from the valley floor. The eagle's keen eyes scoured the valley, expecting to find nothing in particular and did. He was alone with his thoughts, as he liked to be, alone and free. "Vilmos, no magic!" an alarmed voice in his head screamed out and he awoke.

Propelled back, Vilmos sprang to his feet. A distant ruffling noise, perhaps hoofed feet upon dry leaves, brought him through the kitchen to the porch.

Finding nothing, he returned to the empty house, pouring over thoughts of the past, memories that rushed upon him until he could no longer persevere them. He rushed out the door back onto the porch again, staring down the empty road, looking for any signs of his mother and father.

He longed to see a single, horse-drawn coach approach with two occupants. The driver a stern-faced man with a whip in one hand and the reins tucked in the other hand—that was how his father liked to ride. The other occupant would sit quietly beside him; her face would be gentle and kind, aged pleasantly with the years. A familiar figure did eventually approach, not from the road, but from the path that led to the forest and not until hours later.

All delusion faded as the beckoning voice called out. "Vilmos, come!" it commanded.

Vilmos walked to the path, saying, "I thought it was all a dream." Something along the path caught Vilmos' attention, but only for an instant. "How did you find me?"

The reply came in a voice that could only be Xith's, "You found me but that is beside the point."

"Edward, is he…?" asked Vilmos

"Edward is in a good place and he would be happy to know that you are safe."

After a lengthy walk, the two came to an opening that led to a point overlooking the valley. The suspicion that his life was moving in circles and that no matter how far away from it he went he would always come back to the same place, occurred to Vilmos, just as Xith said "We'll stop here to rest for a few moments."

Vilmos sat down on the ground with a thump. He was about to ask Xith if he had anything to eat when Xith stopped him.

"Silence!" Vilmos had only seen Xith like this once before and he didn't like the expression he saw. He started to say something again, and again Xith cut him off.

Xith didn't make a sound after that or move. Vilmos knew something was definitely wrong.

A moment later Xith yelled, "Duck!"

Vilmos fell to the ground, on his belly. As Vilmos lay motionless, he had a strong feeling that he had been in this situation before. He looked to the shaman who shook his head in agreement. Vilmos asked, "But why?"

The shaman turned his eyes heavenward, apparently seeing things that Vilmos couldn't. He waited for a moment before he responded, indicating as he did so that it was all right for Vilmos to sit back up.

"Vilmos, life can be complicated or simple, often times you take a step forward only to find that you have taken two steps backward. Do you understand?"

Vilmos wavered his head. He had no idea what Xith was talking about.

"That is good," said Xith, "don't try to figure it out. It is best just to accept it. Life is a series of circles that sometimes lead you back to the beginning, so instead of giving up you must keep your head high and start again. There will be times when you are not sure whether you are in the past or the present, or whether perhaps you are without time and are never really far away from the place you are trying to reach. Do you understand?"

"I don't," admitted Vilmos honestly.

A sullenness fell over Xith's face and Vilmos could see dark circles under his companion's eyes. "You will, I promise. Edward would not have sacrificed himself for you otherwise. You see, he was the first, the one that was taken from me before you. You are truly he, Vilmos, and the time will soon be upon us."

The shaman raised his eyes to meet Vilmos' then and as he did so a glowing orb of brilliant white appeared in his outstretched hand. In the orb, Vilmos saw the visage of the Princess Adrina and there were tears streaming down her cheeks. As the image grew clearer, he could see that she sat at a great table, around which many were gathered. To her left was the elf Seth, and to Seth's left was Galan. Seth's skin was pale and his great round eyes stared up at the heavens.

***

Ominously the last words of the Queen Mother hung in the air about the chamber. A tear, single and crystalline, shimmered down Queen Mother's cheek. Tiny though it was, it conveyed a feeling of deepest sadness.

Galan clasped Seth's hand tightly; his will had nearly drained away. Her heart raced and her tears flowed ceaselessly.

Adrina gripped Seth's other hand, feeling it grow from warm, full of life, to cool and balmy. Her anguish matched the deep unbroken lines of tears cascading down her cheeks.

My son, you have done all that you could. You have done what you must, what you were meant to do. You shall be remembered, you shall not be forgotten, the sacrifice shall not go unaccounted for... and in a barely audible voice Queen Mother added, *... may the Great Father grant you passage into his very house, so that you may sit by his side, my son.*

The Queen Mother's voice faded away and the link was broken. All eyes remained in place, focusing now on Seth. A smile touched his lips at the gift of his mother, words of praise reserved only for the very great, said only at the passing of a king or queen.

As he breathed his last breath, the smile broadened to the corners of his lips. He fancied the smell of the kingdom garden he had been in earlier and revelled in the flow of nature he had felt. With that one last thought of peace, of life, and of nature, Seth collapsed to the table. No one doubted that he was indeed dead.

Galan whispered into their minds, *This is the holy light of the Great Father reclaiming his son, as are all at the last.* She let the faithful see the wondrous—but otherwise invisible—shimmering light surrounding Seth's fallen form. *Few are able to see the spirit pass thus, so if you can see it, you are truly blessed. You have found faith and sincerity in your heart.*

A pitiful wail, almost a plea, filled their minds as Galan unleashed her sorrows to all in the room. *No!* she cried out, *Please, no!*

Further words were broken by long sobs, followed by an unsettling calm. She held back the tears and the pain, saying *As such is the way of my will, I cannot allow this to happen.*

A blast of icy air defiled the chamber. Galan reached her hands upward chasing after Seth in thought, forcing her will to take her to the place where the Father gathered up his son, knowing she had to hurry because the journey was almost complete.

She pursued the last shard of his life, the tiny light hurtling upward into the heavens. Her own brilliant light, full of life, quickly caught and surpassed it.

Father, I must, she begged. *Father, hear me!*

Responding to a voice only she heard, she replied, "Yes, I understand." These words were spoken aloud and in thought.

The thread that guided Seth's way severed, and his soul plummeted back earthward. His spirit collided with his body, taking with it the light of Galan's life and the place Galan had occupied suddenly emptied.

The council hall was absolutely quiet. No one moved, no one said a word, until Adrina took Seth's hand and led him from the room. King Andrew spoke then, and he said four words, "It shall be done."

The story continues with:

Ruin Mist:
Fields of Honor

About the Author

Robert Stanek is the author of many previously published books, including several bestsellers. Currently, he lives in the Pacific Northwest with his wife and children. Robert is proud to have served in the Persian Gulf War as a combat crewmember on an electronic warfare aircraft. During the war, he flew numerous combat and combat support missions, logging over two hundred combat flight hours.

His distinguished accomplishments during the Persian Gulf War earned him nine medals, including the United States of America's highest flying honor, the Air Force Distinguished Flying Cross. His career total was 17 medals in only 11 years of military service, making him one of the most highly decorated veterans of the Persian Gulf War.

Overwhelmingly, readers agree that Robert's books are among the best they've ever read. His books have very vocal supporters who aren't afraid to voice their opinion, and they frequently do so in online communities and lists, such as at Amazon.com, where you'll find that his books are consistently listed at the top of their class. Strong reader support has led to strong sales.

About Reagent Press

Reagent Press is a small press that publishes both fiction and non-fiction titles. Current fiction titles include *Keeper Martin's Tale* and *Elf Queen's Quest* from the Ruin Mist Chronicles, *The Kingdoms & The Elves of the Reaches Book I* and *Book II* from Keeper Martin's Tales, and *The Elf Queen & The King Book I* and *Book II* from Ruin Mist Tales. Current non-fiction titles include: *Effective Writing for Business, College & Life*, *Essential Windows 2000 Commands Reference*, and *Essential Windows XP Commands Reference*.

Thank you for your continued support! Without the help of you, the reader, we will not be able to produce future works. If you liked this book, please tell your friends!

Edited by nSight, Inc.

Editor: Erin Connaughton, Kristen Ford
Special thanks to Sarah Hains for acting as the project coordinator!

Keeper Martin's Tale

The first book in the light path through Ruin Mist's history. Three heroes set out on an epic journey of discovery only to find that nothing is what they thought it was and that their world is undergoing a transformation that will change everything. Survival in a changing world depends on their ability to adapt and if they fail, their world and everything they believe in will perish.

Kingdom Alliance

The second book in the light path through Ruin Mist's history. Two dozen elves set out from Leklorall, the capital of East Reach. After an ambush at sea only a handful survived, of those only two reached the far shores of the Great Sea. Their names were Seth and Galan and they sided with Great Kingdom during the Battle of Quashan', helping to defend the valley city with skills and speeds no living man had ever seen before. But success on the battlefield could not undo the past. Elves and men are mortal enemies, as it has been since the Great War when the elves of Under-Earth sought to enslave all peoples of Ruin Mist. Now even as Seth attempts to sway Great Kingdom's leaders to stop the coming darkness, there are few who will truly listen—and even fewer who can look beyond the treachery of days past.

Ruin Mist Heroes, Legends & Beyond

Just about everyone that has read about Ruin Mist has wondered about the back story, where it all began, how the story all fits together, and now you can find answers in *Ruin Mist Heroes, Legends & Beyond*, a companion volume to the top-selling Ruin Mist books. *Ruin Mist Heroes, Legends & Beyond* allows you to learn about the dark elves of Under-Earth, common trades in the kingdoms, and beasts that go bump in the night. You can read the complete rules for King's Mate: the game, explore dozens of maps detailing the known realms, learn about the author, and more. In short, this is one book you shouldn't be without.

Sovereign Rule

A tautly told and suspenseful thriller from a hell of a storyteller!

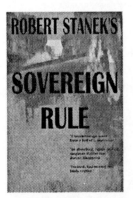

Between fear and freedom lies the shadowed reality through which Scott Evers must go. If he lets them know that he's afraid for, and therefore cares about, those around him, the powerbrokers will take them away one by one until Scott's the only one left between us and those that want to control us. He's desperate to keep his wife and unborn child alive but as Scott's about to find out, the rules of the game have changed and those that control the rules, control the game. The weak and rash take power using bombs and terror; the strong and resolute by sovereign rule. Only one man is in a position to take back control, but can Scott Evers unravel the secrets and lies before it's too late?

Printed in the United States
35958LVS00004B/103-108